THE INFINITE ADVENTURES OF SUPERNOVA
PEPPER PAGE
SAVES THE UNIVERSE!

THE INFINITE ADVENTURES OF SUPERNOVA

PEPPER PAGE

SAVES THE UNIVERSE!

Story by

Landry Q. Walker
and **Eric Jones**

Script: **Landry Q. Walker**
Art: **Eric Jones**
Colors: **Eric Jones, Michael "Rusty" Drake, Pannel Vaughn**
Letters: **Patrick Brosseau**
Producer: **Jon Guhl**

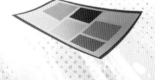

:01
First Second
New York

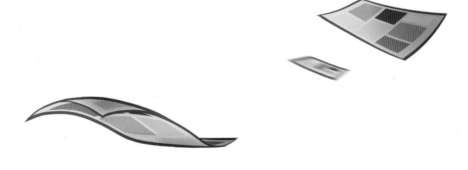

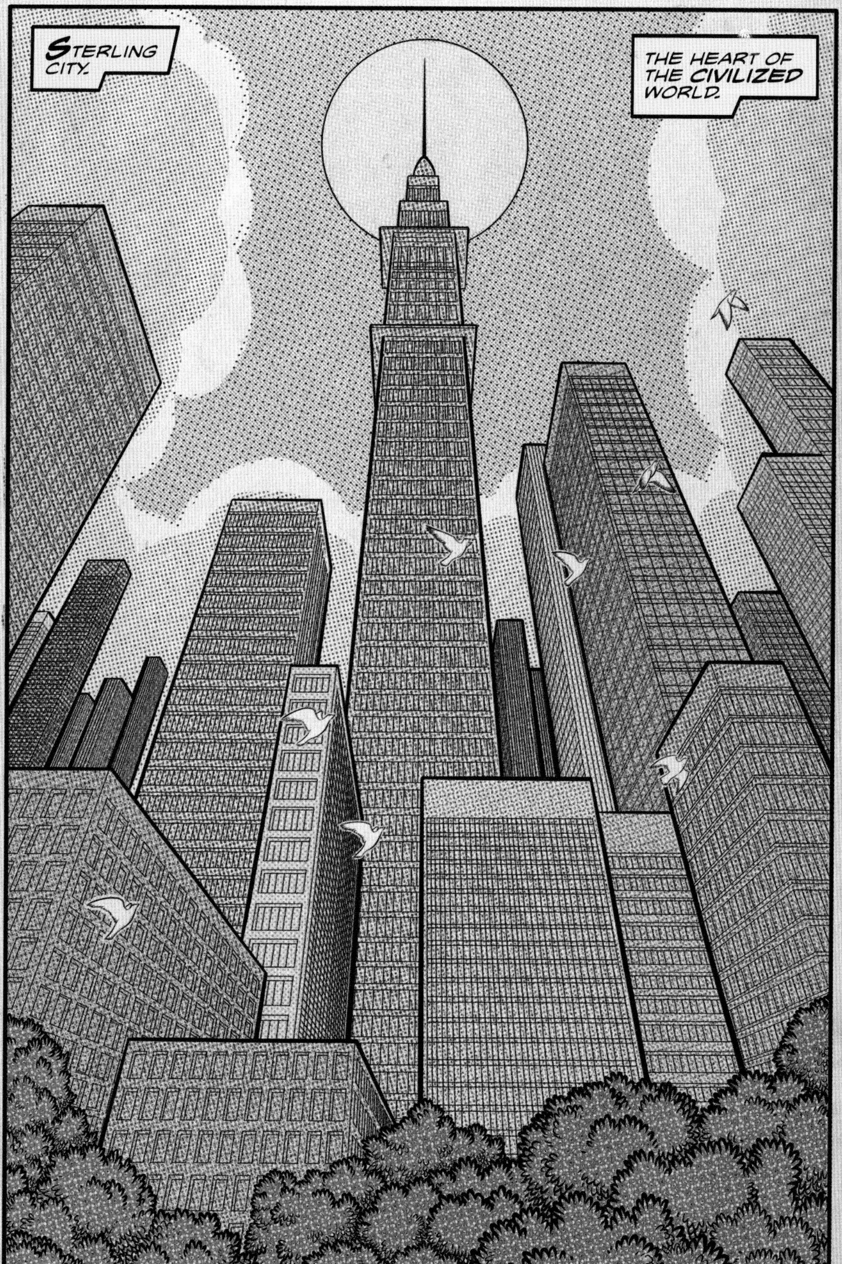
STERLING CITY.
THE HEART OF THE CIVILIZED WORLD.

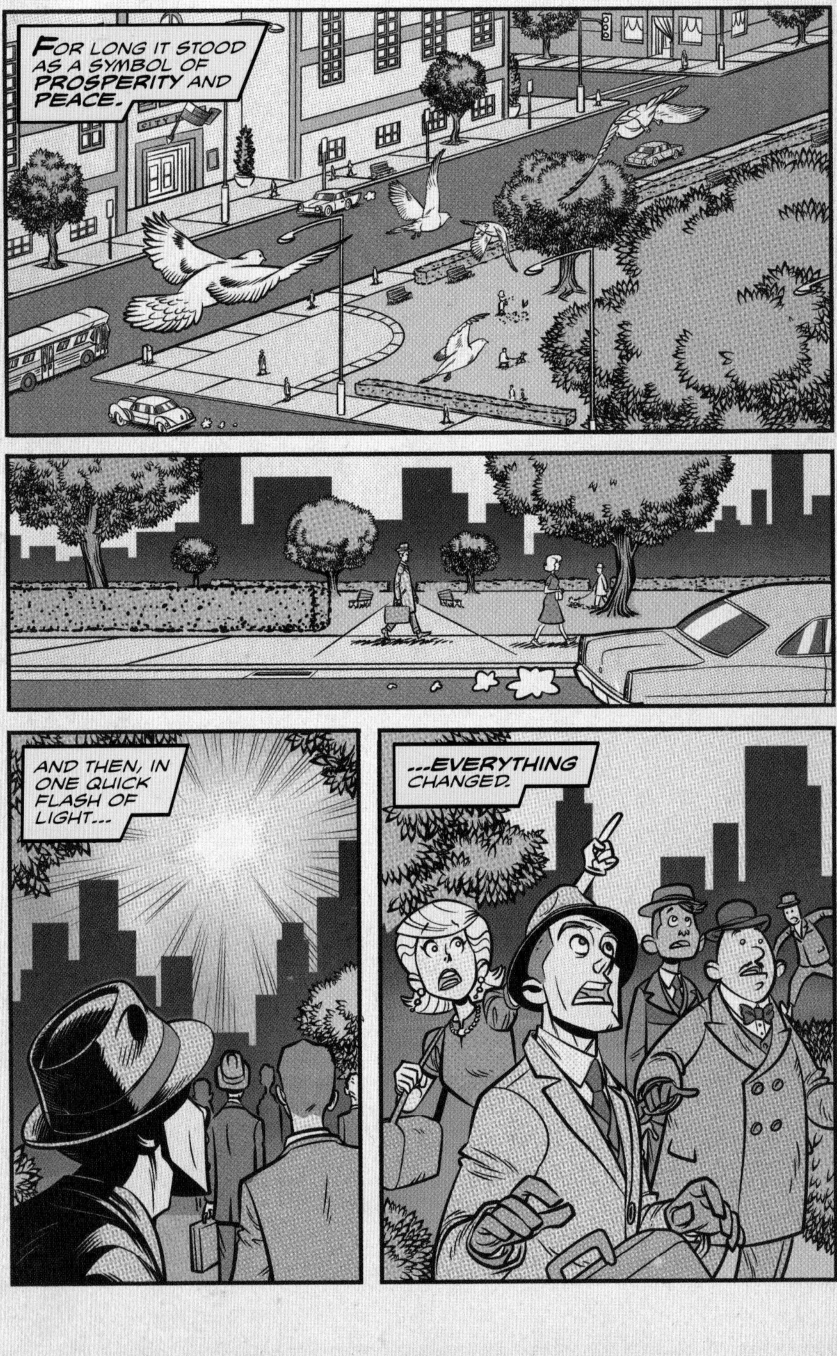
FOR LONG IT STOOD AS A SYMBOL OF **PROSPERITY** AND **PEACE.**
AND THEN, IN ONE QUICK FLASH OF LIGHT...
...**EVERYTHING** CHANGED.

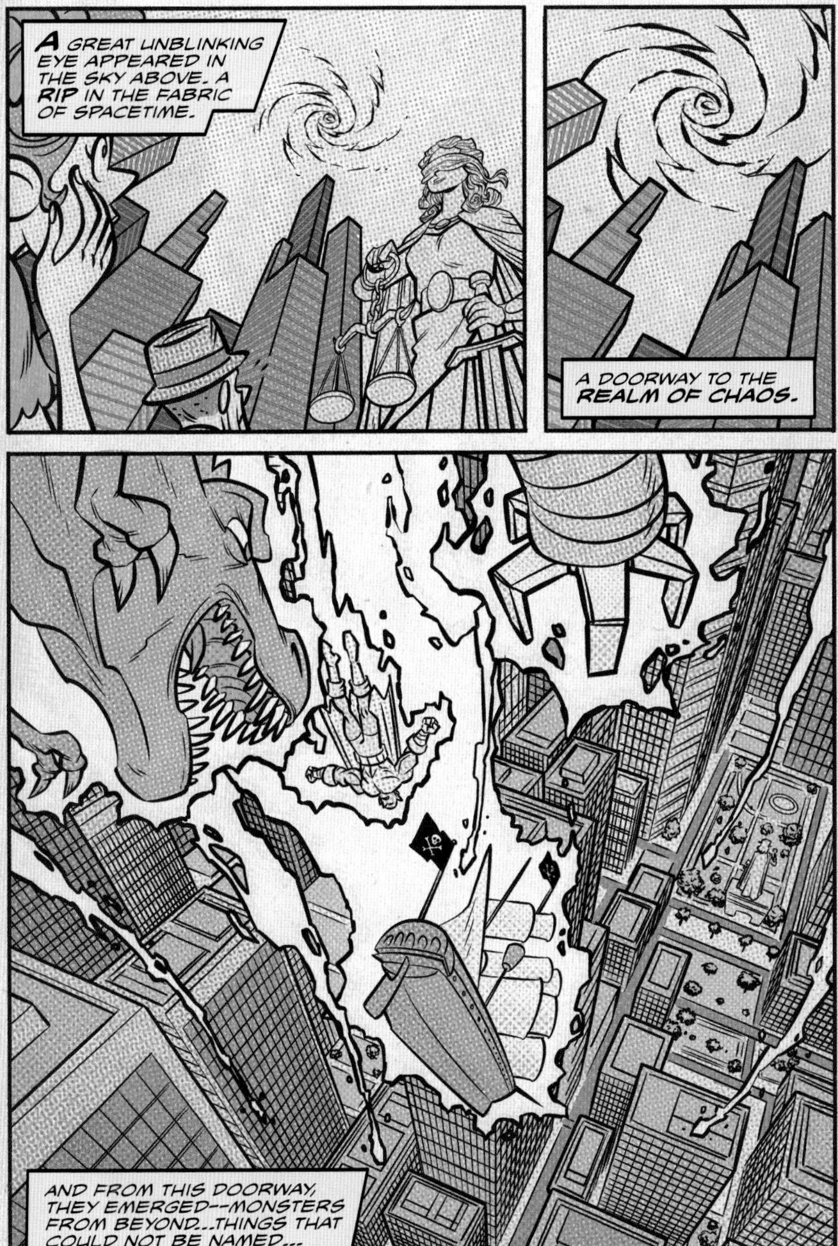
A GREAT UNBLINKING EYE APPEARED IN THE SKY ABOVE. A RIP IN THE FABRIC OF SPACETIME.
A DOORWAY TO THE REALM OF CHAOS.
AND FROM THIS DOORWAY, THEY EMERGED--MONSTERS FROM BEYOND...THINGS THAT COULD NOT BE NAMED...

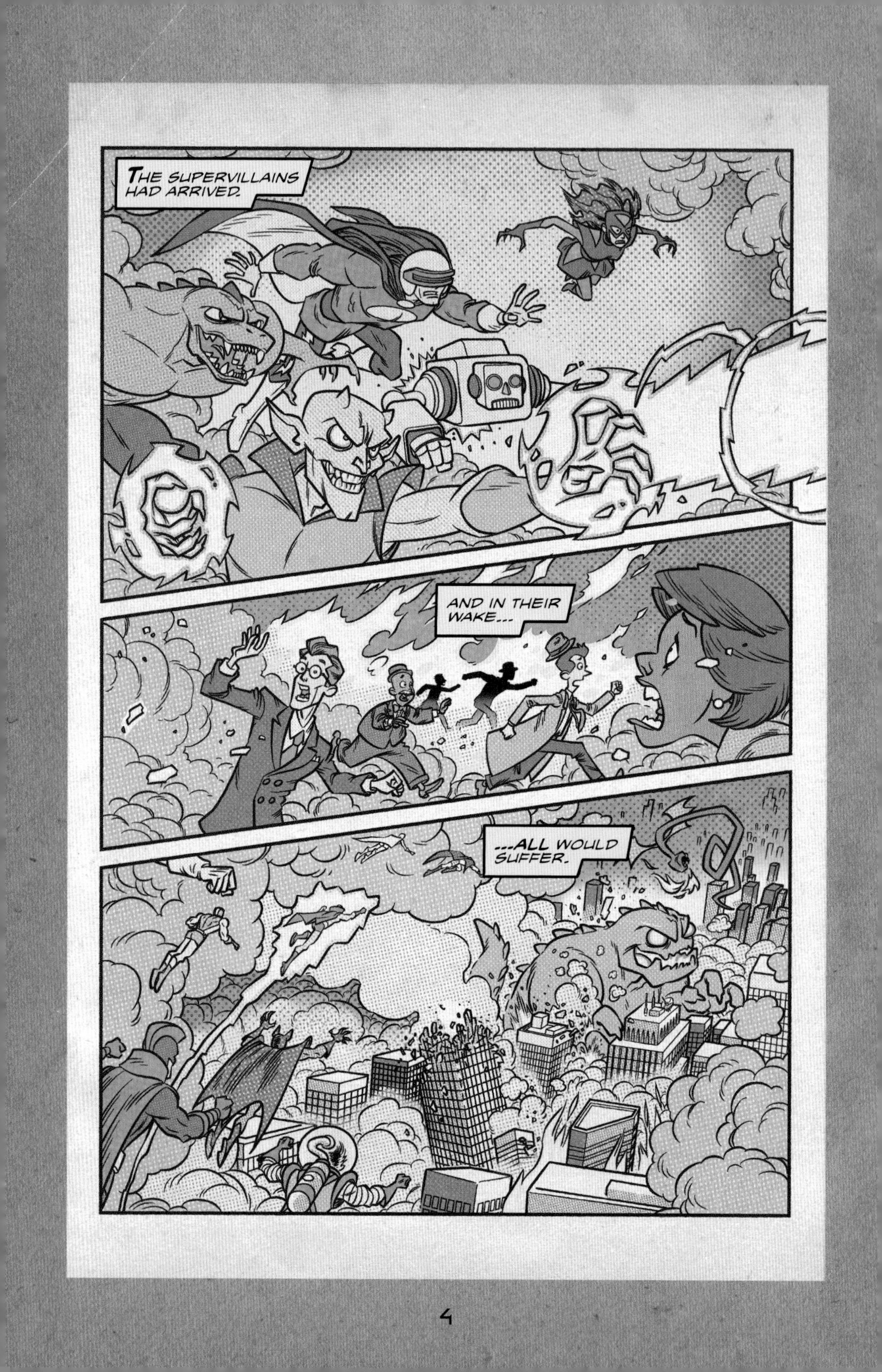
THE SUPERVILLAINS HAD ARRIVED.
AND IN THEIR WAKE...
...ALL WOULD SUFFER.

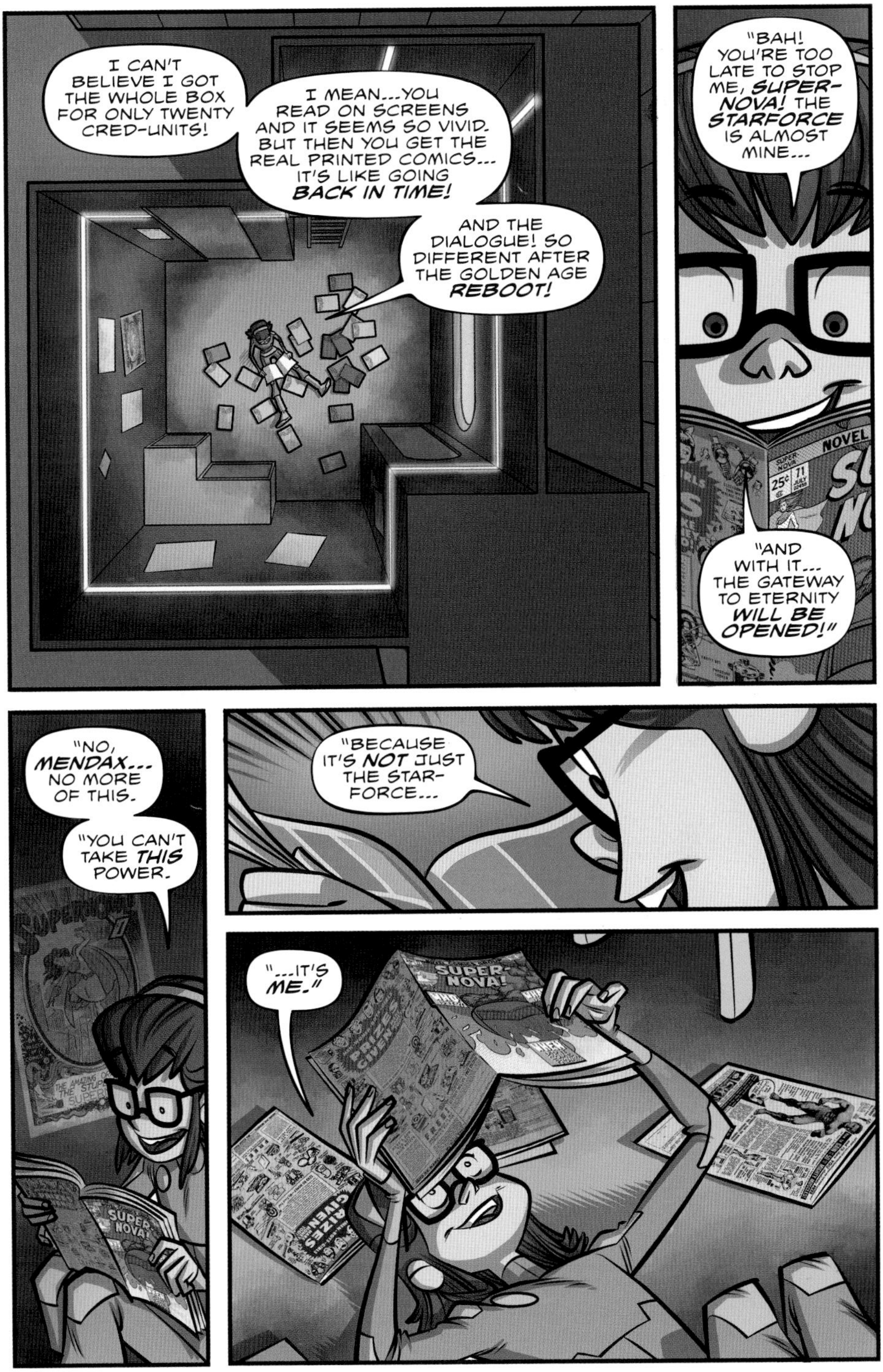
I CAN'T BELIEVE I GOT THE WHOLE BOX FOR ONLY TWENTY CRED-UNITS!
I MEAN...YOU READ ON SCREENS AND IT SEEMS SO VIVID. BUT THEN YOU GET THE REAL PRINTED COMICS... IT'S LIKE GOING BACK IN TIME!
AND THE DIALOGUE! SO DIFFERENT AFTER THE GOLDEN AGE REBOOT!
"BAH! YOU'RE TOO LATE TO STOP ME, SUPER-NOVA! THE STARFORCE IS ALMOST MINE...
"AND WITH IT... THE GATEWAY TO ETERNITY WILL BE OPENED!"
"NO, MENDAX... NO MORE OF THIS.
"YOU CAN'T TAKE THIS POWER.
"BECAUSE IT'S NOT JUST THE STAR-FORCE...
"...IT'S ME."

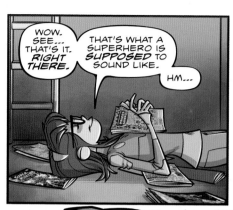

WOW. SEE... THAT'S IT. **RIGHT THERE.**

THAT'S WHAT A SUPERHERO IS **SUPPOSED** TO SOUND LIKE.

HM....

ALERT! ALERT! ALERT!

GAH!

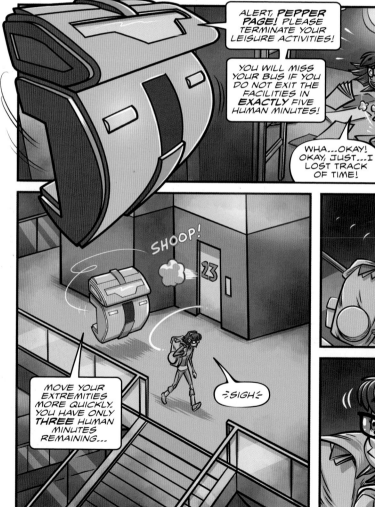

ALERT, **PEPPER PAGE!** PLEASE TERMINATE YOUR LEISURE ACTIVITIES!

YOU WILL MISS YOUR BUS IF YOU DO NOT EXIT THE FACILITIES IN **EXACTLY** FIVE HUMAN MINUTES!

WHA...OKAY! OKAY, JUST...I LOST TRACK OF TIME!

SHOOP!

23

MOVE YOUR EXTREMITIES MORE QUICKLY. YOU HAVE ONLY **THREE** HUMAN MINUTES REMAINING...

÷SIGH÷

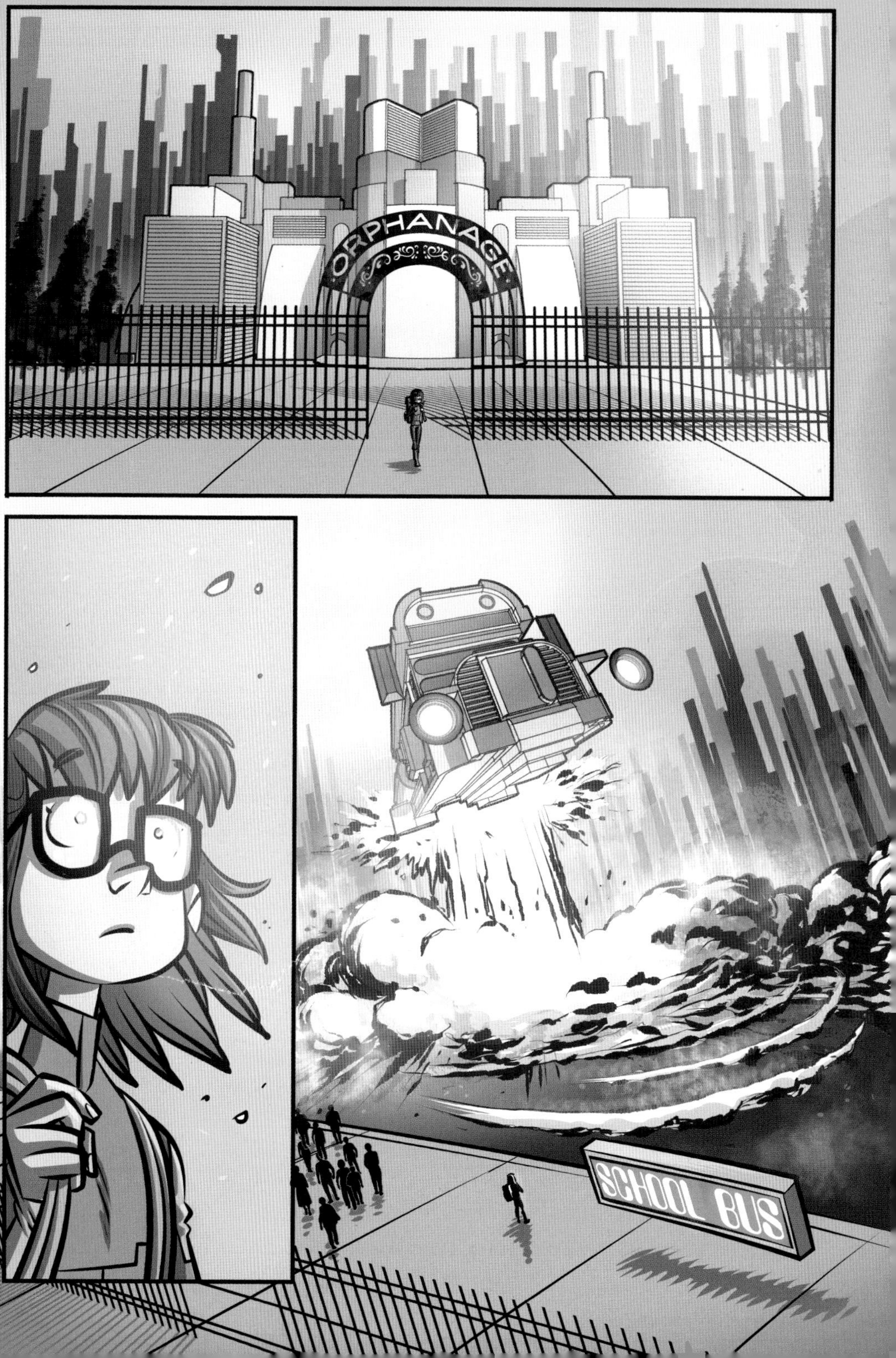
ORPHANAGE
SCHOOL BUS

SUPERNOVA MET *GRIMDARK THE DREAD DETECTIVE* BEFORE THEY JOINED THE *DANGER CLUB?* OH, RIGHT...THEY REWROTE THAT WHEN CHRONOS ERASED THE *TIMELINE...*

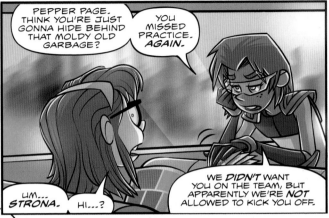

PEPPER PAGE. THINK YOU'RE JUST GONNA HIDE BEHIND THAT MOLDY OLD GARBAGE?

YOU MISSED PRACTICE. *AGAIN.*

UM... *STRONA.* HI...?

WE *DIDN'T* WANT YOU ON THE TEAM, BUT APPARENTLY WE'RE *NOT* ALLOWED TO KICK YOU OFF.

SEE...I DON'T KNOW IF YOU NOTICED, BUT OUR TEAM IS *O FOR 8.* AND YOU KNOW *WHY?*

BECAUSE WE'RE *TERRIBLE?*

BECAUSE *YOU'RE* TERRIBLE. YOU DRAG THE WHOLE TEAM *DOWN.* BUT WE NEED A THIRD-STOP OR WE GET *DISQUALIFIED!*

WON'T MISS THE GAME. I *REALLY* WON'T.

THAT'S WHAT YOU *ALWAYS* SAY!

HEY!

YOU'RE GONNA WRINKLE THAT! IT'S A *COLLECTIBLE!*

SERIOUSLY? *THIS* IS WHAT YOU WASTE TIME ON INSTEAD OF PRACTICE?

JUST GIVE IT *BACK!*

"NIGHT FALLS WHEN *ECLIPSA* STRIKES!"

PFF! WAS THIS WRITTEN BY *BABIES?*

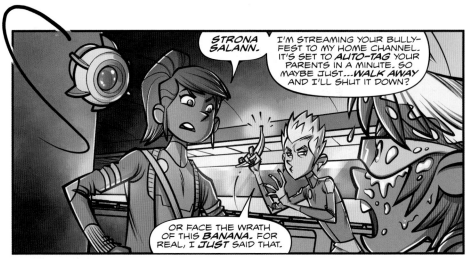

STRONA SALANN.

I'M STREAMING YOUR BULLY-FEST TO MY HOME CHANNEL. IT'S SET TO *AUTO-TAG* YOUR PARENTS IN A MINUTE. SO MAYBE JUST...*WALK AWAY* AND I'LL SHUT IT DOWN?

OR FACE THE WRATH OF THIS *BANANA.* FOR REAL, I *JUST* SAID THAT.

PAH! WHATEVER, TALLY. DO YOU THINK I CARE IF MY PARENTS SEE YOUR *STUPID* LIVESTREAM? I'M LOOKING OUT FOR MY *TEAM!*

YOU *HEAR* THAT? YOUR FRIEND IS TOO AFRAID TO EVEN *TRY.*

YOU *BETTER* NOT COST US ANY MORE GAMES, PAGE. I'M *WARNING* YOU.

CAREFUL!

KEEP WALKING...I'M *STILL* STREAMING THIS...

BAH.

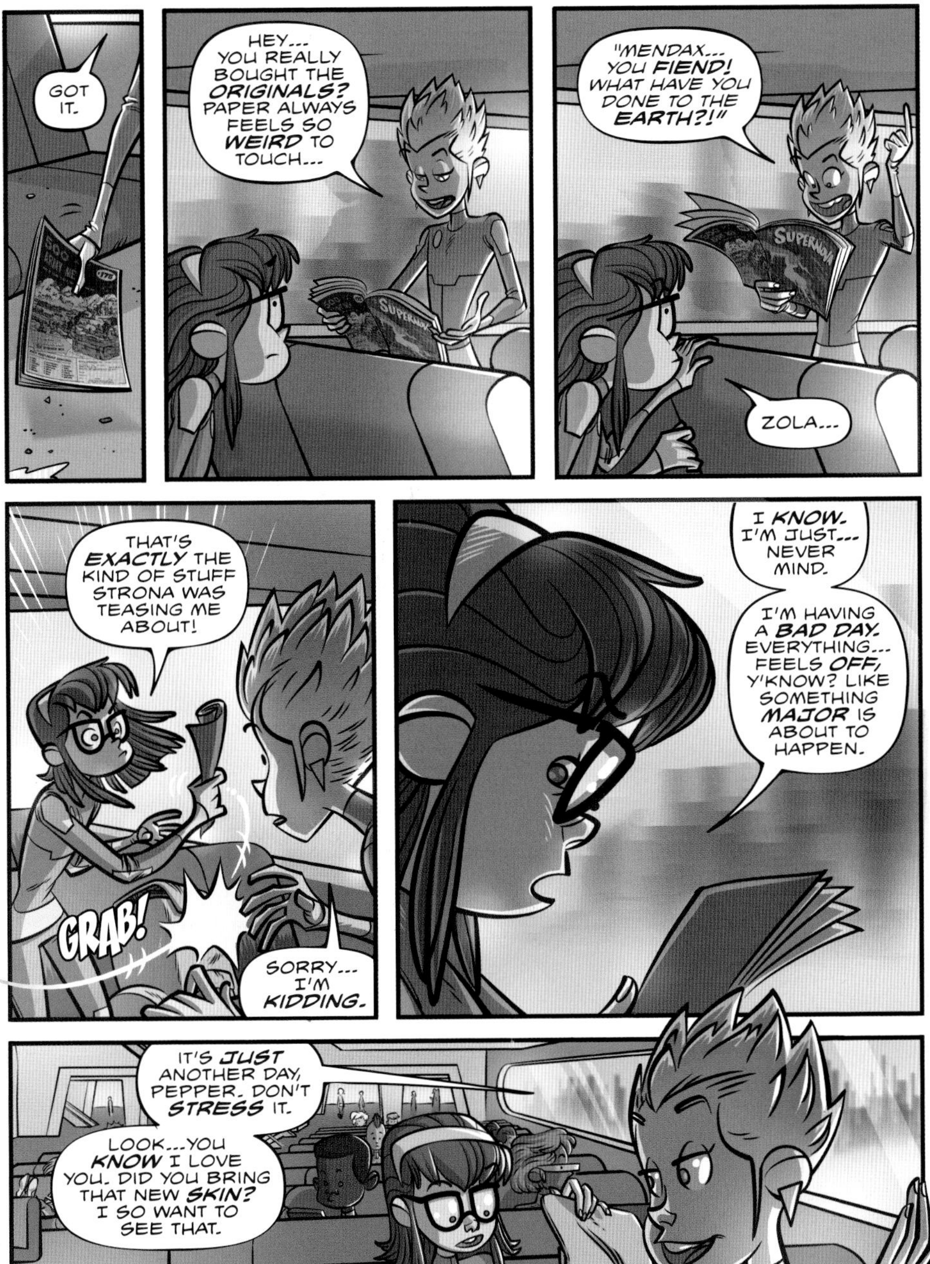

GOT IT.
HEY... YOU REALLY BOUGHT THE ORIGINALS? PAPER ALWAYS FEELS SO WEIRD TO TOUCH...
"MENDAX... YOU FIEND! WHAT HAVE YOU DONE TO THE EARTH?!"
ZOLA...
THAT'S EXACTLY THE KIND OF STUFF STRONA WAS TEASING ME ABOUT!
GRAB!
SORRY... I'M KIDDING.
I KNOW. I'M JUST... NEVER MIND.
I'M HAVING A BAD DAY. EVERYTHING... FEELS OFF, Y'KNOW? LIKE SOMETHING MAJOR IS ABOUT TO HAPPEN.
IT'S JUST ANOTHER DAY, PEPPER. DON'T STRESS IT.
LOOK...YOU KNOW I LOVE YOU. DID YOU BRING THAT NEW SKIN? I SO WANT TO SEE THAT.
YEAH... HOLD ON.

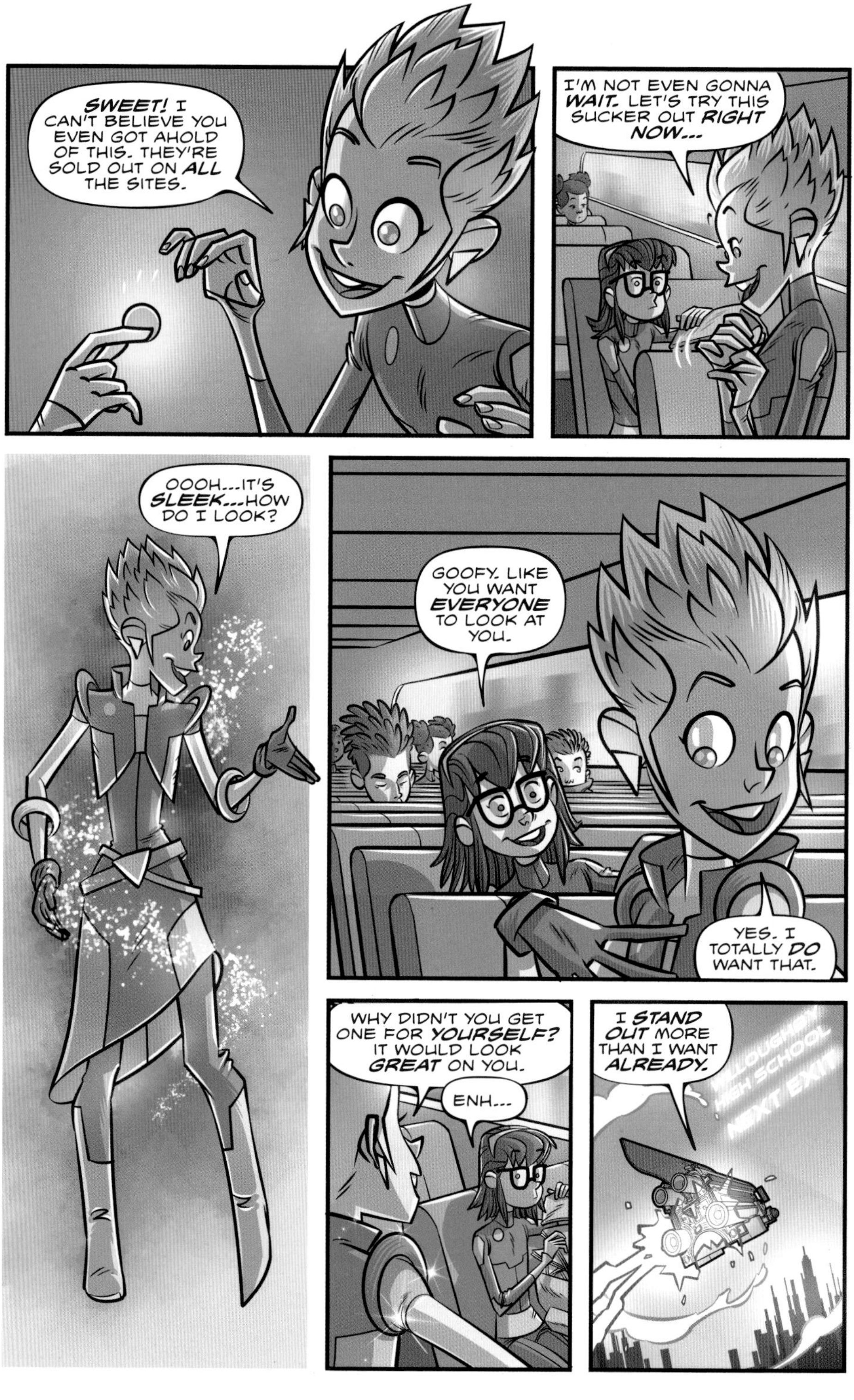
SWEET! I CAN'T BELIEVE YOU EVEN GOT AHOLD OF THIS. THEY'RE SOLD OUT ON ALL THE SITES.
I'M NOT EVEN GONNA WAIT. LET'S TRY THIS SUCKER OUT RIGHT NOW...
OOOH...IT'S SLEEK...HOW DO I LOOK?
GOOFY. LIKE YOU WANT EVERYONE TO LOOK AT YOU.
YES. I TOTALLY DO WANT THAT.
WHY DIDN'T YOU GET ONE FOR YOURSELF? IT WOULD LOOK GREAT ON YOU.
ENH...
I STAND OUT MORE THAN I WANT ALREADY.
WILLOUGHBY HIGH SCHOOL NEXT EXIT

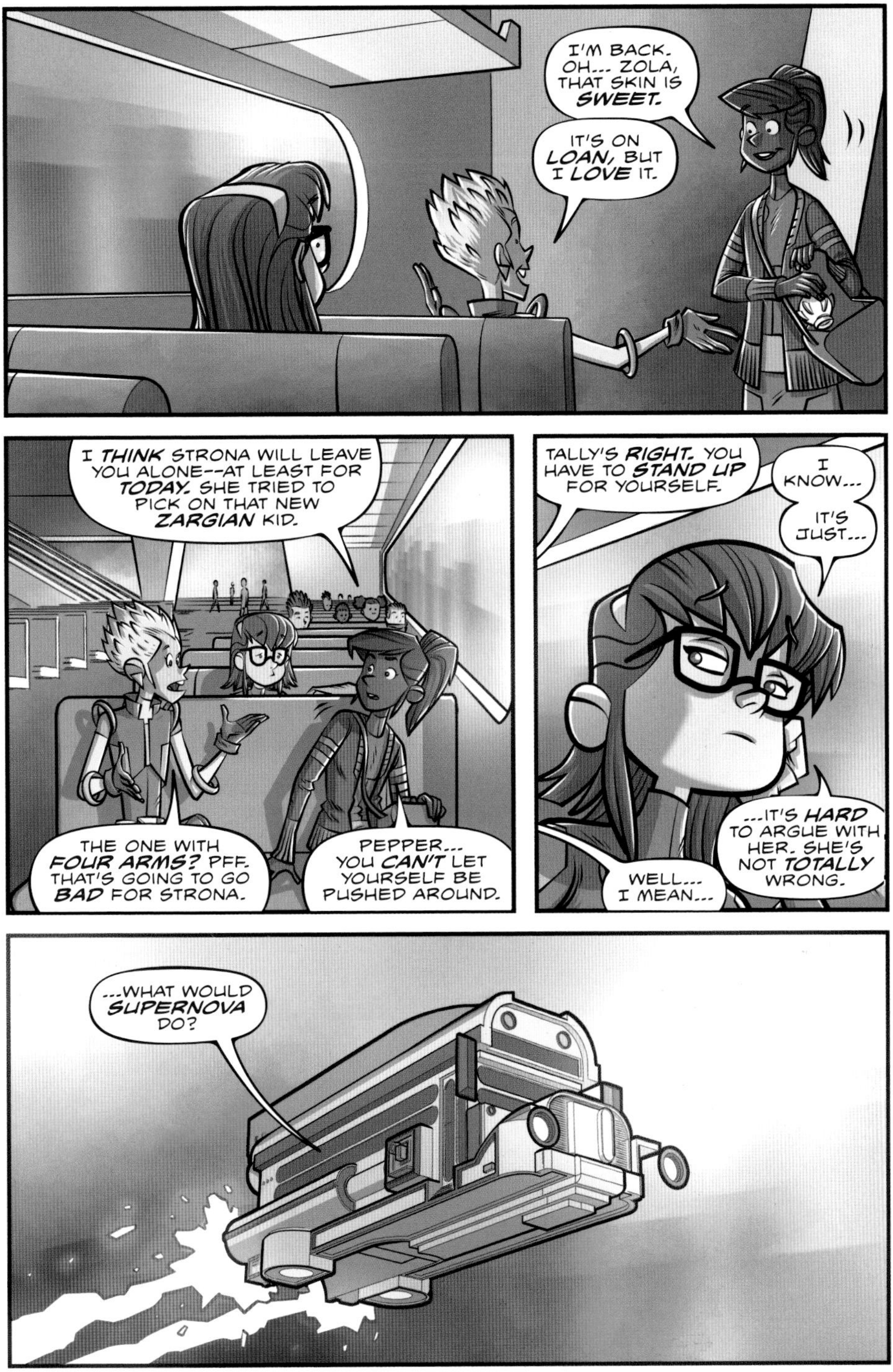
I'M BACK. OH... ZOLA, THAT SKIN IS SWEET.
IT'S ON LOAN, BUT I LOVE IT.
I THINK STRONA WILL LEAVE YOU ALONE--AT LEAST FOR TODAY. SHE TRIED TO PICK ON THAT NEW ZARGIAN KID.
THE ONE WITH FOUR ARMS? PFF. THAT'S GOING TO GO BAD FOR STRONA.
PEPPER... YOU CAN'T LET YOURSELF BE PUSHED AROUND.
TALLY'S RIGHT. YOU HAVE TO STAND UP FOR YOURSELF.
I KNOW...
IT'S JUST...
WELL... I MEAN...
...IT'S HARD TO ARGUE WITH HER. SHE'S NOT TOTALLY WRONG.
...WHAT WOULD SUPERNOVA DO?

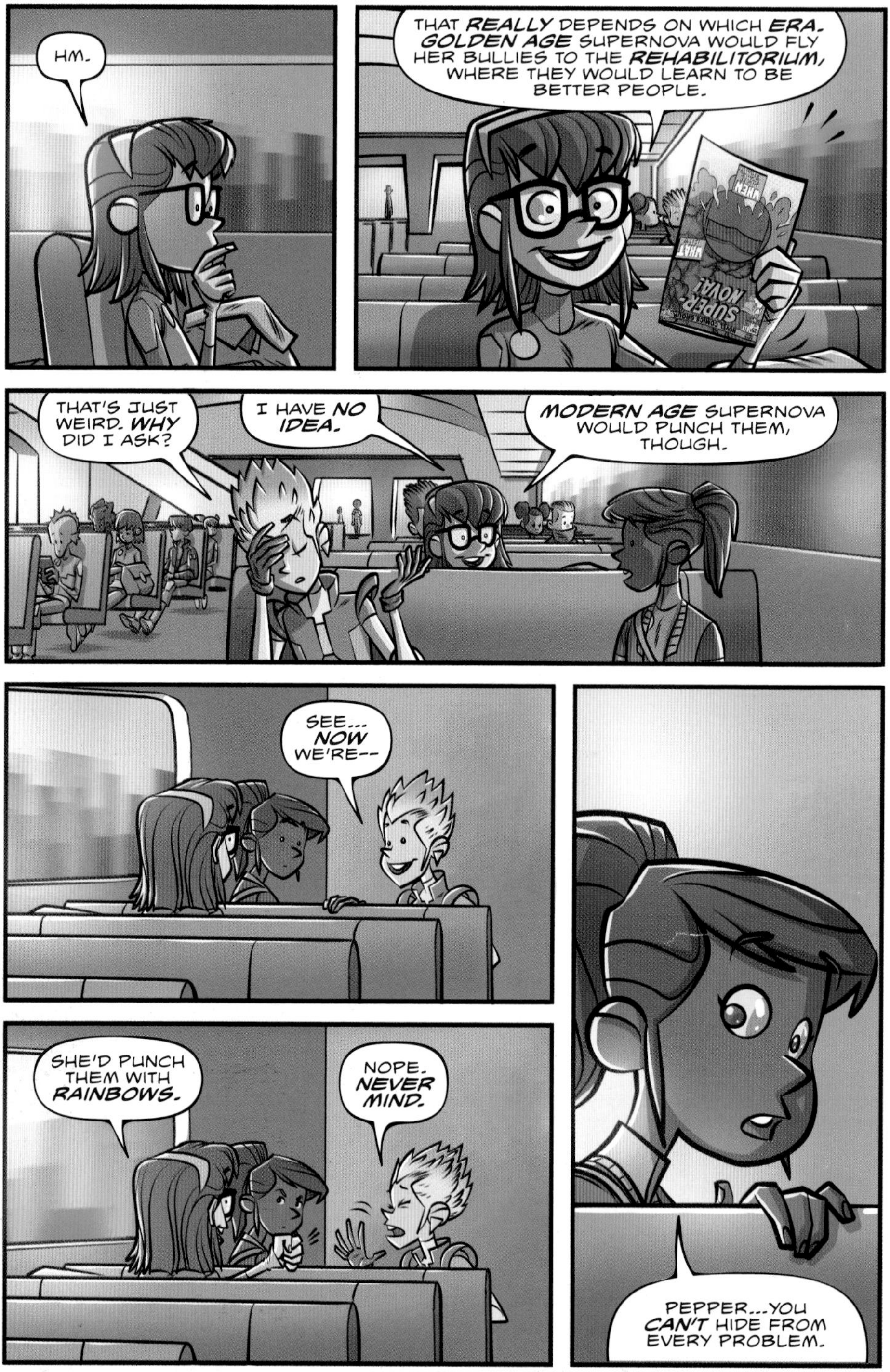
HM.
THAT REALLY DEPENDS ON WHICH ERA. GOLDEN AGE SUPERNOVA WOULD FLY HER BULLIES TO THE REHABILITORIUM, WHERE THEY WOULD LEARN TO BE BETTER PEOPLE.
SUPER-NOVA!
THAT'S JUST WEIRD. WHY DID I ASK?
I HAVE NO IDEA.
MODERN AGE SUPERNOVA WOULD PUNCH THEM, THOUGH.
SEE... NOW WE'RE--
SHE'D PUNCH THEM WITH RAINBOWS.
NOPE. NEVER MIND.
PEPPER...YOU CAN'T HIDE FROM EVERY PROBLEM.

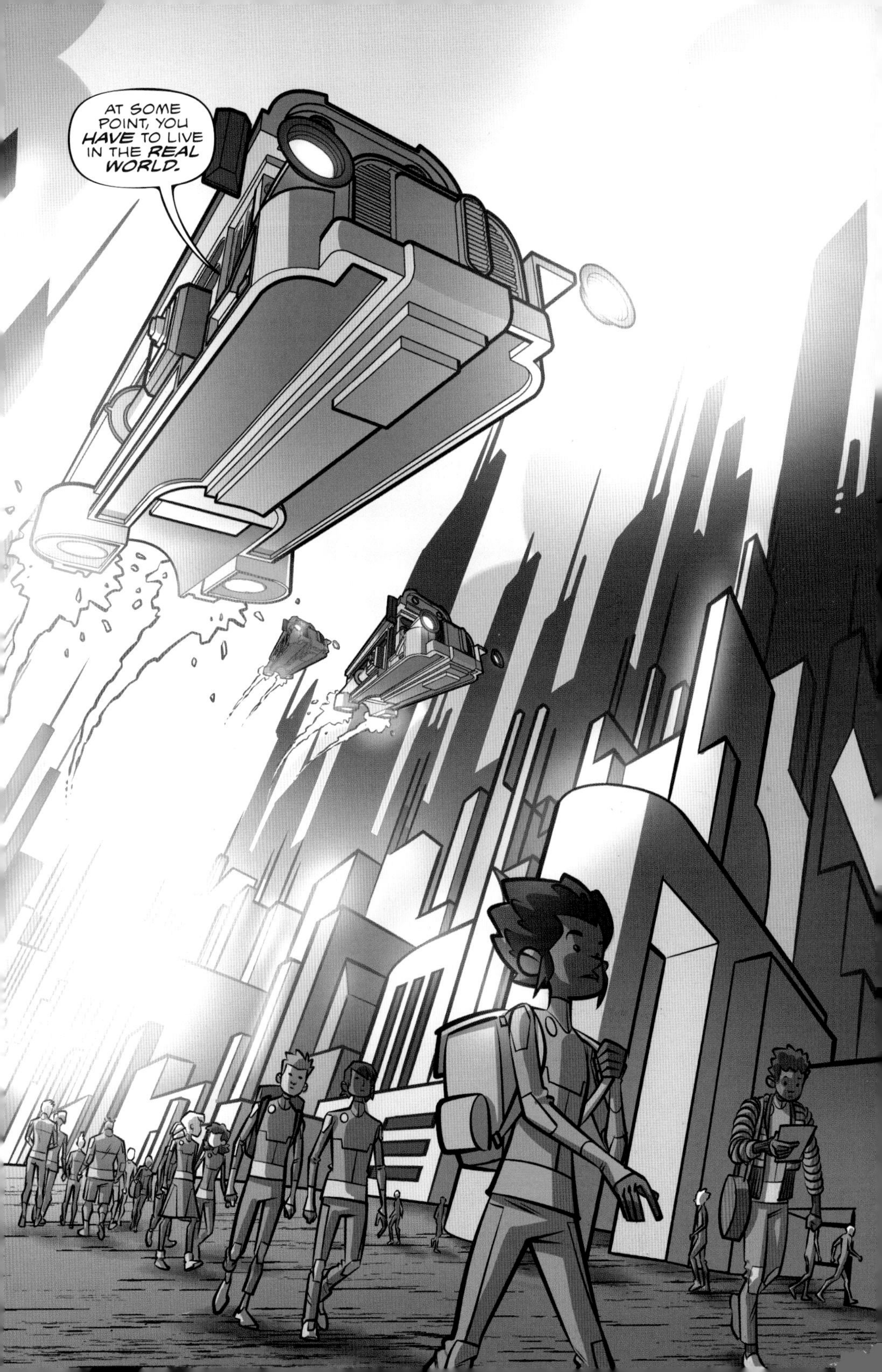
AT SOME POINT, YOU HAVE TO LIVE IN THE REAL WORLD.

GOOD AND EVIL.
WILLOUGHBY
WILLOUGHBY
WILLOUGHBY
PLEASE REPORT TO CLASS
DARKNESS AND LIGHT.
THE REALM OF THE VOID GROWS STRONGER.
THE POWER OF THE SUNS WE MUST REIGNITE.

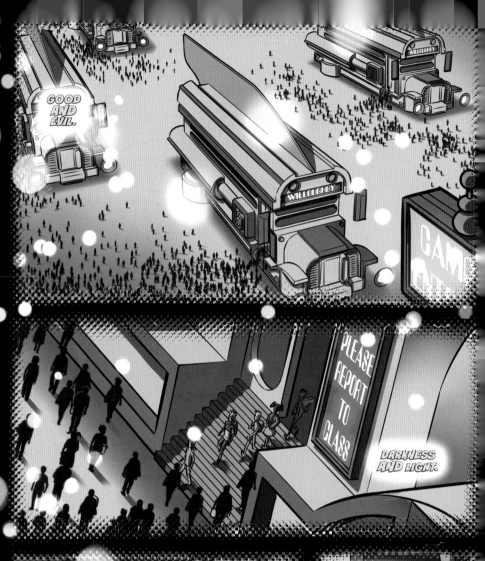

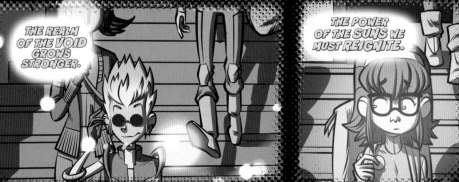

STUDENTS...OPEN YOUR SCREENS TO TAB 478.B.

PLEASE NOTE-- YOUR GRADES FOR THIS SESSION WILL BE CALCULATED ON A *CURVE.* YOUR RETENTION SKILLS, THOUGH *WOEFULLY* UNDERDEVELOPED, ARE SUFFICIENT FOR THESE *SIMPLE* SUBJECTS.

NOW...

·MOON HISTORY·

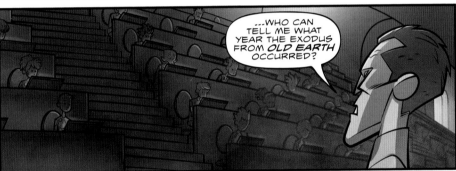

...WHO CAN TELL ME WHAT YEAR THE EXODUS FROM *OLD EARTH* OCCURRED?

OH! UH...*PROFESSOR KILLIAN,* I KNOW...IT WAS, LIKE, 2792!

HM. AN *ADEQUATE* ANSWER FOR A LOW-LEVEL QUESTION.

AND CAN ANYONE NAME THE *ORIGINAL* THREE COLONY WORLDS?

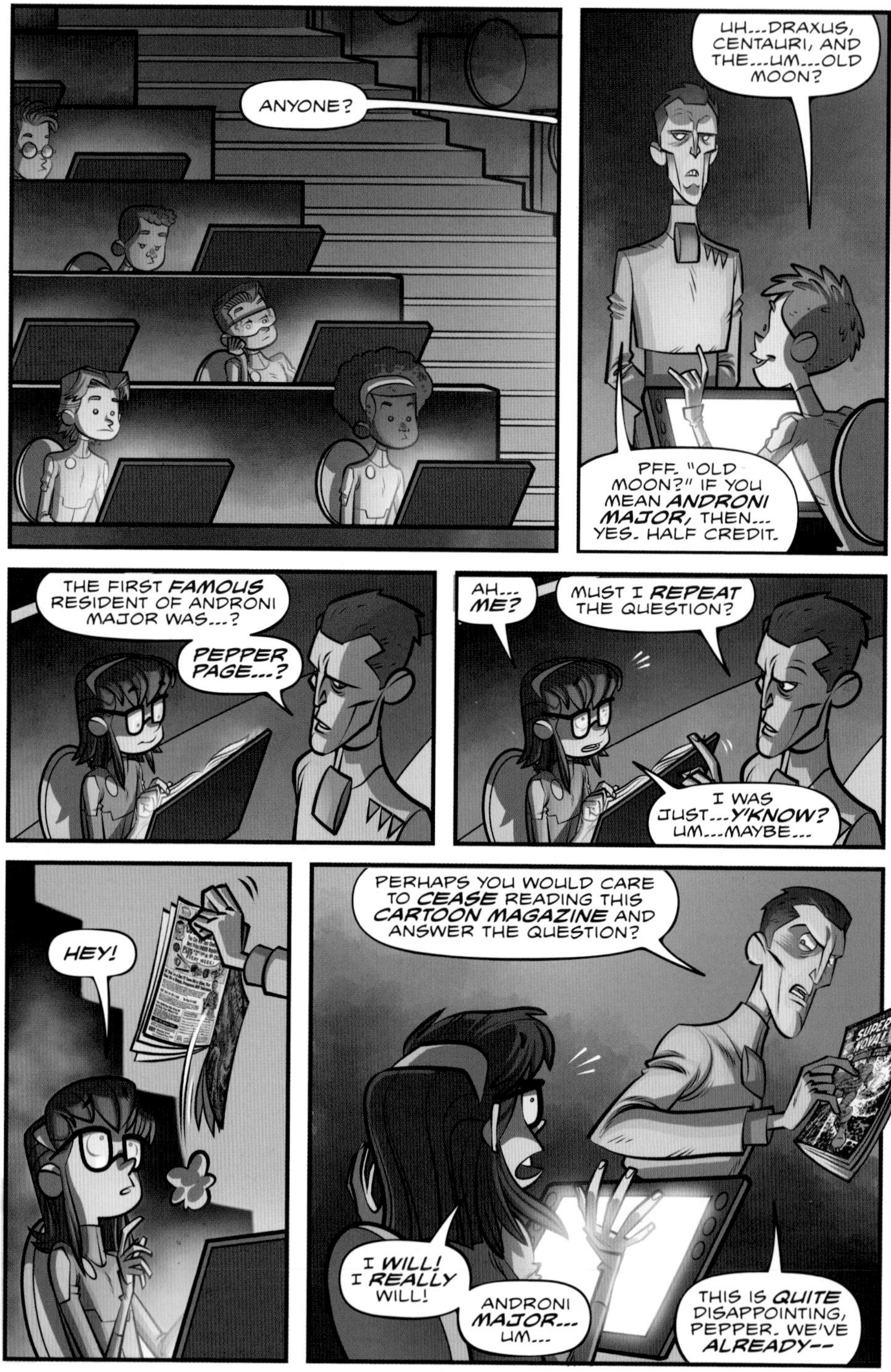
ANYONE?
UH...DRAXUS, CENTAURI, AND THE...UM...OLD MOON?
PFF. "OLD MOON?" IF YOU MEAN ANDRONI MAJOR, THEN... YES. HALF CREDIT.
THE FIRST FAMOUS RESIDENT OF ANDRONI MAJOR WAS...?
PEPPER PAGE...?
AH... ME?
MUST I REPEAT THE QUESTION?
I WAS JUST...Y'KNOW? UM...MAYBE...
HEY!
PERHAPS YOU WOULD CARE TO CEASE READING THIS CARTOON MAGAZINE AND ANSWER THE QUESTION?
I WILL! I REALLY WILL!
ANDRONI MAJOR... UM...
THIS IS QUITE DISAPPOINTING, PEPPER. WE'VE ALREADY--

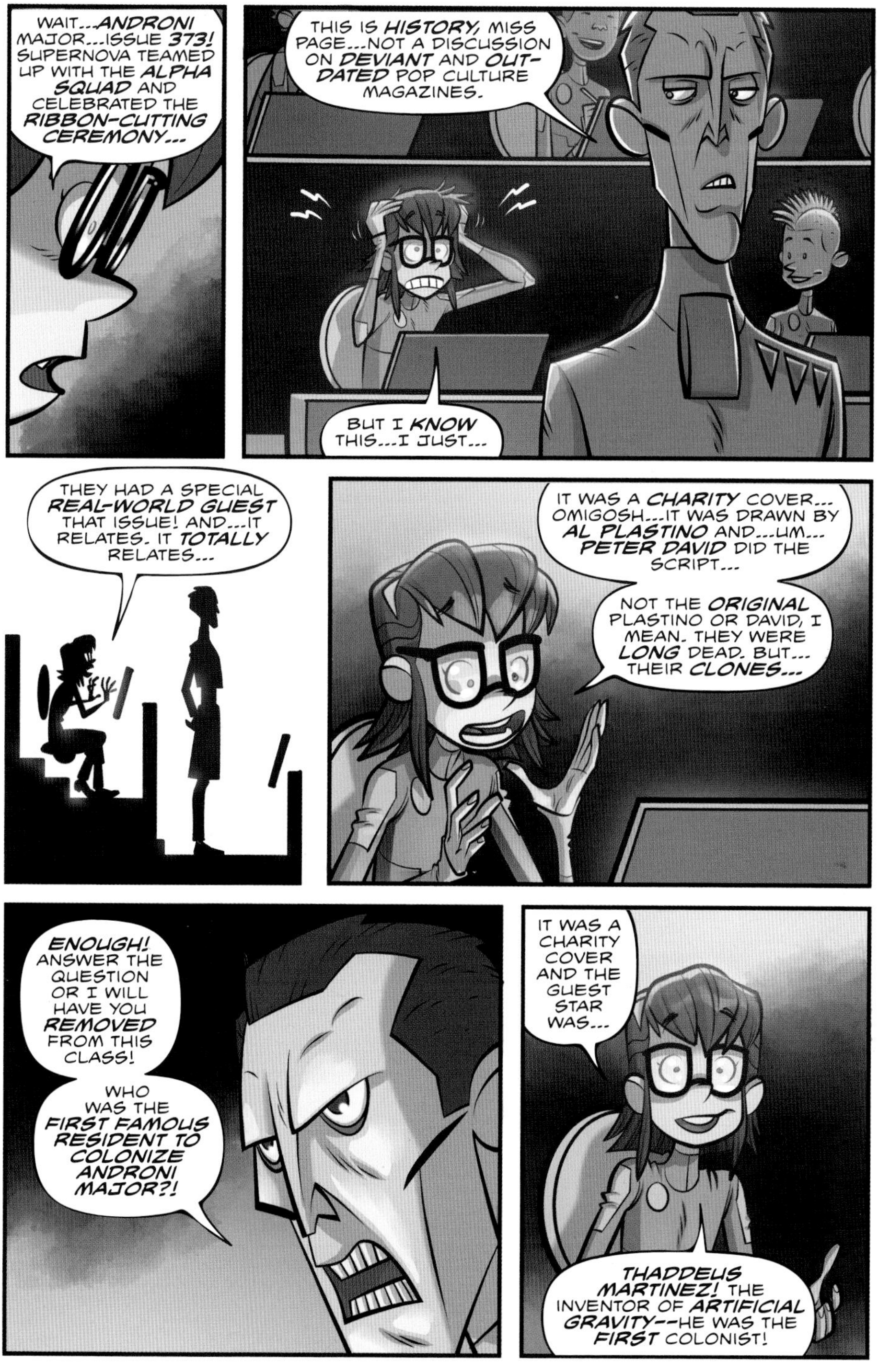
WAIT...ANDRONI MAJOR...ISSUE 373! SUPERNOVA TEAMED UP WITH THE ALPHA SQUAD AND CELEBRATED THE RIBBON-CUTTING CEREMONY...
THIS IS HISTORY, MISS PAGE...NOT A DISCUSSION ON DEVIANT AND OUTDATED POP CULTURE MAGAZINES.
BUT I KNOW THIS...I JUST...
THEY HAD A SPECIAL REAL-WORLD GUEST THAT ISSUE! AND...IT RELATES. IT TOTALLY RELATES...
IT WAS A CHARITY COVER... OMIGOSH...IT WAS DRAWN BY AL PLASTINO AND...UM... PETER DAVID DID THE SCRIPT...
NOT THE ORIGINAL PLASTINO OR DAVID, I MEAN. THEY WERE LONG DEAD. BUT... THEIR CLONES...
ENOUGH! ANSWER THE QUESTION OR I WILL HAVE YOU REMOVED FROM THIS CLASS!
WHO WAS THE FIRST FAMOUS RESIDENT TO COLONIZE ANDRONI MAJOR?!
IT WAS A CHARITY COVER AND THE GUEST STAR WAS...
THADDEUS MARTINEZ! THE INVENTOR OF ARTIFICIAL GRAVITY--HE WAS THE FIRST COLONIST!

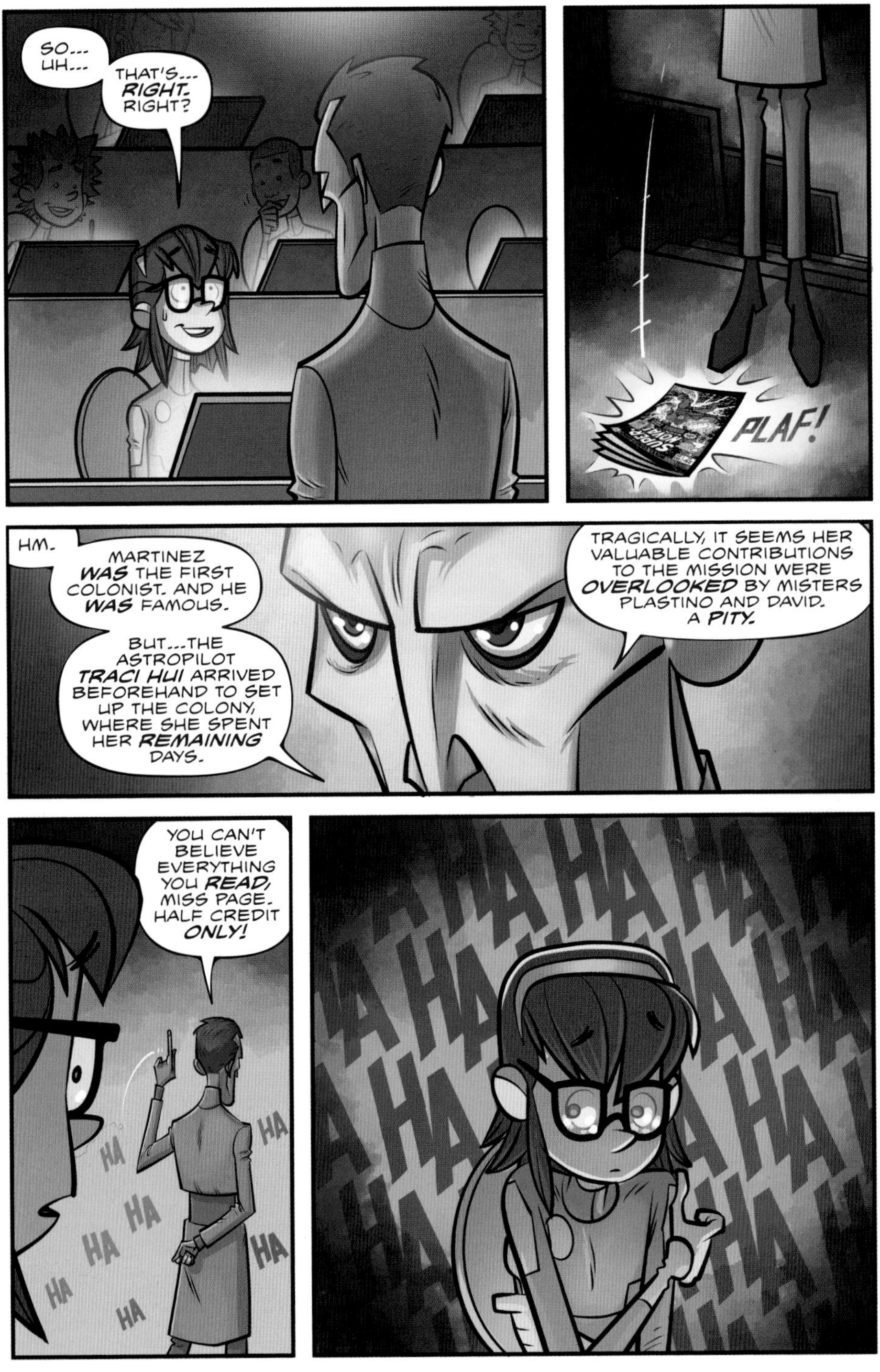
SO... UH...
THAT'S... RIGHT. RIGHT?
PLAF!
HM.
MARTINEZ WAS THE FIRST COLONIST. AND HE WAS FAMOUS.
BUT...THE ASTROPILOT TRACI HUI ARRIVED BEFOREHAND TO SET UP THE COLONY, WHERE SHE SPENT HER REMAINING DAYS.
TRAGICALLY, IT SEEMS HER VALUABLE CONTRIBUTIONS TO THE MISSION WERE OVERLOOKED BY MISTERS PLASTINO AND DAVID. A PITY.
YOU CAN'T BELIEVE EVERYTHING YOU READ, MISS PAGE. HALF CREDIT ONLY!
HA HA HA HA HA HA HA
HA HA HA HA HA HA HA HA HA HA HA HA

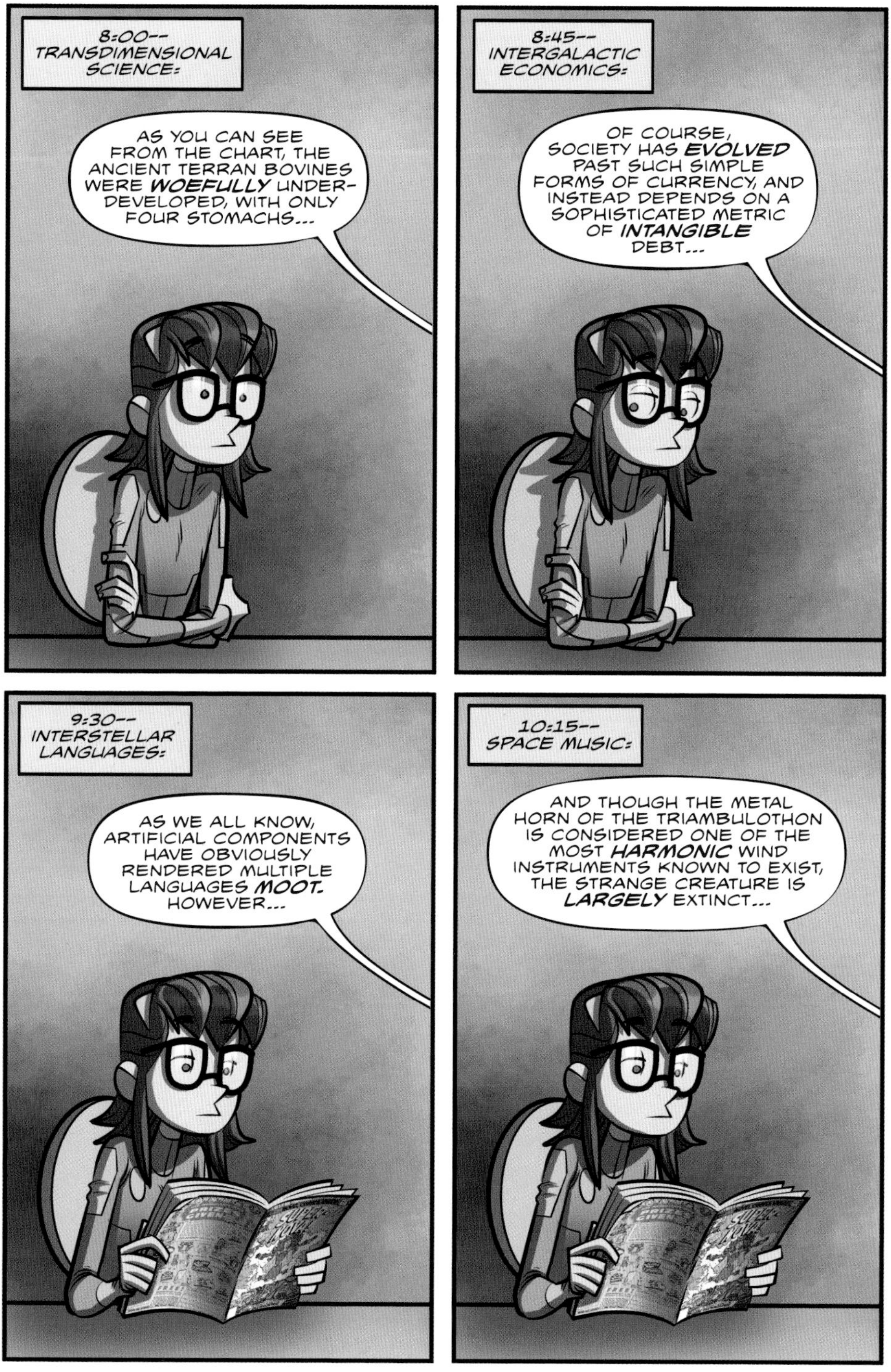
8:00-- TRANSDIMENSIONAL SCIENCE:
AS YOU CAN SEE FROM THE CHART, THE ANCIENT TERRAN BOVINES WERE ***WOEFULLY*** UNDER-DEVELOPED, WITH ONLY FOUR STOMACHS...
8:45-- INTERGALACTIC ECONOMICS:
OF COURSE, SOCIETY HAS ***EVOLVED*** PAST SUCH SIMPLE FORMS OF CURRENCY, AND INSTEAD DEPENDS ON A SOPHISTICATED METRIC OF ***INTANGIBLE*** DEBT...
9:30-- INTERSTELLAR LANGUAGES:
AS WE ALL KNOW, ARTIFICIAL COMPONENTS HAVE OBVIOUSLY RENDERED MULTIPLE LANGUAGES ***MOOT.*** HOWEVER...
10:15-- SPACE MUSIC:
AND THOUGH THE METAL HORN OF THE TRIAMBULOTHON IS CONSIDERED ONE OF THE MOST ***HARMONIC*** WIND INSTRUMENTS KNOWN TO EXIST, THE STRANGE CREATURE IS ***LARGELY*** EXTINCT...

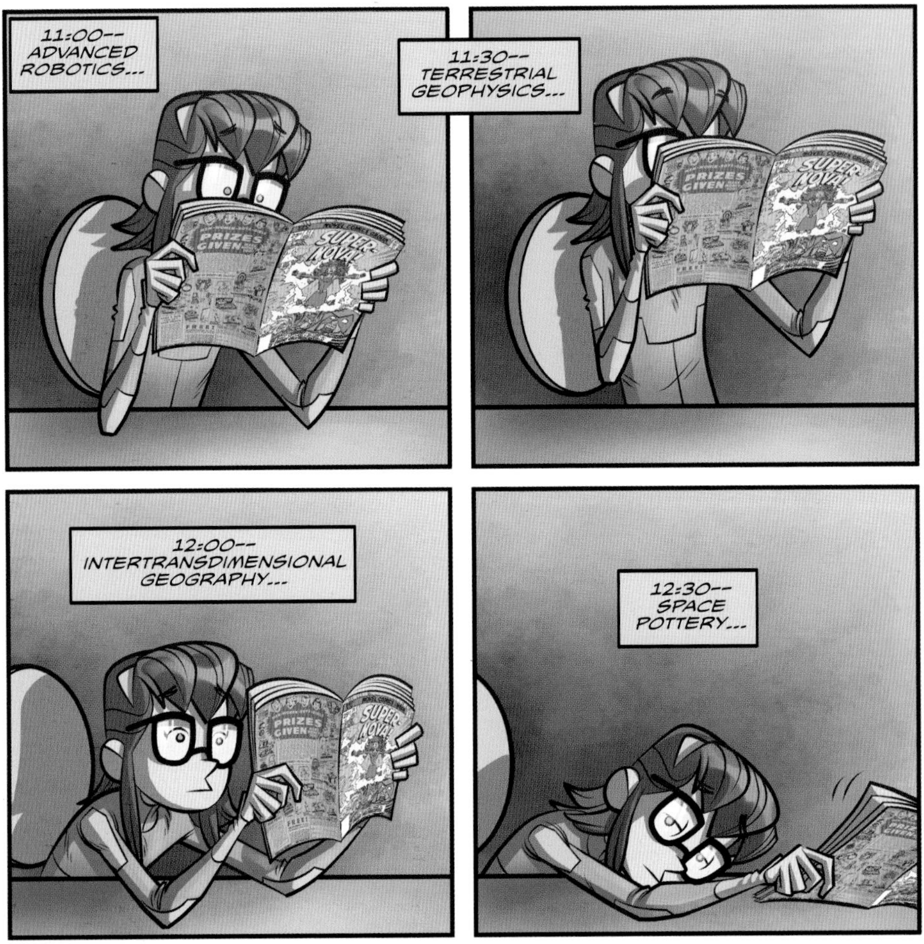
11:00-- ADVANCED ROBOTICS...
11:30-- TERRESTRIAL GEOPHYSICS...
12:00-- INTERTRANSDIMENSIONAL GEOGRAPHY...
12:30-- SPACE POTTERY...
1:15-- QUASI-POLITICAL SCIENCE...
2:15-- ANTIMATTER CALLIGRAPHY...

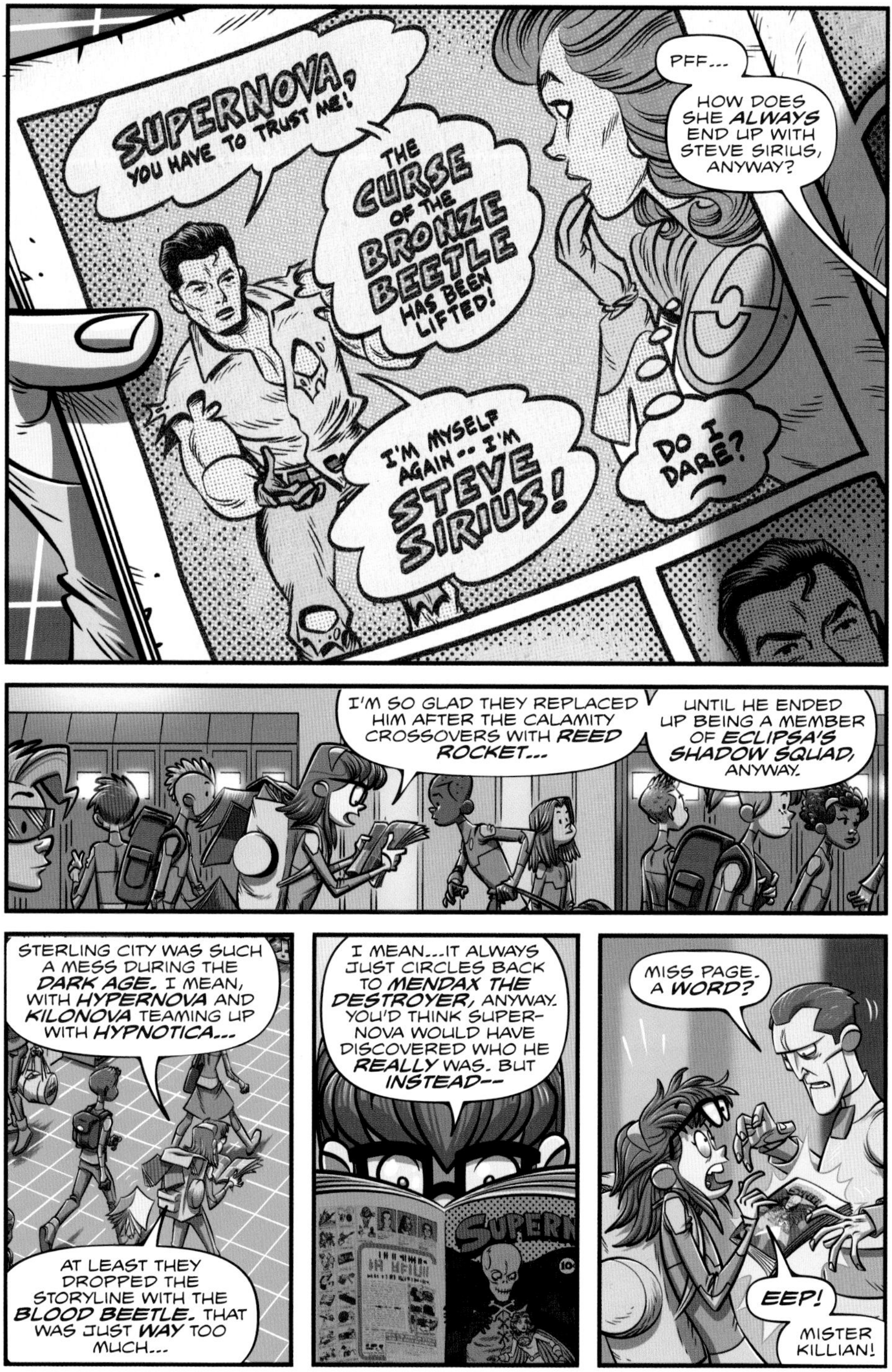
SUPERNOVA, YOU HAVE TO TRUST ME!
THE CURSE OF THE BRONZE BEETLE HAS BEEN LIFTED!
I'M MYSELF AGAIN-- I'M STEVE SIRIUS!
DO I DARE?
PFF...
HOW DOES SHE ALWAYS END UP WITH STEVE SIRIUS, ANYWAY?
I'M SO GLAD THEY REPLACED HIM AFTER THE CALAMITY CROSSOVERS WITH REED ROCKET...
UNTIL HE ENDED UP BEING A MEMBER OF ECLIPSA'S SHADOW SQUAD, ANYWAY.
STERLING CITY WAS SUCH A MESS DURING THE DARK AGE. I MEAN, WITH HYPERNOVA AND KILONOVA TEAMING UP WITH HYPNOTICA...
AT LEAST THEY DROPPED THE STORYLINE WITH THE BLOOD BEETLE. THAT WAS JUST WAY TOO MUCH...
I MEAN...IT ALWAYS JUST CIRCLES BACK TO MENDAX THE DESTROYER, ANYWAY. YOU'D THINK SUPER-NOVA WOULD HAVE DISCOVERED WHO HE REALLY WAS. BUT INSTEAD--
SUPERN
MISS PAGE. A WORD?
EEP!
MISTER KILLIAN!

THAT'S *PROFESSOR* KILLIAN. I HAVE *EARNED* MY TITLE, PLEASE DO *NOT* IGNORE IT.

UH... YEAH. YES, SIR. *PROFESSOR.* SIR.

I SEE YOU *REMAIN* HOPELESSLY ENGAGED IN THE REALM OF *MAKE-BELIEVE.*

IT'S... COMICS. YOU KNOW...

MAY I?

UM...

SUPERNOVA. THE FIRST APPEARANCE OF *THE GIGGLING SKULL.*

A *RARE* ORIGINAL COPY.

YOU *KNOW*... COMICS? YOU--

I KNOW A GREAT MANY THINGS.

NEVER FORGET THAT.

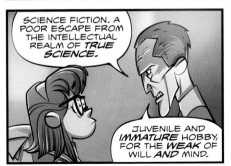

SCIENCE FICTION. A POOR ESCAPE FROM THE INTELLECTUAL REALM OF *TRUE SCIENCE.*

JUVENILE AND *IMMATURE* HOBBY, FOR THE *WEAK* OF WILL *AND* MIND.

TO THAT END...I WAS *SEEKING* YOU.

ME?

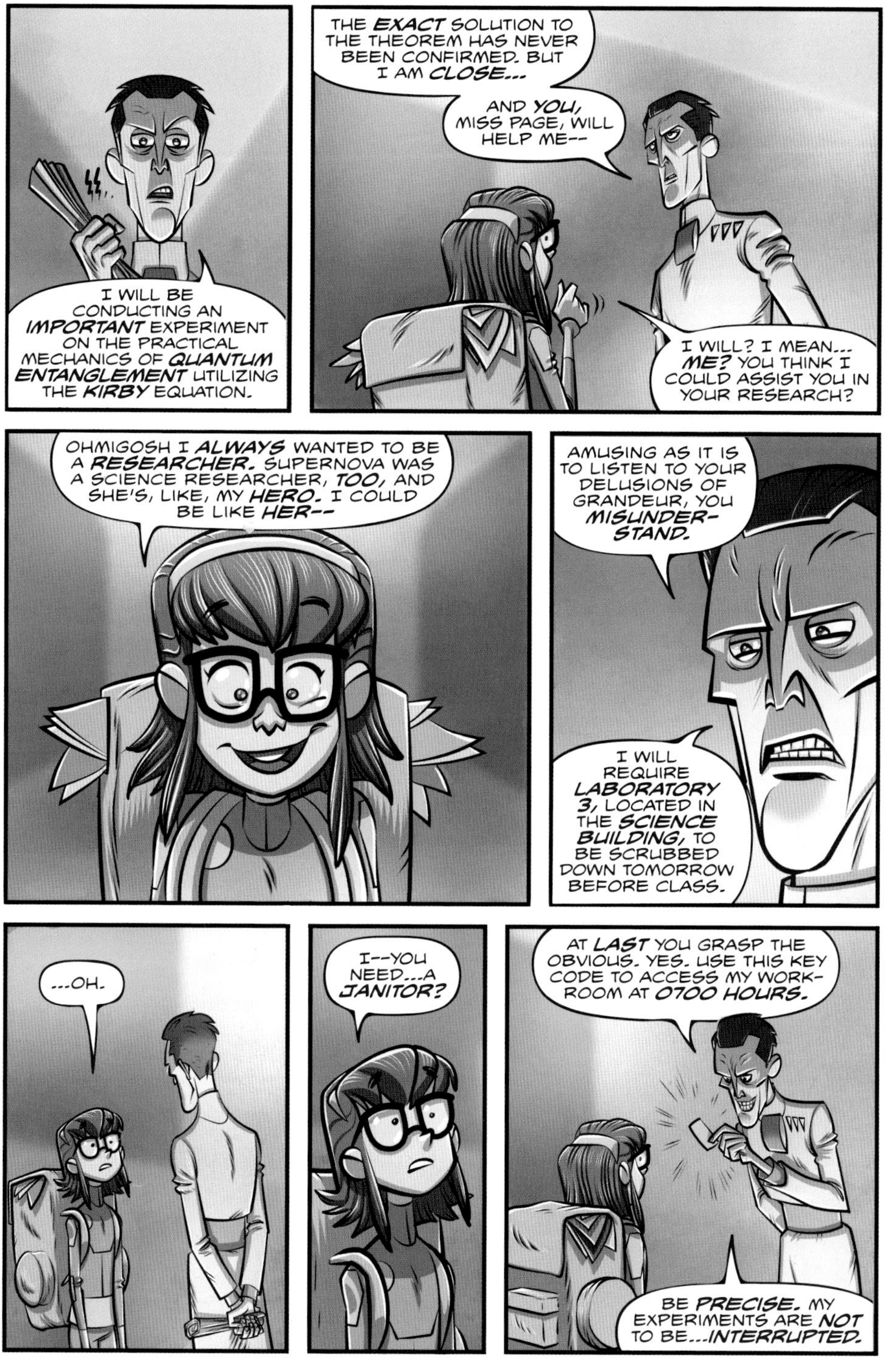
I WILL BE CONDUCTING AN IMPORTANT EXPERIMENT ON THE PRACTICAL MECHANICS OF QUANTUM ENTANGLEMENT UTILIZING THE KIRBY EQUATION.
THE EXACT SOLUTION TO THE THEOREM HAS NEVER BEEN CONFIRMED. BUT I AM CLOSE...
AND YOU, MISS PAGE, WILL HELP ME--
I WILL? I MEAN... ME? YOU THINK I COULD ASSIST YOU IN YOUR RESEARCH?
OHMIGOSH I ALWAYS WANTED TO BE A RESEARCHER. SUPERNOVA WAS A SCIENCE RESEARCHER, TOO, AND SHE'S, LIKE, MY HERO. I COULD BE LIKE HER--
AMUSING AS IT IS TO LISTEN TO YOUR DELUSIONS OF GRANDEUR, YOU MISUNDER-STAND.
I WILL REQUIRE LABORATORY 3, LOCATED IN THE SCIENCE BUILDING, TO BE SCRUBBED DOWN TOMORROW BEFORE CLASS.
...OH.
I--YOU NEED...A JANITOR?
AT LAST YOU GRASP THE OBVIOUS. YES. USE THIS KEY CODE TO ACCESS MY WORK-ROOM AT 0700 HOURS.
BE PRECISE. MY EXPERIMENTS ARE NOT TO BE...INTERRUPTED.

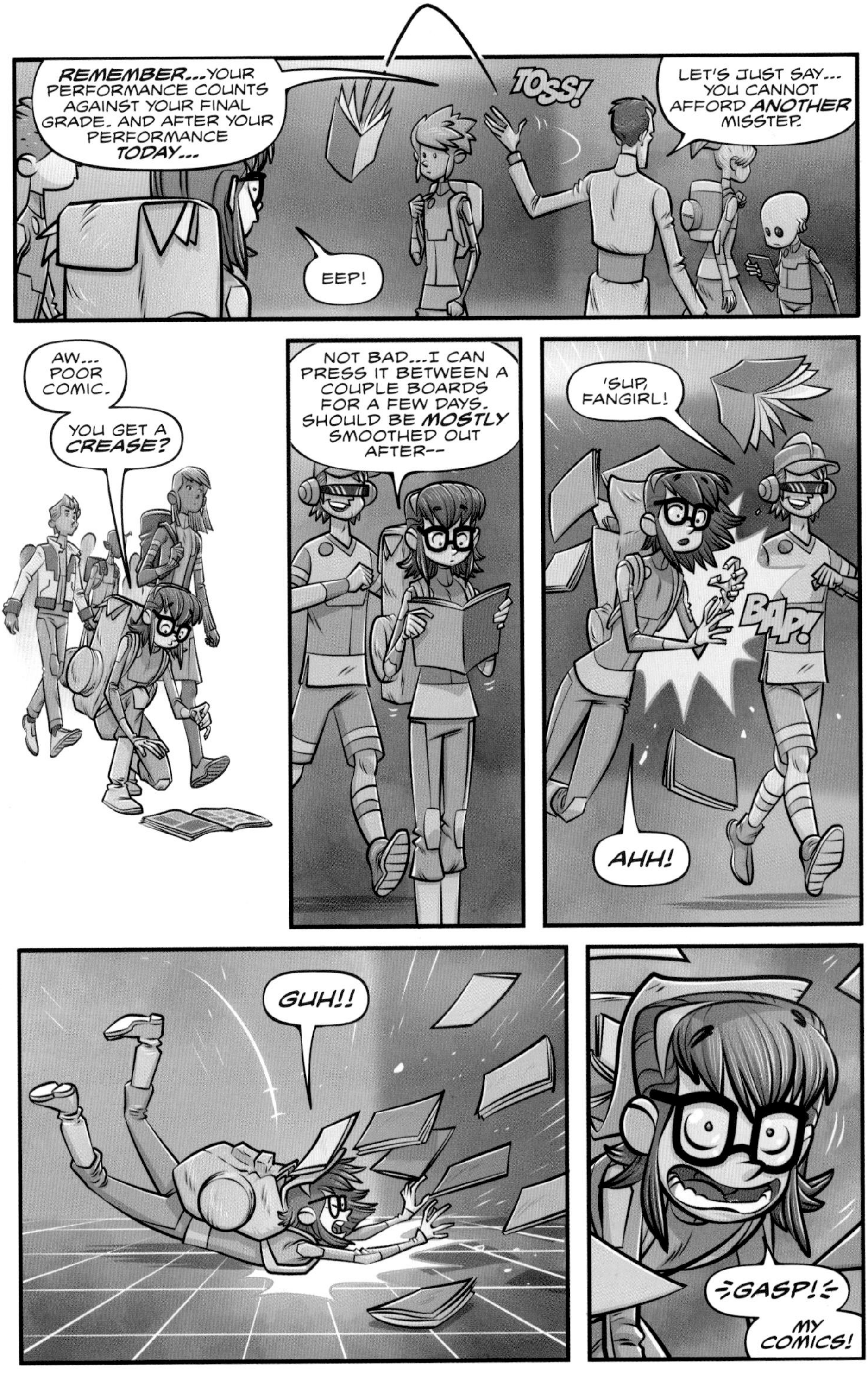
REMEMBER...YOUR PERFORMANCE COUNTS AGAINST YOUR FINAL GRADE. AND AFTER YOUR PERFORMANCE TODAY...
TOSS!
LET'S JUST SAY... YOU CANNOT AFFORD ANOTHER MISSTEP.
EEP!
AW... POOR COMIC.
YOU GET A CREASE?
NOT BAD...I CAN PRESS IT BETWEEN A COUPLE BOARDS FOR A FEW DAYS. SHOULD BE MOSTLY SMOOTHED OUT AFTER--
'SUP, FANGIRL!
BAP!
AHH!
GUH!!
GASP!
MY COMICS!

OKAY...I CAN SAVE THEM...SOON AS THE HALL CLEARS...

THEY'RE STILL *MINT*...

...MAYBE *NEAR MINT*...

...VERY GOOD...

...POOR. *VERY POOR.*

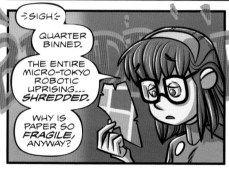

÷SIGH÷

QUARTER BINNED.

THE ENTIRE MICRO-TOKYO ROBOTIC UPRISING... *SHREDDED.*

WHY IS PAPER SO *FRAGILE,* ANYWAY?

WAIT? THE BELL?! *THE BELL!!*

THE HOLO-GAME!!!

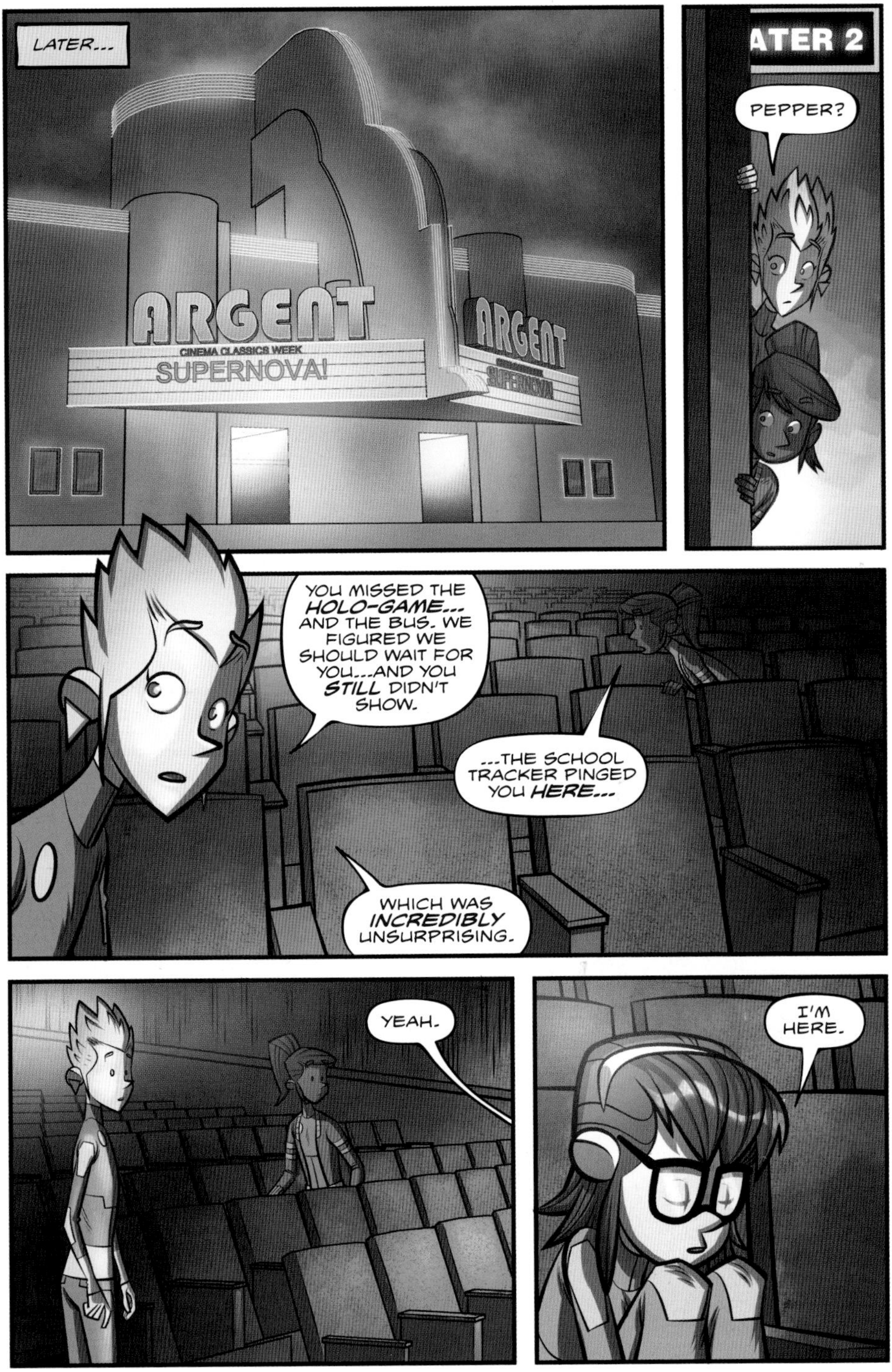
LATER...
ARGENT
CINEMA CLASSICS WEEK
SUPERNOVA!
ARGENT
SUPERNOVA!
ATER 2
PEPPER?
YOU MISSED THE HOLO-GAME... AND THE BUS. WE FIGURED WE SHOULD WAIT FOR YOU...AND YOU STILL DIDN'T SHOW.
...THE SCHOOL TRACKER PINGED YOU HERE...
WHICH WAS INCREDIBLY UNSURPRISING.
YEAH.
I'M HERE.

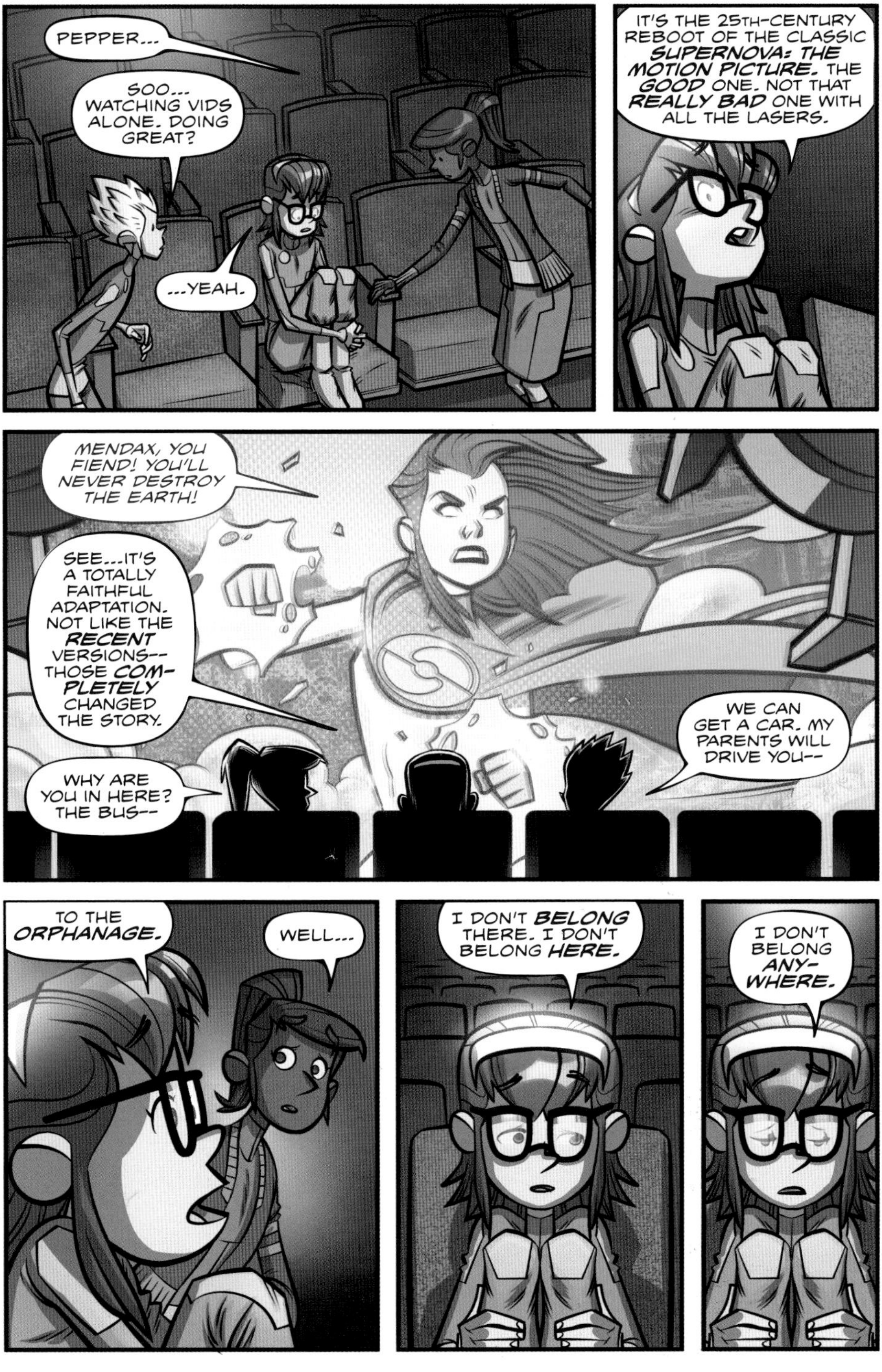
PEPPER...
SOO... WATCHING VIDS ALONE. DOING GREAT?
...YEAH.
IT'S THE 25TH-CENTURY REBOOT OF THE CLASSIC SUPERNOVA: THE MOTION PICTURE. THE GOOD ONE. NOT THAT REALLY BAD ONE WITH ALL THE LASERS.
MENDAX, YOU FIEND! YOU'LL NEVER DESTROY THE EARTH!
SEE...IT'S A TOTALLY FAITHFUL ADAPTATION. NOT LIKE THE RECENT VERSIONS-- THOSE COMPLETELY CHANGED THE STORY.
WHY ARE YOU IN HERE? THE BUS--
WE CAN GET A CAR. MY PARENTS WILL DRIVE YOU--
TO THE ORPHANAGE.
WELL...
I DON'T BELONG THERE. I DON'T BELONG HERE.
I DON'T BELONG ANYWHERE.

WHEN I WAS LITTLE... *REALLY* LITTLE, BEFORE KINDER, WHEN WE MET, I REMEMBER WATCHING THIS MOVIE.

SUPERNOVA.

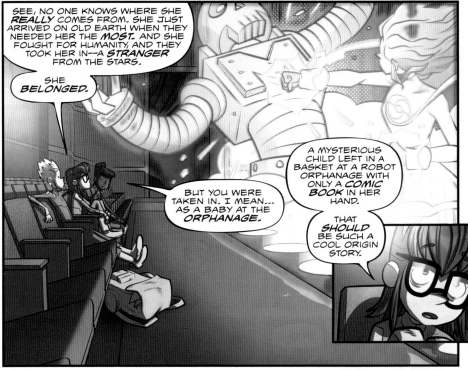

SEE, NO ONE KNOWS WHERE SHE *REALLY* COMES FROM. SHE JUST ARRIVED ON OLD EARTH WHEN THEY NEEDED HER THE *MOST.* AND SHE FOUGHT FOR HUMANITY, AND THEY TOOK HER IN--A *STRANGER* FROM THE STARS.

SHE *BELONGED.*

BUT YOU WERE TAKEN IN. I MEAN... AS A BABY AT THE *ORPHANAGE.*

A MYSTERIOUS CHILD LEFT IN A BASKET AT A ROBOT ORPHANAGE WITH ONLY A *COMIC BOOK* IN HER HAND.

THAT *SHOULD* BE SUCH A COOL ORIGIN STORY.

BUT HONESTLY...IT'S JUST *DEPRESSING.*

IT'D BE NICE TO KNOW WHO I *REALLY* AM.

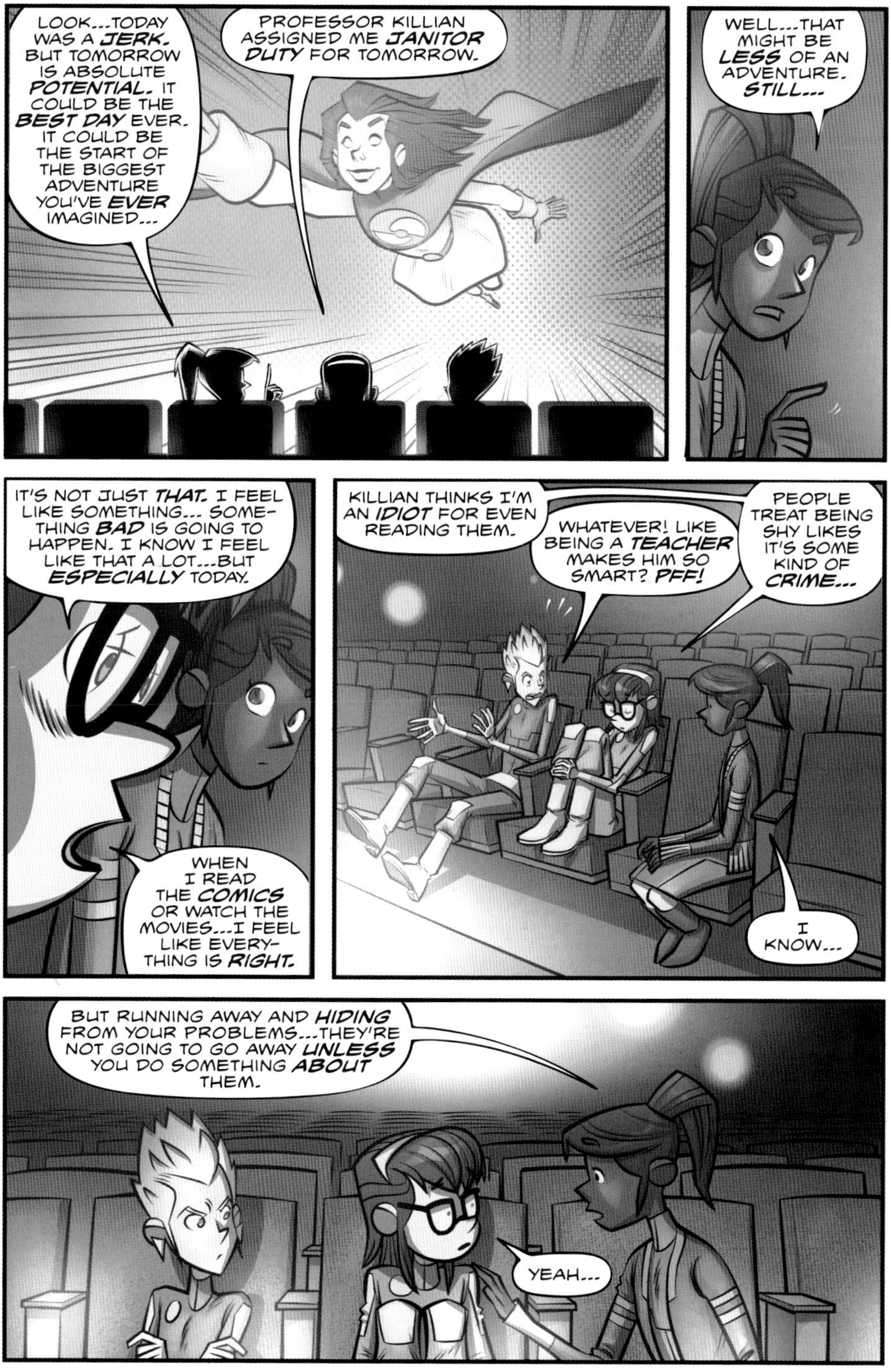
LOOK...TODAY WAS A JERK. BUT TOMORROW IS ABSOLUTE POTENTIAL. IT COULD BE THE BEST DAY EVER. IT COULD BE THE START OF THE BIGGEST ADVENTURE YOU'VE EVER IMAGINED...
PROFESSOR KILLIAN ASSIGNED ME JANITOR DUTY FOR TOMORROW.
WELL...THAT MIGHT BE LESS OF AN ADVENTURE. STILL...
IT'S NOT JUST THAT. I FEEL LIKE SOMETHING... SOMETHING BAD IS GOING TO HAPPEN. I KNOW I FEEL LIKE THAT A LOT...BUT ESPECIALLY TODAY.
WHEN I READ THE COMICS OR WATCH THE MOVIES...I FEEL LIKE EVERYTHING IS RIGHT.
KILLIAN THINKS I'M AN IDIOT FOR EVEN READING THEM.
PEOPLE TREAT BEING SHY LIKES IT'S SOME KIND OF CRIME...
WHATEVER! LIKE BEING A TEACHER MAKES HIM SO SMART? PFF!
I KNOW...
BUT RUNNING AWAY AND HIDING FROM YOUR PROBLEMS...THEY'RE NOT GOING TO GO AWAY UNLESS YOU DO SOMETHING ABOUT THEM.
YEAH...

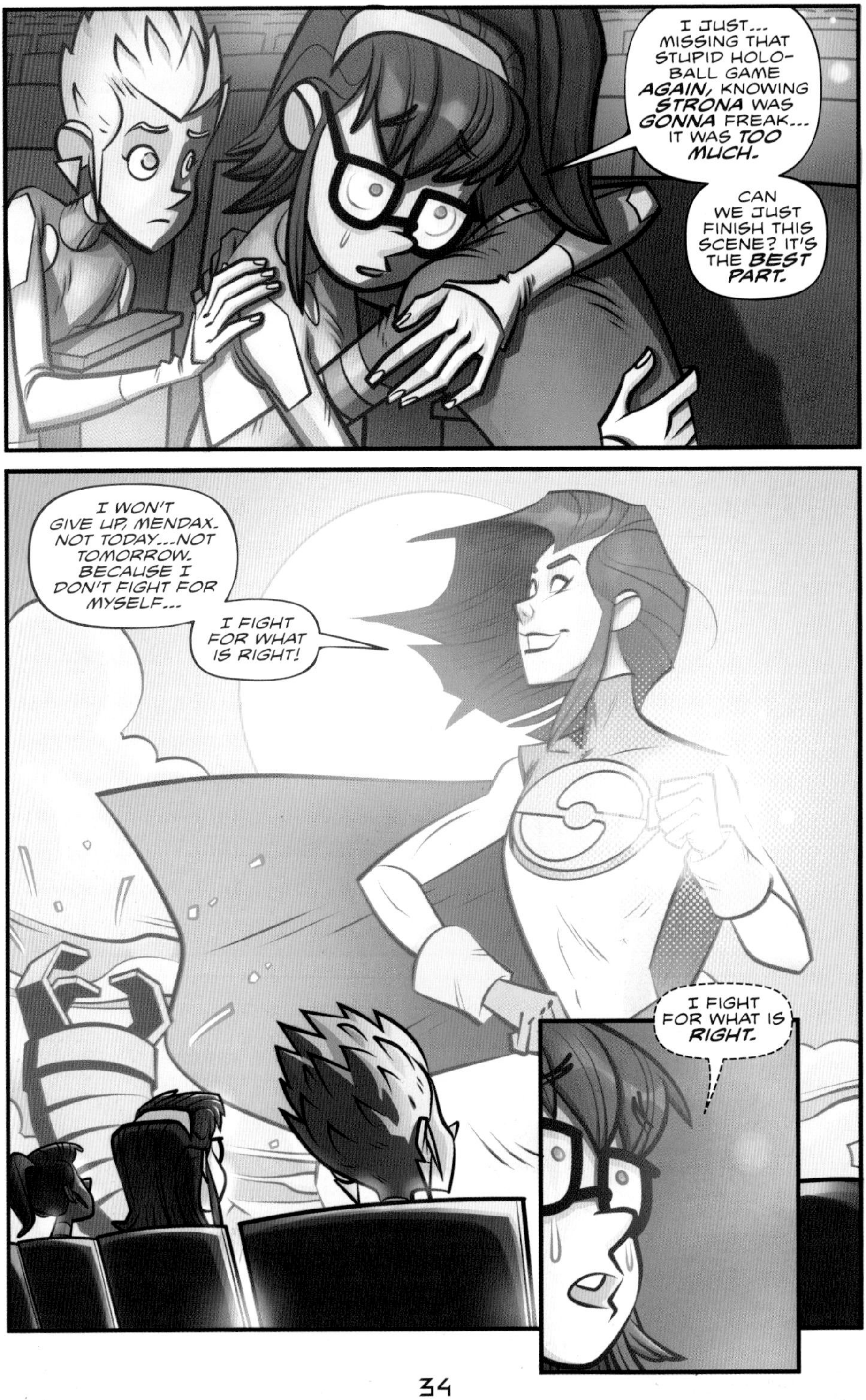
I JUST... MISSING THAT STUPID HOLO-BALL GAME AGAIN, KNOWING STRONA WAS GONNA FREAK... IT WAS TOO MUCH.
CAN WE JUST FINISH THIS SCENE? IT'S THE BEST PART.
I WON'T GIVE UP, MENDAX. NOT TODAY...NOT TOMORROW. BECAUSE I DON'T FIGHT FOR MYSELF...
I FIGHT FOR WHAT IS RIGHT!
I FIGHT FOR WHAT IS RIGHT.

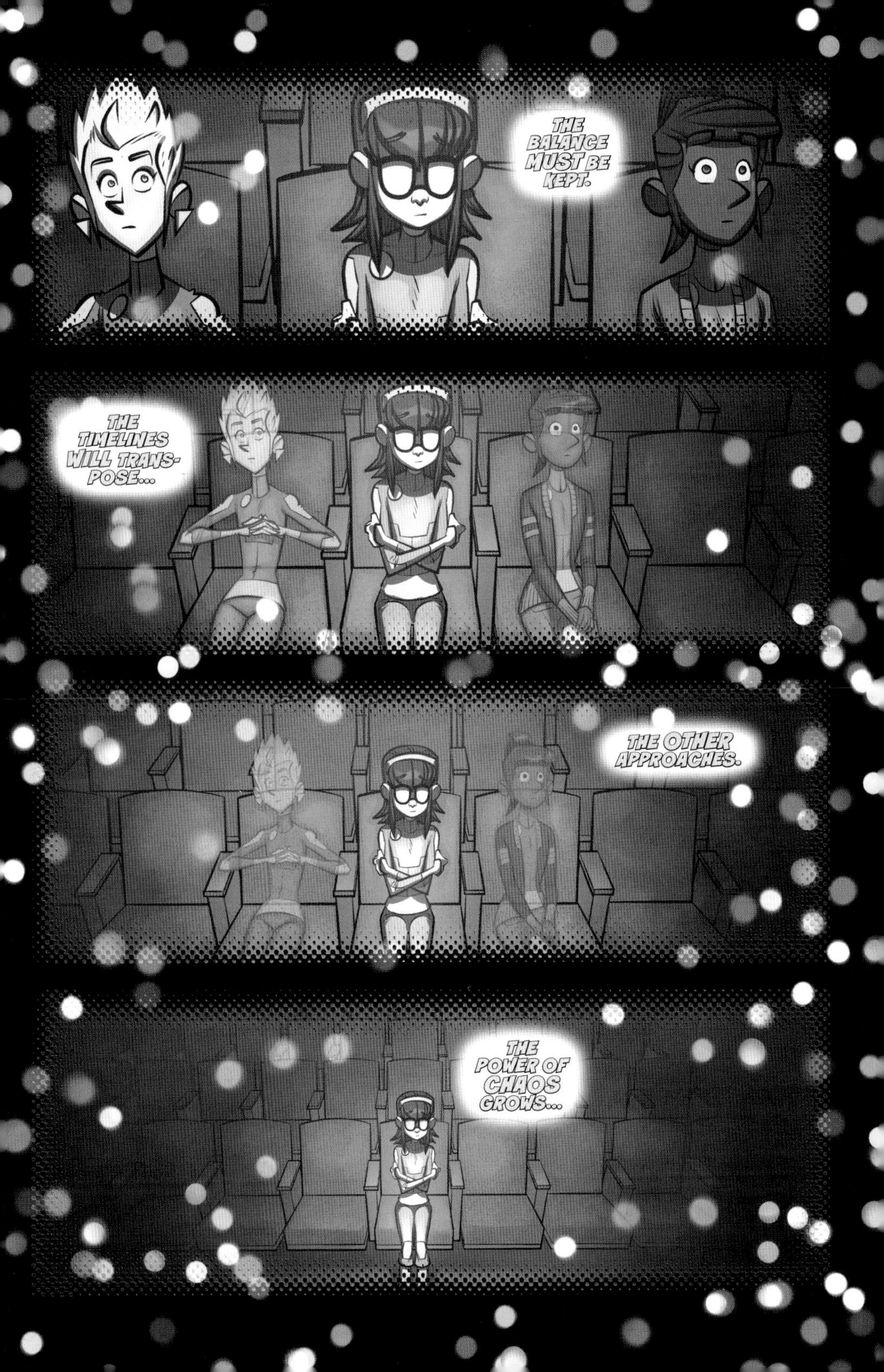
THE BALANCE MUST BE KEPT.
THE TIMELINES WILL TRANS-POSE...
THE OTHER APPROACHES.
THE POWER OF CHAOS GROWS...

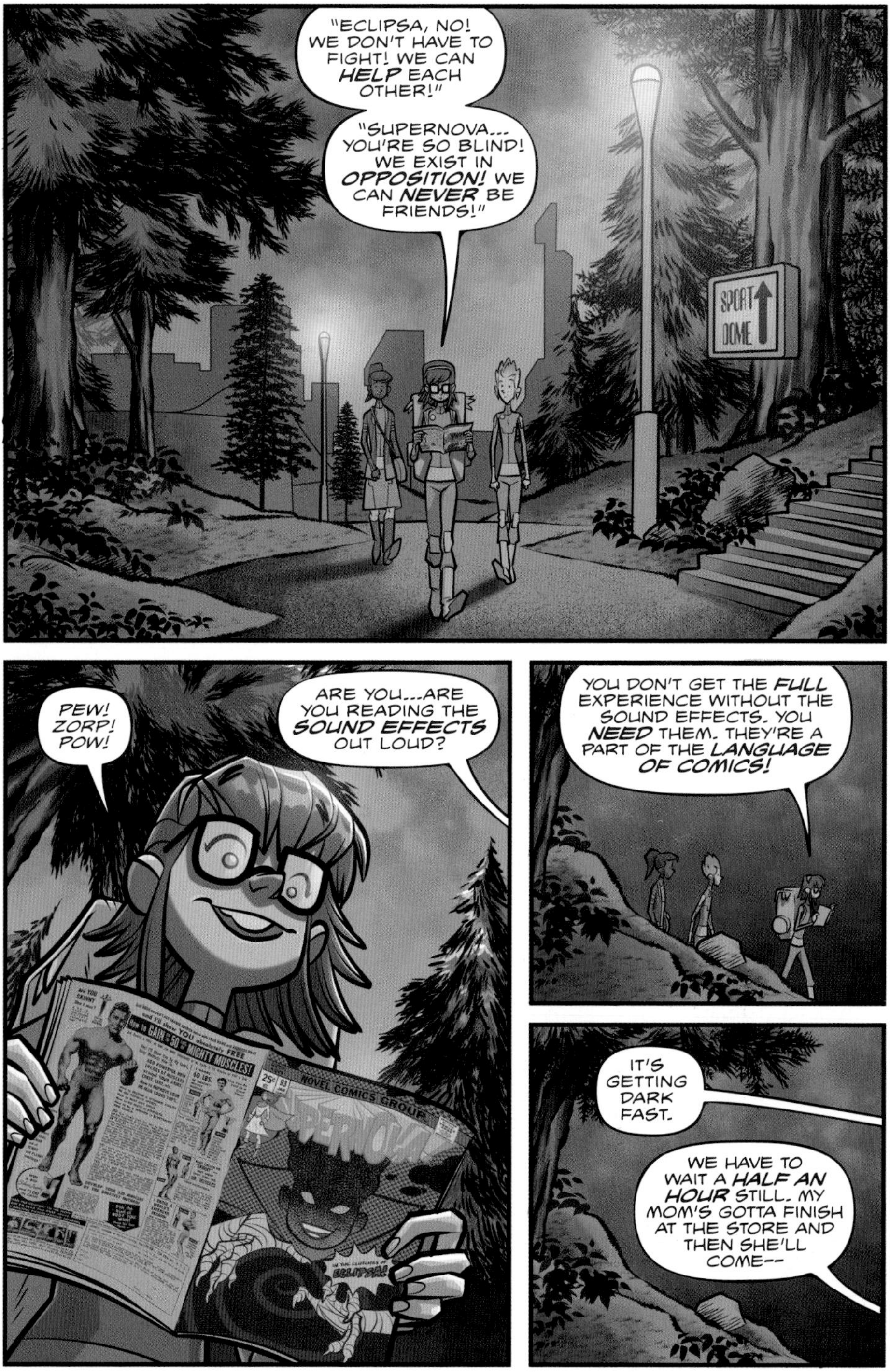

"ECLIPSA, NO! WE DON'T HAVE TO FIGHT! WE CAN HELP EACH OTHER!"
"SUPERNOVA... YOU'RE SO BLIND! WE EXIST IN OPPOSITION! WE CAN NEVER BE FRIENDS!"
SPORT DOME
PEW! ZORP! POW!
ARE YOU...ARE YOU READING THE SOUND EFFECTS OUT LOUD?
NOVEL COMICS GROUP
MIGHTY MUSCLES!
YOU DON'T GET THE FULL EXPERIENCE WITHOUT THE SOUND EFFECTS. YOU NEED THEM. THEY'RE A PART OF THE LANGUAGE OF COMICS!
IT'S GETTING DARK FAST.
WE HAVE TO WAIT A HALF AN HOUR STILL. MY MOM'S GOTTA FINISH AT THE STORE AND THEN SHE'LL COME--

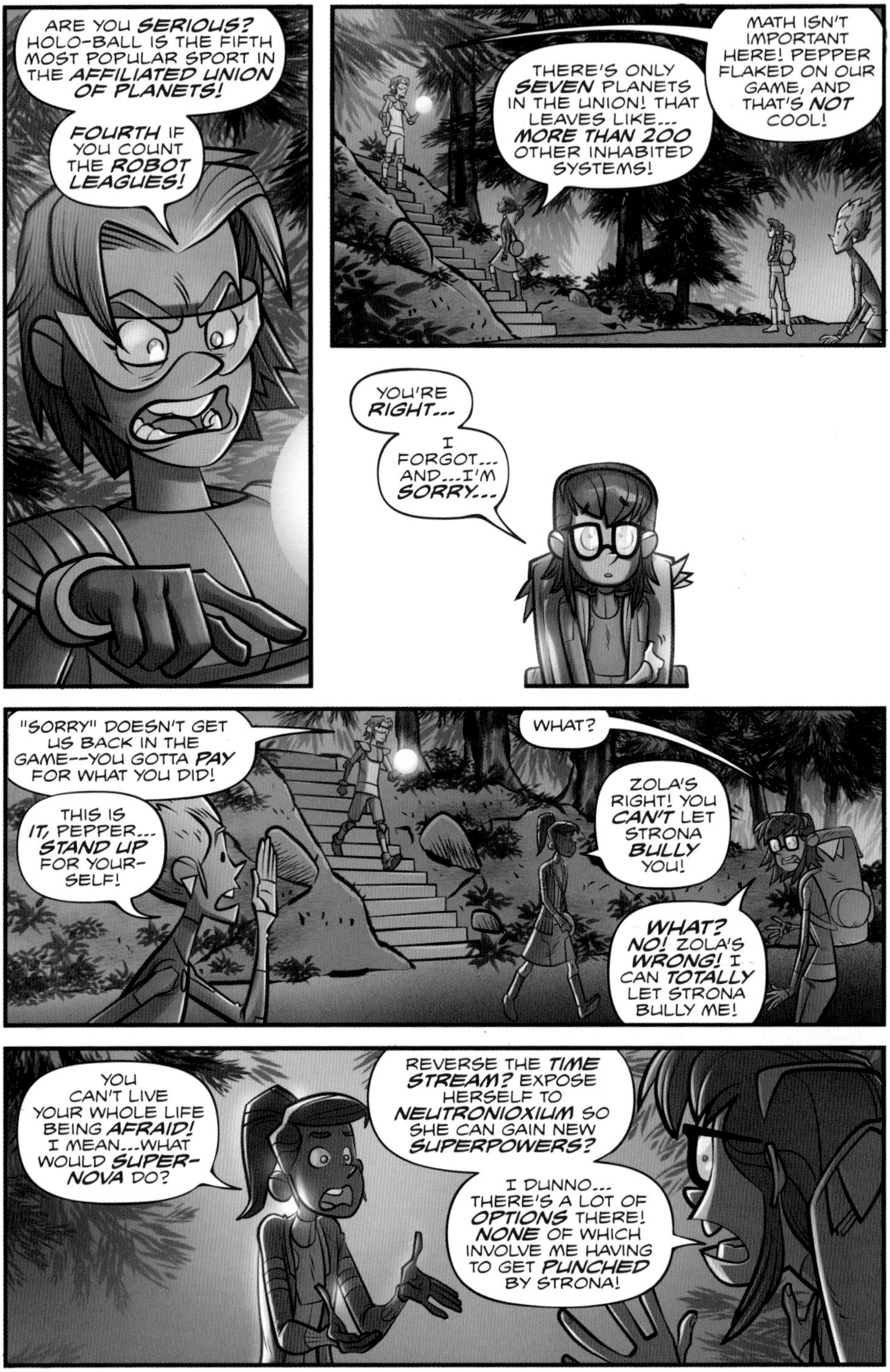
ARE YOU SERIOUS? HOLO-BALL IS THE FIFTH MOST POPULAR SPORT IN THE AFFILIATED UNION OF PLANETS!
FOURTH IF YOU COUNT THE ROBOT LEAGUES!
THERE'S ONLY SEVEN PLANETS IN THE UNION! THAT LEAVES LIKE... MORE THAN 200 OTHER INHABITED SYSTEMS!
MATH ISN'T IMPORTANT HERE! PEPPER FLAKED ON OUR GAME, AND THAT'S NOT COOL!
YOU'RE RIGHT...
I FORGOT... AND...I'M SORRY...
"SORRY" DOESN'T GET US BACK IN THE GAME--YOU GOTTA PAY FOR WHAT YOU DID!
WHAT?
THIS IS IT, PEPPER... STAND UP FOR YOUR-SELF!
ZOLA'S RIGHT! YOU CAN'T LET STRONA BULLY YOU!
WHAT? NO! ZOLA'S WRONG! I CAN TOTALLY LET STRONA BULLY ME!
YOU CAN'T LIVE YOUR WHOLE LIFE BEING AFRAID! I MEAN...WHAT WOULD SUPER-NOVA DO?
REVERSE THE TIME STREAM? EXPOSE HERSELF TO NEUTRONIOXIUM SO SHE CAN GAIN NEW SUPERPOWERS?
I DUNNO... THERE'S A LOT OF OPTIONS THERE! NONE OF WHICH INVOLVE ME HAVING TO GET PUNCHED BY STRONA!

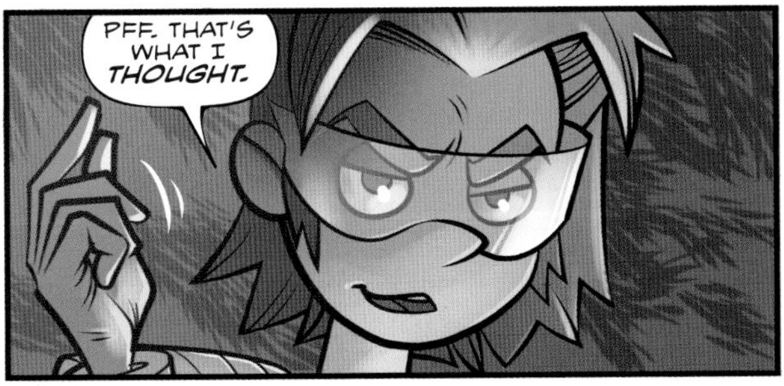
PFF. THAT'S WHAT I *THOUGHT.*
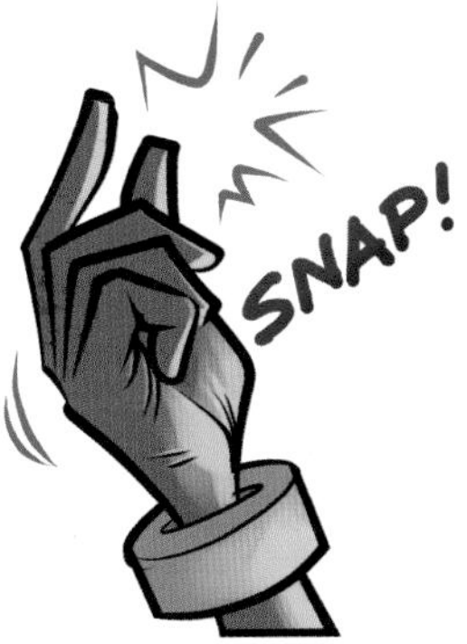
SNAP!
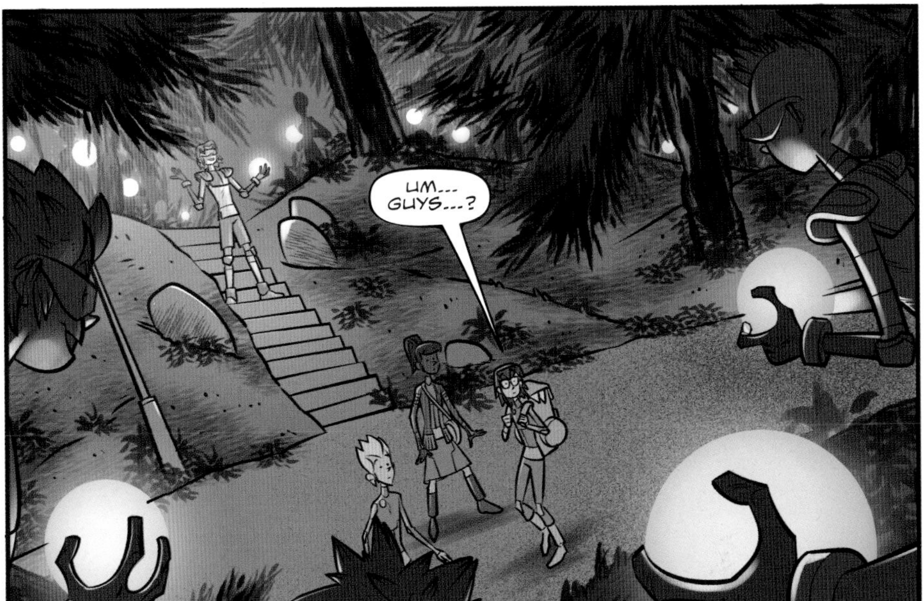
UM... GUYS...?
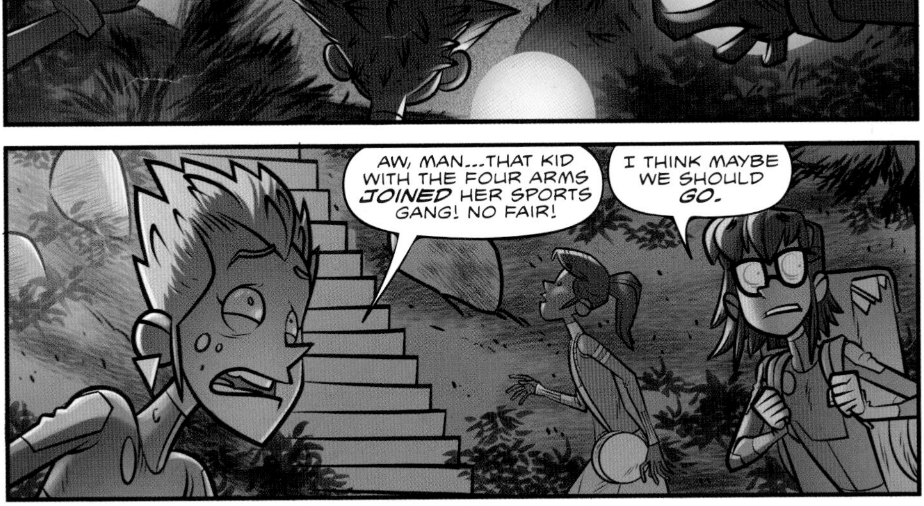
AW, MAN...THAT KID WITH THE FOUR ARMS *JOINED* HER SPORTS GANG! NO FAIR!
I THINK MAYBE WE SHOULD *GO.*

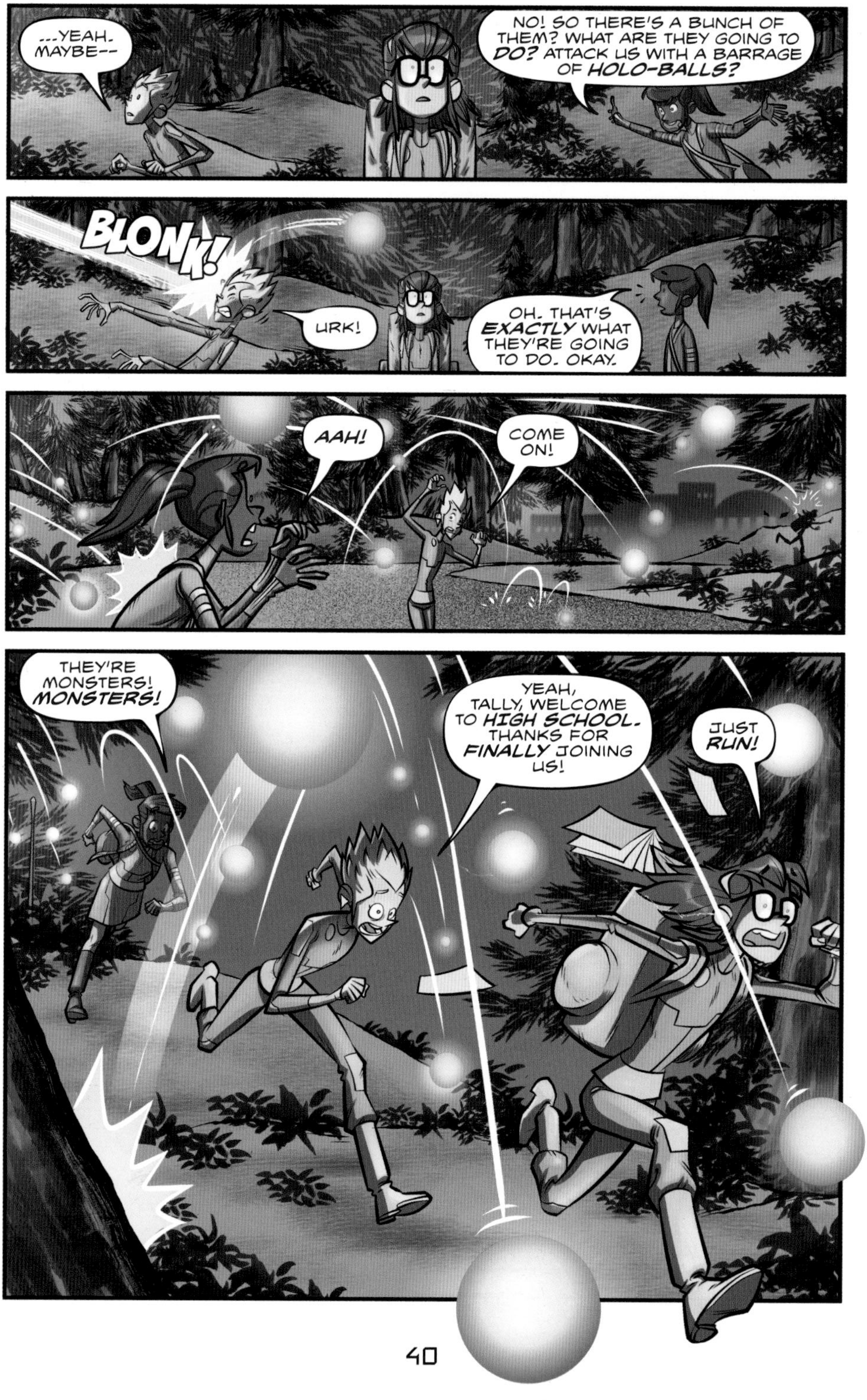

---YEAH. MAYBE--
NO! SO THERE'S A BUNCH OF THEM? WHAT ARE THEY GOING TO DO? ATTACK US WITH A BARRAGE OF HOLO-BALLS?
BLONK!
URK!
OH. THAT'S EXACTLY WHAT THEY'RE GOING TO DO. OKAY.
AAH!
COME ON!
THEY'RE MONSTERS! MONSTERS!
YEAH, TALLY, WELCOME TO HIGH SCHOOL. THANKS FOR FINALLY JOINING US!
JUST RUN!

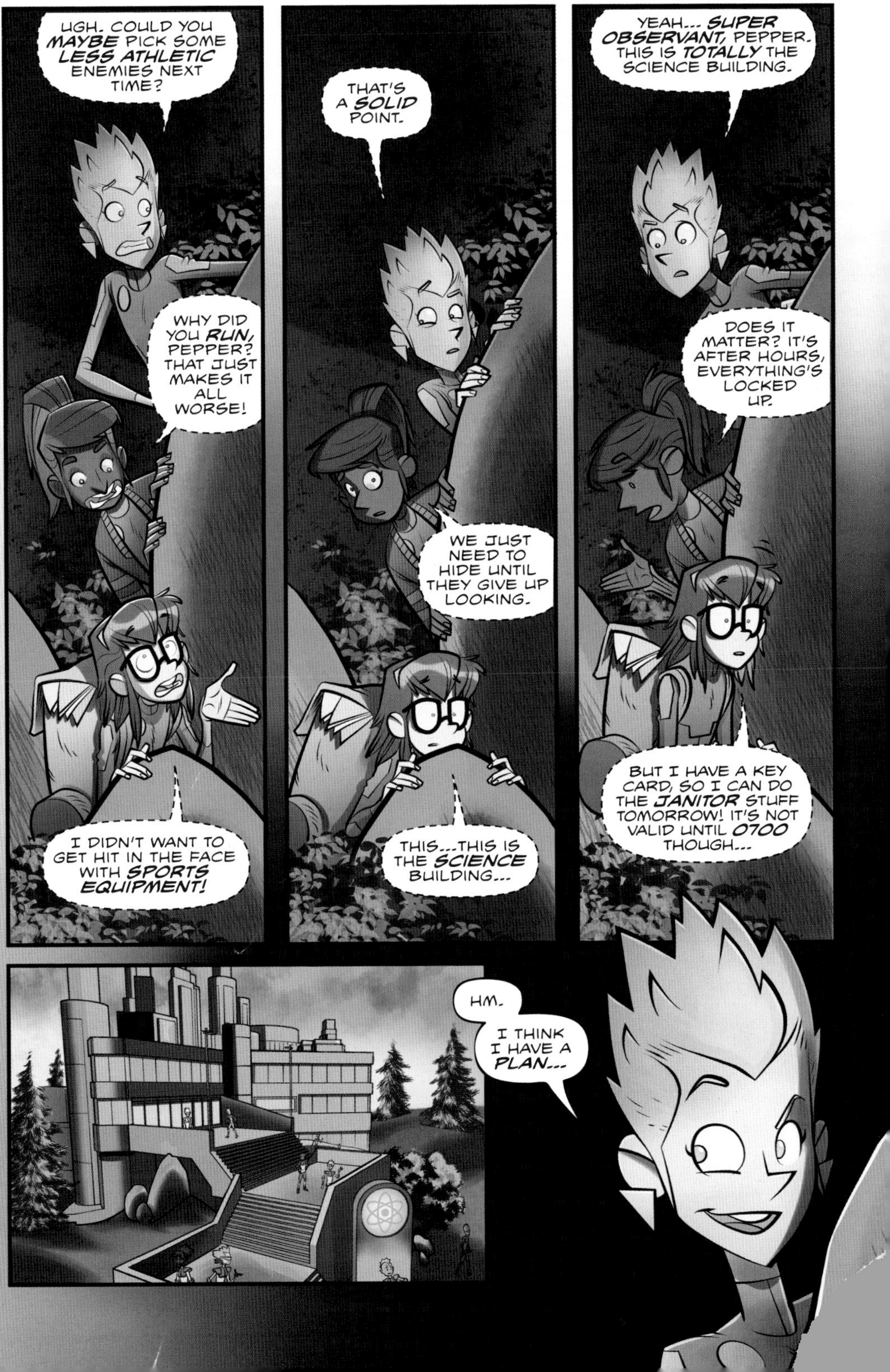
UGH. COULD YOU MAYBE PICK SOME LESS ATHLETIC ENEMIES NEXT TIME?
WHY DID YOU RUN, PEPPER? THAT JUST MAKES IT ALL WORSE!
I DIDN'T WANT TO GET HIT IN THE FACE WITH SPORTS EQUIPMENT!
THAT'S A SOLID POINT.
WE JUST NEED TO HIDE UNTIL THEY GIVE UP LOOKING.
THIS...THIS IS THE SCIENCE BUILDING...
YEAH... SUPER OBSERVANT, PEPPER. THIS IS TOTALLY THE SCIENCE BUILDING.
DOES IT MATTER? IT'S AFTER HOURS, EVERYTHING'S LOCKED UP.
BUT I HAVE A KEY CARD, SO I CAN DO THE JANITOR STUFF TOMORROW! IT'S NOT VALID UNTIL 0700 THOUGH...
HM.
I THINK I HAVE A PLAN...

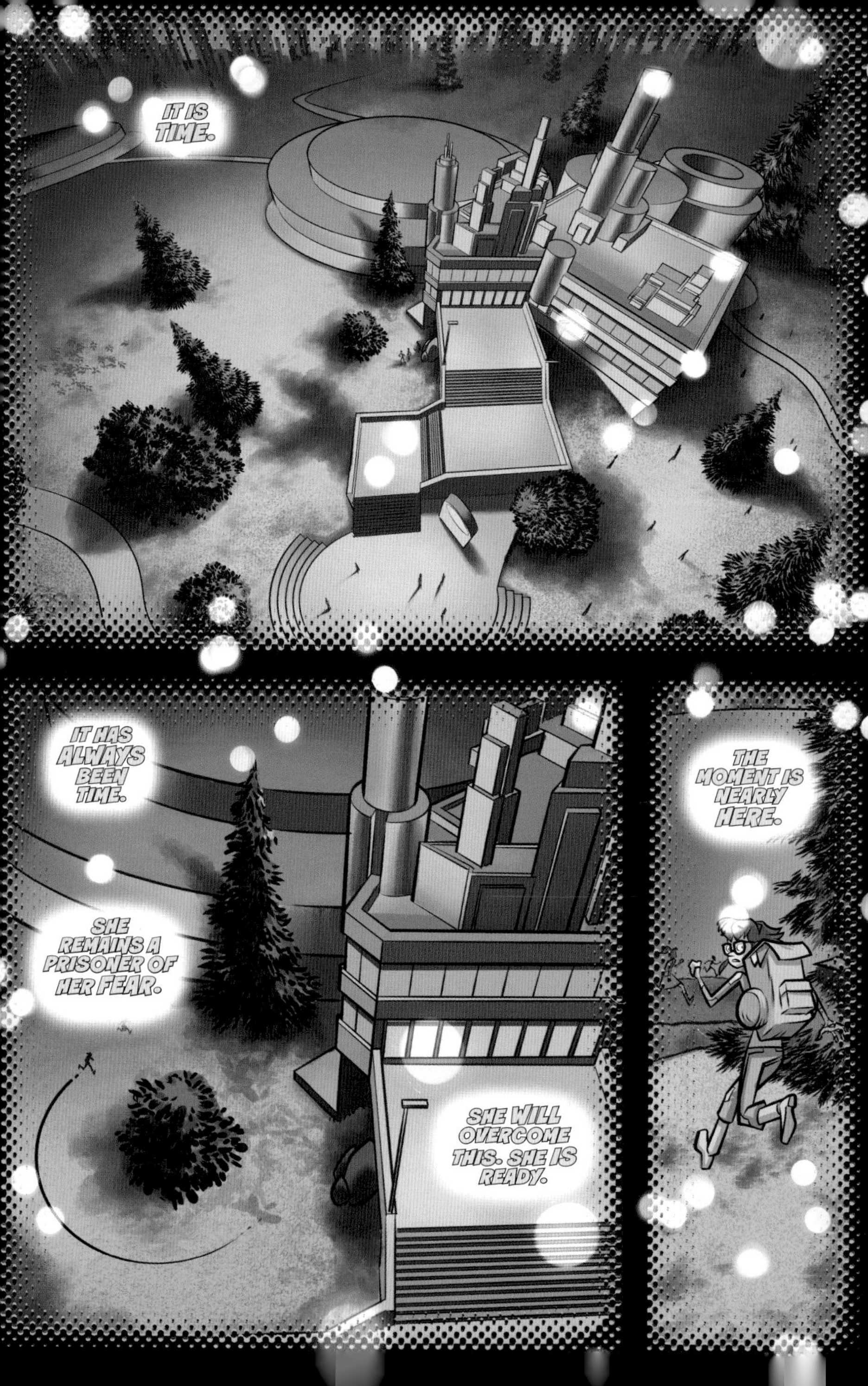
IT IS TIME.
IT HAS ALWAYS BEEN TIME.
SHE REMAINS A PRISONER OF HER FEAR.
SHE WILL OVERCOME THIS. SHE IS READY.
THE MOMENT IS NEARLY HERE.

THIS IS A **TERRIBLE** PLAN.

ALMOST GOT IT.

HURRY BEFORE THEY **COME BACK**...

OH...I'M JUST HACKING THE SCHOOL LOCKS SLOW-LIKE FOR **FUN**. BECAUSE **WHY NOT?**

THIS IS AGAINST THE **LAW**. IF WE GET **CAUGHT**, WE'LL BE **SUSPENDED** OR SOMETHING...

OR **SOMETHING?** SOMETHING **WORSE** THAN SUSPENSION? THEY CAN DO **THAT?** LIKE PRISON? ARE WE GOING TO **PRISON?!**

TOO FAR, PEPPER.

OHMIGOSH...I'M GOING TO BE IN PRISON **FOREVER** AND I'M GOING TO HAVE TO LEARN TO **MAKE LICENSE PLATES** AND WEAR **BLACK AND WHITE STRIPES**--

PEPPER!

GOT IT!

FSSSSHHHHHHHHHH

HA! **HERE** WE GO...

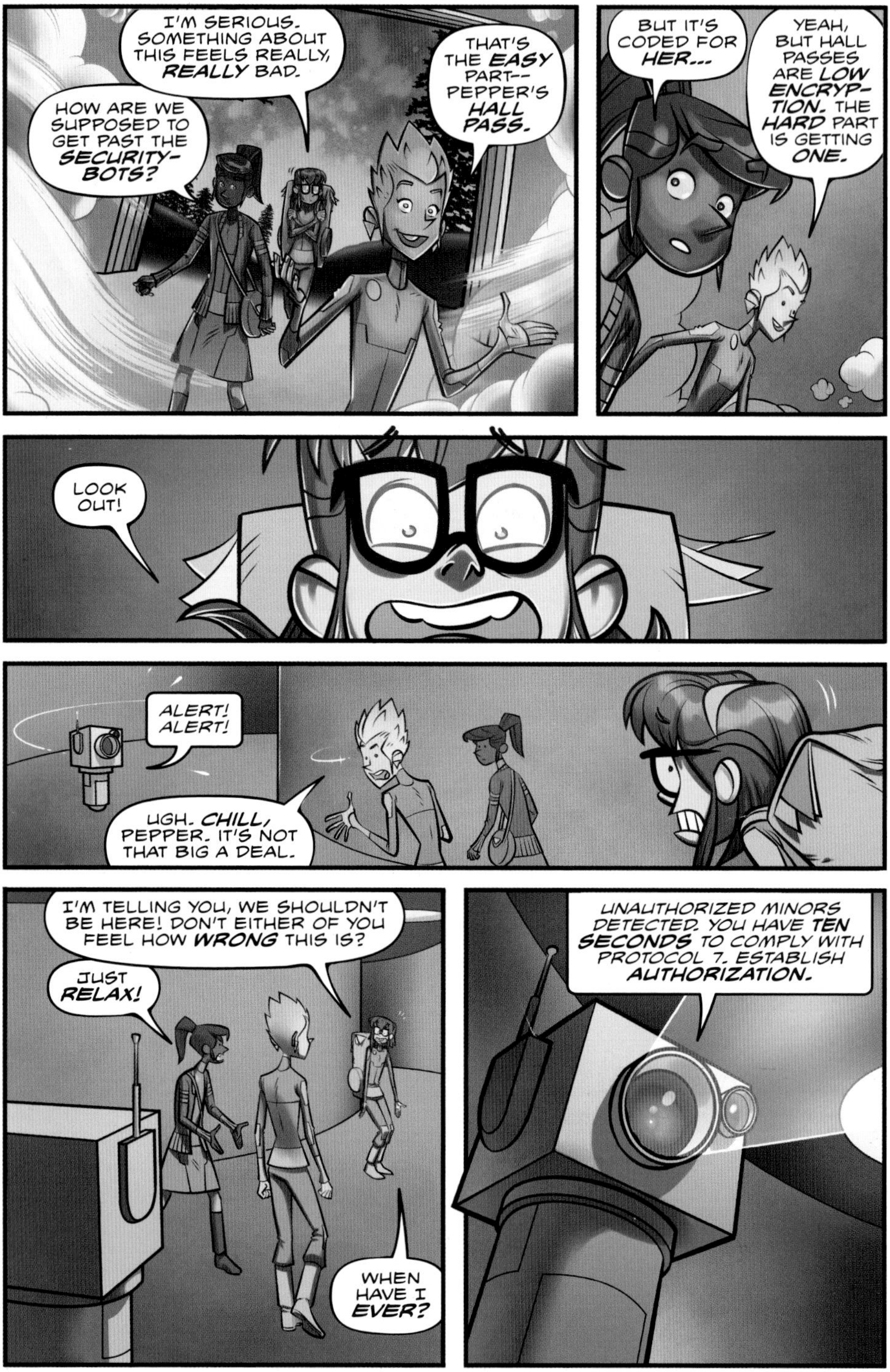
I'M SERIOUS. SOMETHING ABOUT THIS FEELS REALLY, REALLY BAD.
HOW ARE WE SUPPOSED TO GET PAST THE SECURITY-BOTS?
THAT'S THE EASY PART-- PEPPER'S HALL PASS.
BUT IT'S CODED FOR HER...
YEAH, BUT HALL PASSES ARE LOW ENCRYPTION. THE HARD PART IS GETTING ONE.
LOOK OUT!
ALERT! ALERT!
UGH. CHILL, PEPPER. IT'S NOT THAT BIG A DEAL.
I'M TELLING YOU, WE SHOULDN'T BE HERE! DON'T EITHER OF YOU FEEL HOW WRONG THIS IS?
JUST RELAX!
WHEN HAVE I EVER?
UNAUTHORIZED MINORS DETECTED. YOU HAVE TEN SECONDS TO COMPLY WITH PROTOCOL 7. ESTABLISH AUTHORIZATION.

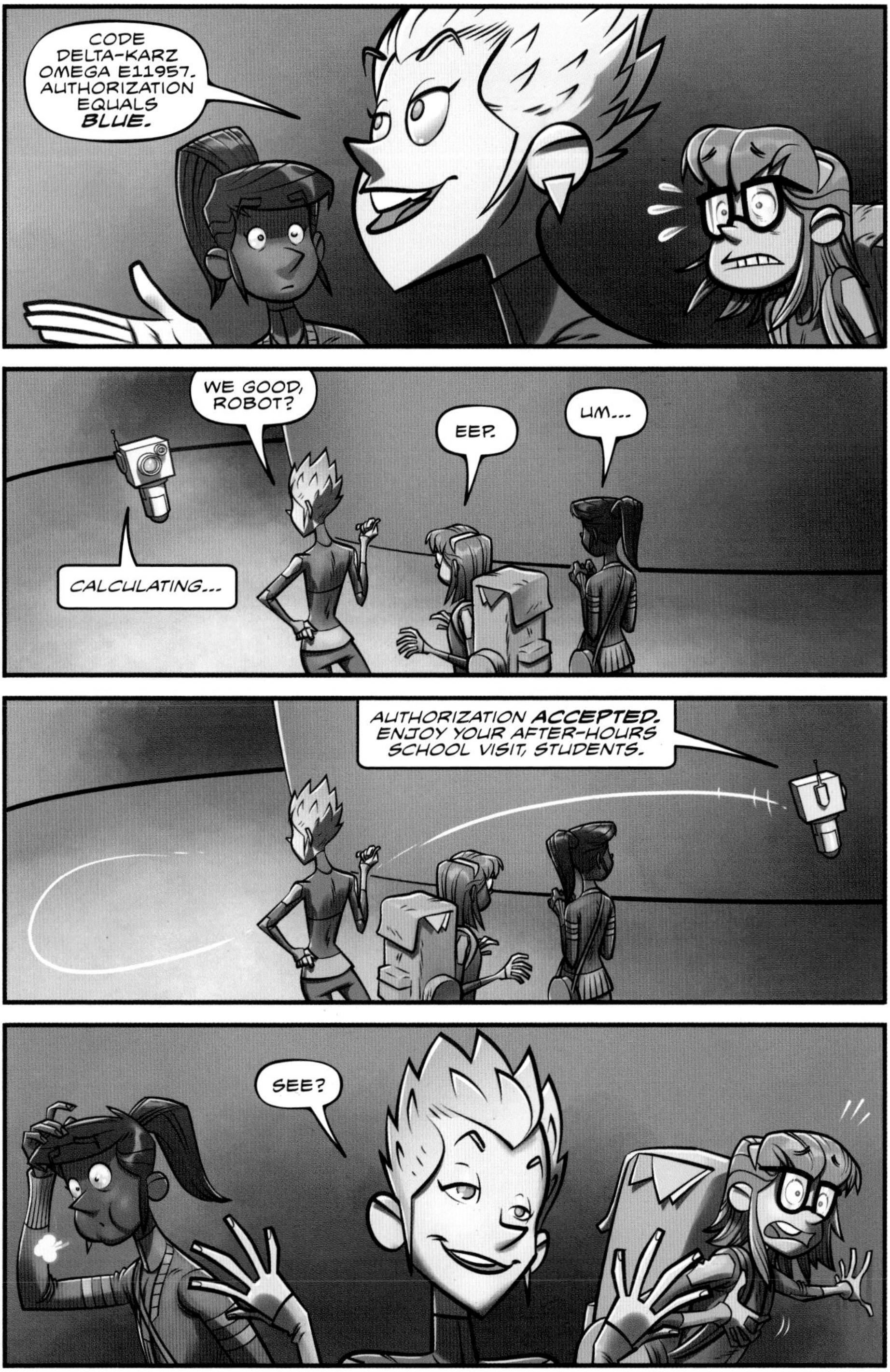
CODE DELTA-KARZ OMEGA E11957. AUTHORIZATION EQUALS **BLUE.**
WE GOOD, ROBOT?
EEP.
UM...
CALCULATING...
AUTHORIZATION **ACCEPTED.** ENJOY YOUR AFTER-HOURS SCHOOL VISIT, STUDENTS.
SEE?

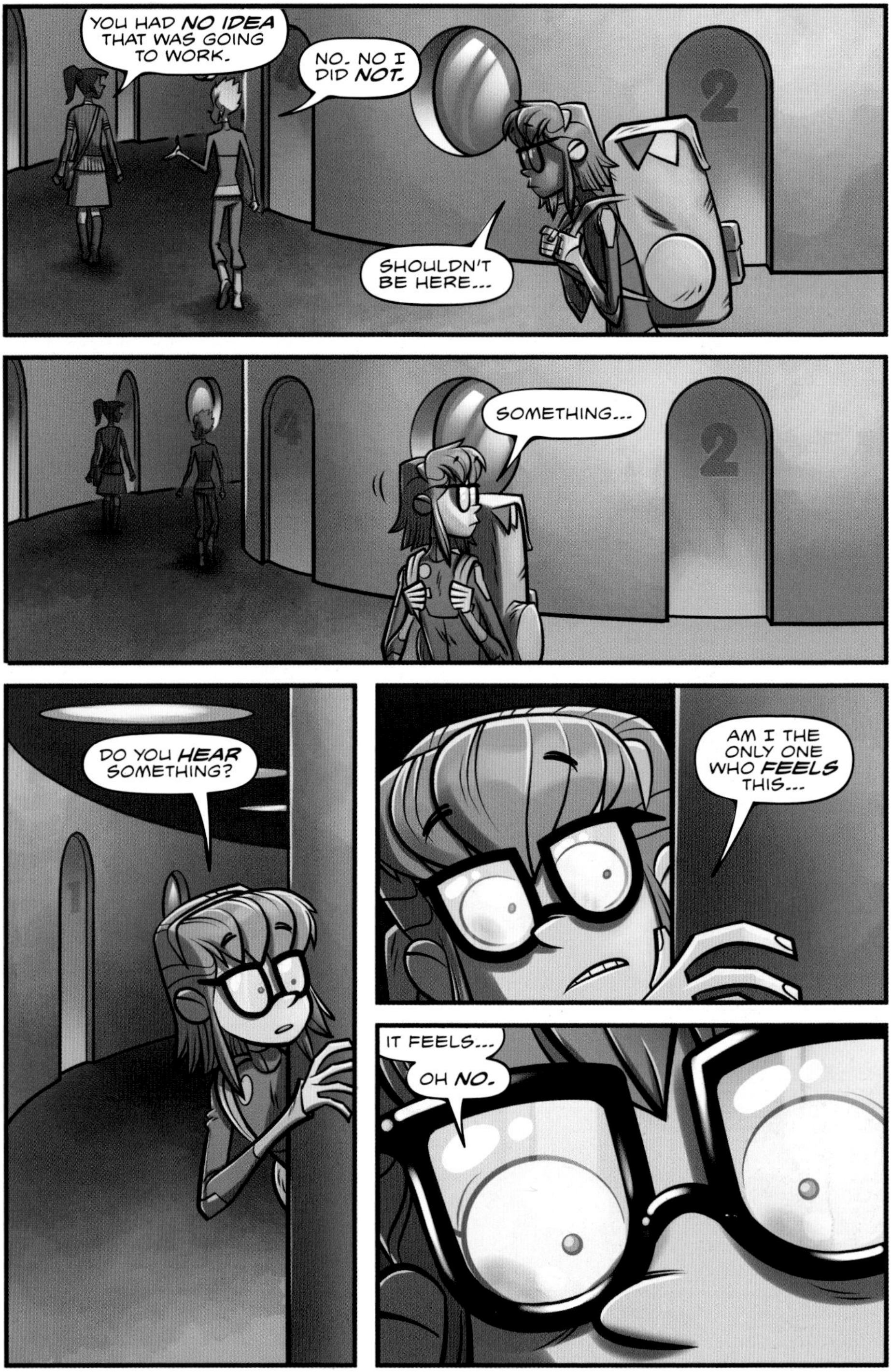
YOU HAD **NO IDEA** THAT WAS GOING TO WORK.
NO. NO I DID **NOT.**
SHOULDN'T BE HERE...
SOMETHING...
DO YOU **HEAR** SOMETHING?
AM I THE ONLY ONE WHO **FEELS** THIS...
IT FEELS...
OH **NO.**

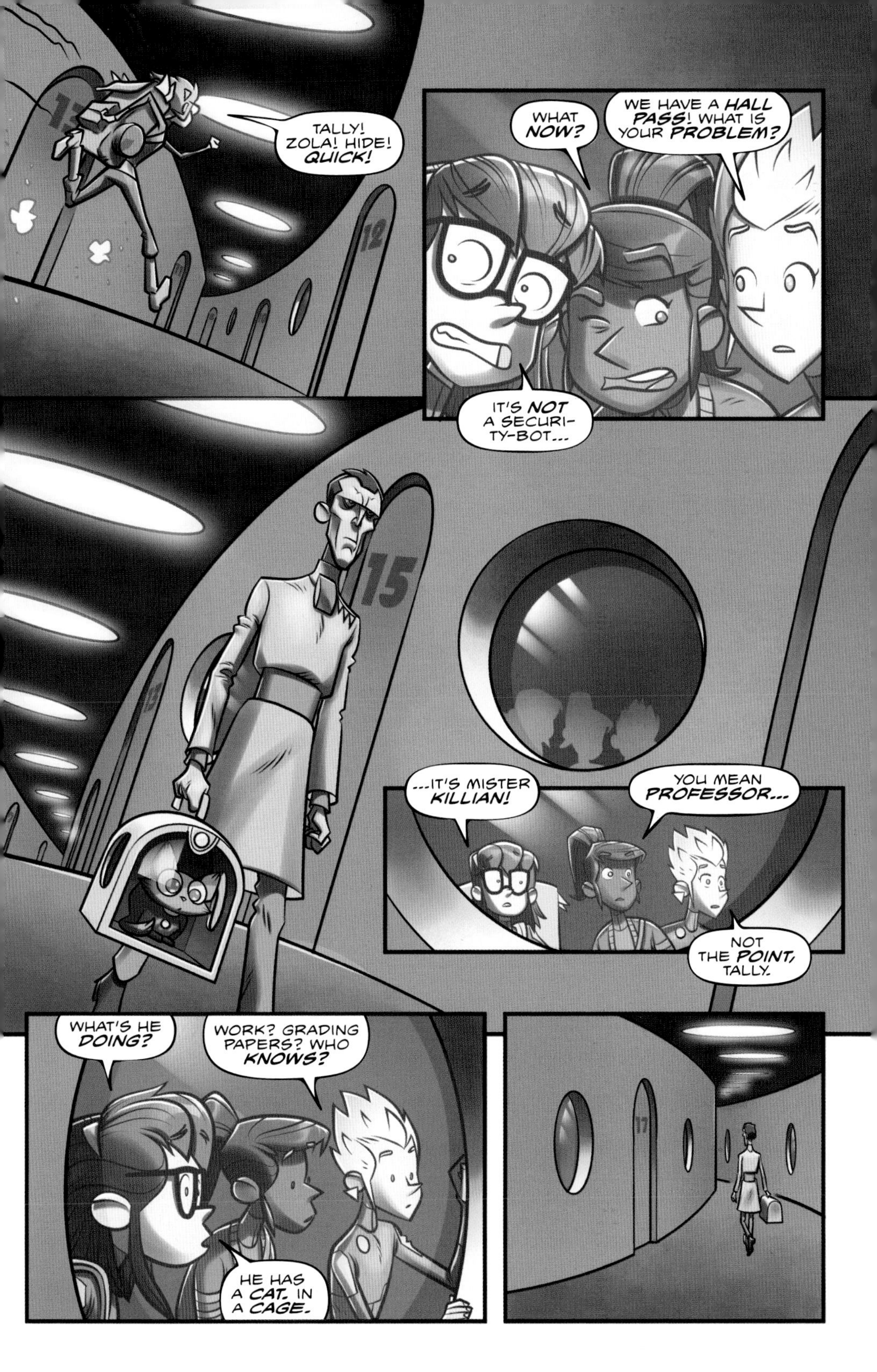
TALLY! ZOLA! HIDE! QUICK!
WHAT NOW?
WE HAVE A HALL PASS! WHAT IS YOUR PROBLEM?
IT'S NOT A SECURI-TY-BOT...
...IT'S MISTER KILLIAN!
YOU MEAN PROFESSOR...
NOT THE POINT, TALLY.
WHAT'S HE DOING?
WORK? GRADING PAPERS? WHO KNOWS?
HE HAS A CAT. IN A CAGE.

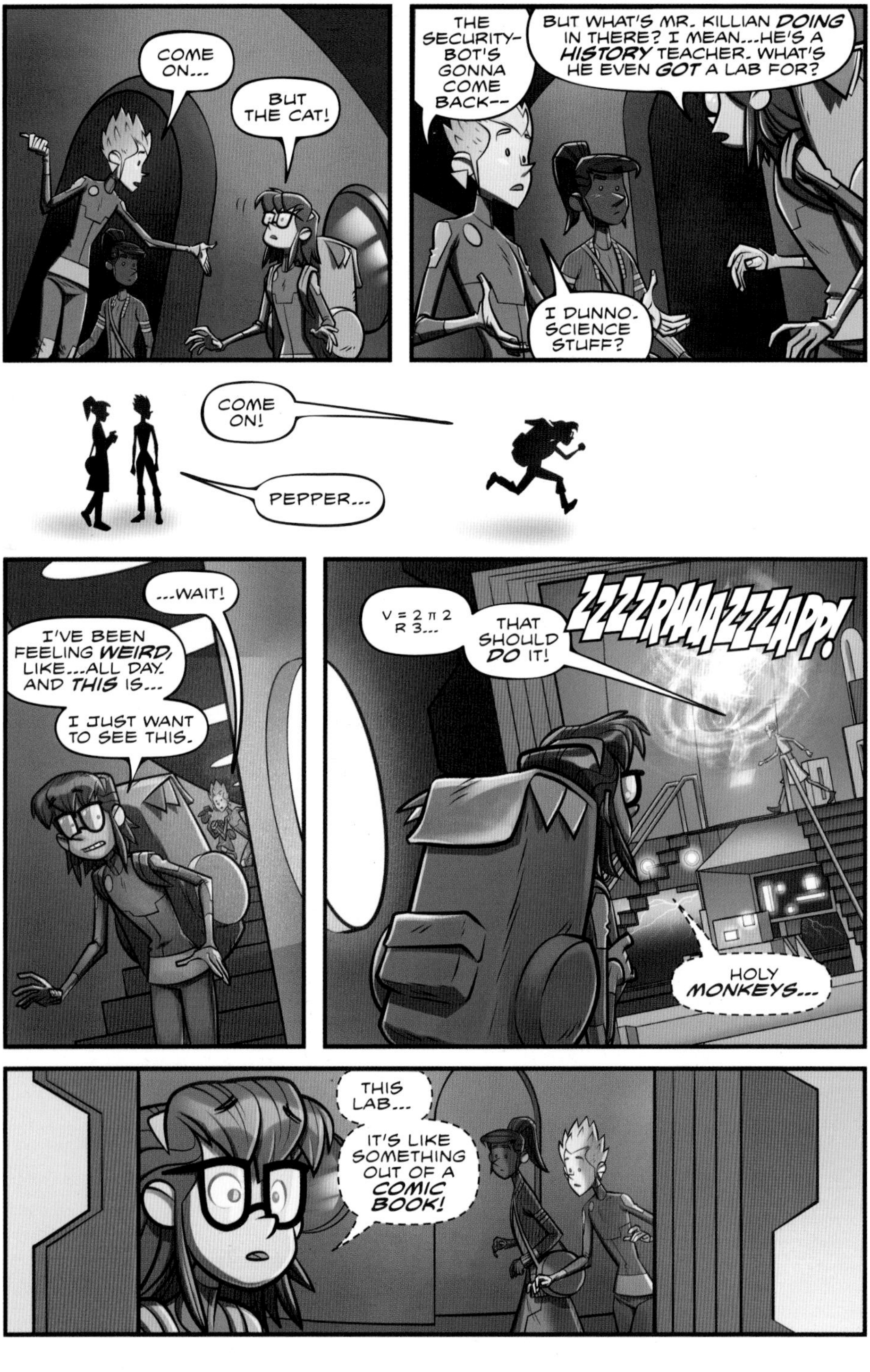

COME ON...
BUT THE CAT!
THE SECURITY-BOT'S GONNA COME BACK--
BUT WHAT'S MR. KILLIAN *DOING* IN THERE? I MEAN...HE'S A *HISTORY* TEACHER. WHAT'S HE EVEN *GOT* A LAB FOR?
I DUNNO. SCIENCE STUFF?
COME ON!
PEPPER...
...WAIT!
I'VE BEEN FEELING *WEIRD,* LIKE...ALL DAY. AND *THIS* IS...
I JUST WANT TO SEE THIS.
V = 2 π 2 R 3...
THAT SHOULD *DO* IT!
ZZZZRAAAZZZAPP!
HOLY *MONKEYS...*
THIS LAB...
IT'S LIKE SOMETHING OUT OF A *COMIC BOOK!*

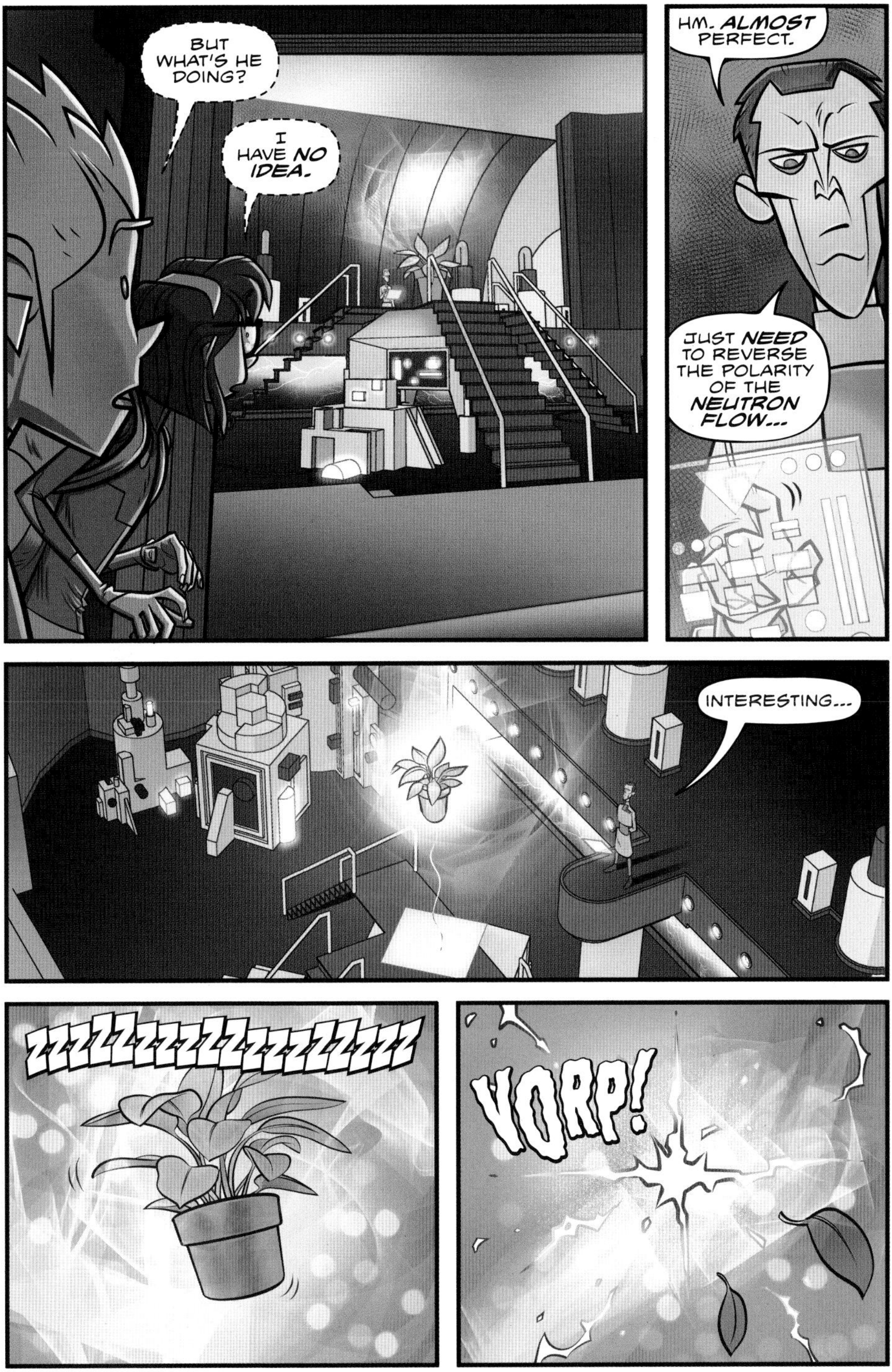
BUT WHAT'S HE DOING?
I HAVE NO IDEA.
HM. ALMOST PERFECT.
JUST NEED TO REVERSE THE POLARITY OF THE NEUTRON FLOW...
INTERESTING...
ZZZZZZZZZZZZZZZZZZZ
VORP!

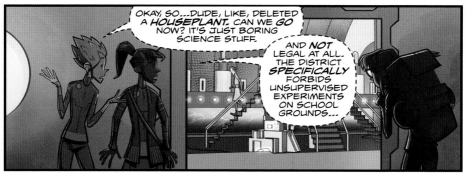

OKAY, SO....DUDE, LIKE, DELETED A *HOUSEPLANT.* CAN WE *GO* NOW? IT'S JUST BORING SCIENCE STUFF.

AND *NOT* LEGAL AT ALL. THE DISTRICT *SPECIFICALLY* FORBIDS UNSUPERVISED EXPERIMENTS ON SCHOOL GROUNDS...

YES.

PERHAPS A *SLIGHT* VARIATION TO THE MODULATION OF THE *ENERGY FIELD*...

...AND WE'LL BE READY FOR A *TRUE TEST* OF THE *QUANTUM FIELD MANIPULATOR.*

MEW?

UHH...

NO!

WHOA. HE'S LIKE A *LEGIT* MAD SCIENTIST? NO *WAY* THIS IS REAL...

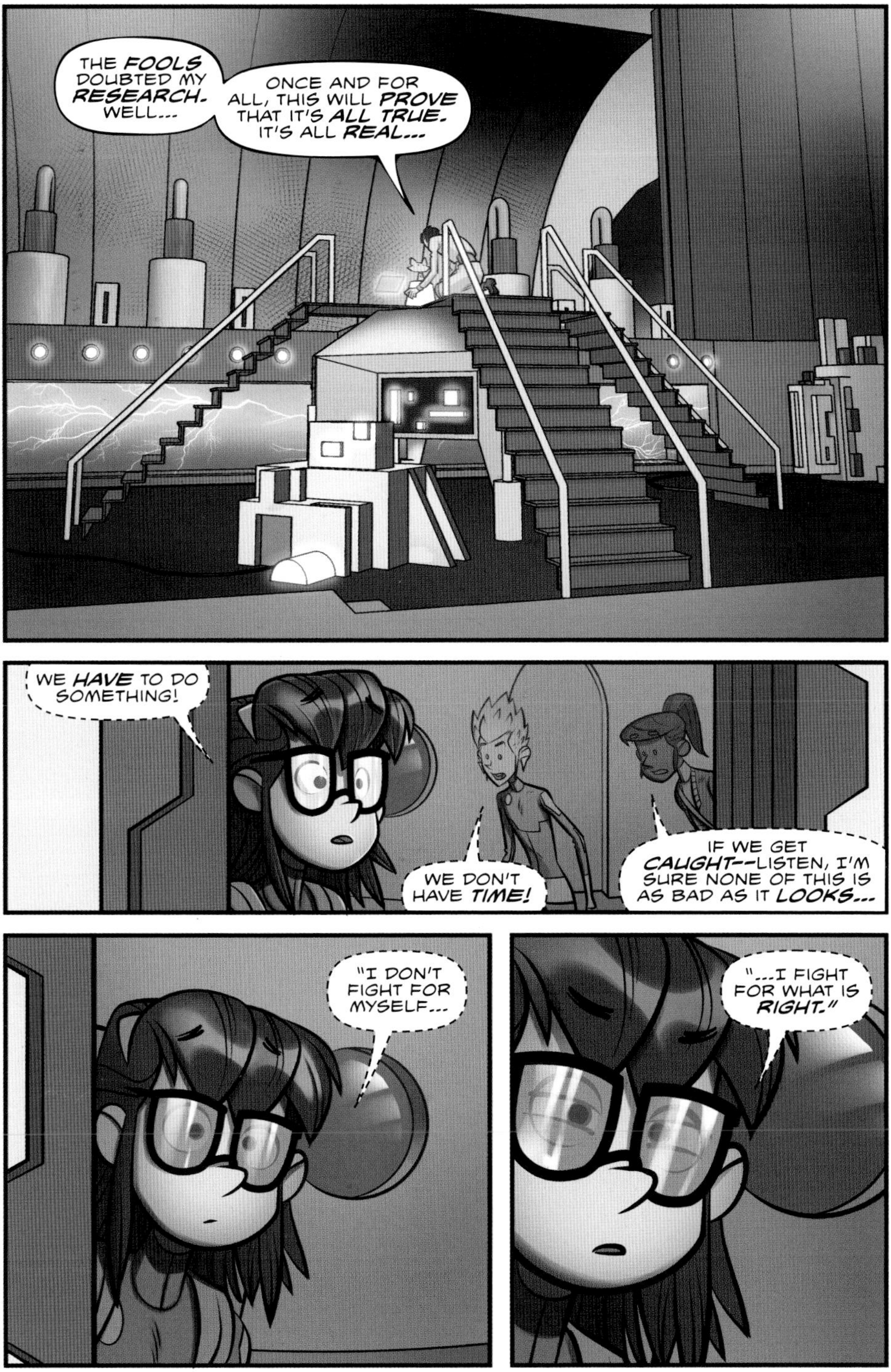
THE *FOOLS* DOUBTED MY *RESEARCH.* WELL...
ONCE AND FOR ALL, THIS WILL *PROVE* THAT IT'S *ALL TRUE.* IT'S ALL *REAL...*
WE *HAVE* TO DO SOMETHING!
WE DON'T HAVE *TIME!*
IF WE GET *CAUGHT*--LISTEN, I'M SURE NONE OF THIS IS AS BAD AS IT *LOOKS...*
"I DON'T FIGHT FOR MYSELF...
"...I FIGHT FOR WHAT IS *RIGHT.*"

THE TEST SUBJECT IS HEALTHY...AND **WELL PREPARED** FOR THE PROCESS.

THAT WILL LEAVE ONLY **ONE MORE HURDLE.** ONE THAT WILL BE PASSED COME THE MORNING.

A **HUMAN SUBJECT.**

PEPPER!

WHAT ARE YOU **DOING?!**

SHH... JUST GIVE ME A **SECOND!**

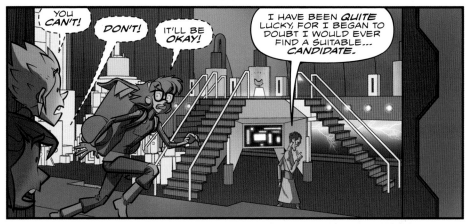

YOU **CAN'T!**

DON'T!

IT'LL BE **OKAY!**

I HAVE BEEN **QUITE** LUCKY, FOR I BEGAN TO DOUBT I WOULD EVER FIND A SUITABLE... **CANDIDATE.**

LUCKILY...**THIS** ONE IS UNLIKELY TO BE MISSED. HER NAME IS--

KLIK!

EH?

UM...

MEW!

PEPPER PAGE?!!

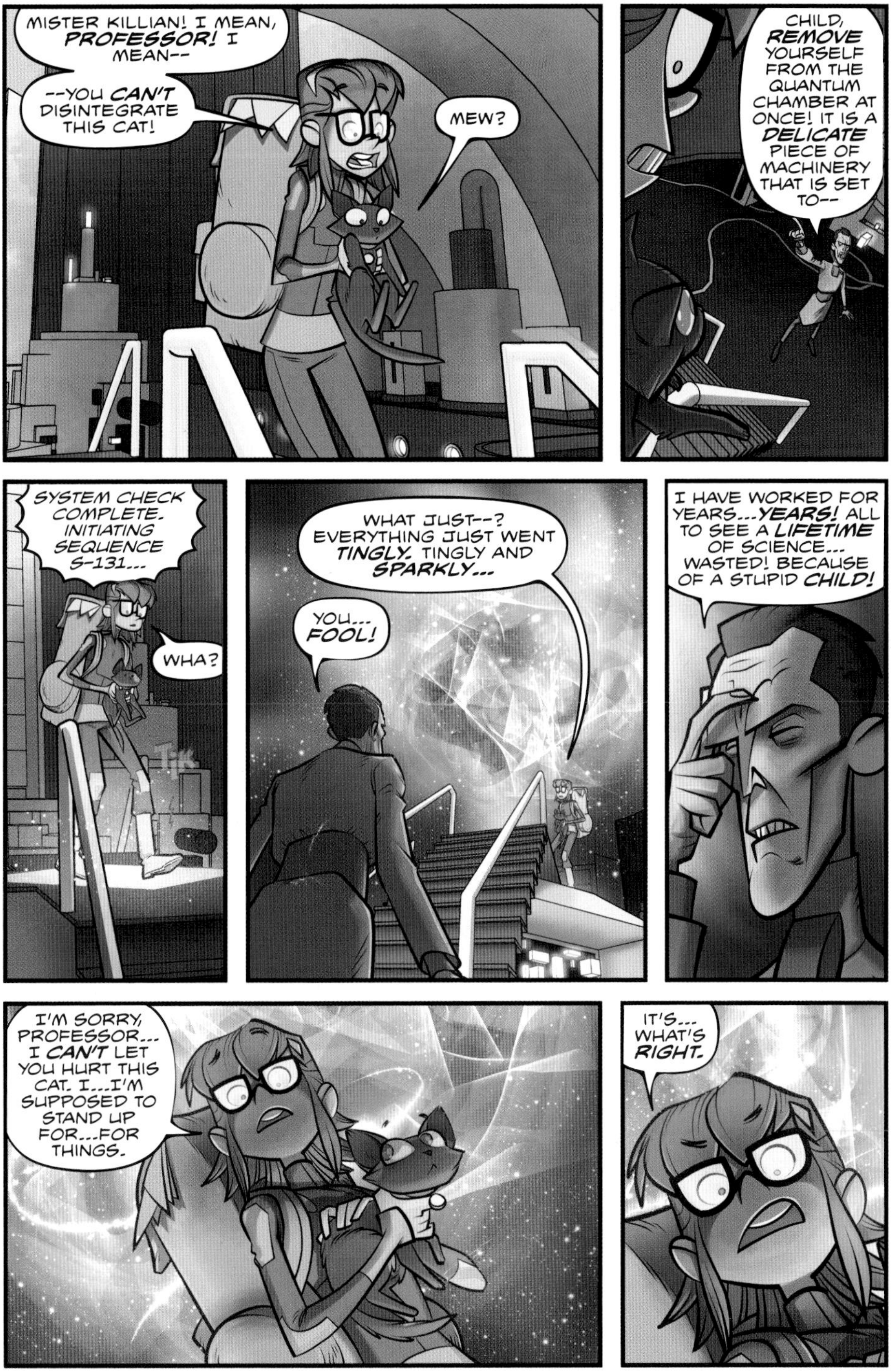
MISTER KILLIAN! I MEAN, PROFESSOR! I MEAN--
--YOU CAN'T DISINTEGRATE THIS CAT!
MEW?
CHILD, REMOVE YOURSELF FROM THE QUANTUM CHAMBER AT ONCE! IT IS A DELICATE PIECE OF MACHINERY THAT IS SET TO--
SYSTEM CHECK COMPLETE. INITIATING SEQUENCE S-131...
WHA?
WHAT JUST--? EVERYTHING JUST WENT TINGLY. TINGLY AND SPARKLY...
YOU... FOOL!
I HAVE WORKED FOR YEARS... YEARS! ALL TO SEE A LIFETIME OF SCIENCE... WASTED! BECAUSE OF A STUPID CHILD!
I'M SORRY, PROFESSOR... I CAN'T LET YOU HURT THIS CAT. I...I'M SUPPOSED TO STAND UP FOR...FOR THINGS.
IT'S... WHAT'S RIGHT.

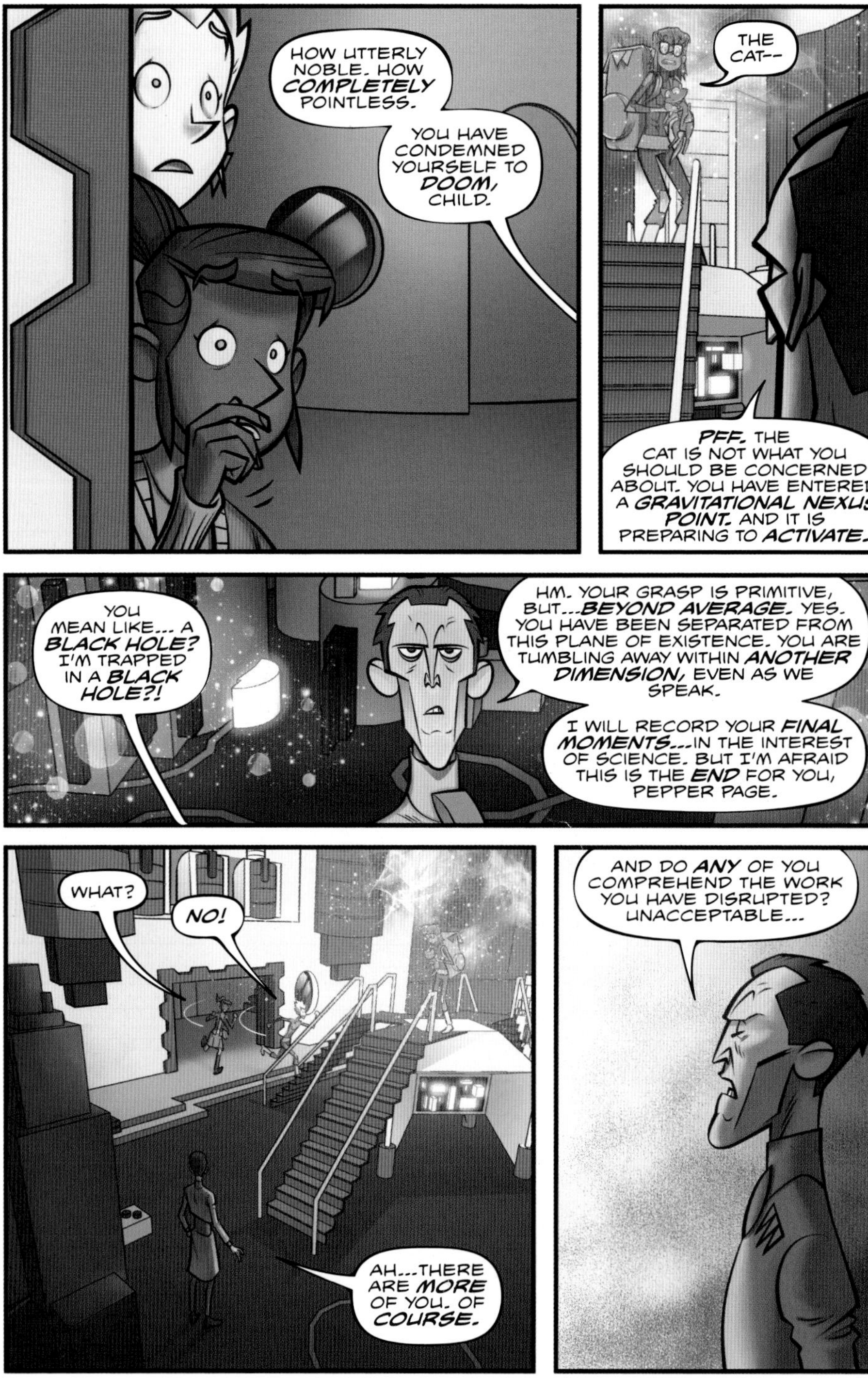

HOW UTTERLY NOBLE. HOW COMPLETELY POINTLESS.
YOU HAVE CONDEMNED YOURSELF TO DOOM, CHILD.
THE CAT--
PFF. THE CAT IS NOT WHAT YOU SHOULD BE CONCERNED ABOUT. YOU HAVE ENTERED A GRAVITATIONAL NEXUS POINT. AND IT IS PREPARING TO ACTIVATE.
YOU MEAN LIKE... A BLACK HOLE? I'M TRAPPED IN A BLACK HOLE?!
HM. YOUR GRASP IS PRIMITIVE, BUT...BEYOND AVERAGE. YES. YOU HAVE BEEN SEPARATED FROM THIS PLANE OF EXISTENCE. YOU ARE TUMBLING AWAY WITHIN ANOTHER DIMENSION, EVEN AS WE SPEAK.
I WILL RECORD YOUR FINAL MOMENTS...IN THE INTEREST OF SCIENCE. BUT I'M AFRAID THIS IS THE END FOR YOU, PEPPER PAGE.
WHAT?
NO!
AH...THERE ARE MORE OF YOU. OF COURSE.
AND DO ANY OF YOU COMPREHEND THE WORK YOU HAVE DISRUPTED? UNACCEPTABLE...

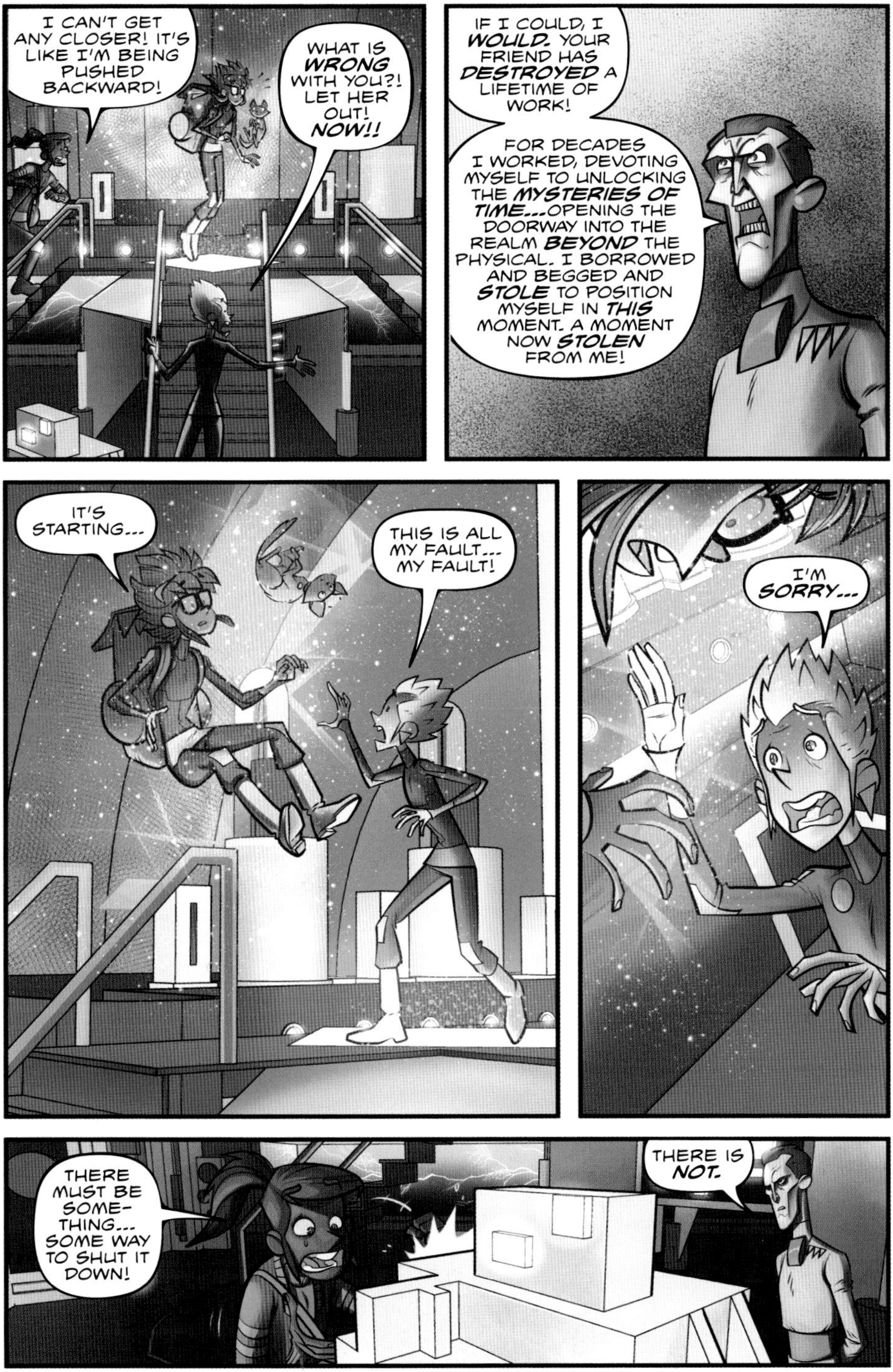
I CAN'T GET ANY CLOSER! IT'S LIKE I'M BEING PUSHED BACKWARD!
WHAT IS *WRONG* WITH YOU?! LET HER OUT! *NOW!!*
IF I COULD, I *WOULD.* YOUR FRIEND HAS *DESTROYED* A LIFETIME OF WORK!
FOR DECADES I WORKED, DEVOTING MYSELF TO UNLOCKING THE *MYSTERIES OF TIME...* OPENING THE DOORWAY INTO THE REALM *BEYOND* THE PHYSICAL. I BORROWED AND BEGGED AND *STOLE* TO POSITION MYSELF IN *THIS* MOMENT. A MOMENT NOW *STOLEN* FROM ME!
IT'S STARTING...
THIS IS ALL MY FAULT... MY FAULT!
I'M *SORRY...*
THERE MUST BE SOME-THING... SOME WAY TO SHUT IT DOWN!
THERE IS *NOT.*

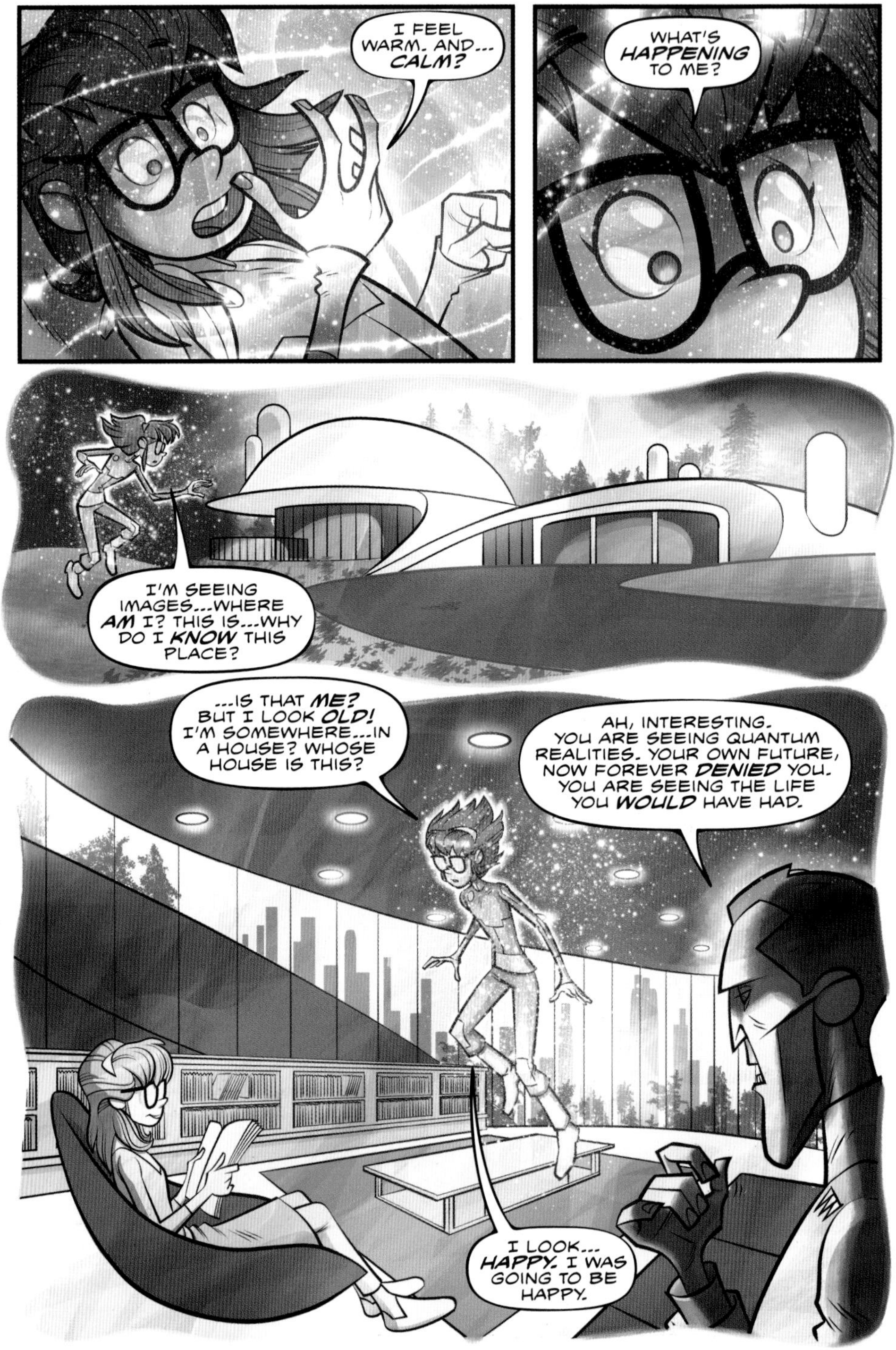

I FEEL WARM. AND... CALM?
WHAT'S HAPPENING TO ME?
I'M SEEING IMAGES...WHERE AM I? THIS IS...WHY DO I KNOW THIS PLACE?
...IS THAT ME? BUT I LOOK OLD! I'M SOMEWHERE...IN A HOUSE? WHOSE HOUSE IS THIS?
AH, INTERESTING. YOU ARE SEEING QUANTUM REALITIES. YOUR OWN FUTURE, NOW FOREVER DENIED YOU. YOU ARE SEEING THE LIFE YOU WOULD HAVE HAD.
I LOOK... HAPPY. I WAS GOING TO BE HAPPY.

THAT MUST BE VERY INTERESTING FOR YOU. FOR ME IT IS SIMPLY A *DISTRACTION.* UNDERSTAND THIS: YOUR MEDDLING MAY HAVE COST ME TIME, BUT I WILL STILL PREVAIL.

YOU'RE A *MONSTER!*

PERHAPS.

GOODBYE, MISS PAGE...

I WILL *NOT* FORGET THIS.

...I DON'T WANT TO GO.

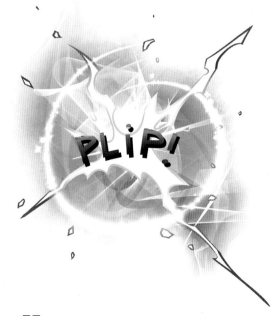

PLIP!

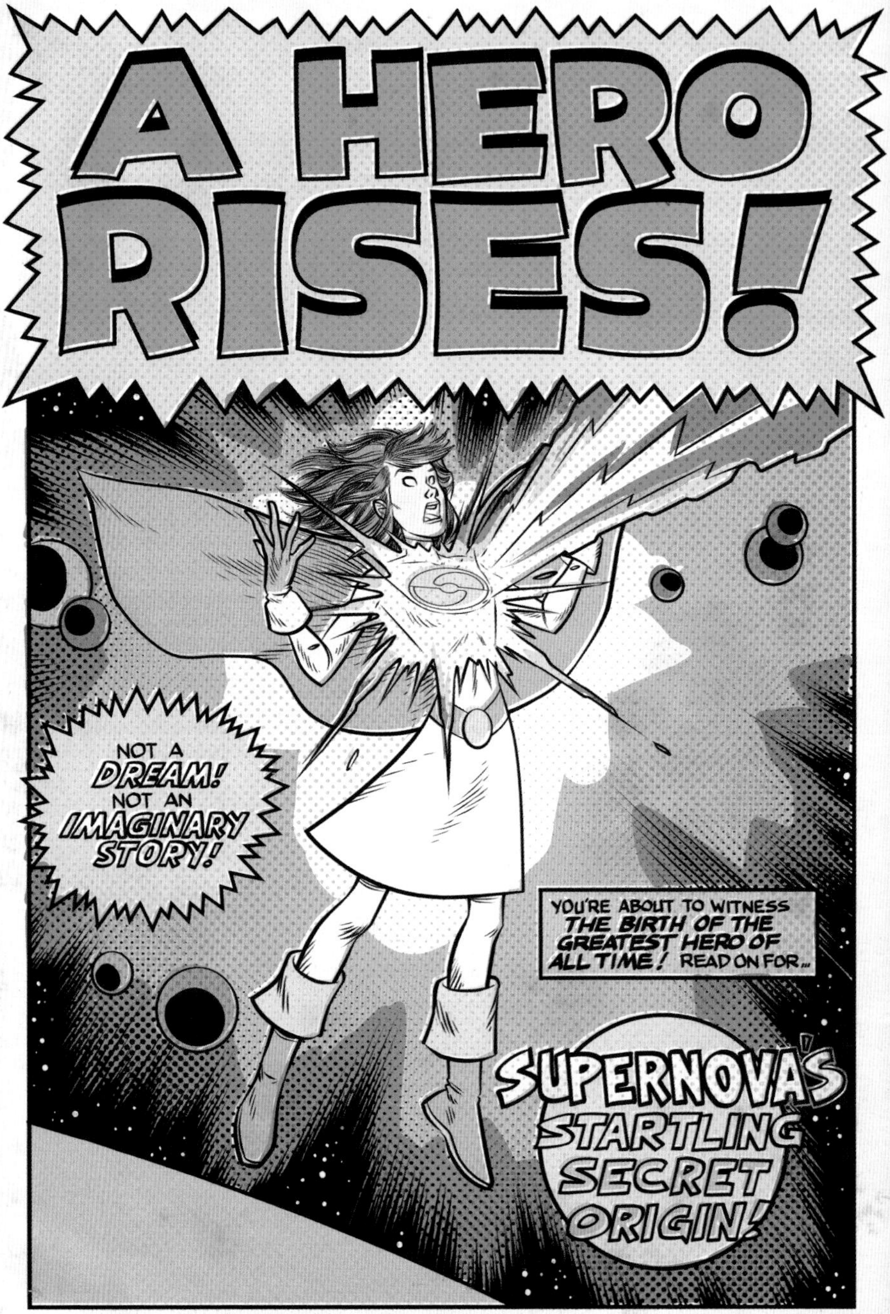
A HERO RISES!
NOT A DREAM! NOT AN IMAGINARY STORY!
YOU'RE ABOUT TO WITNESS THE BIRTH OF THE GREATEST HERO OF ALL TIME! READ ON FOR...
SUPERNOVA'S STARTLING SECRET ORIGIN!

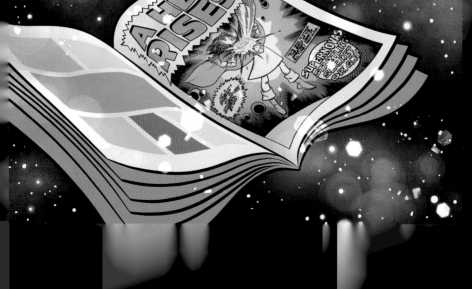

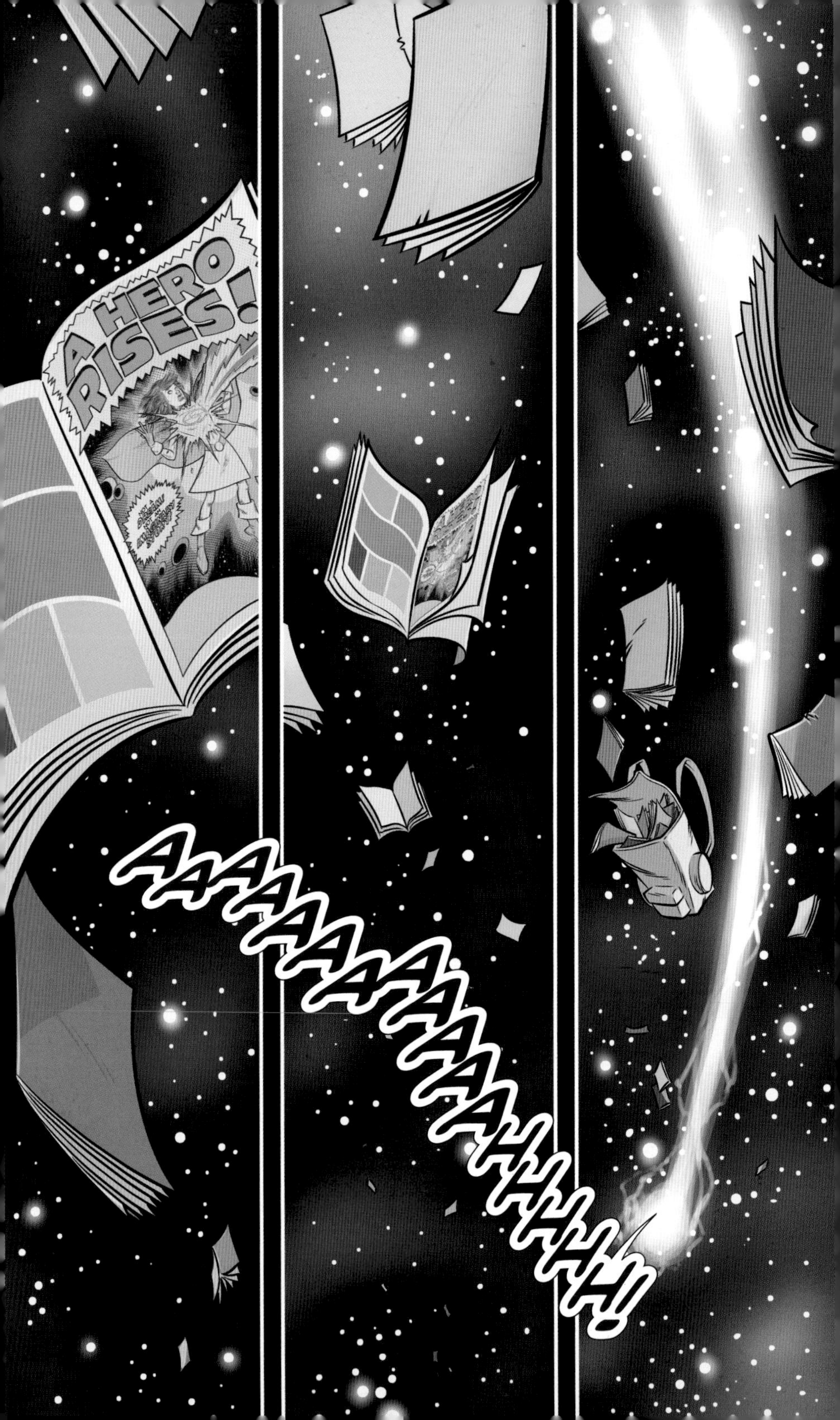
A HERO RISES!
AAAAAAAAAAAHHHHH!

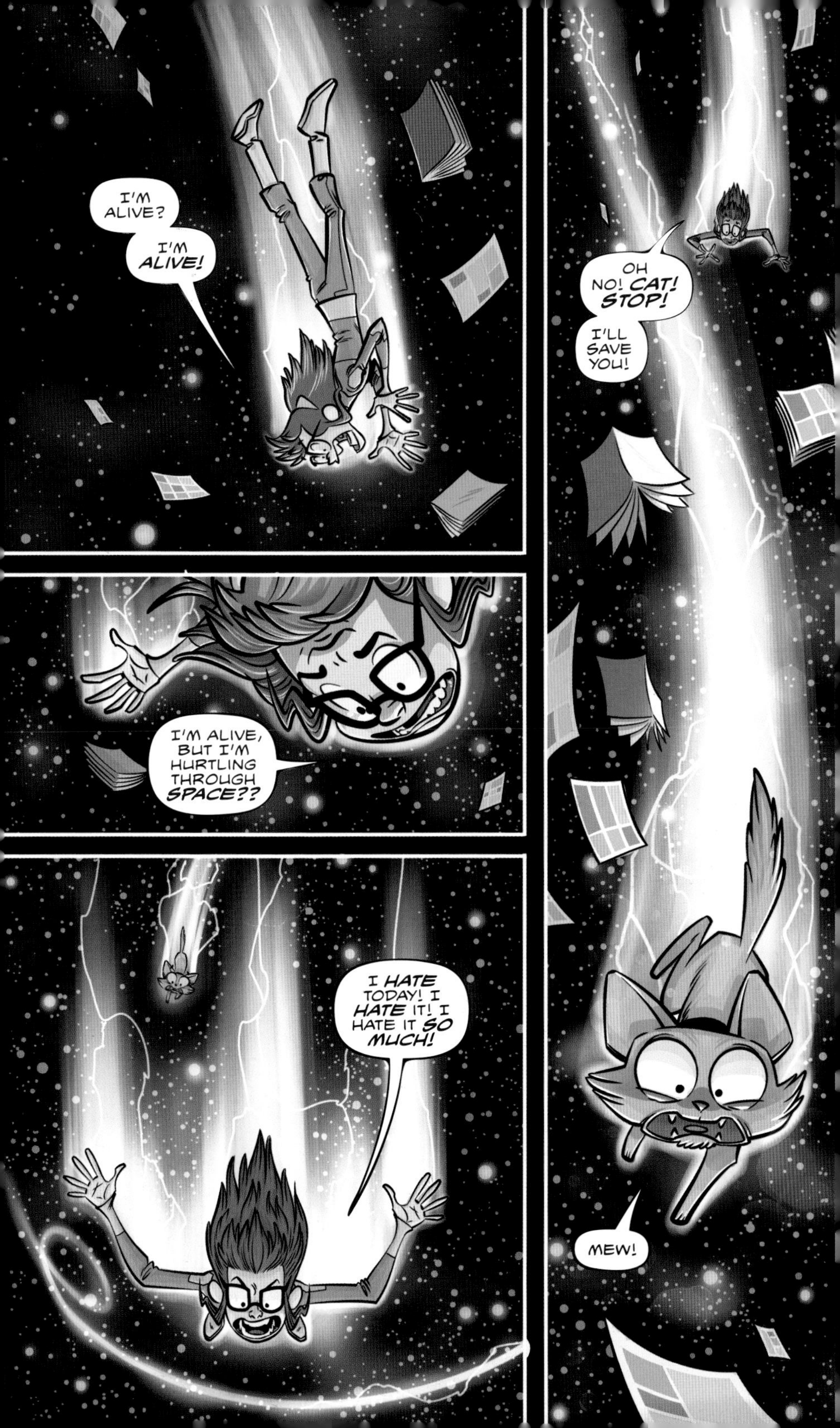
I'M ALIVE?
I'M *ALIVE!*
I'M ALIVE, BUT I'M HURTLING THROUGH *SPACE??*
I *HATE* TODAY! I *HATE* IT! I HATE IT *SO MUCH!*
OH NO! *CAT! STOP!*
I'LL SAVE YOU!
MEW!

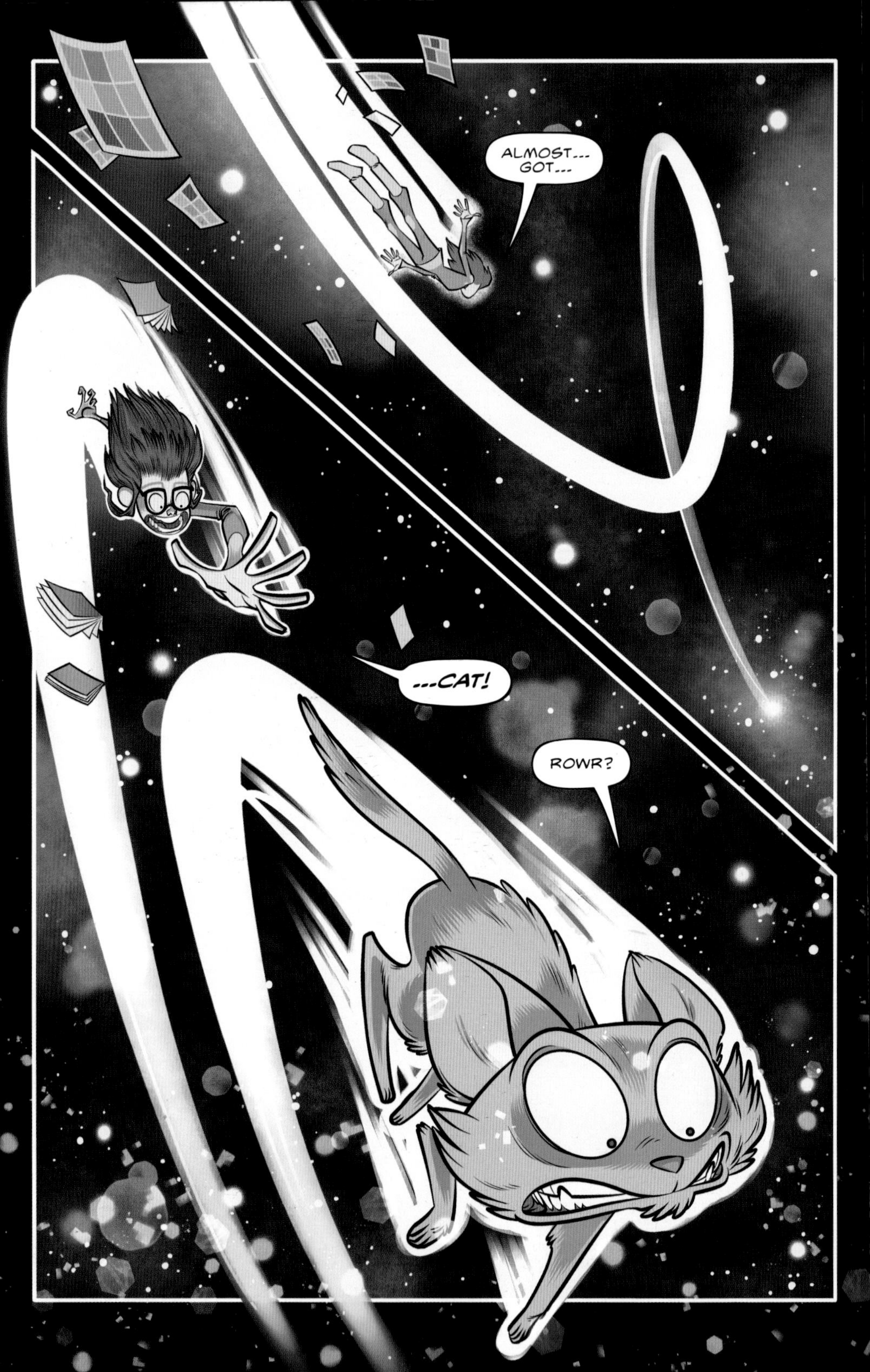
ALMOST... GOT...
...CAT!
ROWR?

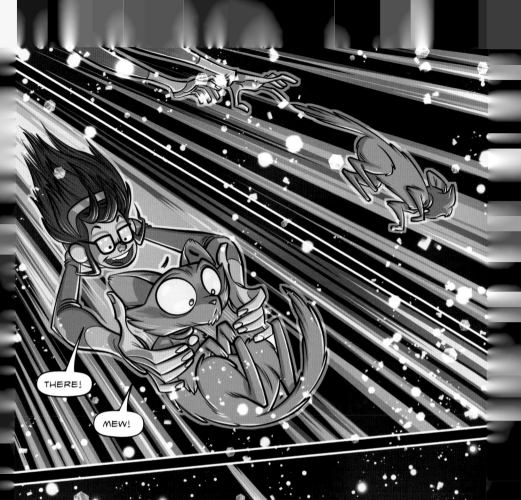

THERE!

MEW!

THE PAST...

...THE HECK WAS THAT?

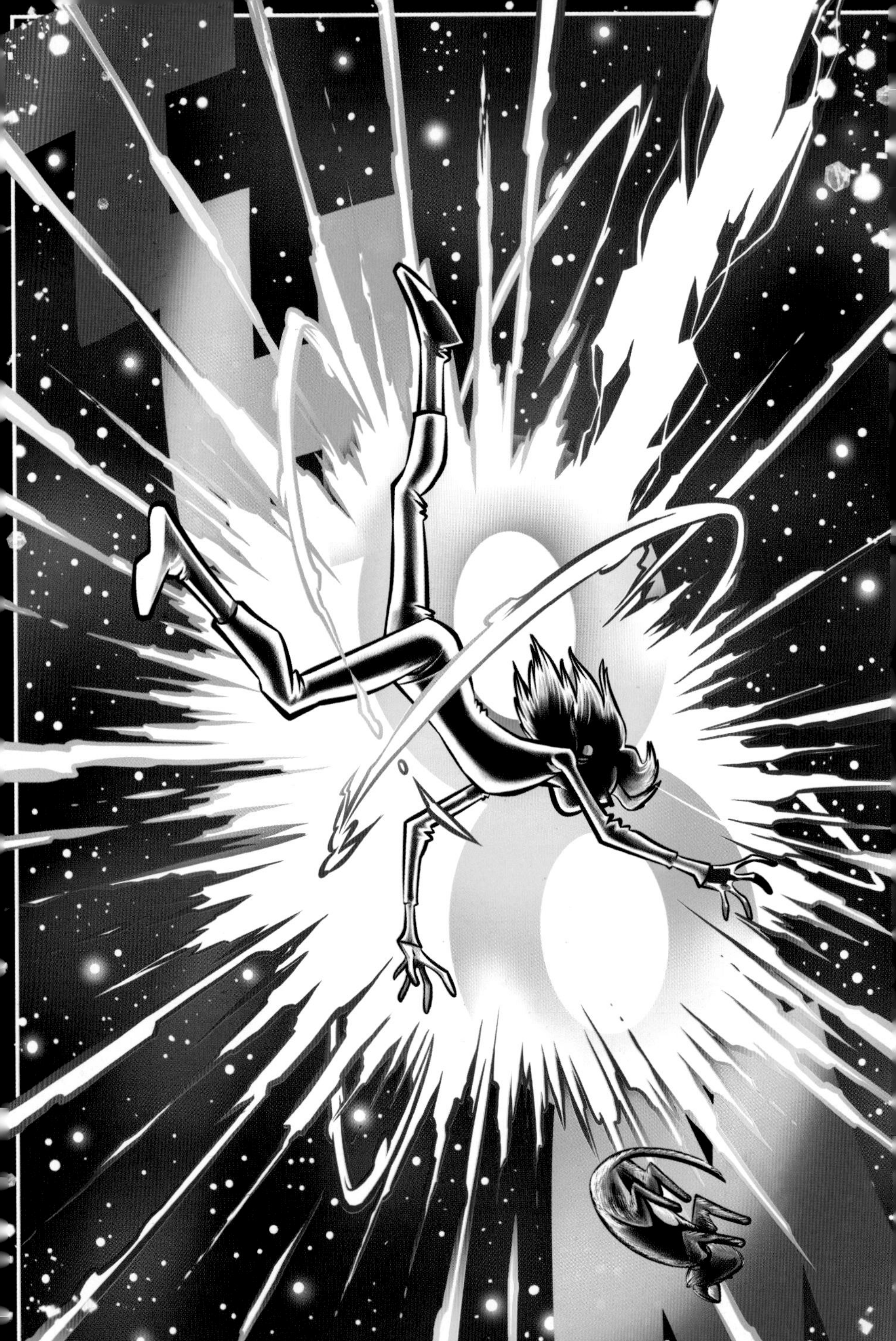

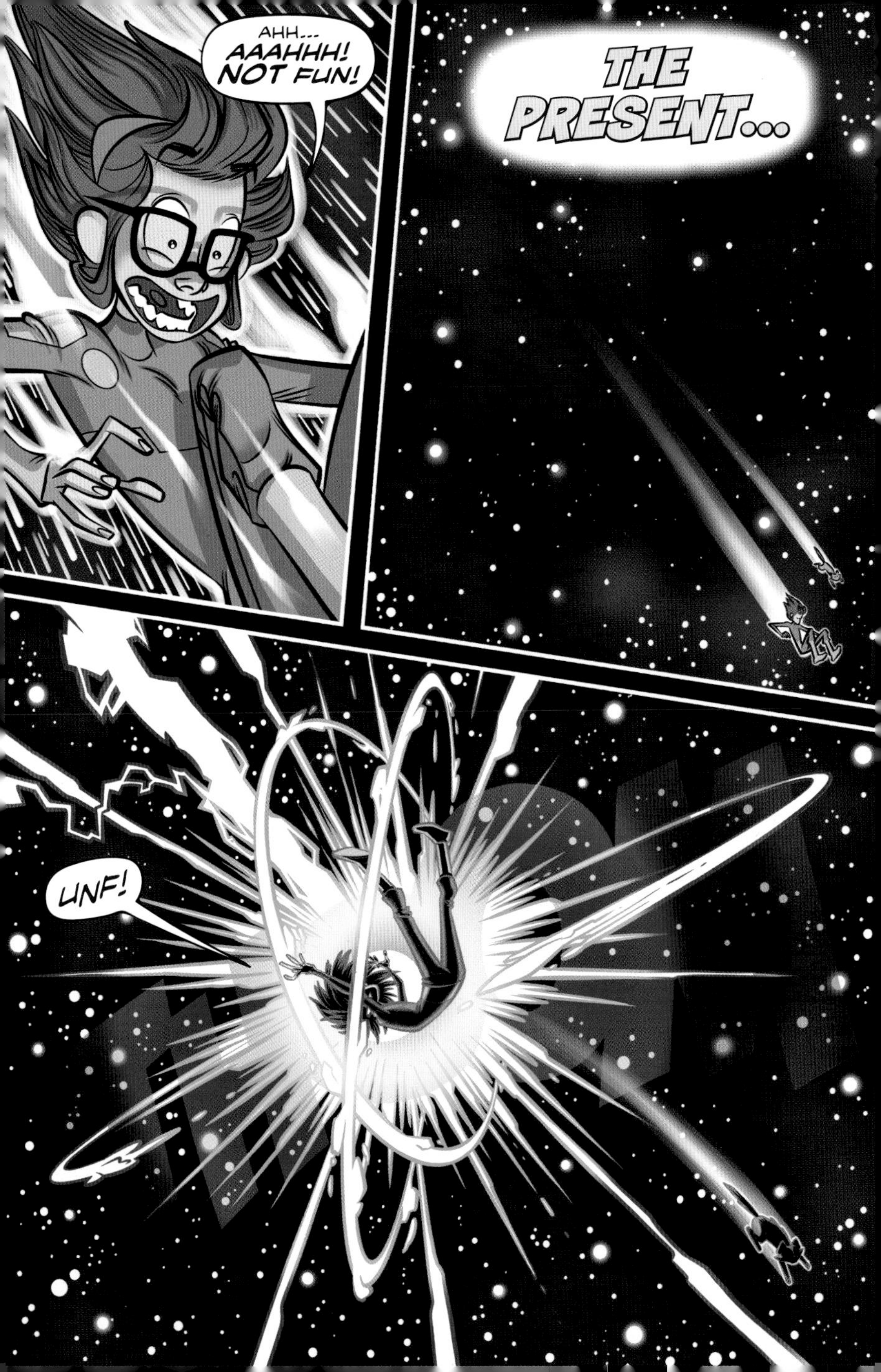
AHH...
AAAHHH!
NOT FUN!
THE PRESENT...
UNF!

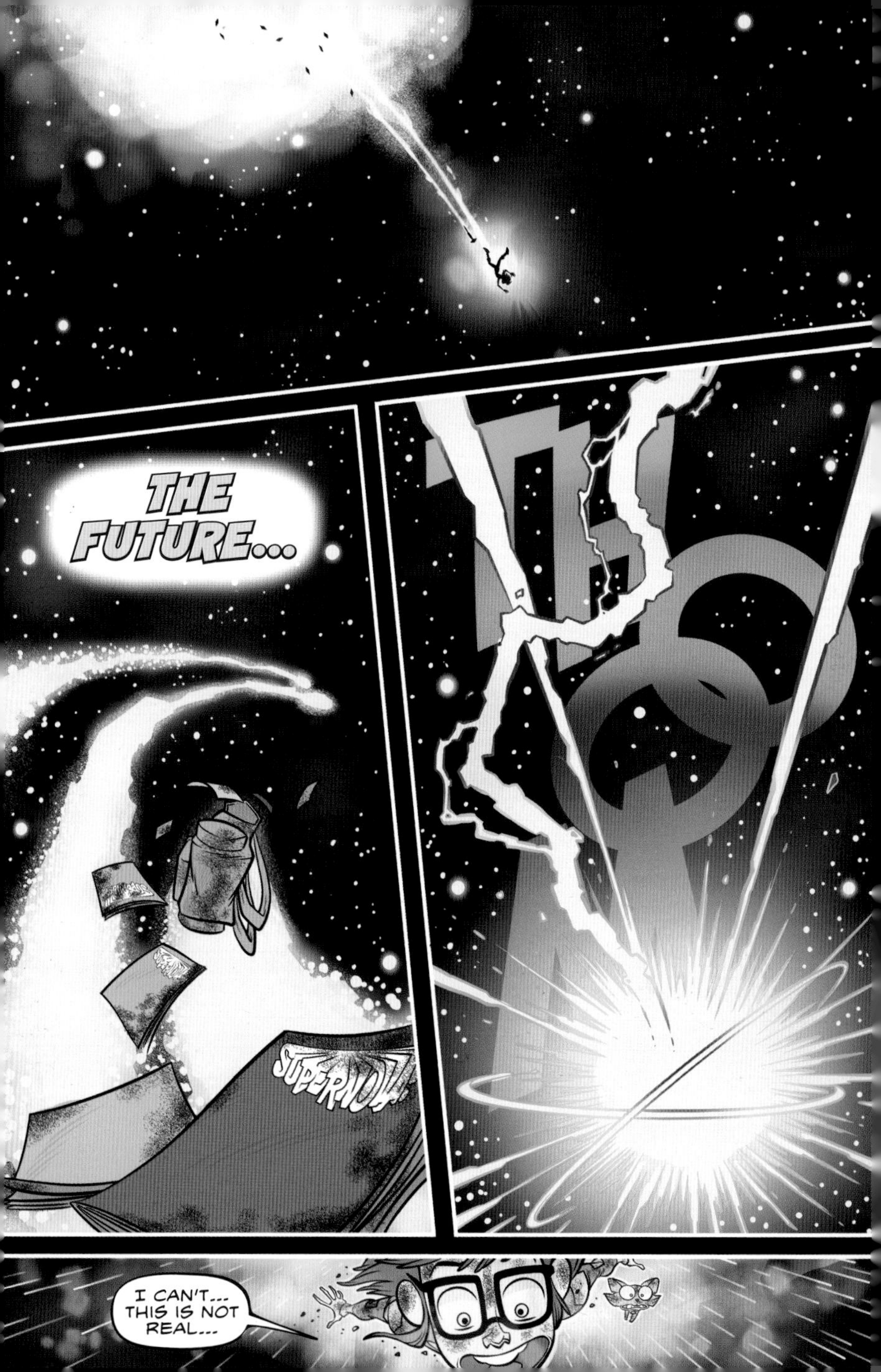
THE FUTURE...
SUPERNOVA
I CAN'T... THIS IS NOT REAL...

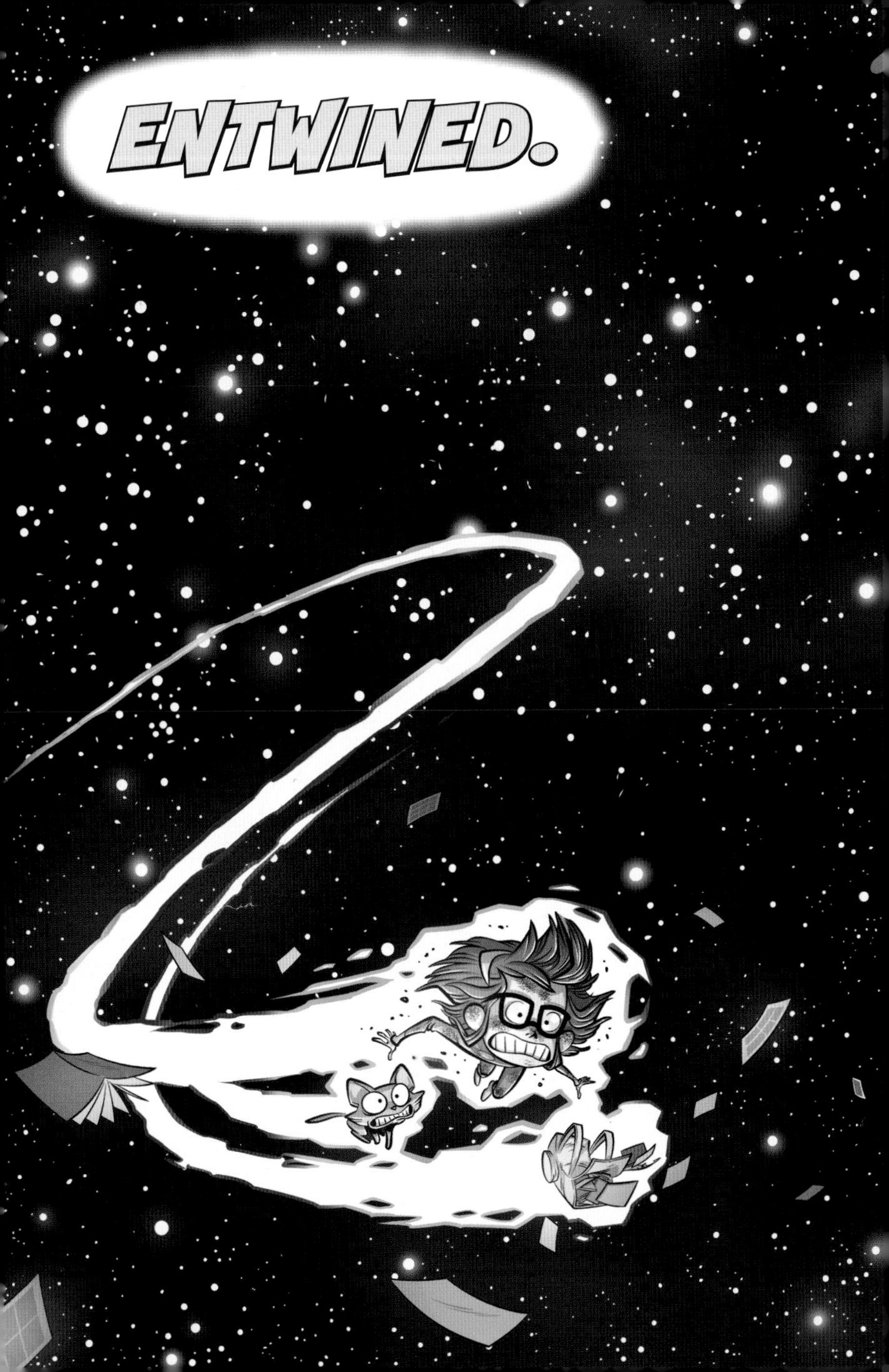
ENTWINED.

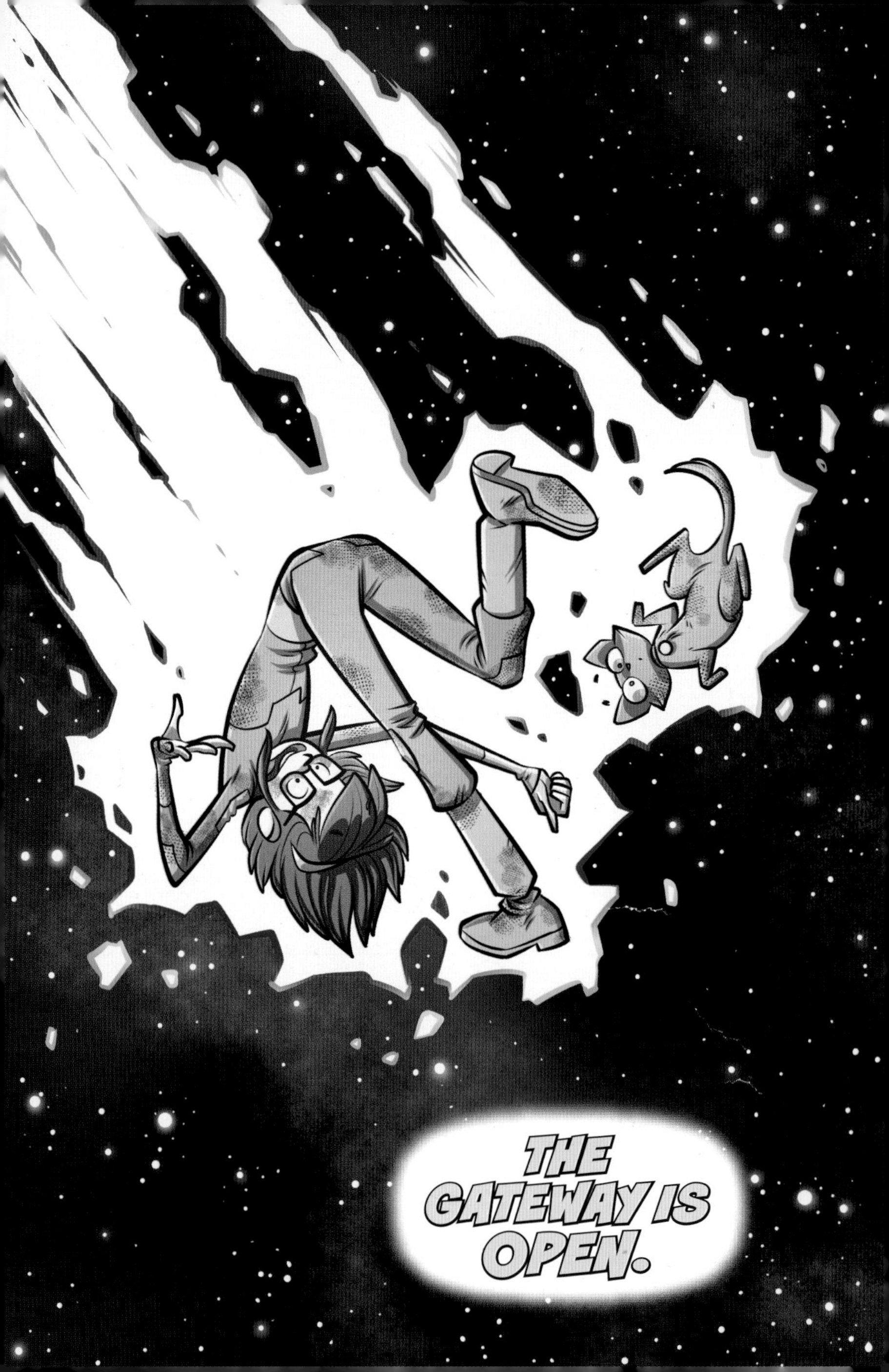
THE GATEWAY IS OPEN.

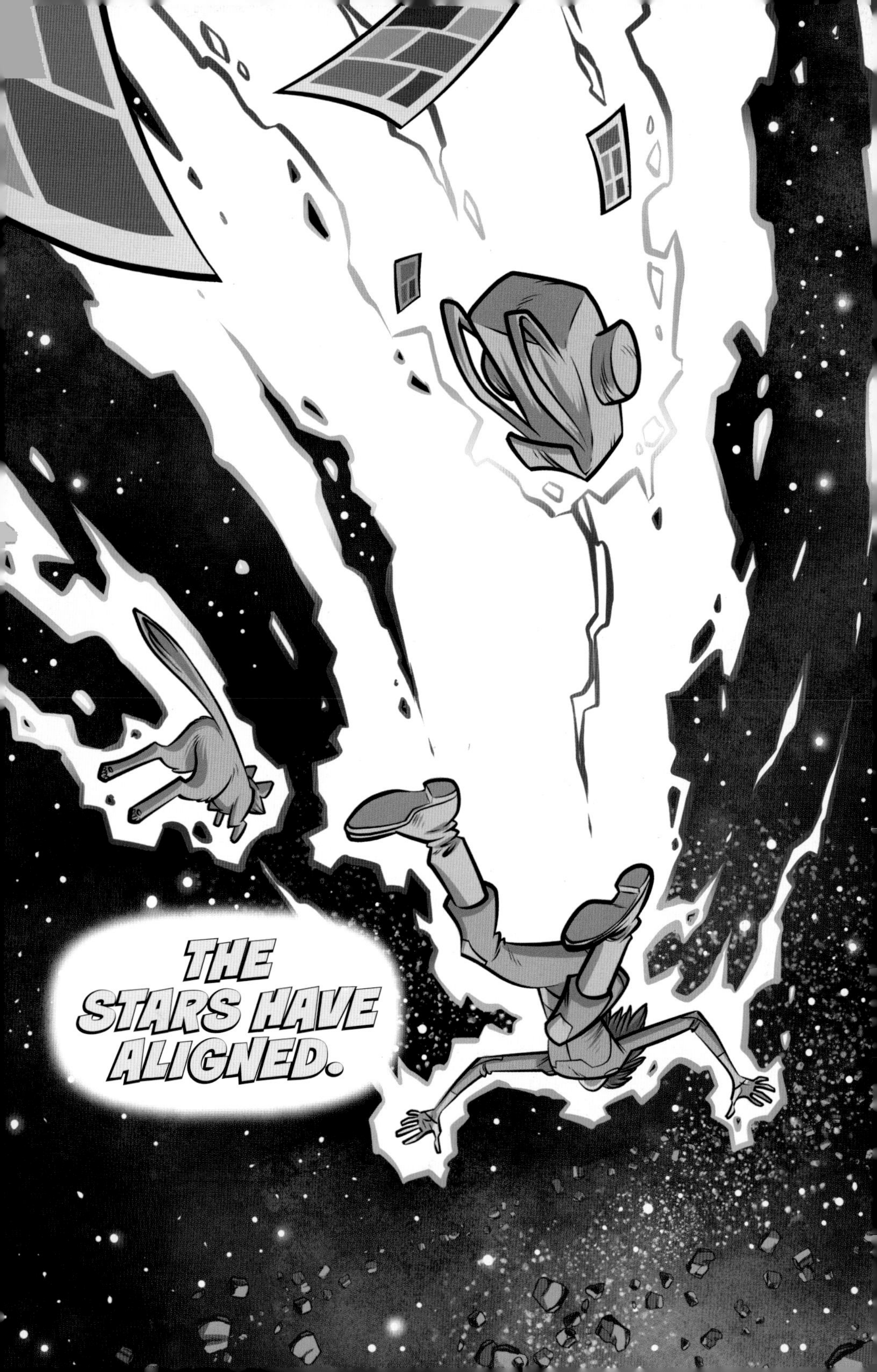
THE STARS HAVE ALIGNED.

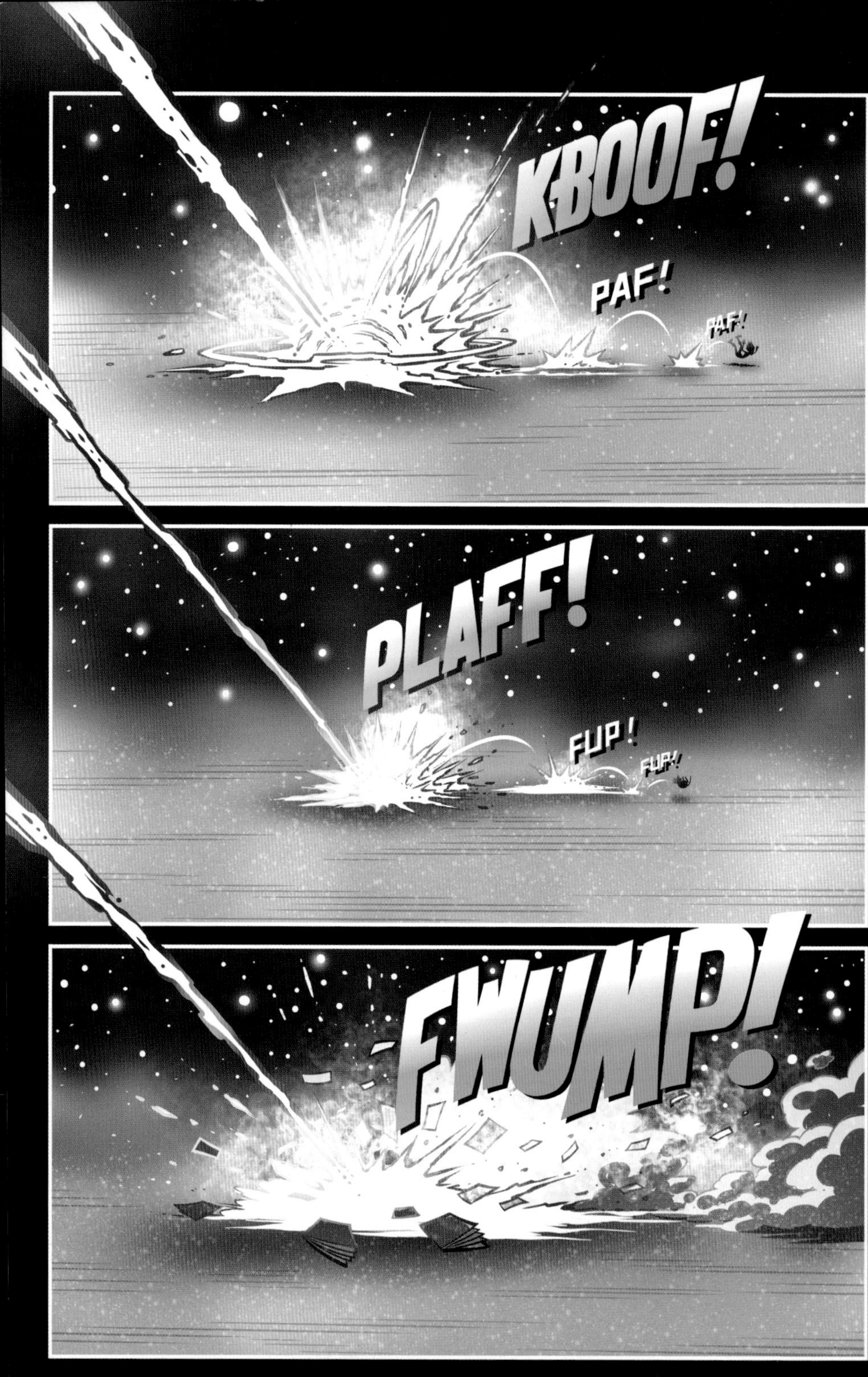
KBOOF!
PAF!
PAF!
PLAFF!
FUP!
FUP!
FWUMP!

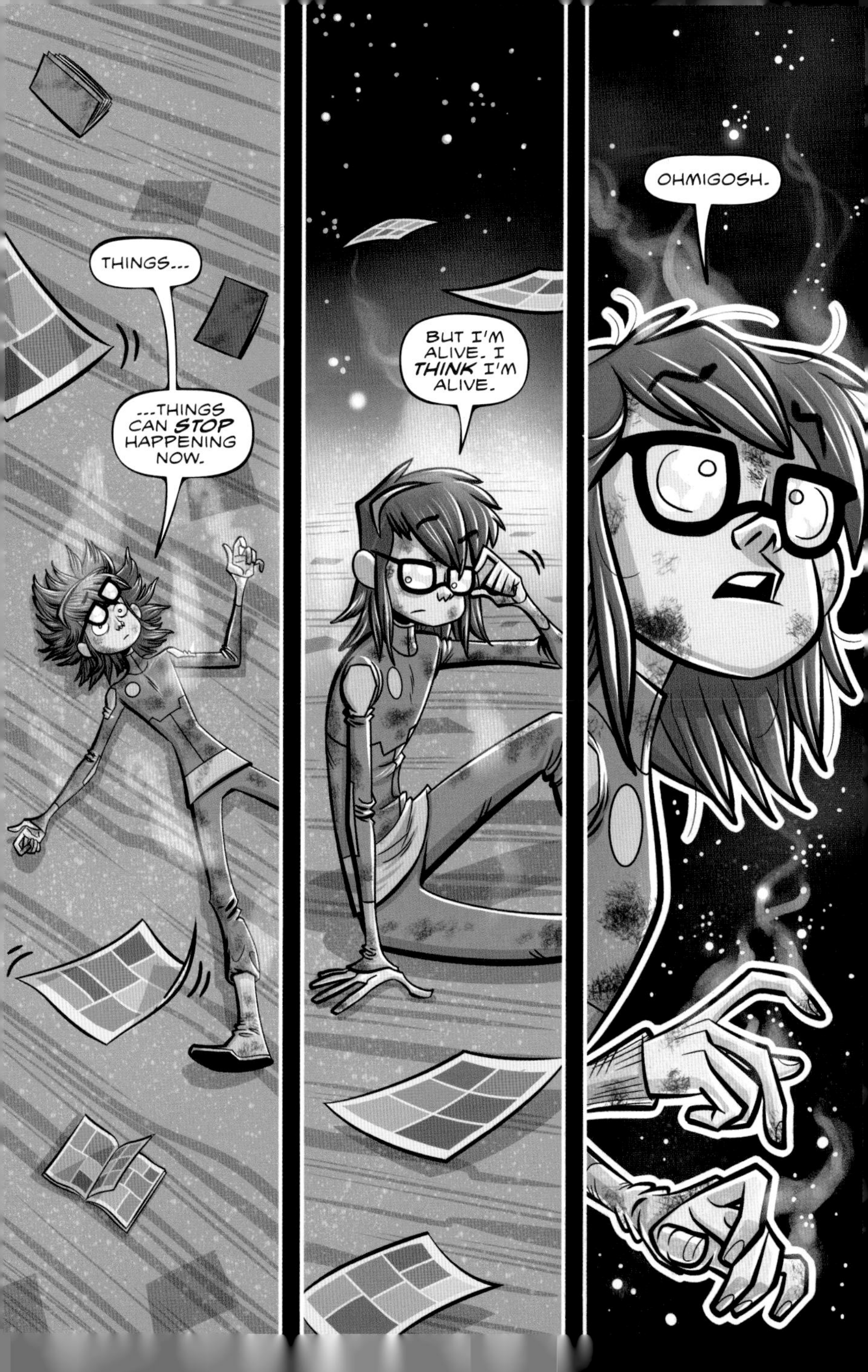
THINGS...
...THINGS CAN STOP HAPPENING NOW.
BUT I'M ALIVE. I THINK I'M ALIVE.
OHMIGOSH.

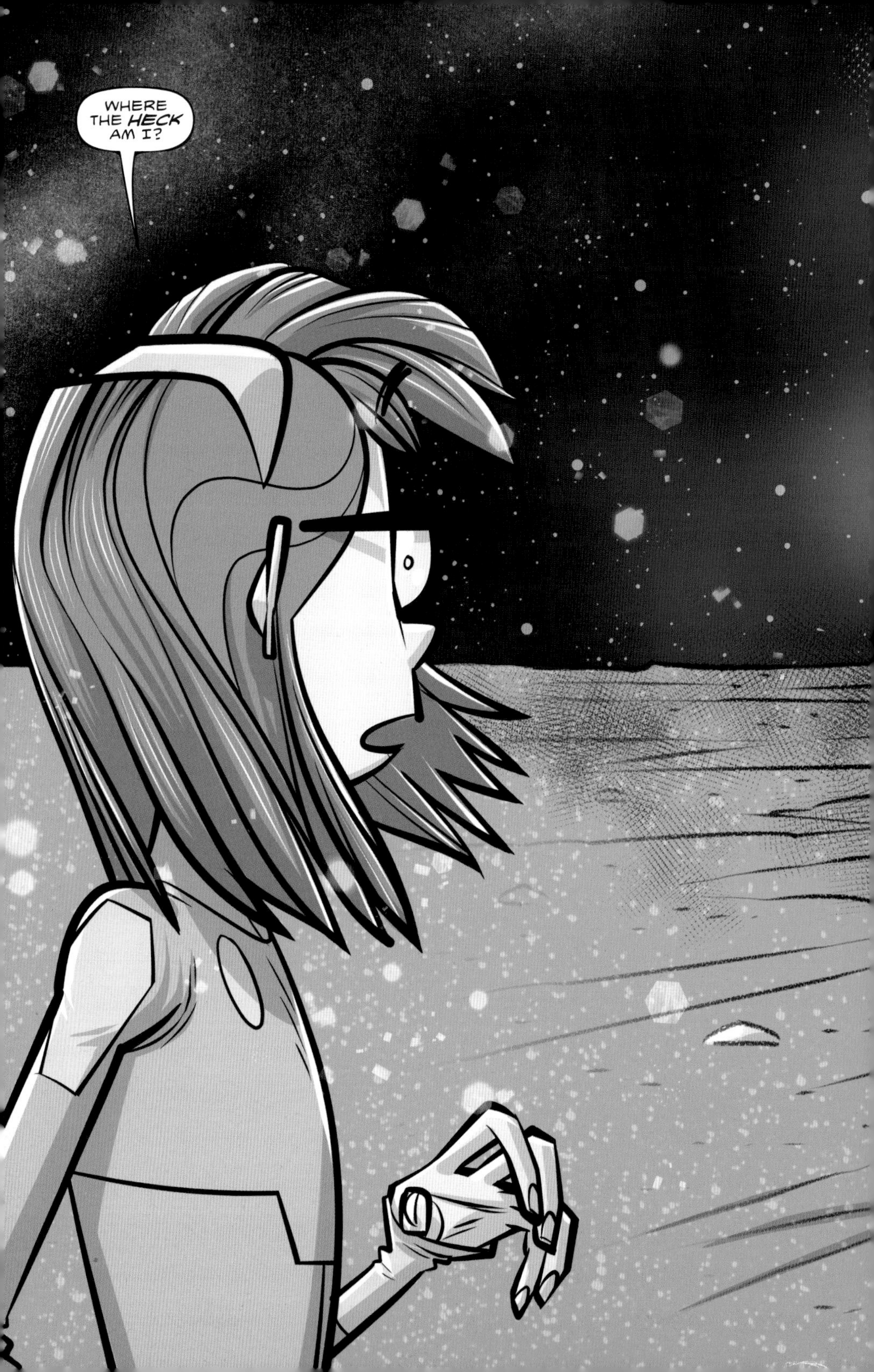
WHERE THE HECK AM I?

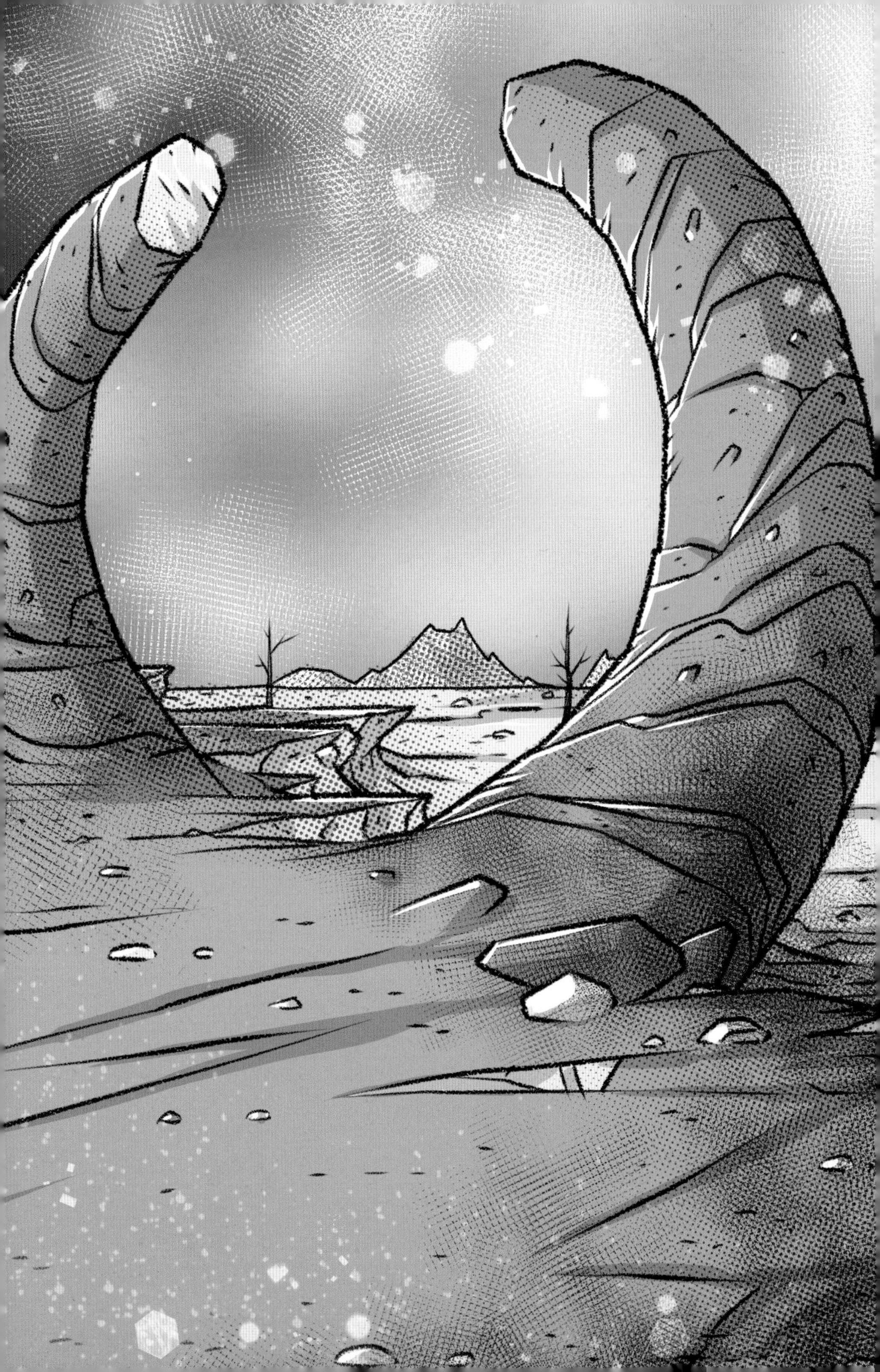

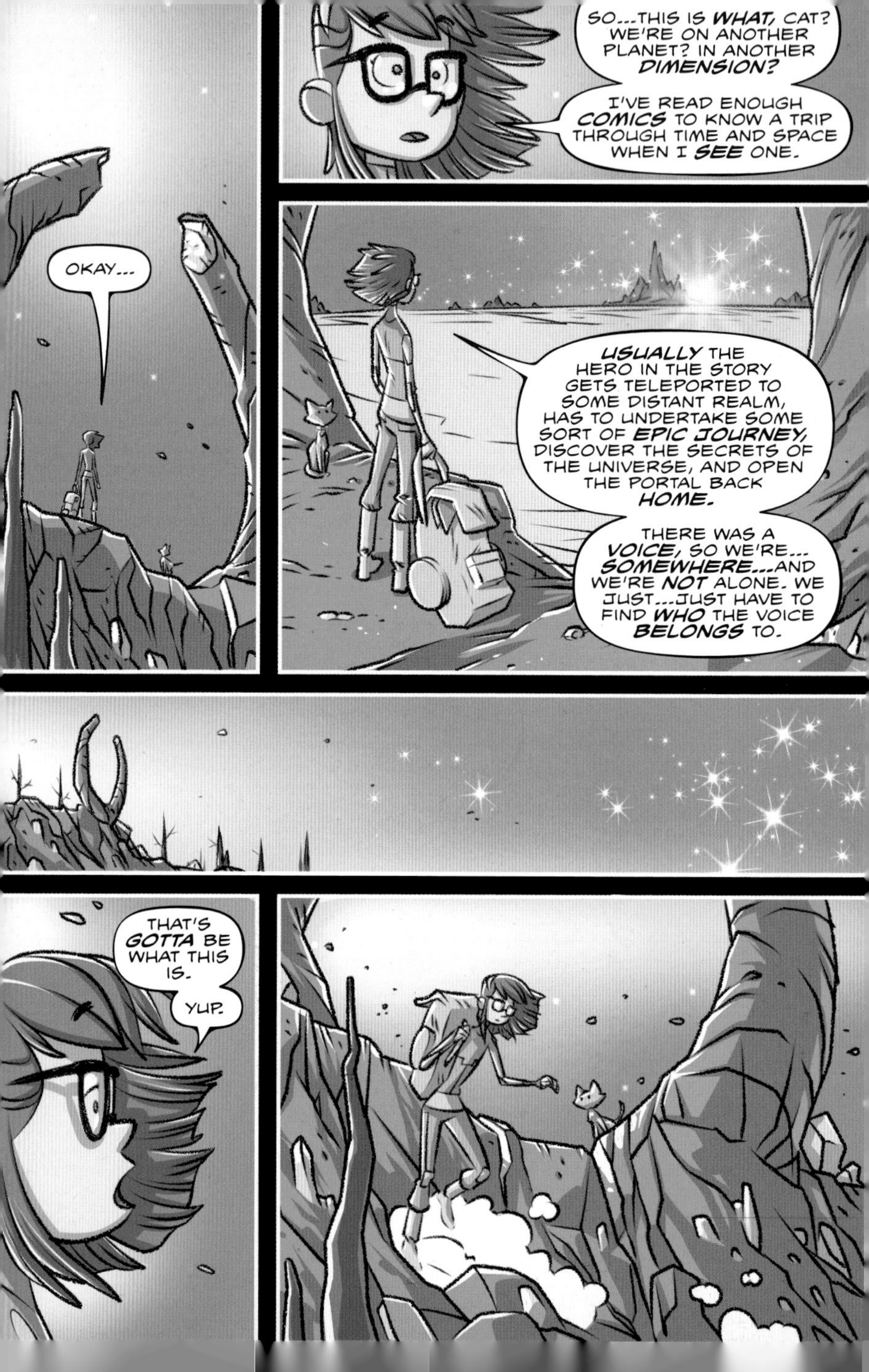
SO...THIS IS WHAT, CAT? WE'RE ON ANOTHER PLANET? IN ANOTHER DIMENSION?
I'VE READ ENOUGH COMICS TO KNOW A TRIP THROUGH TIME AND SPACE WHEN I SEE ONE.
OKAY...
USUALLY THE HERO IN THE STORY GETS TELEPORTED TO SOME DISTANT REALM, HAS TO UNDERTAKE SOME SORT OF EPIC JOURNEY, DISCOVER THE SECRETS OF THE UNIVERSE, AND OPEN THE PORTAL BACK HOME.
THERE WAS A VOICE, SO WE'RE... SOMEWHERE...AND WE'RE NOT ALONE. WE JUST...JUST HAVE TO FIND WHO THE VOICE BELONGS TO.
THAT'S GOTTA BE WHAT THIS IS.
YUP.

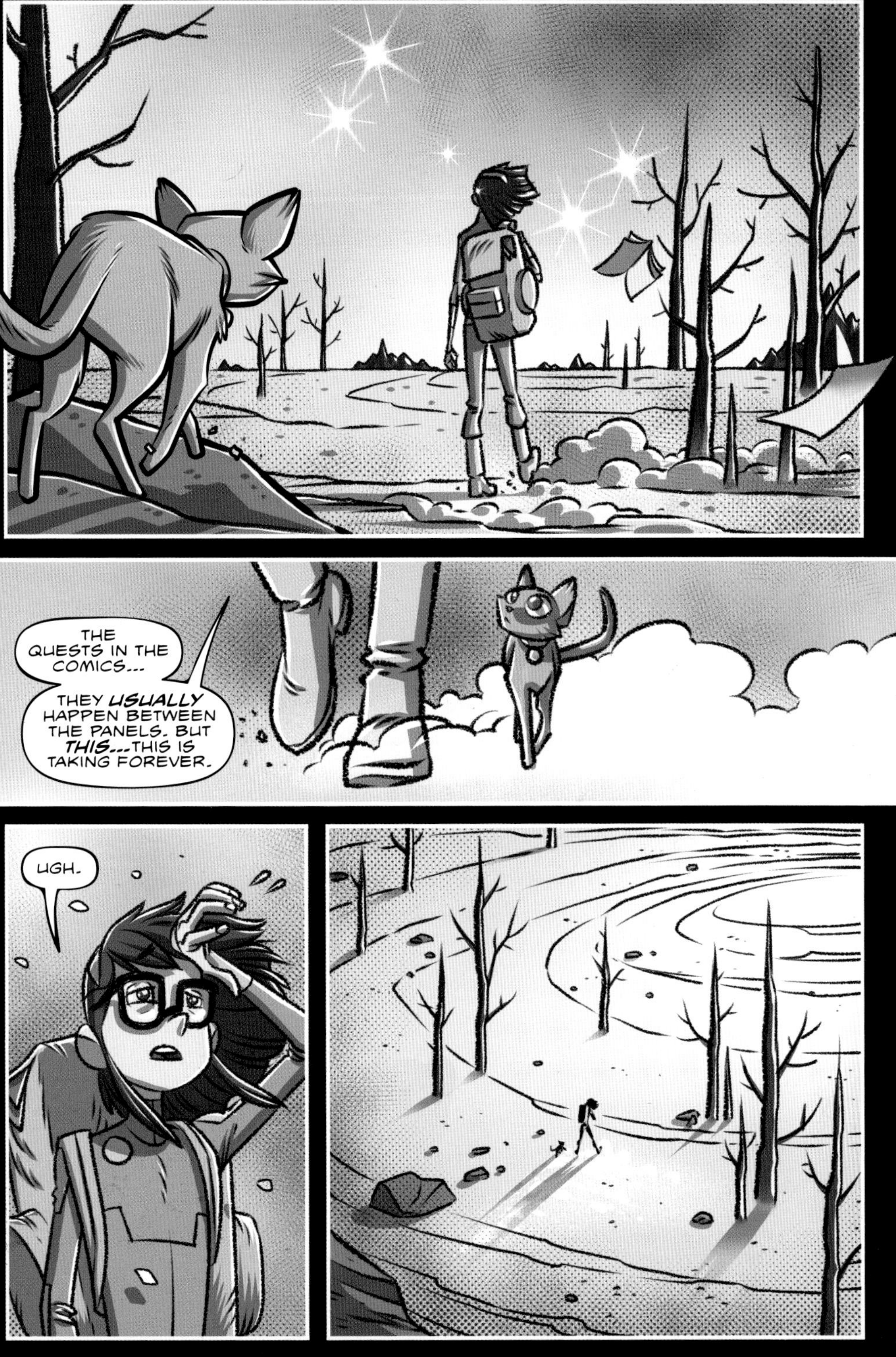
THE QUESTS IN THE COMICS...
THEY *USUALLY* HAPPEN BETWEEN THE PANELS. BUT *THIS*...THIS IS TAKING FOREVER.
UGH.

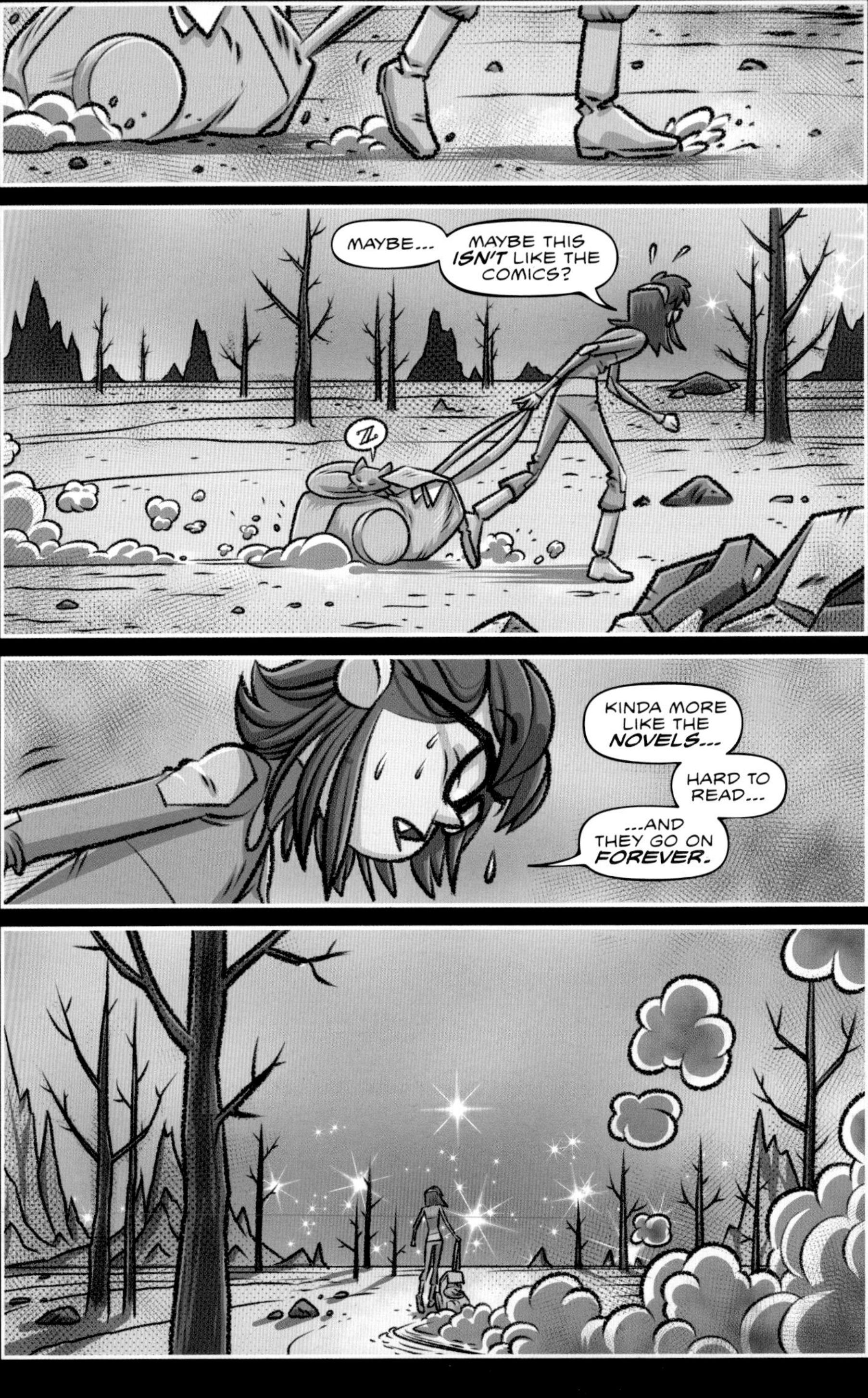
MAYBE...
MAYBE THIS ISN'T LIKE THE COMICS?
Z
KINDA MORE LIKE THE NOVELS...
HARD TO READ...
...AND THEY GO ON FOREVER.

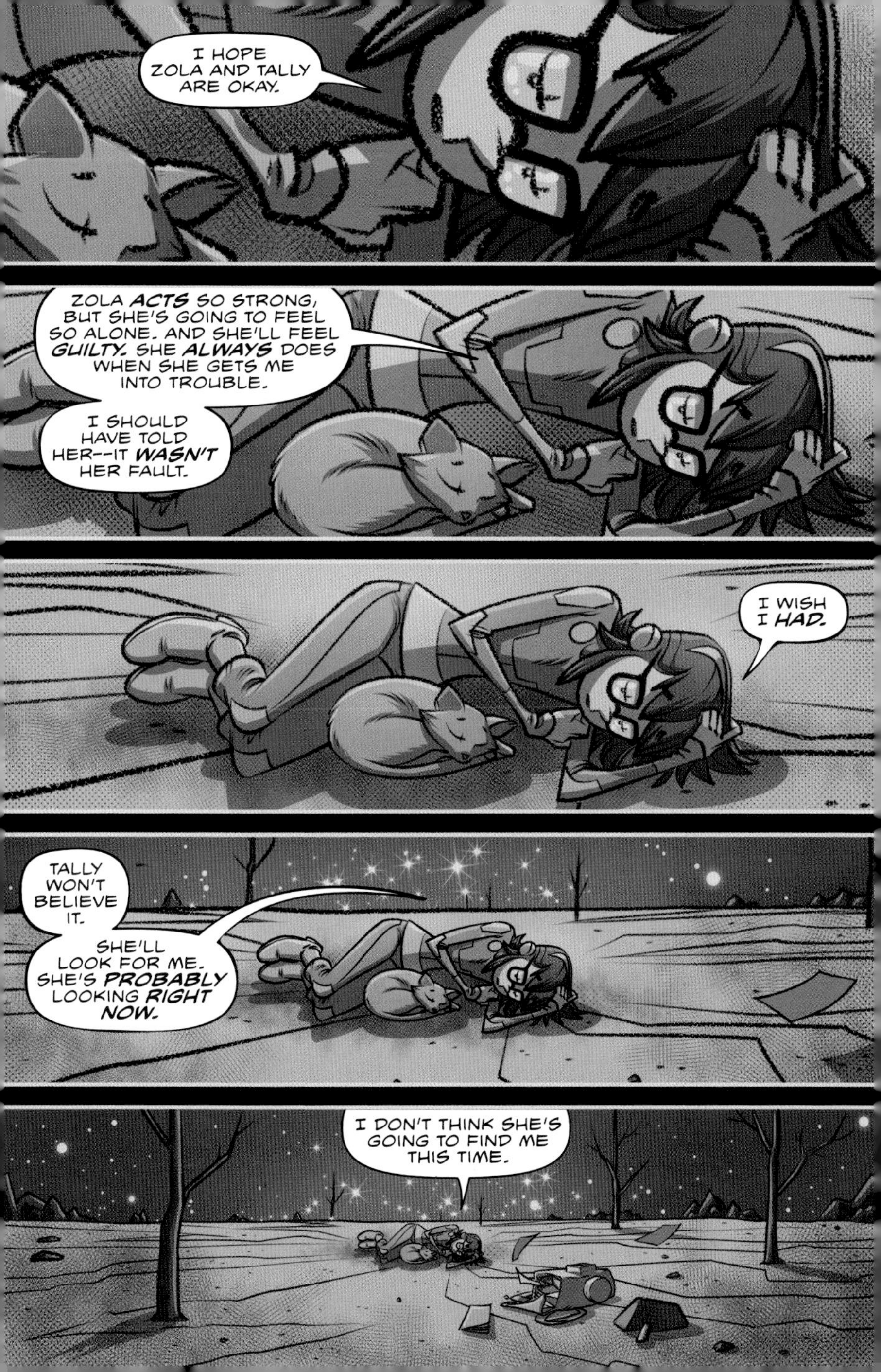
I HOPE ZOLA AND TALLY ARE OKAY.
ZOLA ACTS SO STRONG, BUT SHE'S GOING TO FEEL SO ALONE. AND SHE'LL FEEL GUILTY. SHE ALWAYS DOES WHEN SHE GETS ME INTO TROUBLE.
I SHOULD HAVE TOLD HER--IT WASN'T HER FAULT.
I WISH I HAD.
TALLY WON'T BELIEVE IT.
SHE'LL LOOK FOR ME. SHE'S PROBABLY LOOKING RIGHT NOW.
I DON'T THINK SHE'S GOING TO FIND ME THIS TIME.

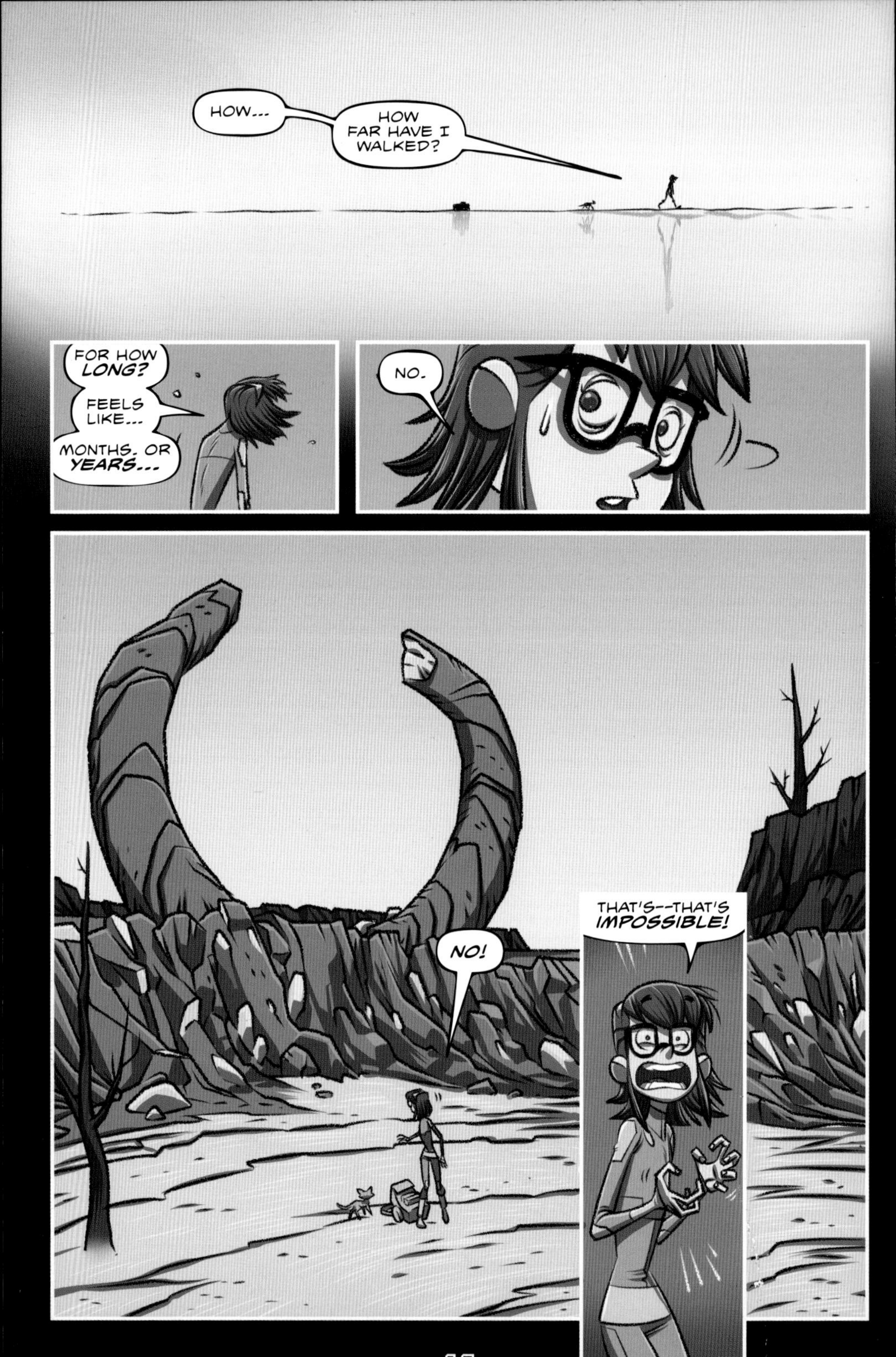
HOW...
HOW FAR HAVE I WALKED?
FOR HOW LONG?
FEELS LIKE...
MONTHS. OR YEARS...
NO.
NO!
THAT'S--THAT'S IMPOSSIBLE!

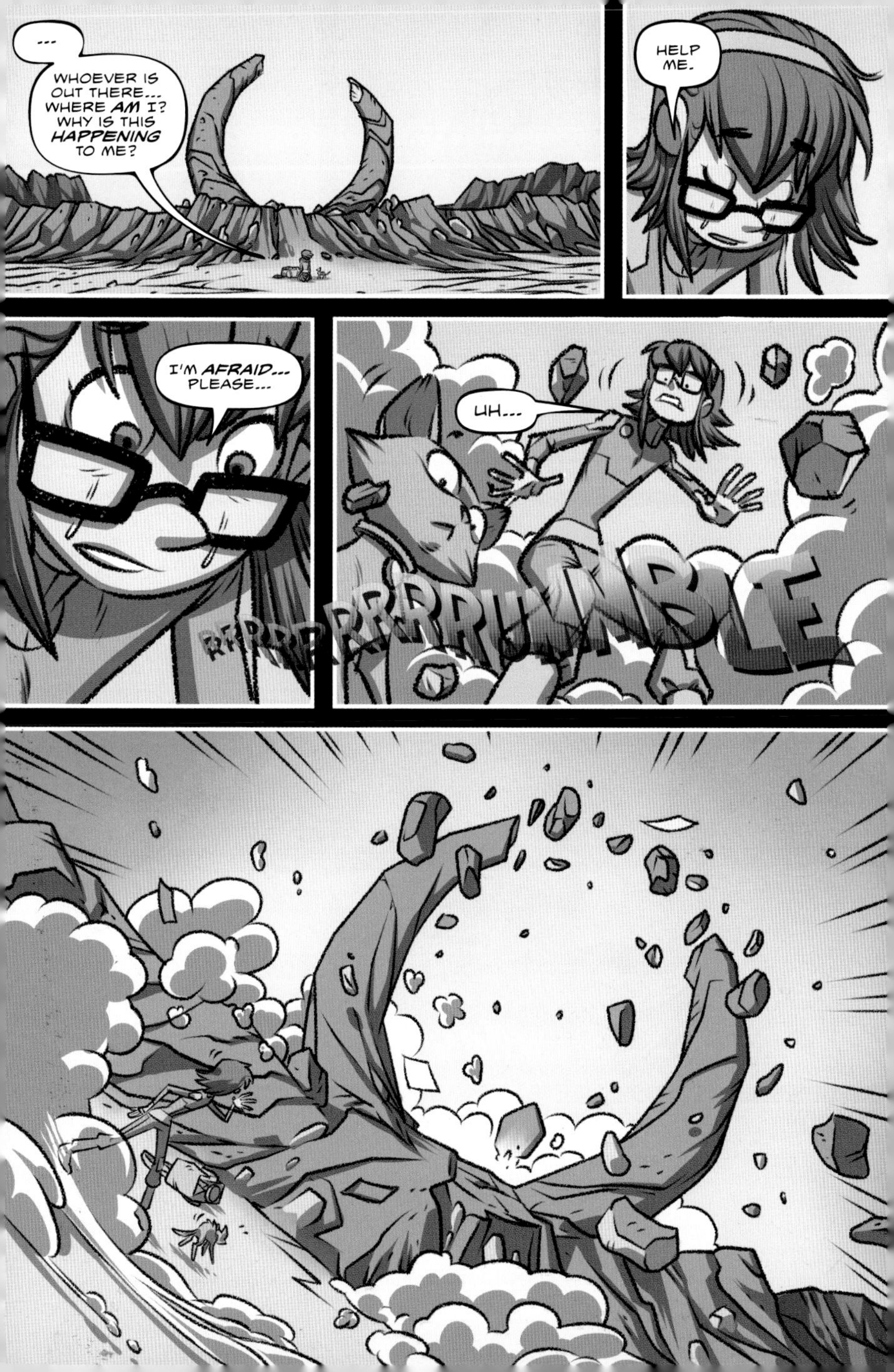

...
WHOEVER IS OUT THERE... WHERE *AM* I? WHY IS THIS *HAPPENING* TO ME?
HELP ME.
I'M *AFRAID...* PLEASE...
UH...
RRRRRRRRRRUMBLE

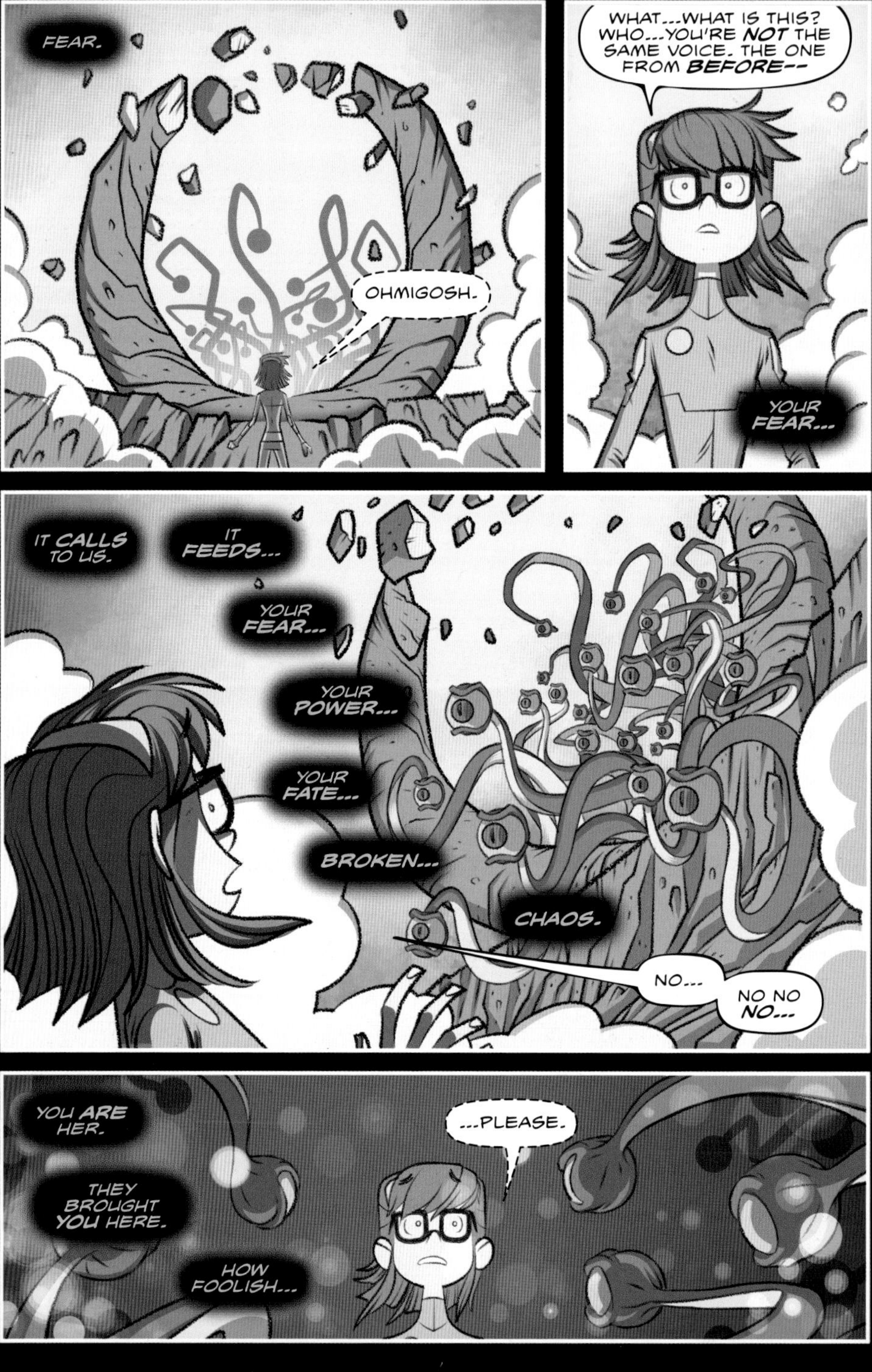
FEAR.
OHMIGOSH.
WHAT...WHAT IS THIS? WHO...YOU'RE NOT THE SAME VOICE. THE ONE FROM BEFORE--
YOUR FEAR...
IT CALLS TO US.
IT FEEDS...
YOUR FEAR...
YOUR POWER...
YOUR FATE...
BROKEN...
CHAOS.
NO...
NO NO NO...
YOU ARE HER.
...PLEASE.
THEY BROUGHT YOU HERE.
HOW FOOLISH...

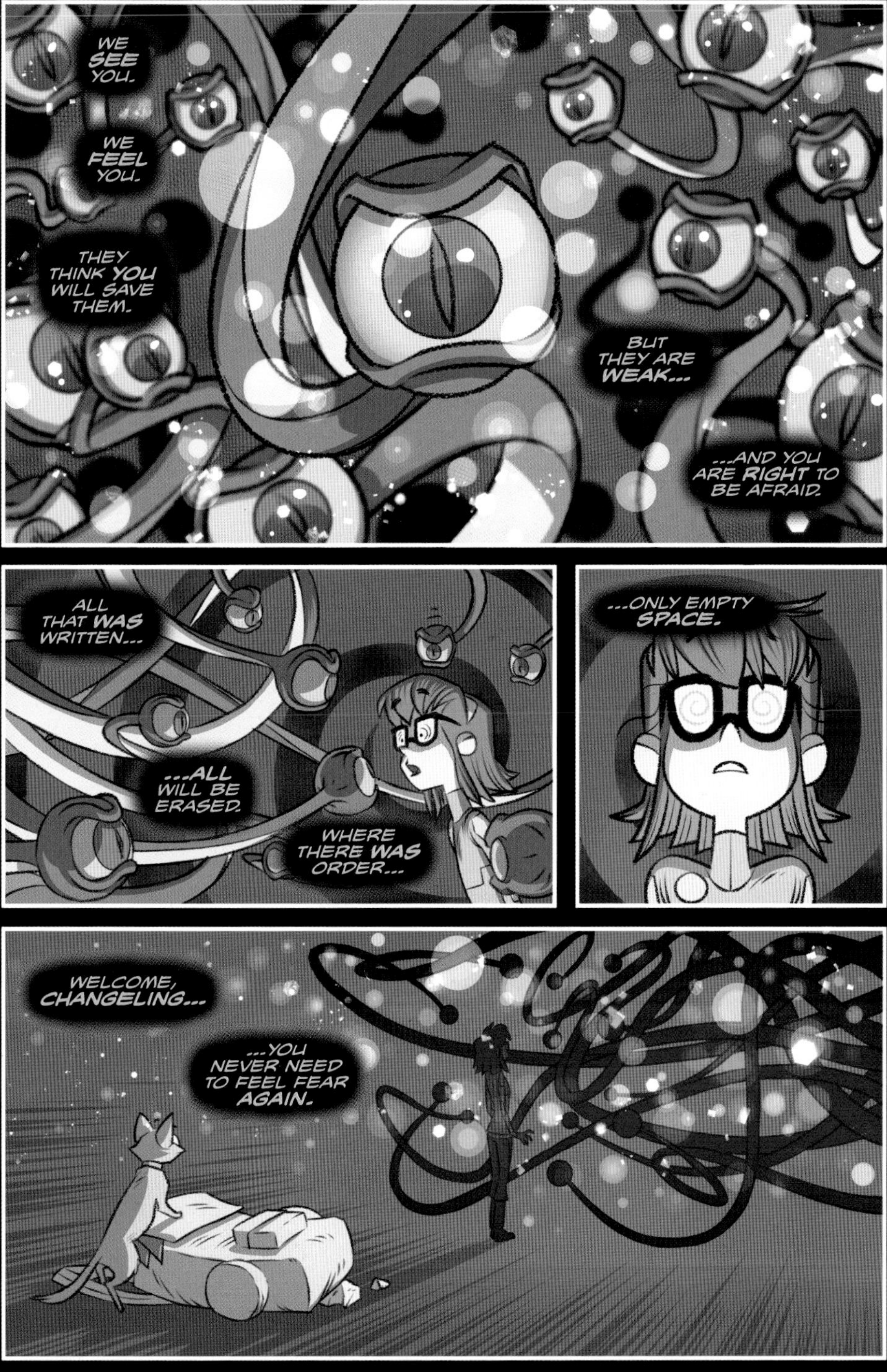
WE SEE YOU.
WE FEEL YOU.
THEY THINK YOU WILL SAVE THEM.
BUT THEY ARE WEAK...
...AND YOU ARE RIGHT TO BE AFRAID.
ALL THAT WAS WRITTEN...
...ALL WILL BE ERASED.
WHERE THERE WAS ORDER...
...ONLY EMPTY SPACE.
WELCOME, CHANGELING...
...YOU NEVER NEED TO FEEL FEAR AGAIN.

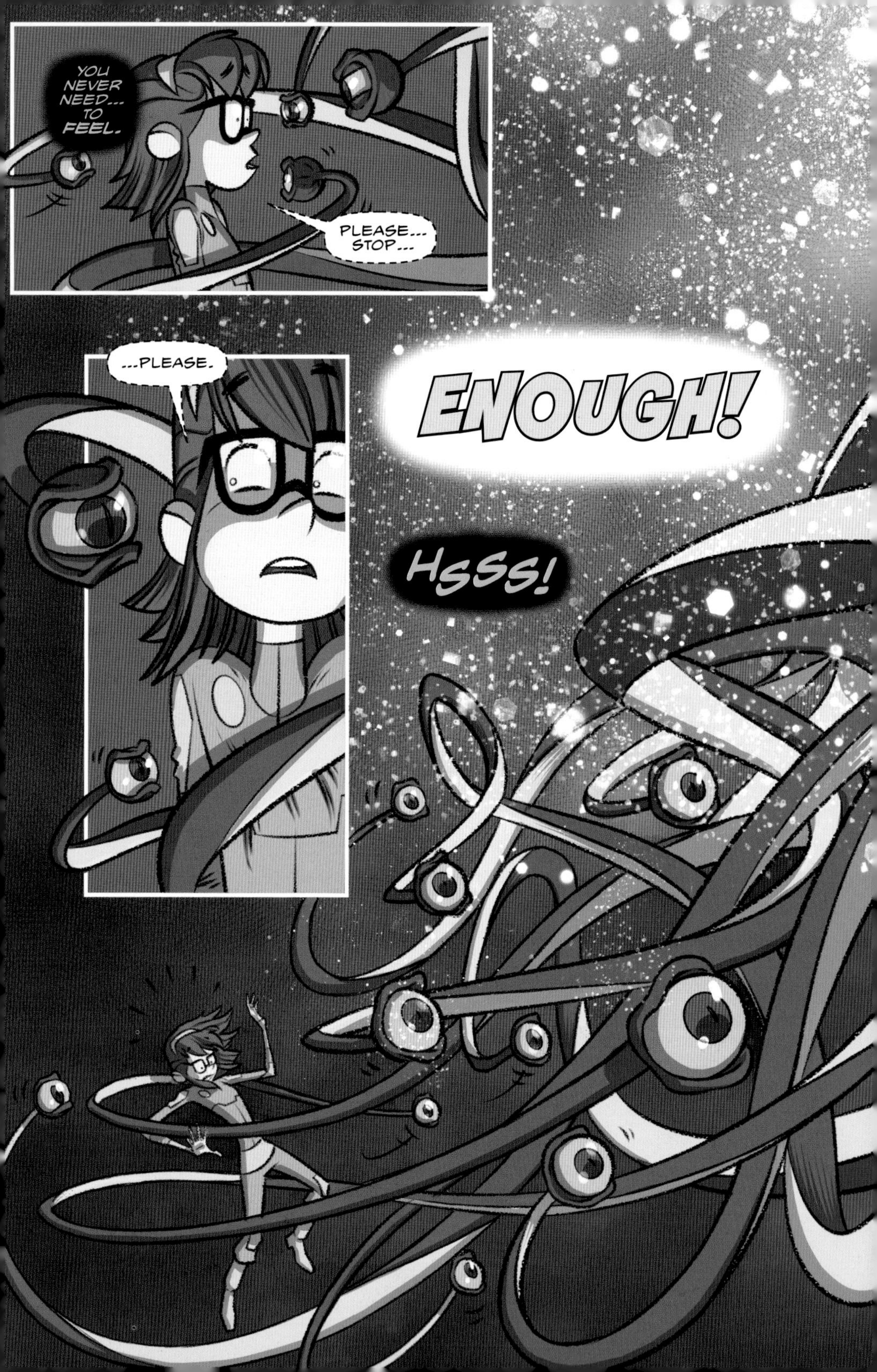
YOU NEVER NEED... TO FEEL.
PLEASE... STOP...
...PLEASE.
ENOUGH!
HSSS!

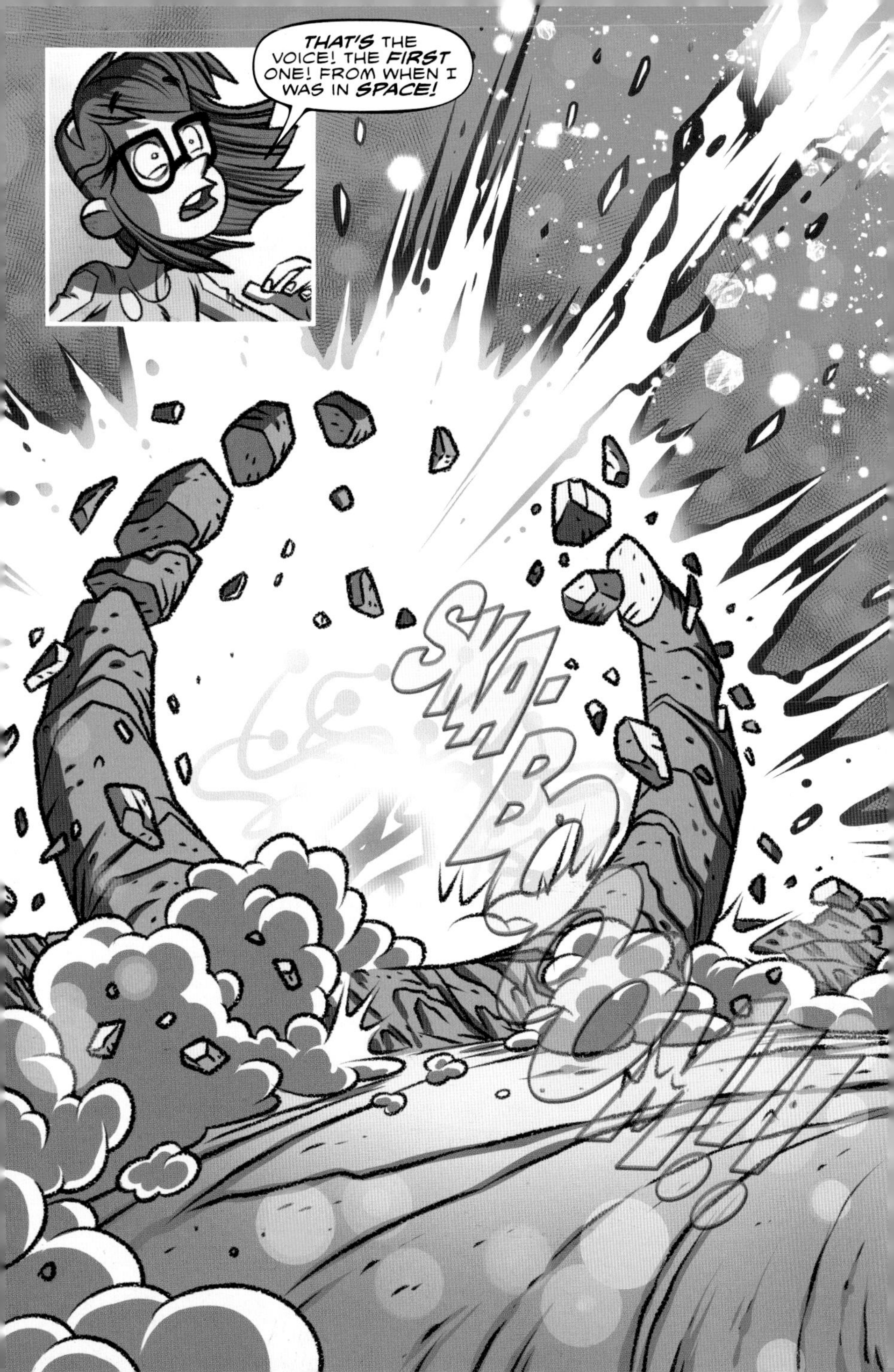
THAT'S THE VOICE! THE FIRST ONE! FROM WHEN I WAS IN SPACE!

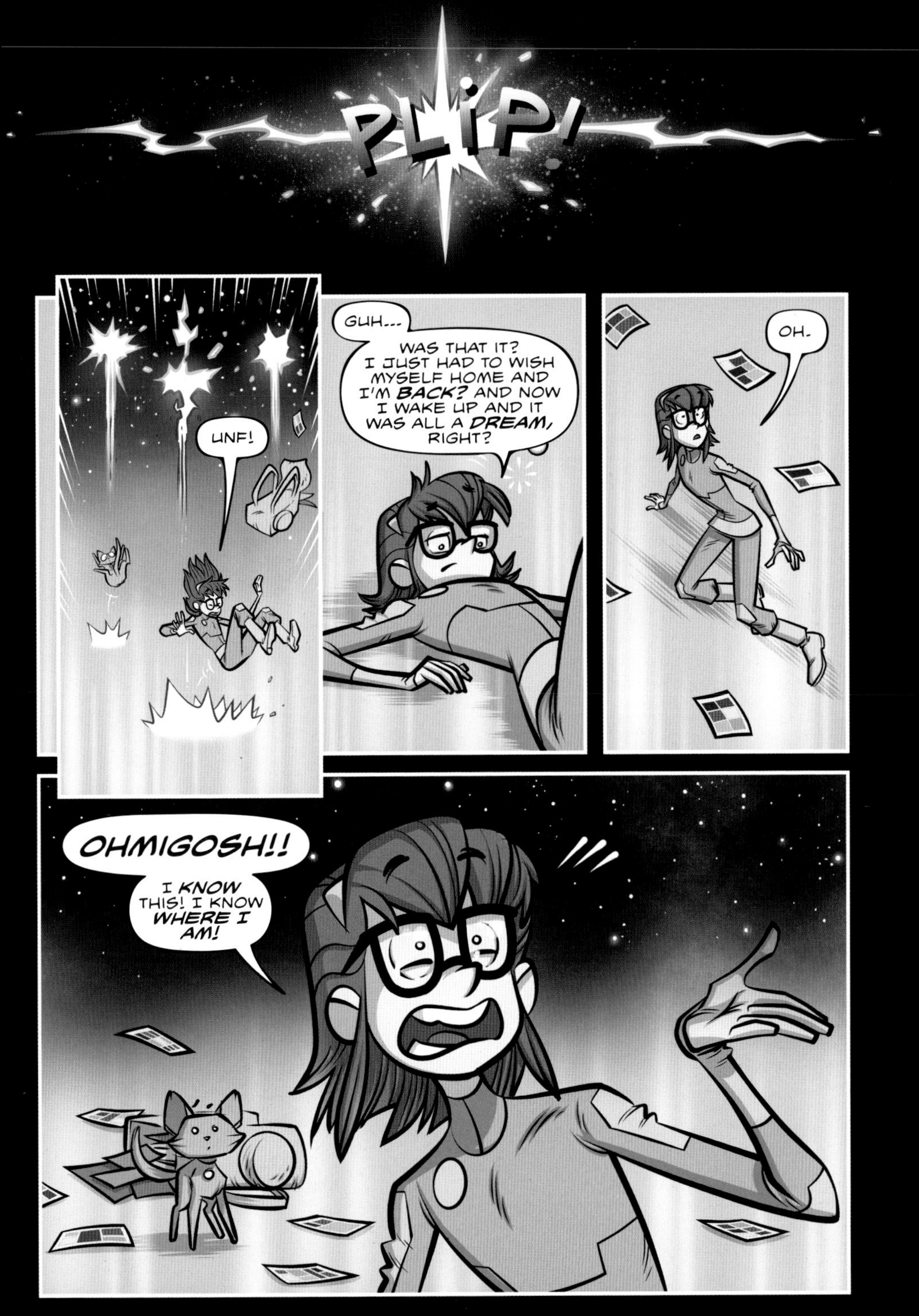
PLIP!
UNF!
GUH...
WAS THAT IT? I JUST HAD TO WISH MYSELF HOME AND I'M *BACK?* AND NOW I WAKE UP AND IT WAS ALL A *DREAM,* RIGHT?
OH.
OHMIGOSH!!
I *KNOW* THIS! I KNOW *WHERE I AM!*

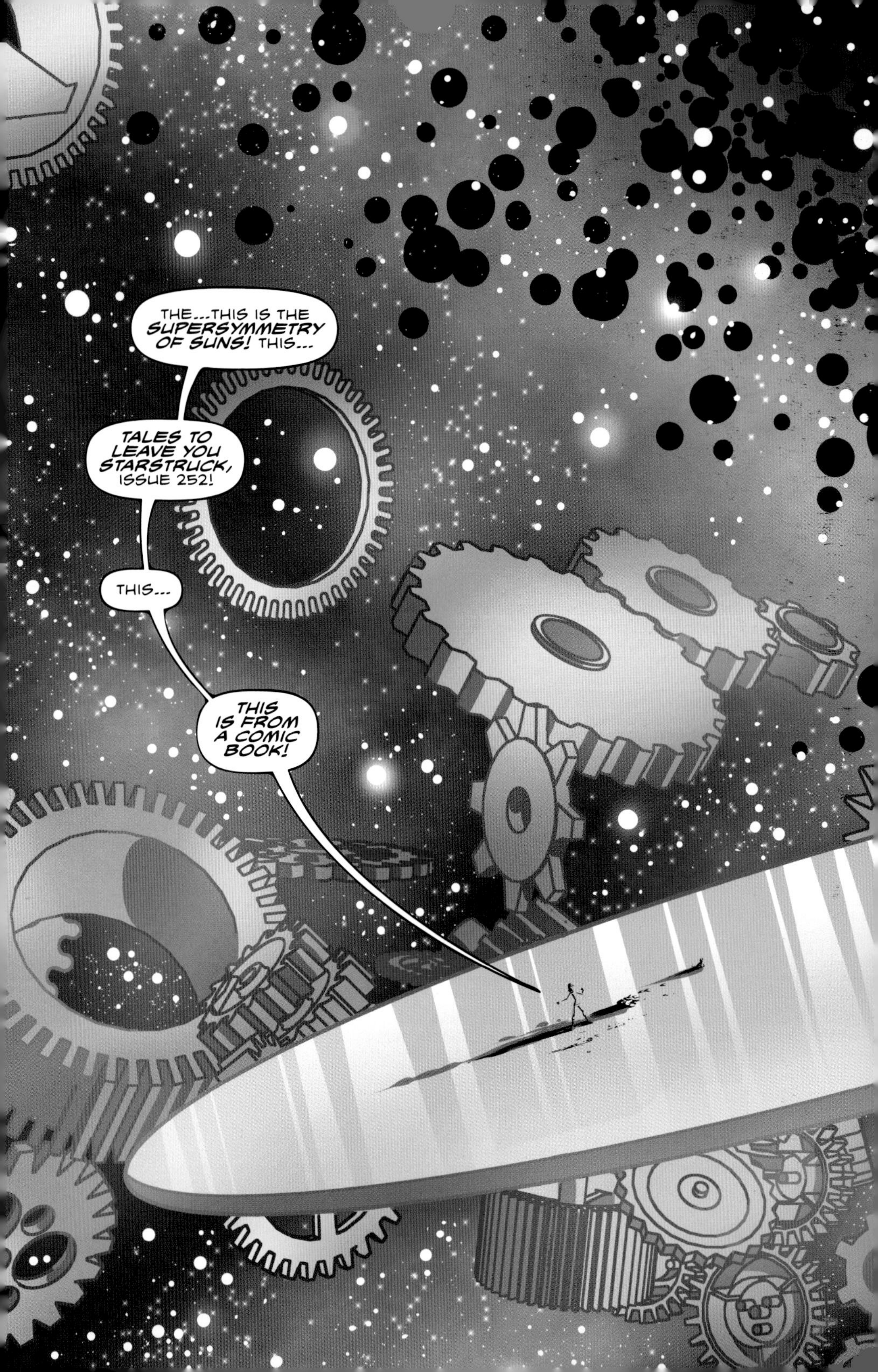
THE...THIS IS THE SUPERSYMMETRY OF SUNS! THIS...
TALES TO LEAVE YOU STARSTRUCK, ISSUE 252!
THIS...
THIS IS FROM A COMIC BOOK!

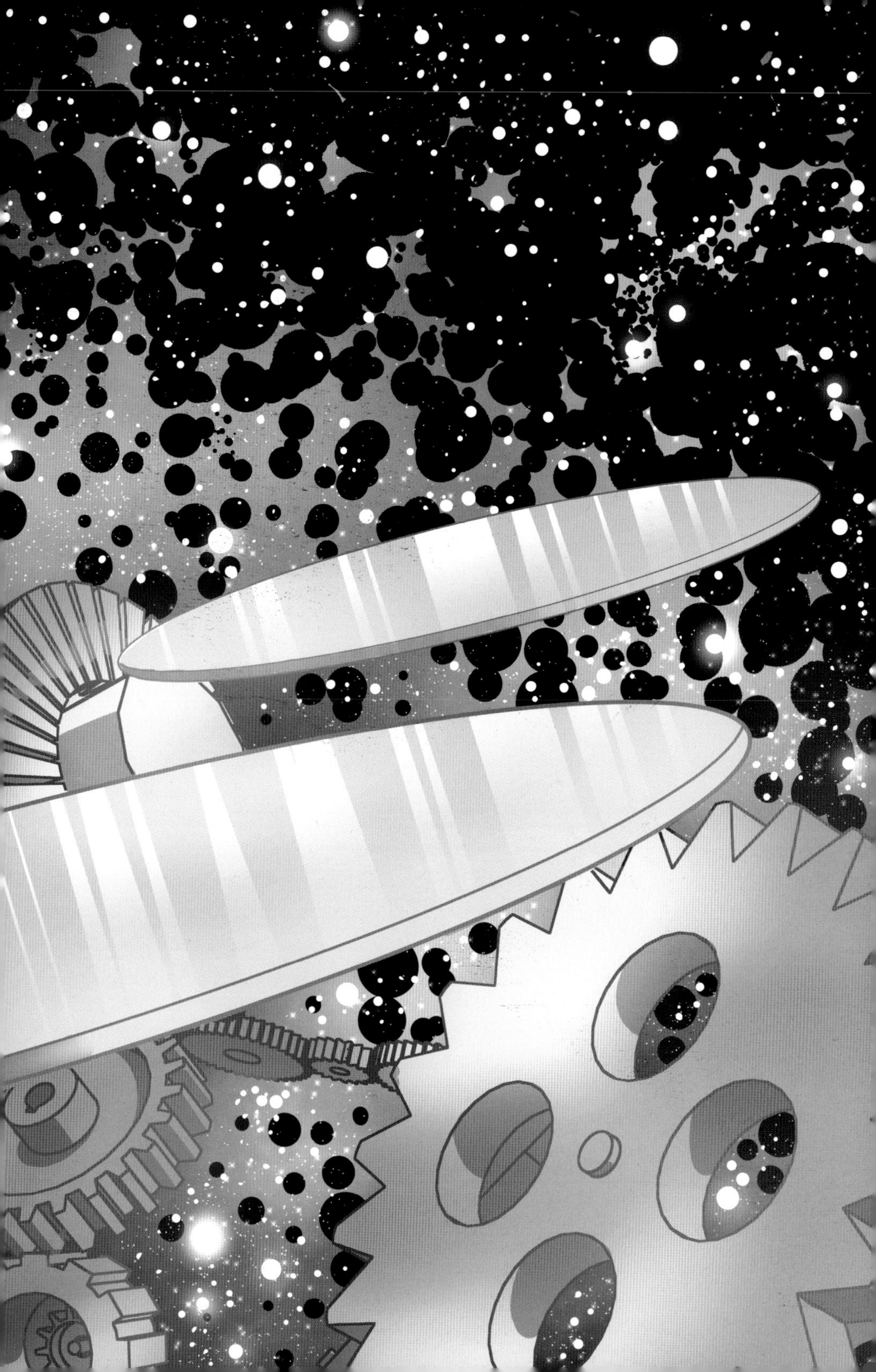

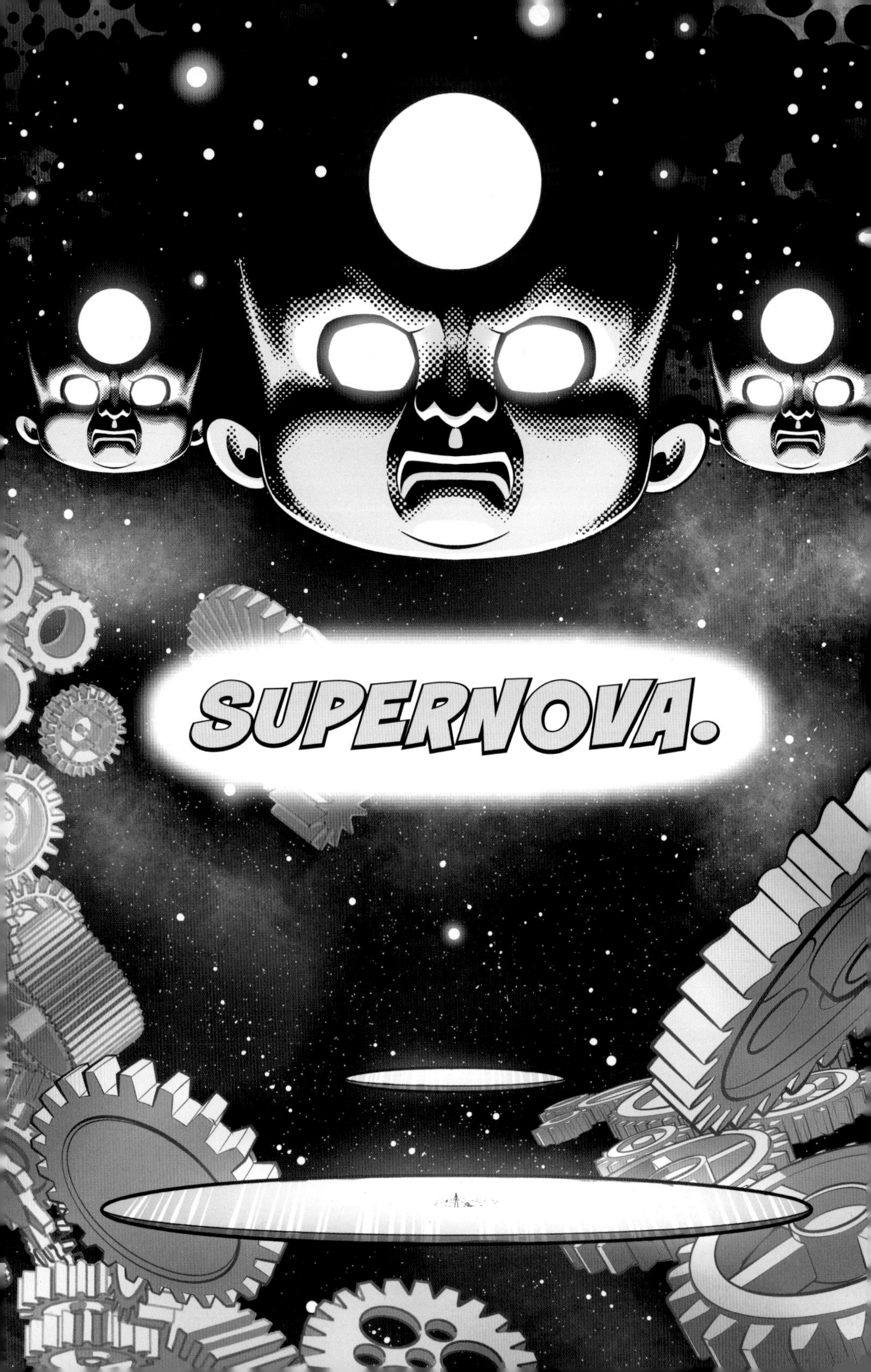
SUPERNOVA.

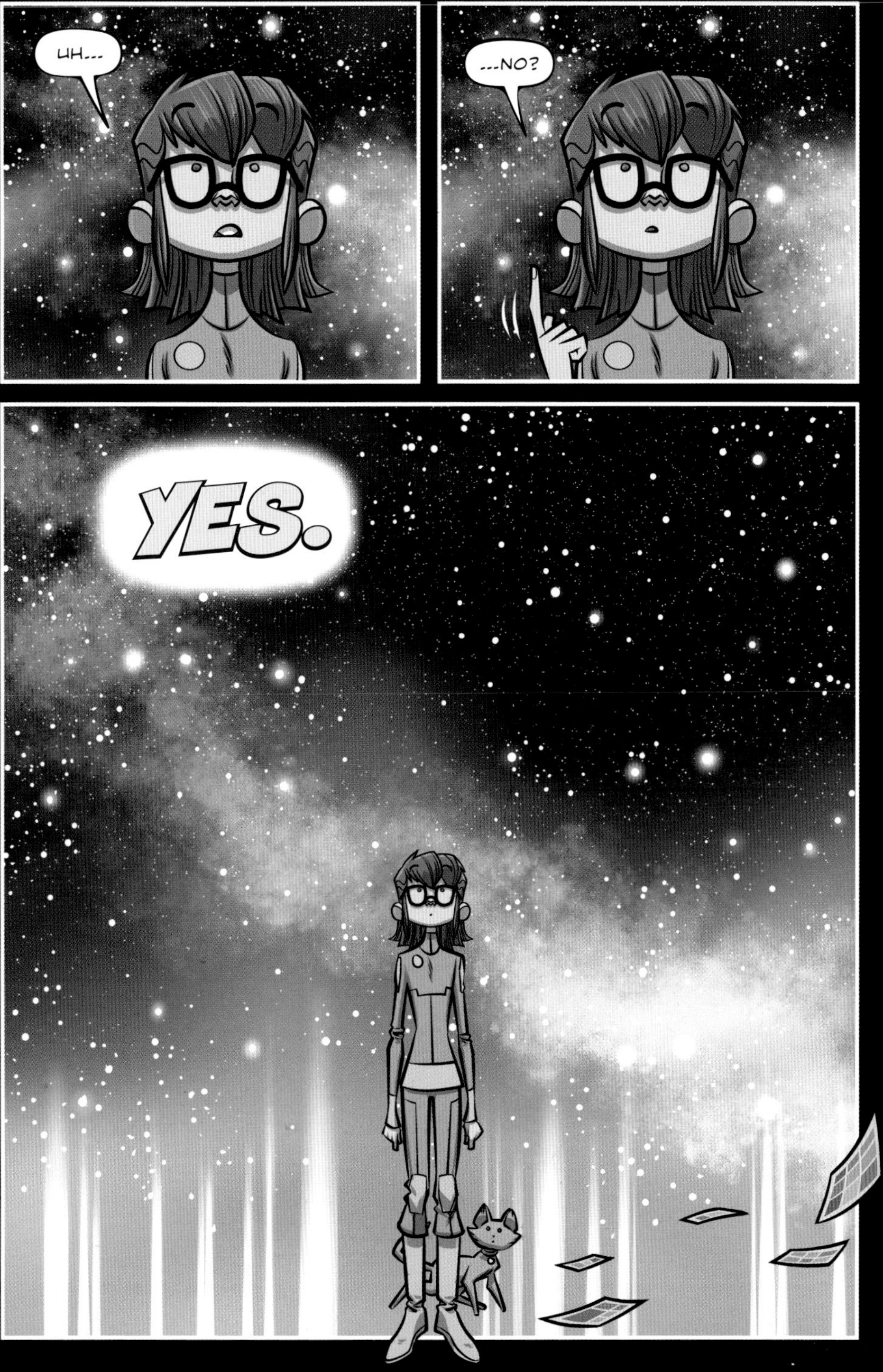
UH...
...NO?
YES.

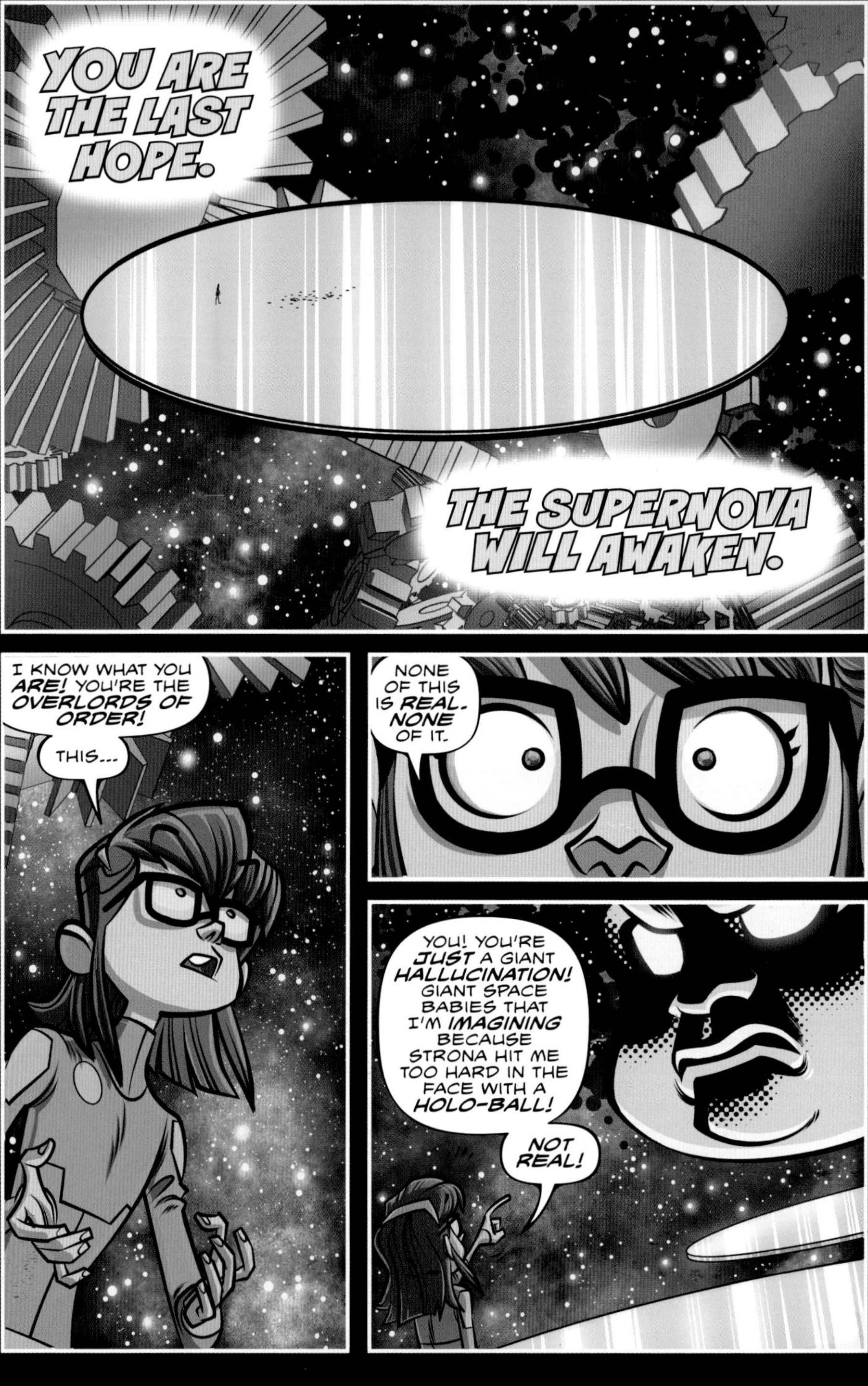
YOU ARE THE LAST HOPE.
THE SUPERNOVA WILL AWAKEN.
I KNOW WHAT YOU ARE! YOU'RE THE OVERLORDS OF ORDER!
THIS...
NONE OF THIS IS REAL. NONE OF IT.
YOU! YOU'RE JUST A GIANT HALLUCINATION! GIANT SPACE BABIES THAT I'M IMAGINING BECAUSE STRONA HIT ME TOO HARD IN THE FACE WITH A HOLO-BALL!
NOT REAL!

BECAUSE YOU *CAN'T* BE.

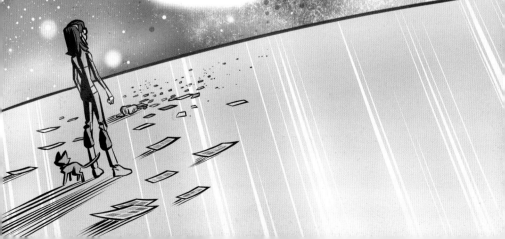

THE ORDER OF EXISTENCE HAS BEEN FORSAKEN.

YOU ARE THE SUPERNOVA. YOU *WILL* AWAKEN.

THE VOID HAS WEAKENED US. CHAOS IS ASCENDING.

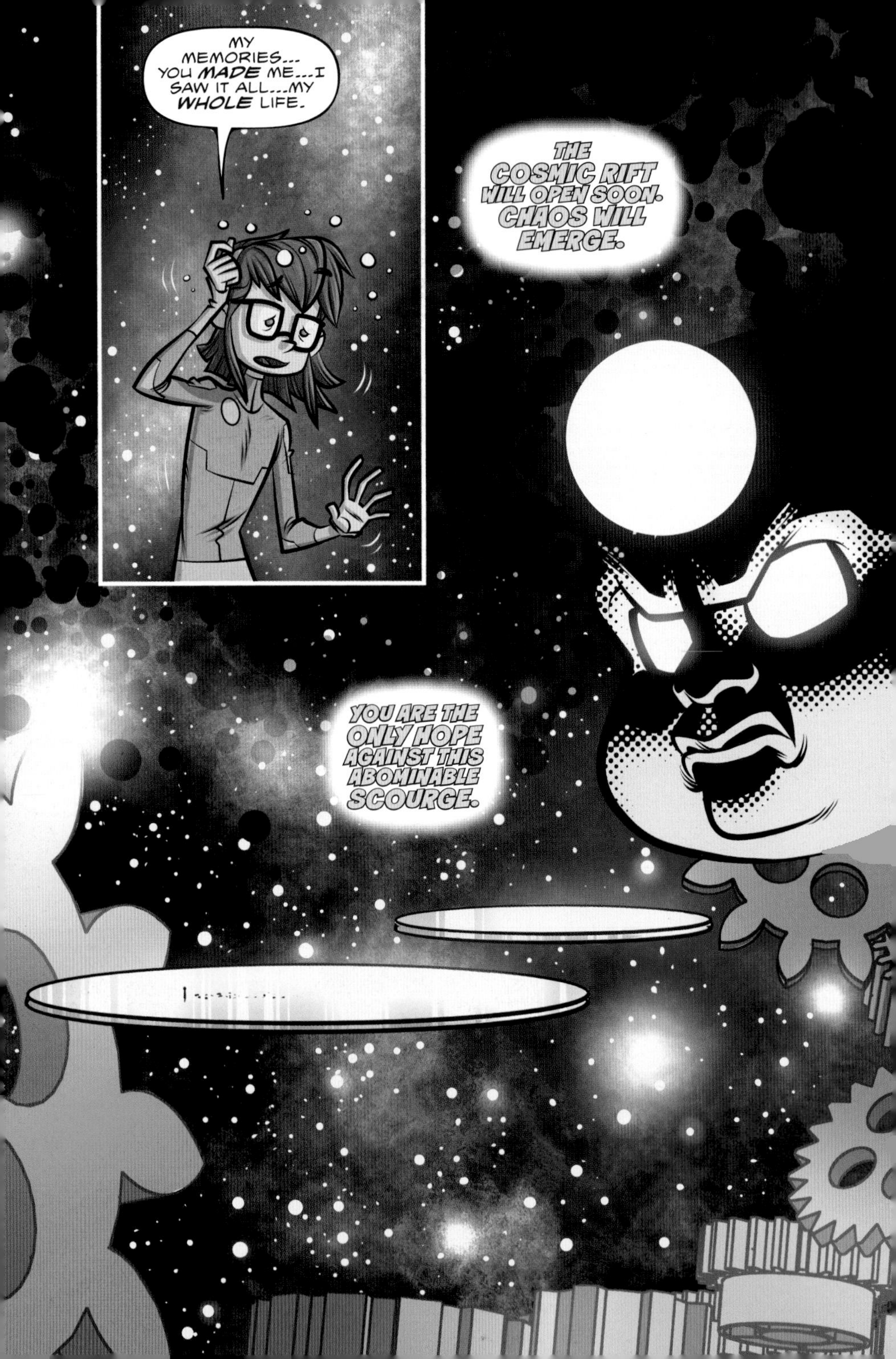
MY MEMORIES... YOU MADE ME...I SAW IT ALL...MY WHOLE LIFE.
THE COSMIC RIFT WILL OPEN SOON. CHAOS WILL EMERGE.
YOU ARE THE ONLY HOPE AGAINST THIS ABOMINABLE SCOURGE.

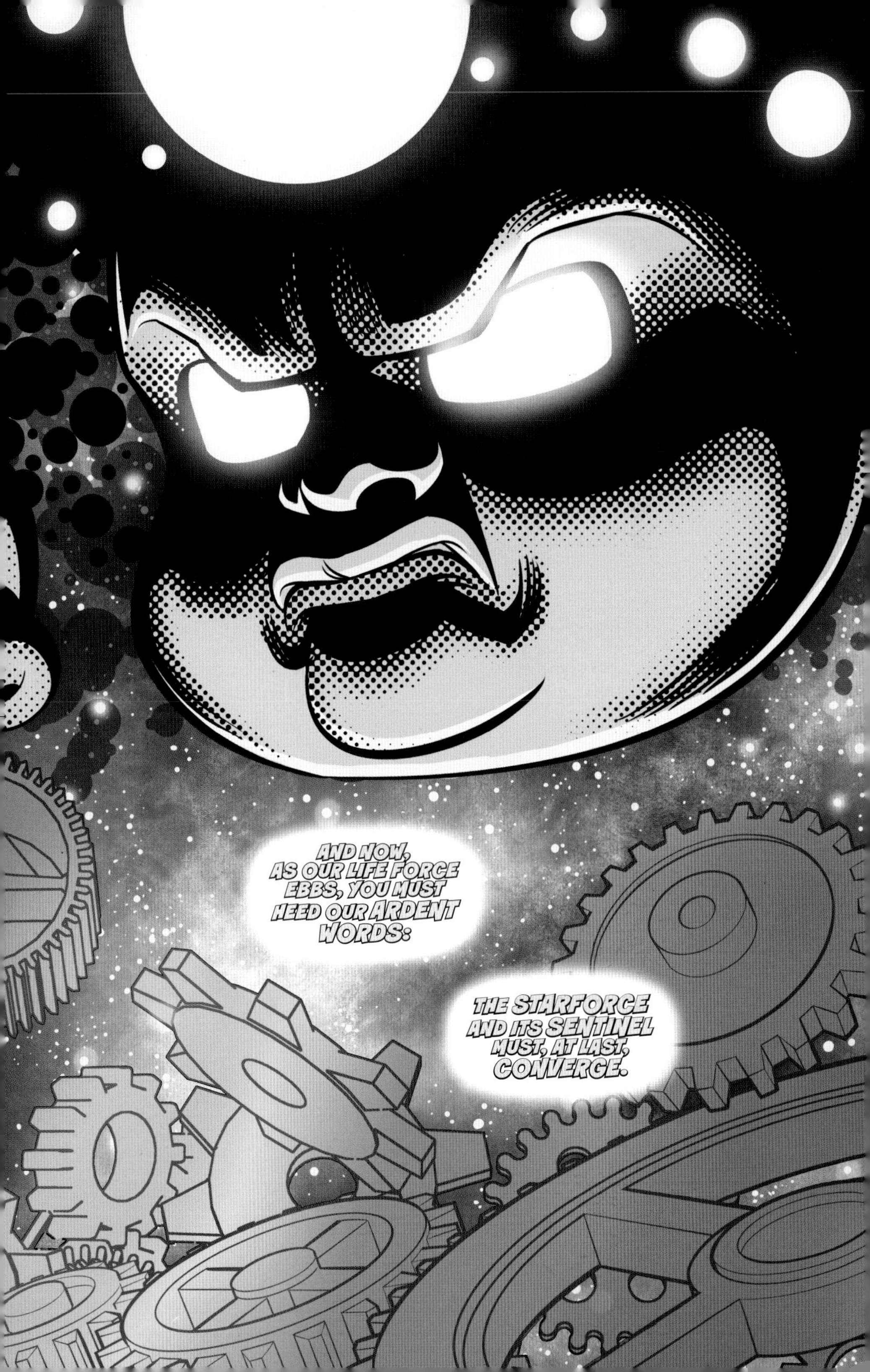
AND NOW, AS OUR LIFE FORCE EBBS, YOU MUST HEED OUR ARDENT WORDS:
THE STARFORCE AND ITS SENTINEL MUST, AT LAST, CONVERGE.

THE DESTROYER? LIKE *MENDAX*? BUT WHAT'S THE *DECEIVER*?

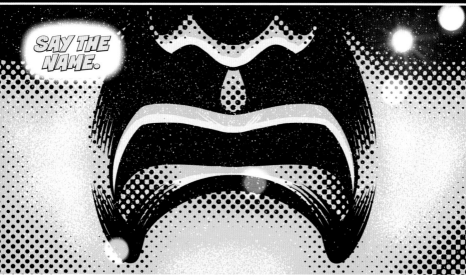

SAY THE NAME.

WHAT?

I JUST WANT TO GO *HOME*! JUST...JUST SEND ME *BACK*!

WHATEVER YOU *THINK* I AM...

I'M *NOT*! OKAY? I'M *JUST PEPPER PAGE*!

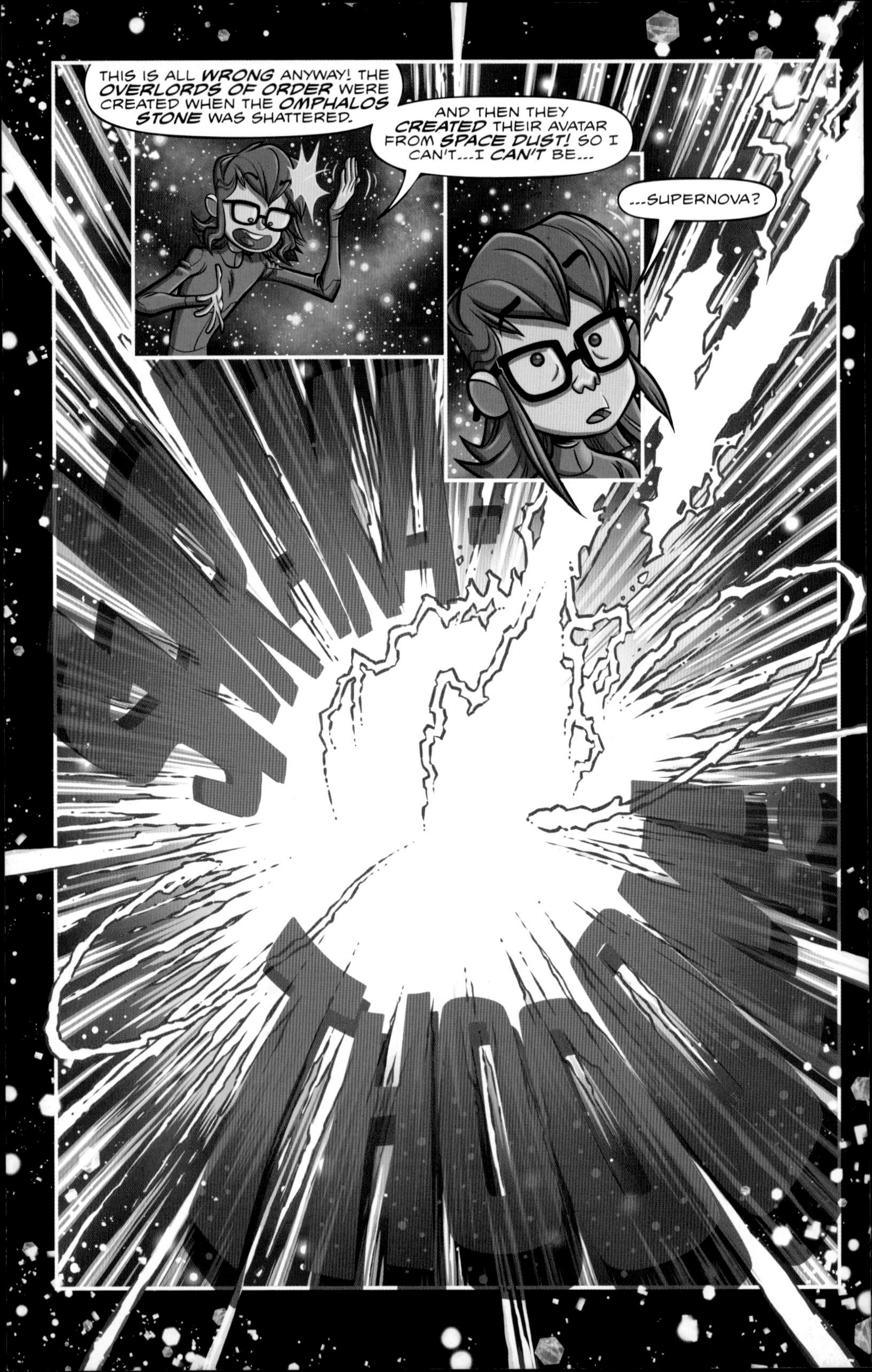
THIS IS ALL WRONG ANYWAY! THE OVERLORDS OF ORDER WERE CREATED WHEN THE OMPHALOS STONE WAS SHATTERED.
AND THEN THEY CREATED THEIR AVATAR FROM SPACE DUST! SO I CAN'T...I CAN'T BE...
...SUPERNOVA?

THE NAME HAS BEEN SPOKEN.

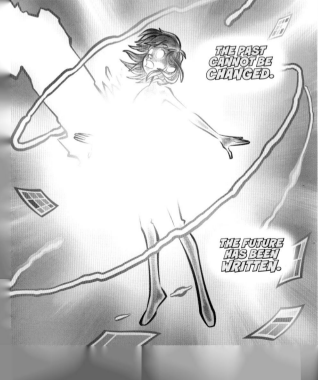

THE PAST CANNOT BE CHANGED.

THE FUTURE HAS BEEN WRITTEN.

HARMONY SUSTAINED.

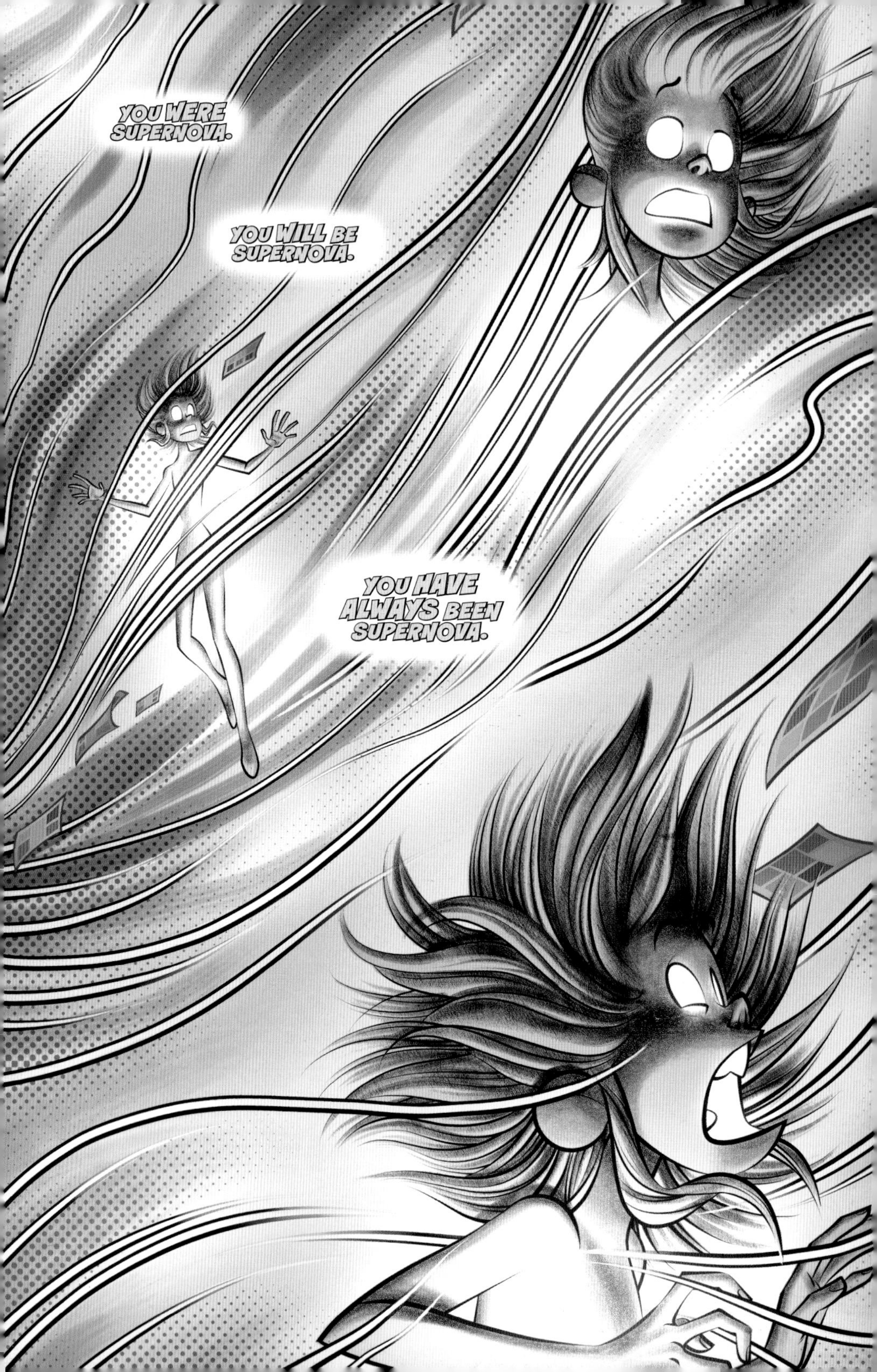
YOU WERE SUPERNOVA.
YOU WILL BE SUPERNOVA.
YOU HAVE ALWAYS BEEN SUPERNOVA.

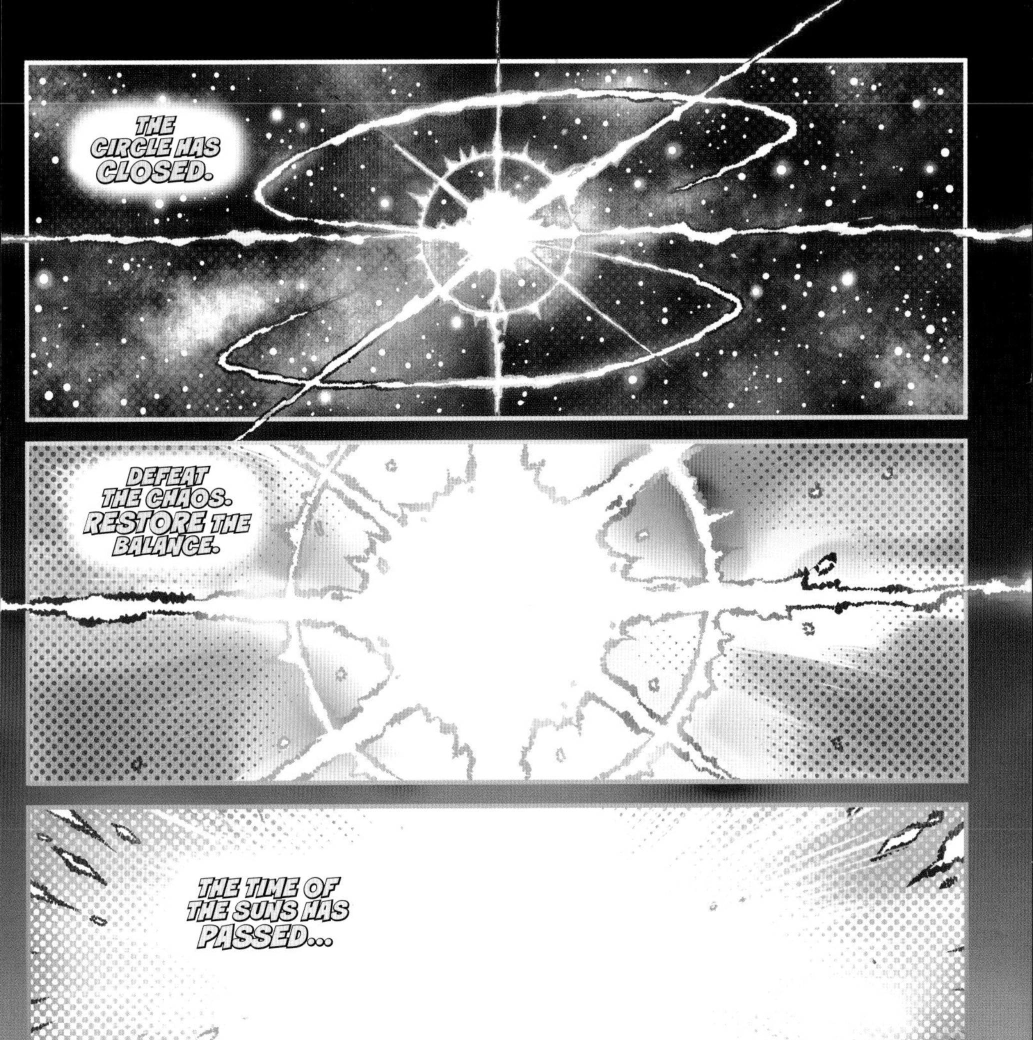
THE CIRCLE HAS CLOSED.
DEFEAT THE CHAOS. RESTORE THE BALANCE.
THE TIME OF THE SUNS HAS PASSED...
...BUT EVIL MUST STILL BE OPPOSED.

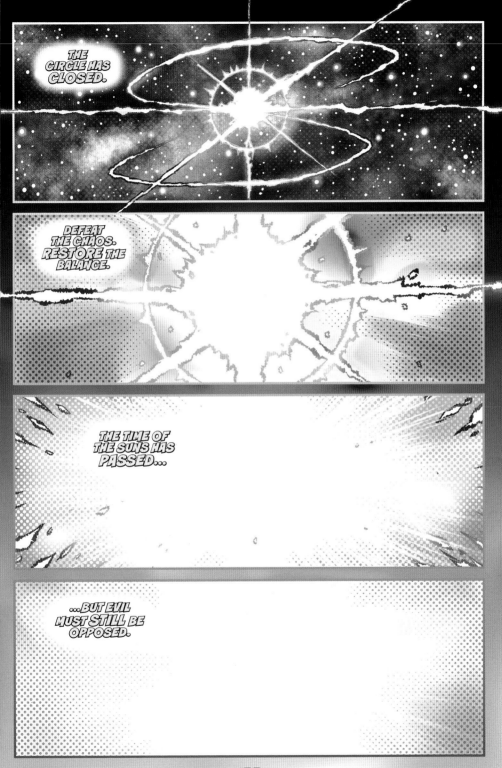

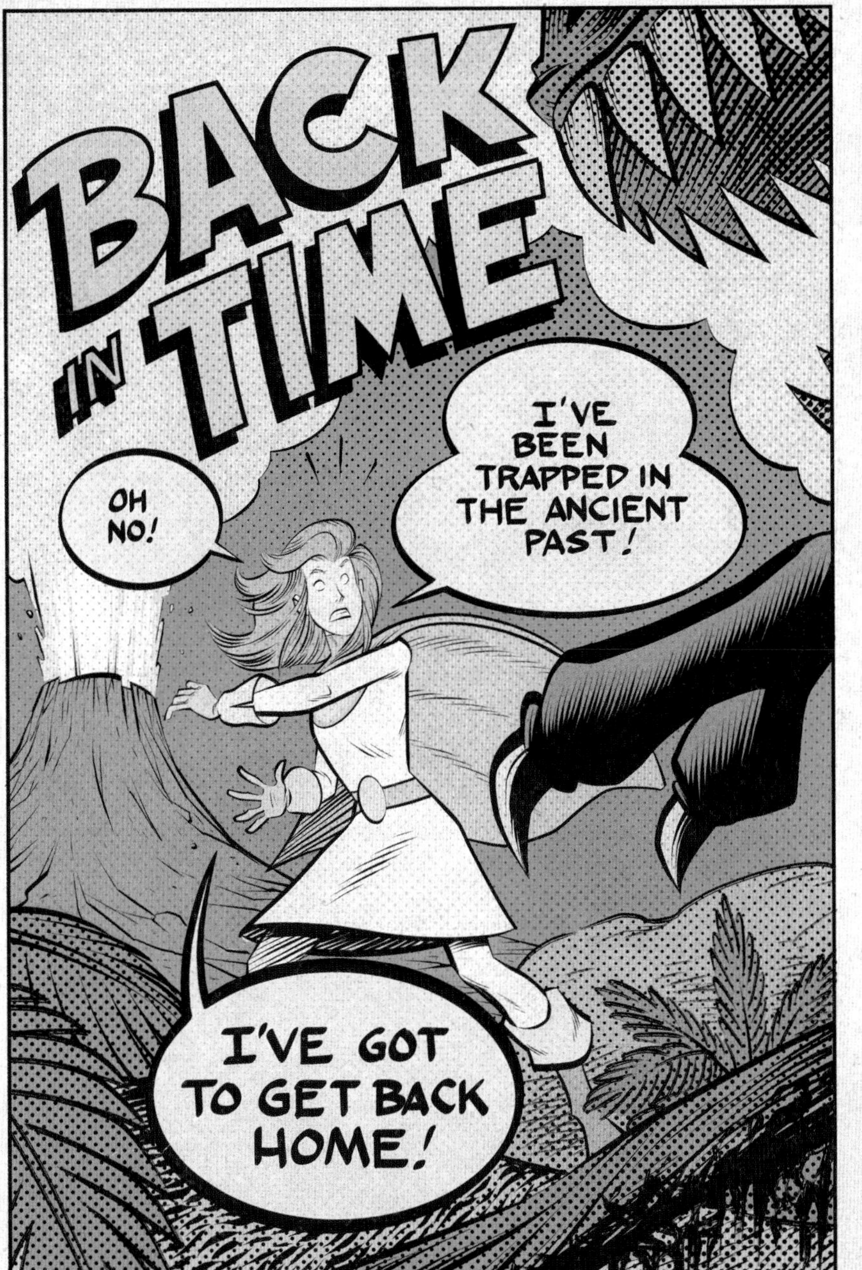
BACK IN TIME
OH NO!
I'VE BEEN TRAPPED IN THE ANCIENT PAST!
I'VE GOT TO GET BACK HOME!

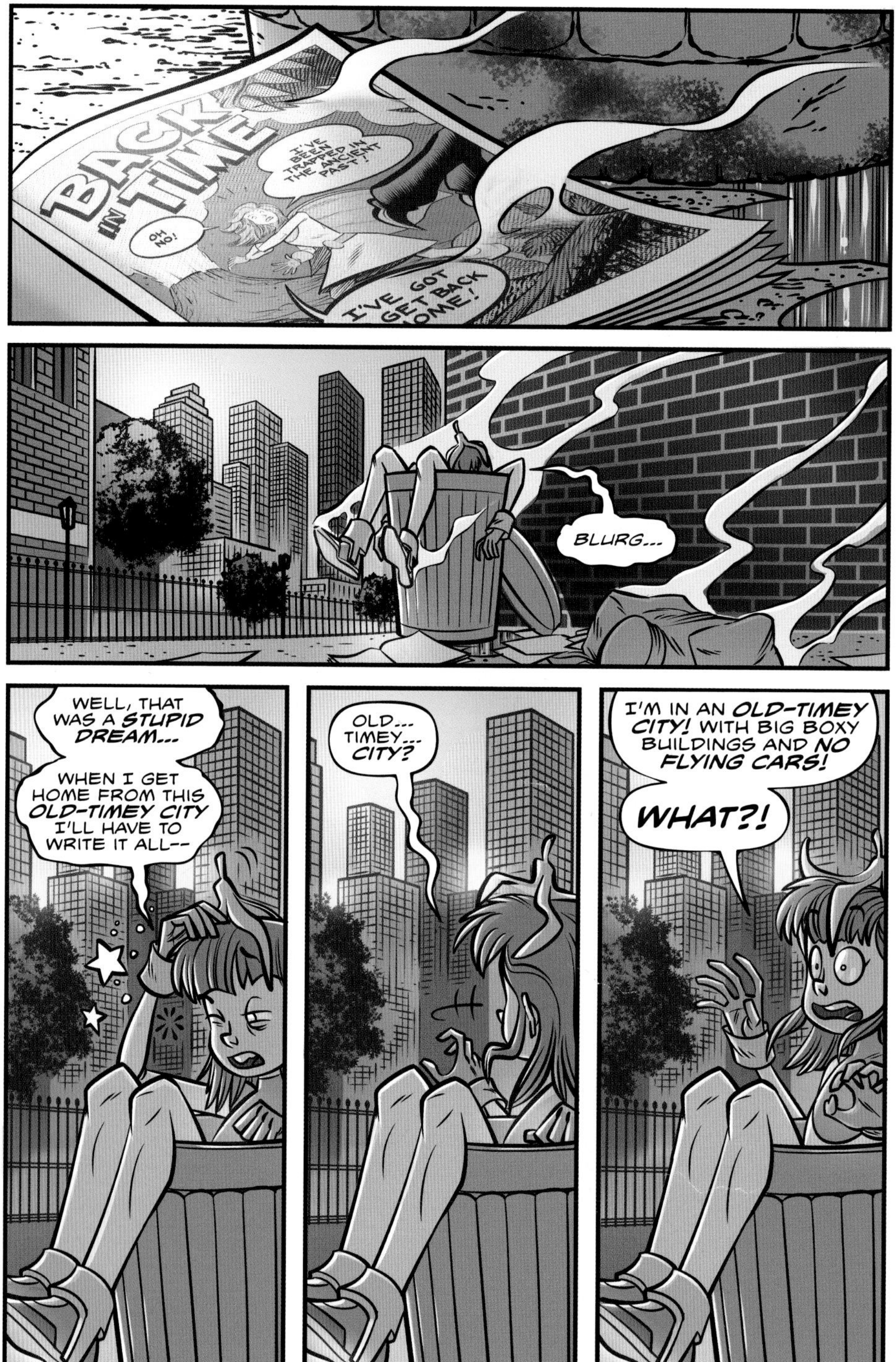
BACK IN TIME
I'VE BEEN TRAPPED IN THE ANCIENT PAST!
OH NO!
I'VE GOT GET BACK HOME!
BLURG...
WELL, THAT WAS A STUPID DREAM...
WHEN I GET HOME FROM THIS OLD-TIMEY CITY I'LL HAVE TO WRITE IT ALL--
OLD... TIMEY... CITY?
I'M IN AN OLD-TIMEY CITY! WITH BIG BOXY BUILDINGS AND NO FLYING CARS!
WHAT?!

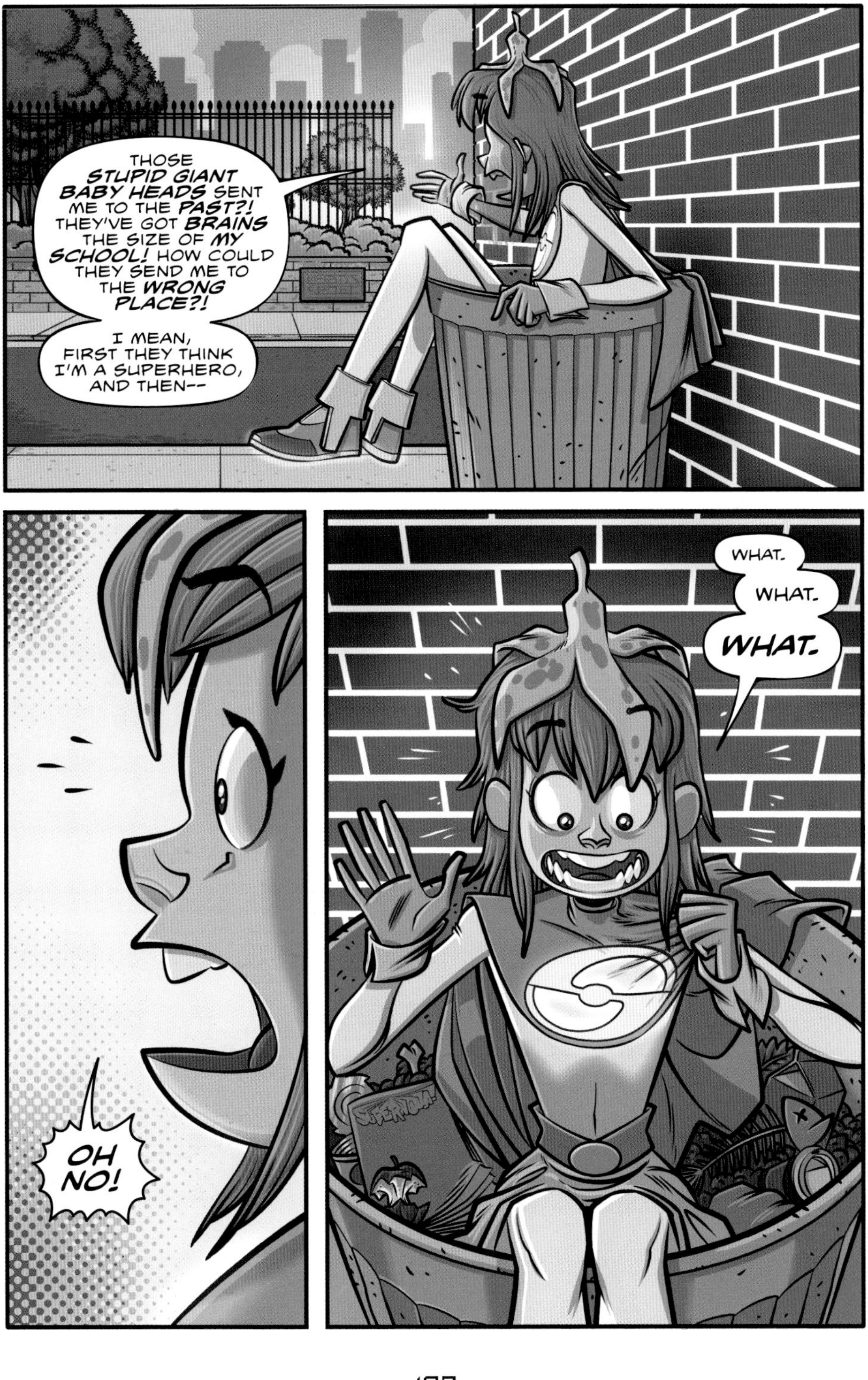
THOSE STUPID GIANT BABY HEADS SENT ME TO THE PAST?! THEY'VE GOT BRAINS THE SIZE OF MY SCHOOL! HOW COULD THEY SEND ME TO THE WRONG PLACE?!
I MEAN, FIRST THEY THINK I'M A SUPERHERO, AND THEN--
OH NO!
WHAT.
WHAT.
WHAT.
SUPERNOVA!

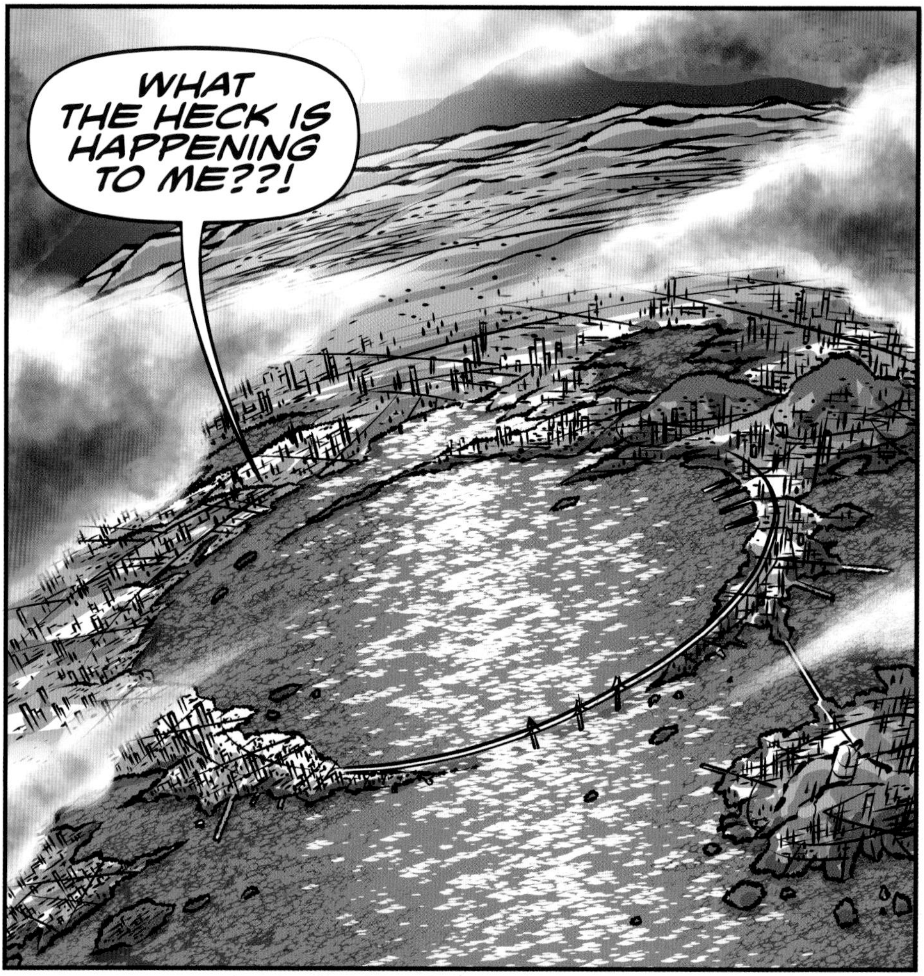
WHAT THE HECK IS HAPPENING TO ME??!

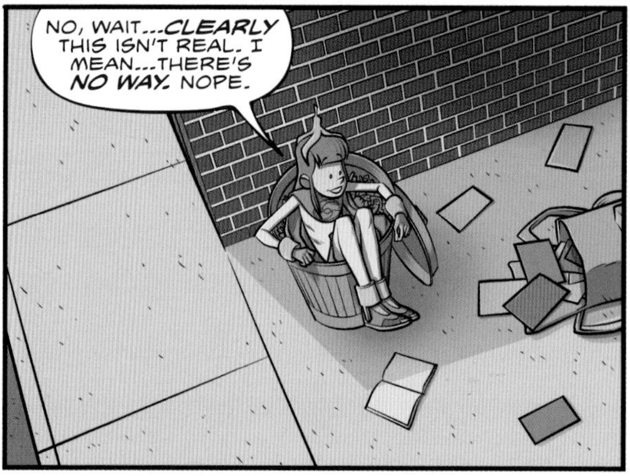
NO, WAIT...CLEARLY THIS ISN'T REAL. I MEAN...THERE'S NO WAY. NOPE.

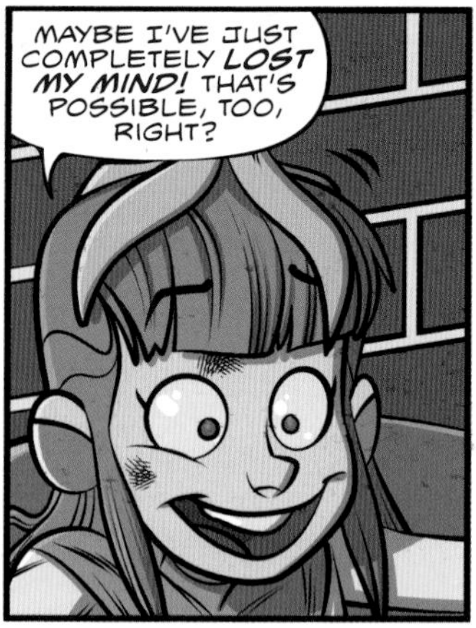
MAYBE I'VE JUST COMPLETELY LOST MY MIND! THAT'S POSSIBLE, TOO, RIGHT?

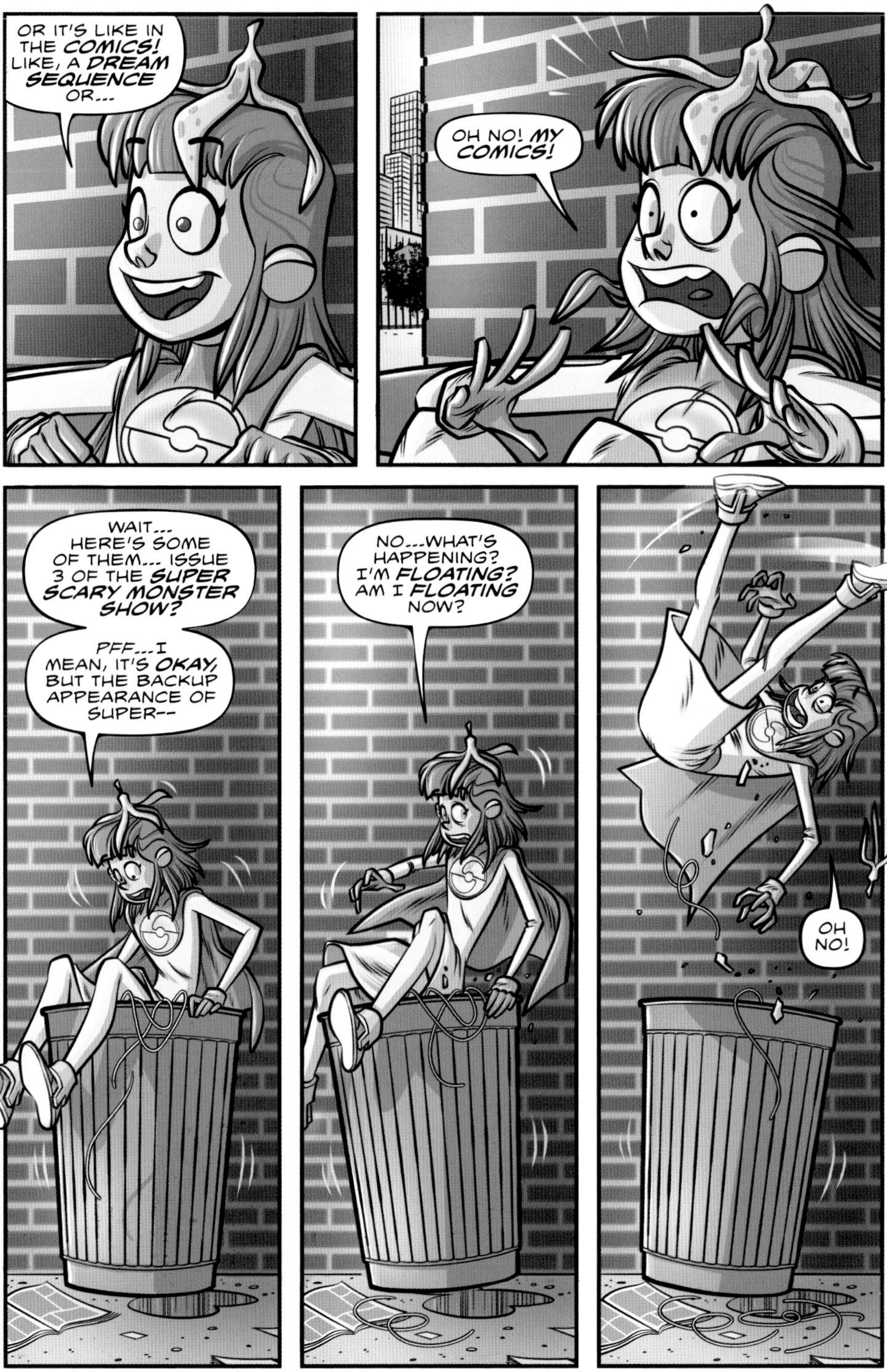
OR IT'S LIKE IN THE COMICS! LIKE, A DREAM SEQUENCE OR...
OH NO! MY COMICS!
WAIT... HERE'S SOME OF THEM... ISSUE 3 OF THE SUPER SCARY MONSTER SHOW?
PFF...I MEAN, IT'S OKAY, BUT THE BACKUP APPEARANCE OF SUPER--
NO...WHAT'S HAPPENING? I'M FLOATING? AM I FLOATING NOW?
OH NO!

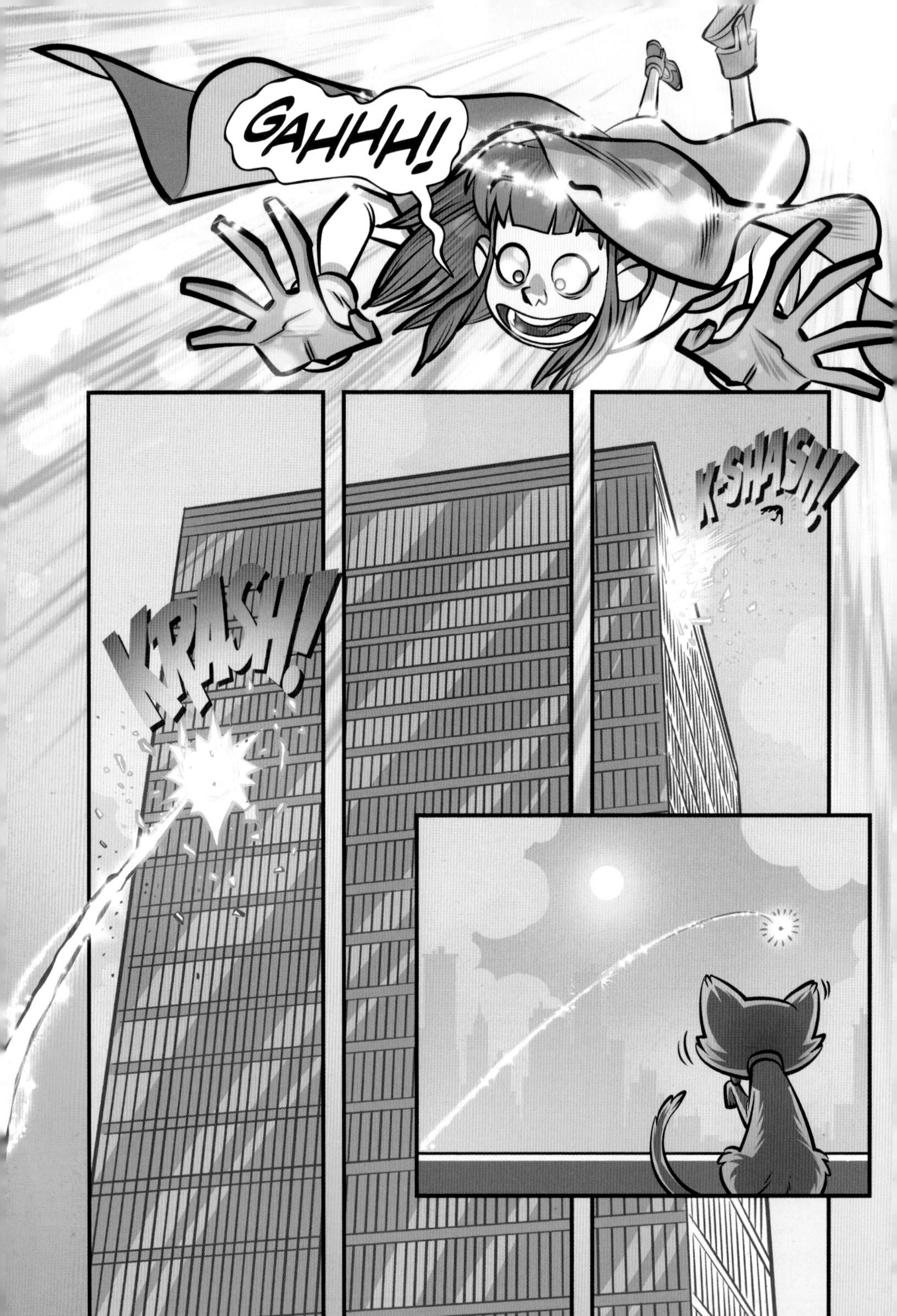
GAHHH!
KRASH!
K-SHASH!

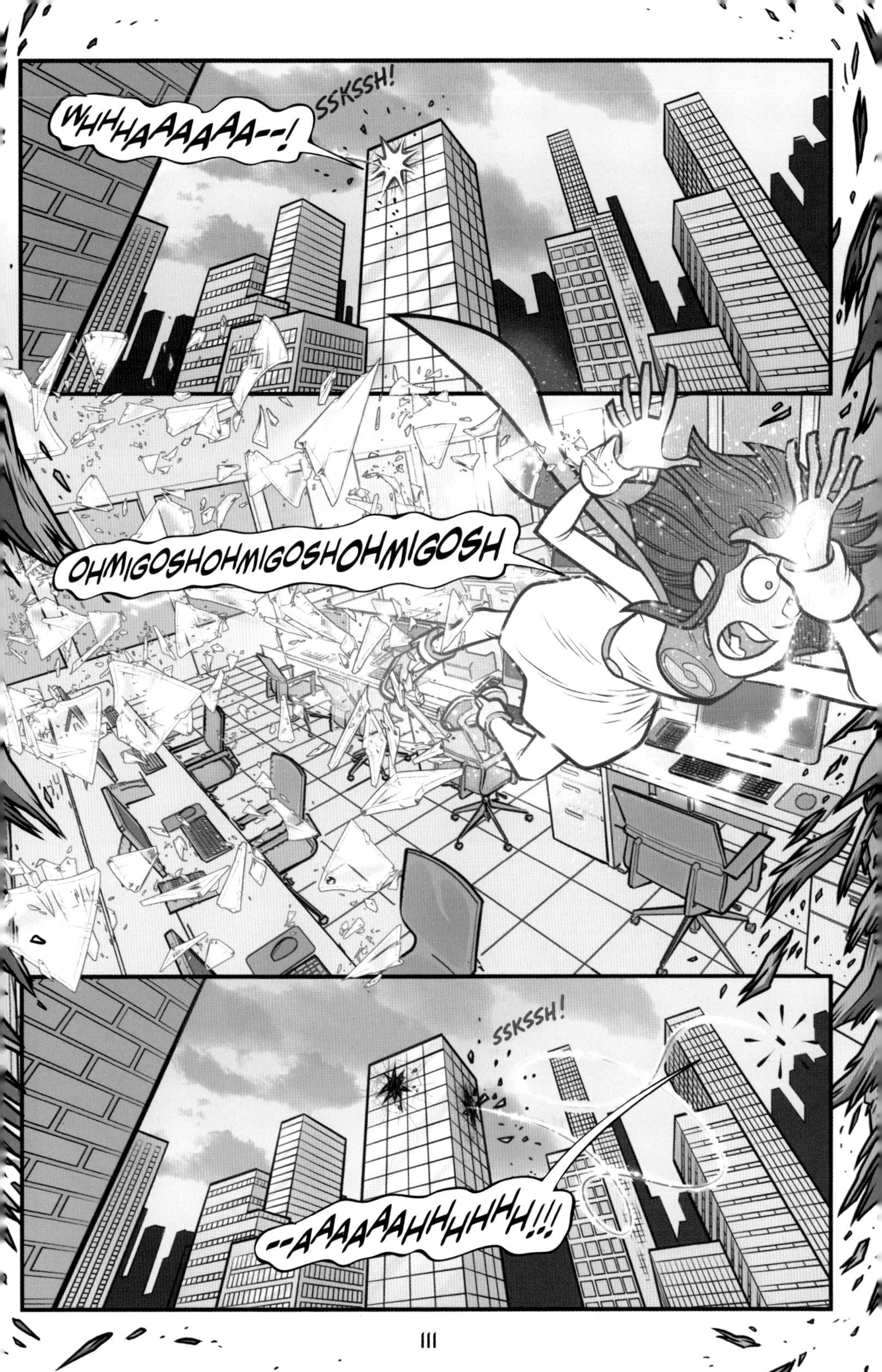
WHHHAAAAAA--!
SSKSSH!
OHMIGOSHOHMIGOSHOHMIGOSH
SSKSSH!
--AAAAAAHHHHHH!!!

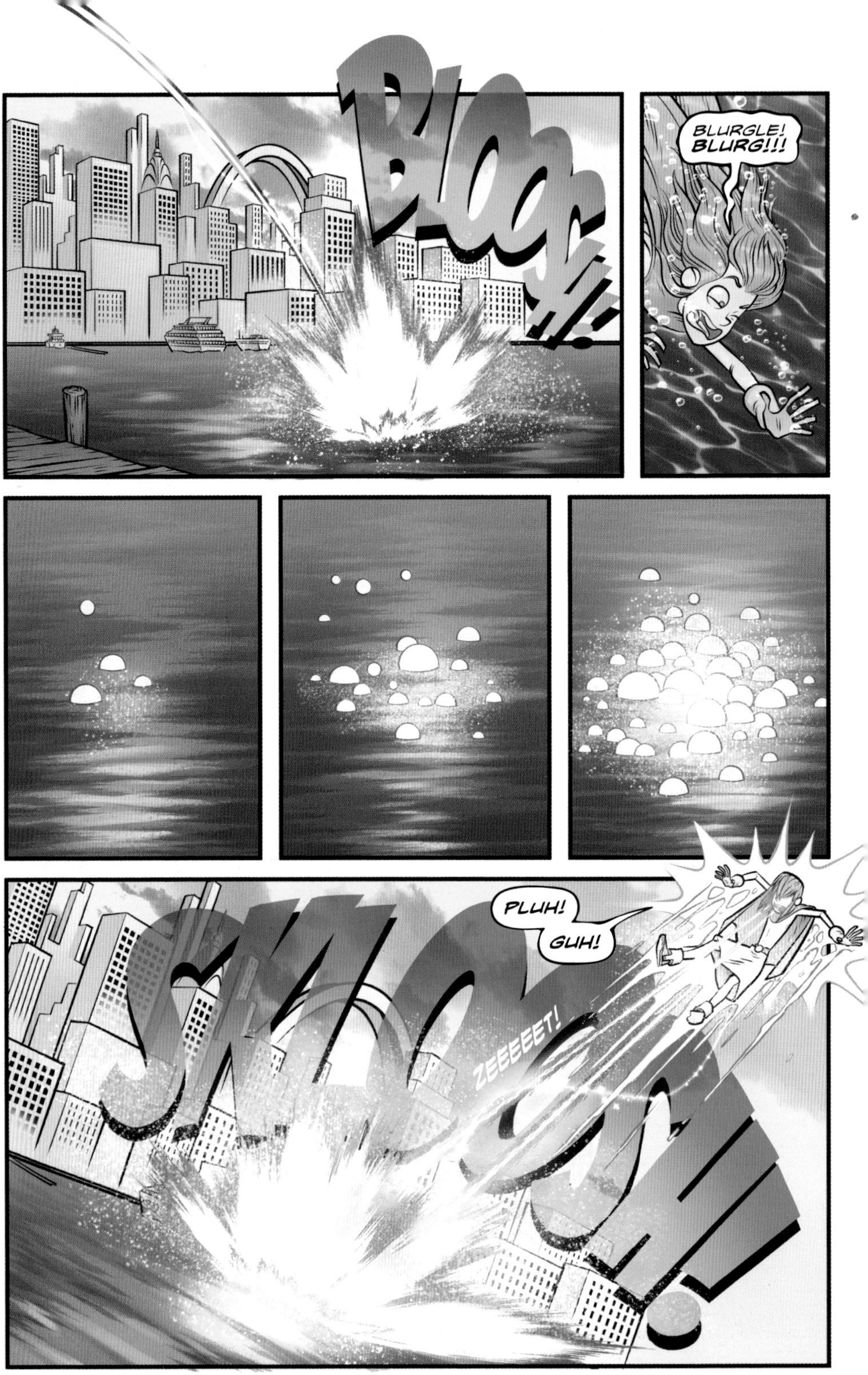
BLOOSH!!
BLURGLE! BLURG!!!
PLUH! GUH!
SPLOOSH!
ZEEEEET!

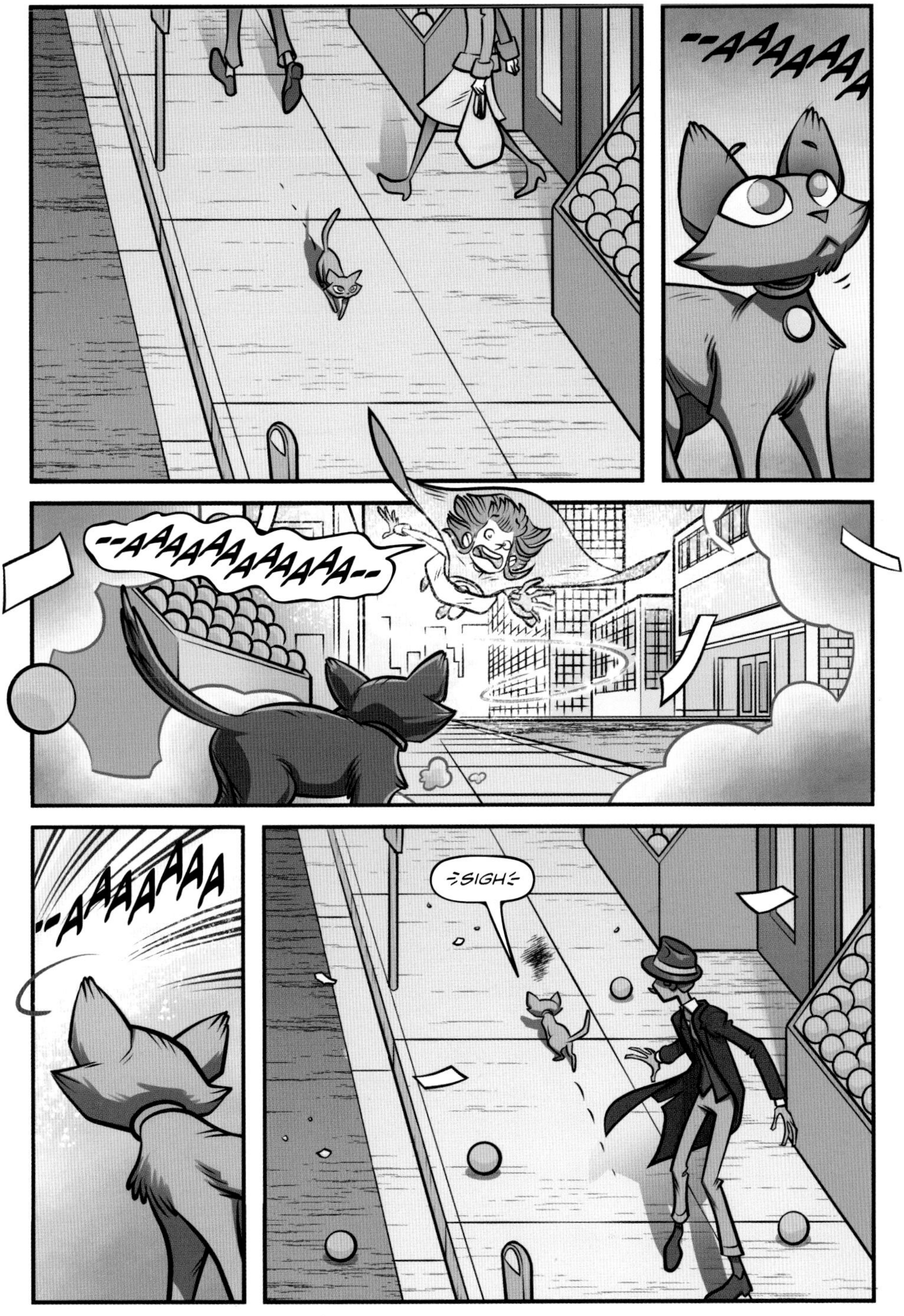
--AAAAAAA
--AAAAAAAAAAAAA--
--AAAAAAA
-SIGH-

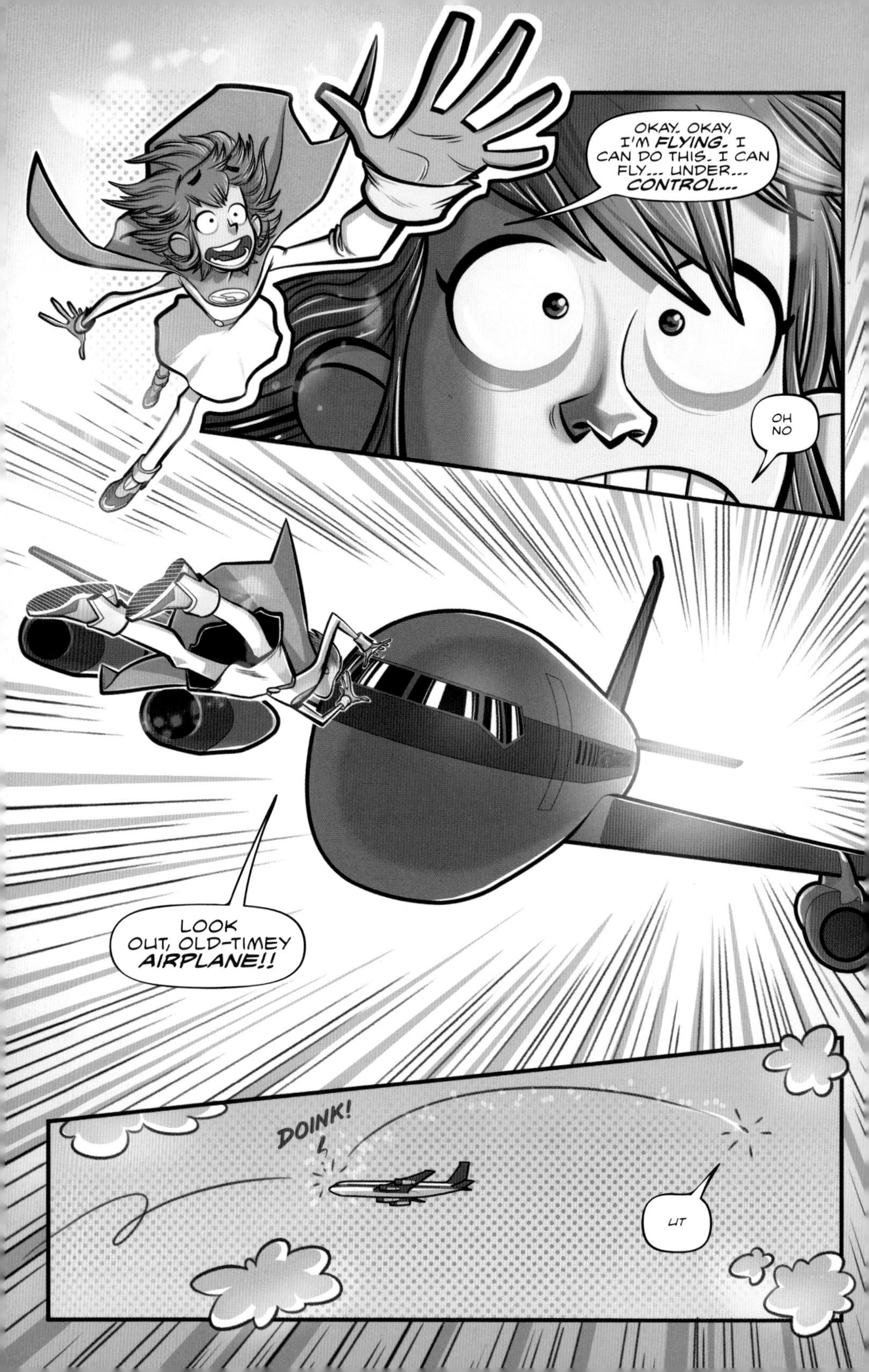
OKAY. OKAY, I'M FLYING. I CAN DO THIS. I CAN FLY... UNDER... CONTROL...
OH NO
LOOK OUT, OLD-TIMEY AIRPLANE!!
DOINK!
UT

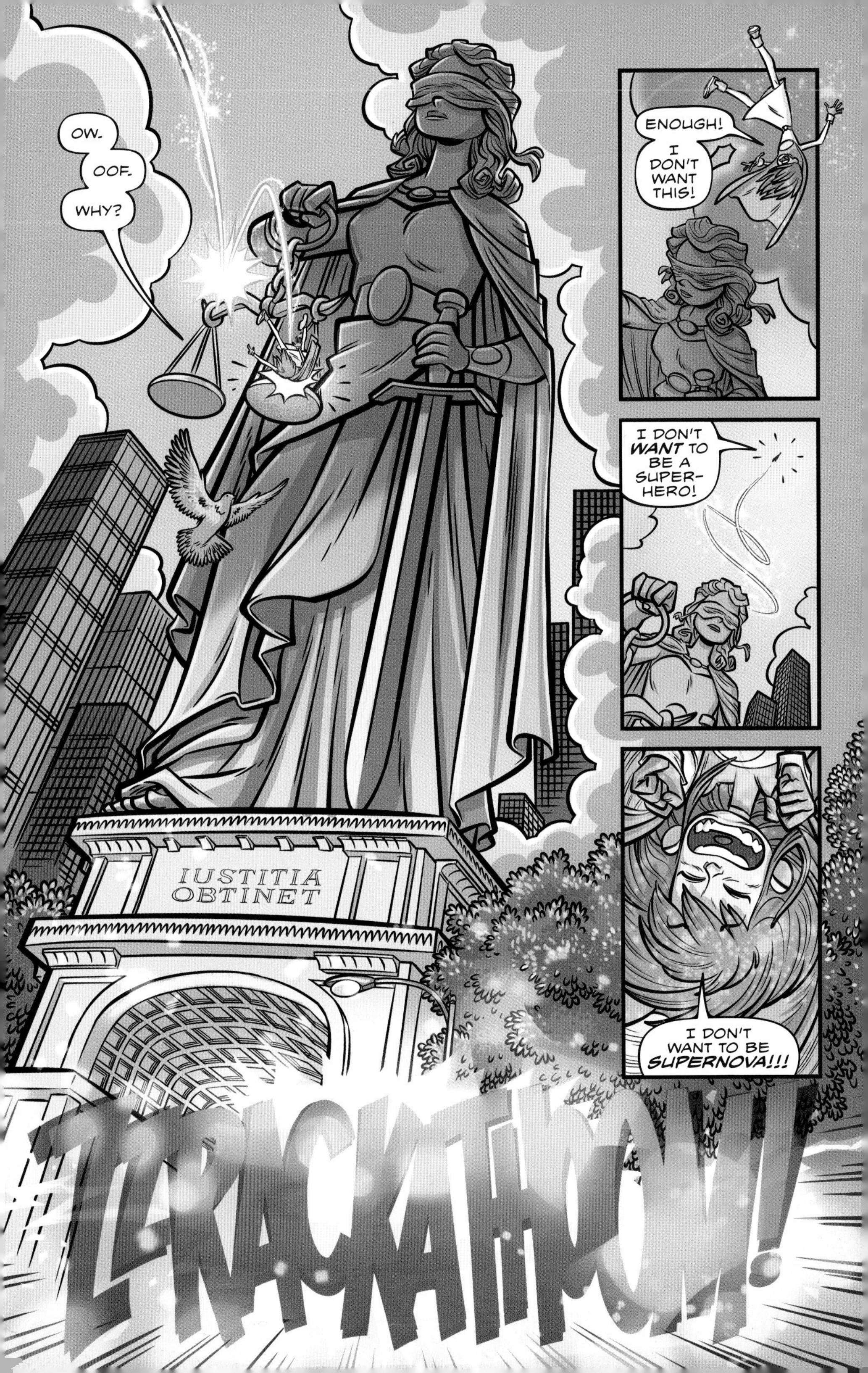
OW-
OOF-
WHY?
IUSTITIA OBTINET
ENOUGH!
I DON'T WANT THIS!
I DON'T WANT TO BE A SUPER-HERO!
I DON'T WANT TO BE SUPERNOVA!!!
ZRACKATHOOM!

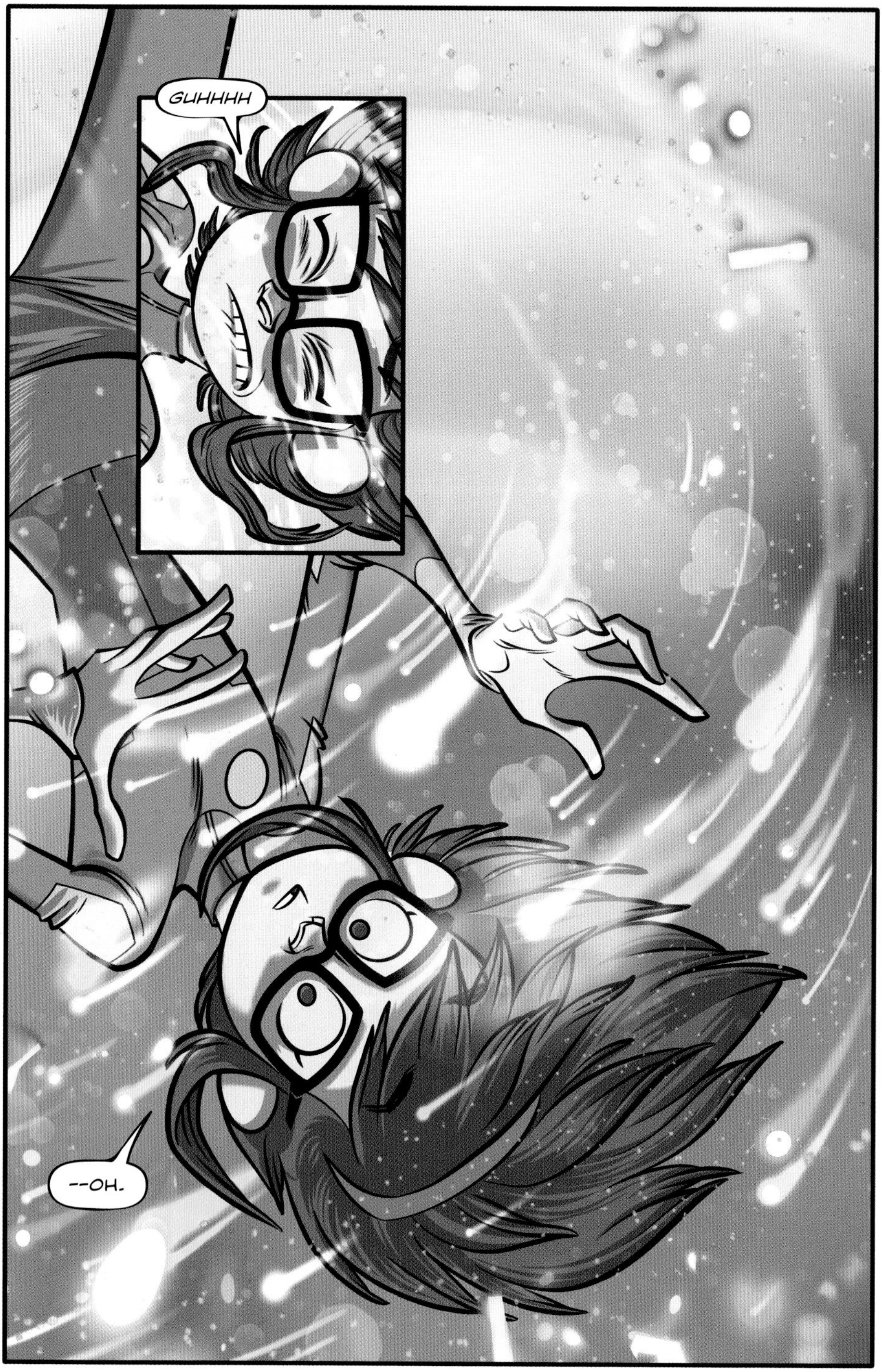
GUHHHH
--OH.

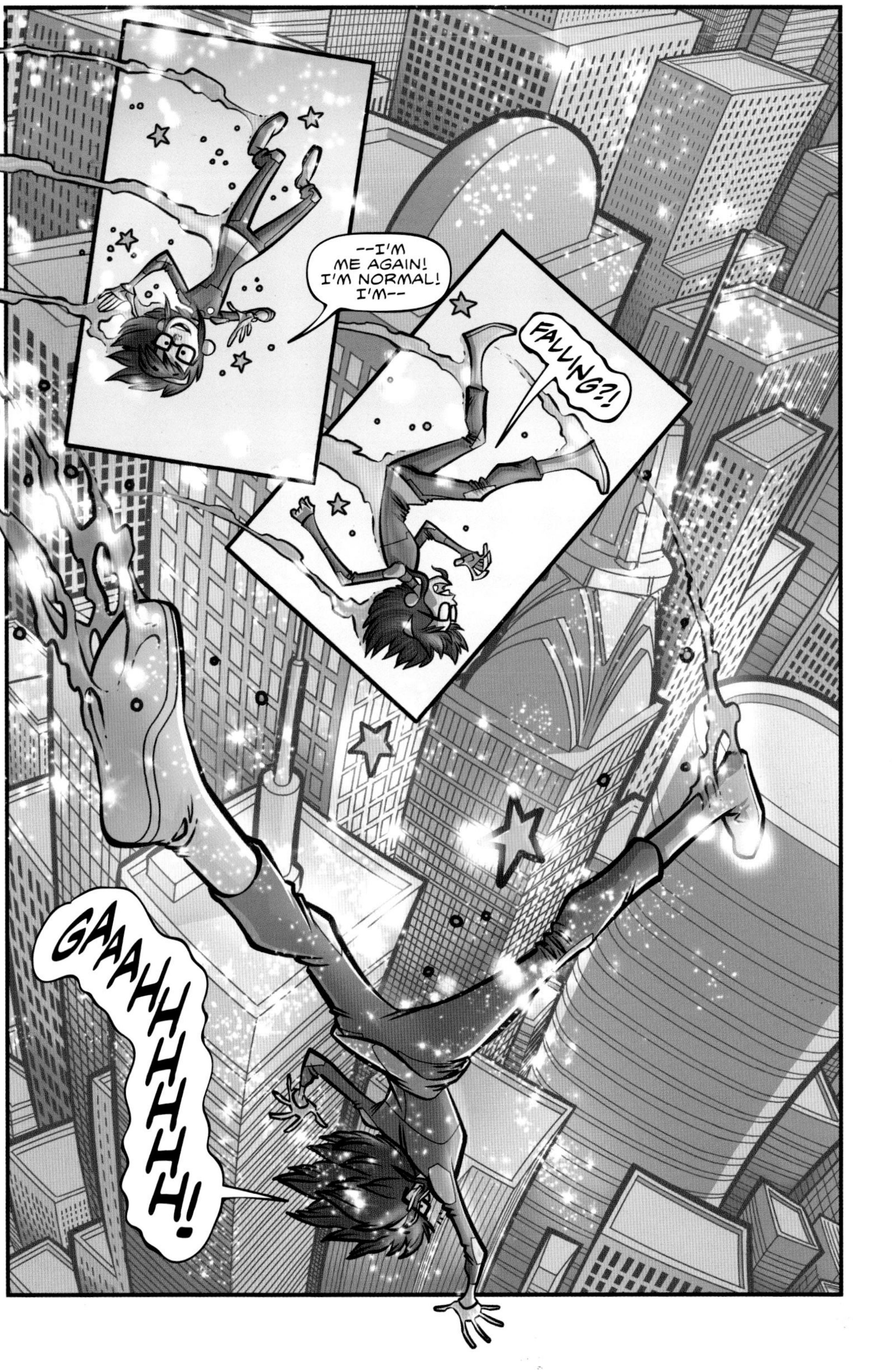
--I'M ME AGAIN! I'M NORMAL! I'M--
FALLING?!
GAAAHHHHHH!

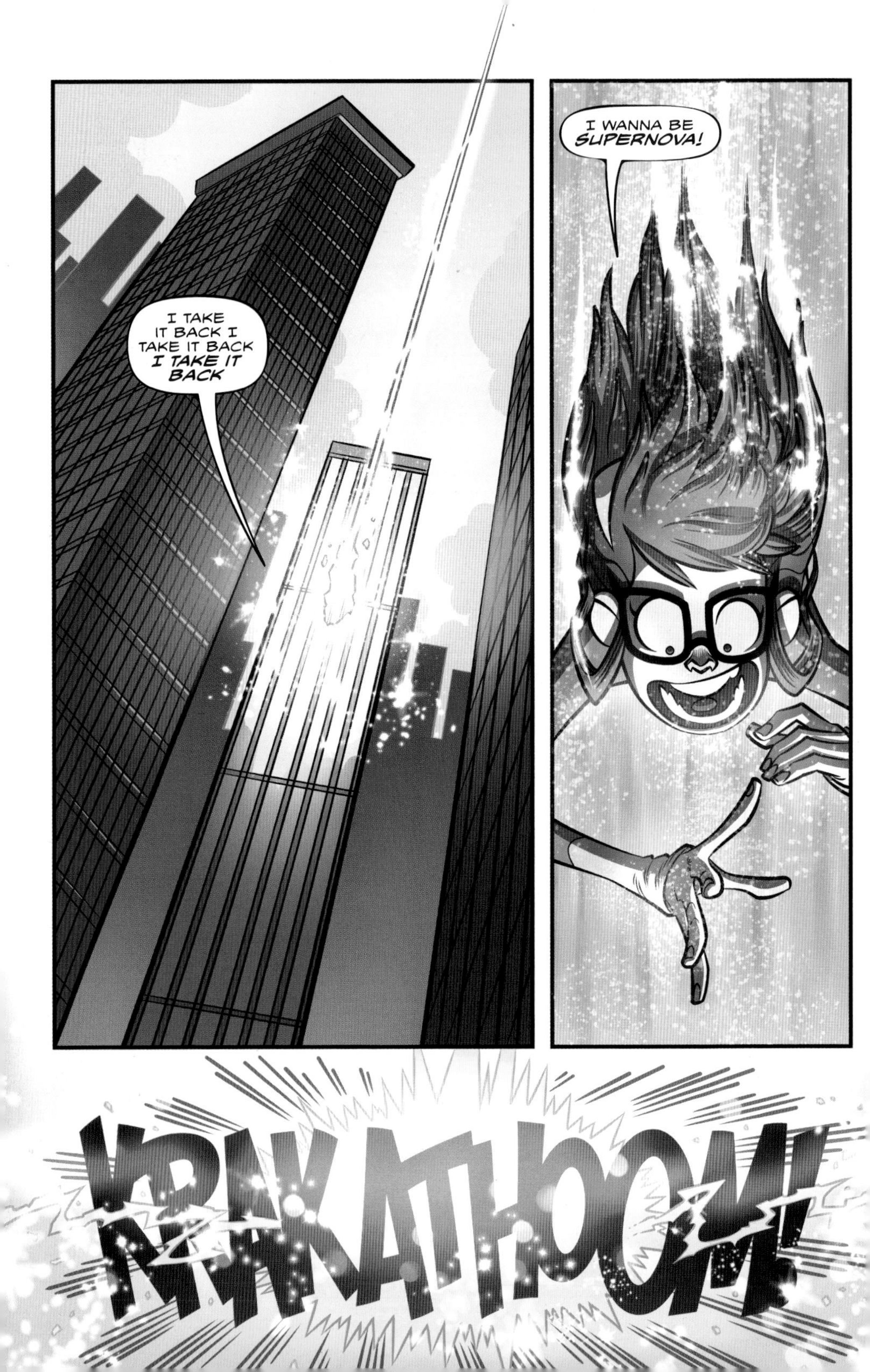
I TAKE IT BACK I TAKE IT BACK *I TAKE IT BACK*
I WANNA BE *SUPERNOVA!*
KRAKATHOOM!

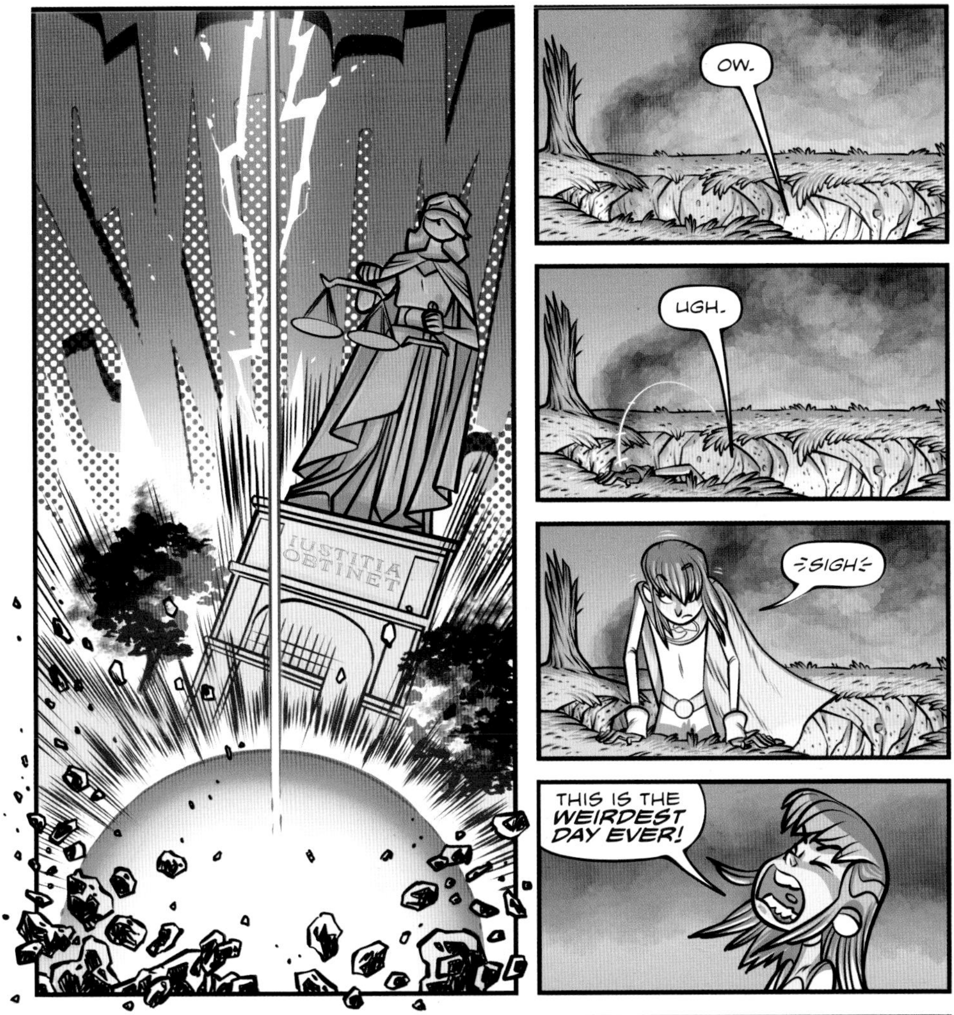
IUSTITIA OBTINET
OW.
UGH.
SIGH
THIS IS THE WEIRDEST DAY EVER!
I'M AFRAID, DEAR SUPERNOVA, THAT IT IS ABOUT TO GET FAR STRANGER.

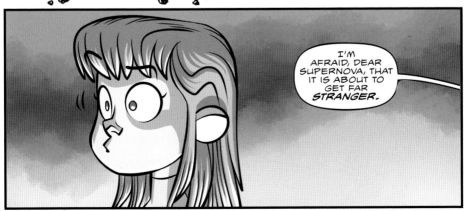

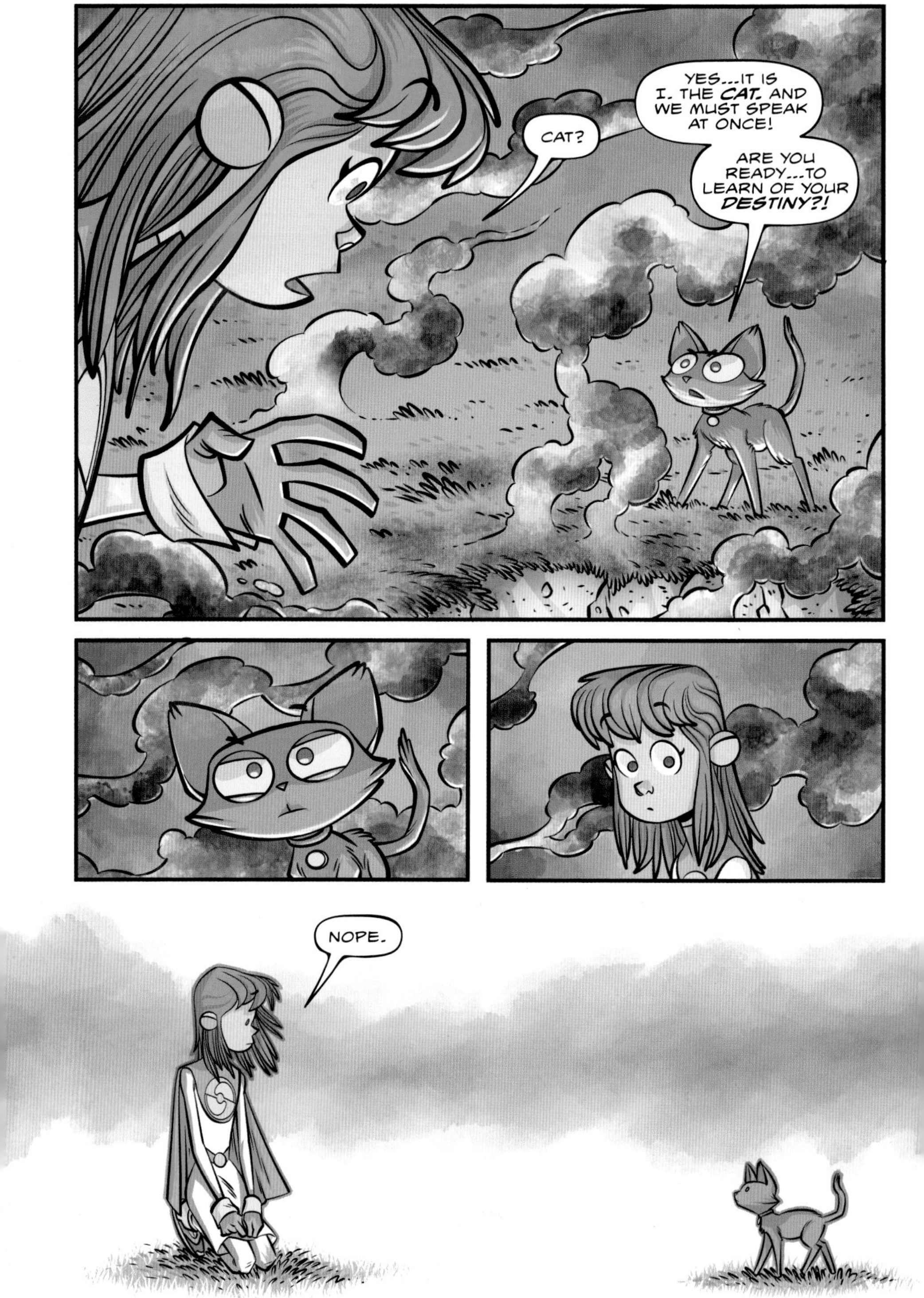
CAT?
YES...IT IS I. THE CAT. AND WE MUST SPEAK AT ONCE!
ARE YOU READY...TO LEARN OF YOUR DESTINY?!
NOPE.

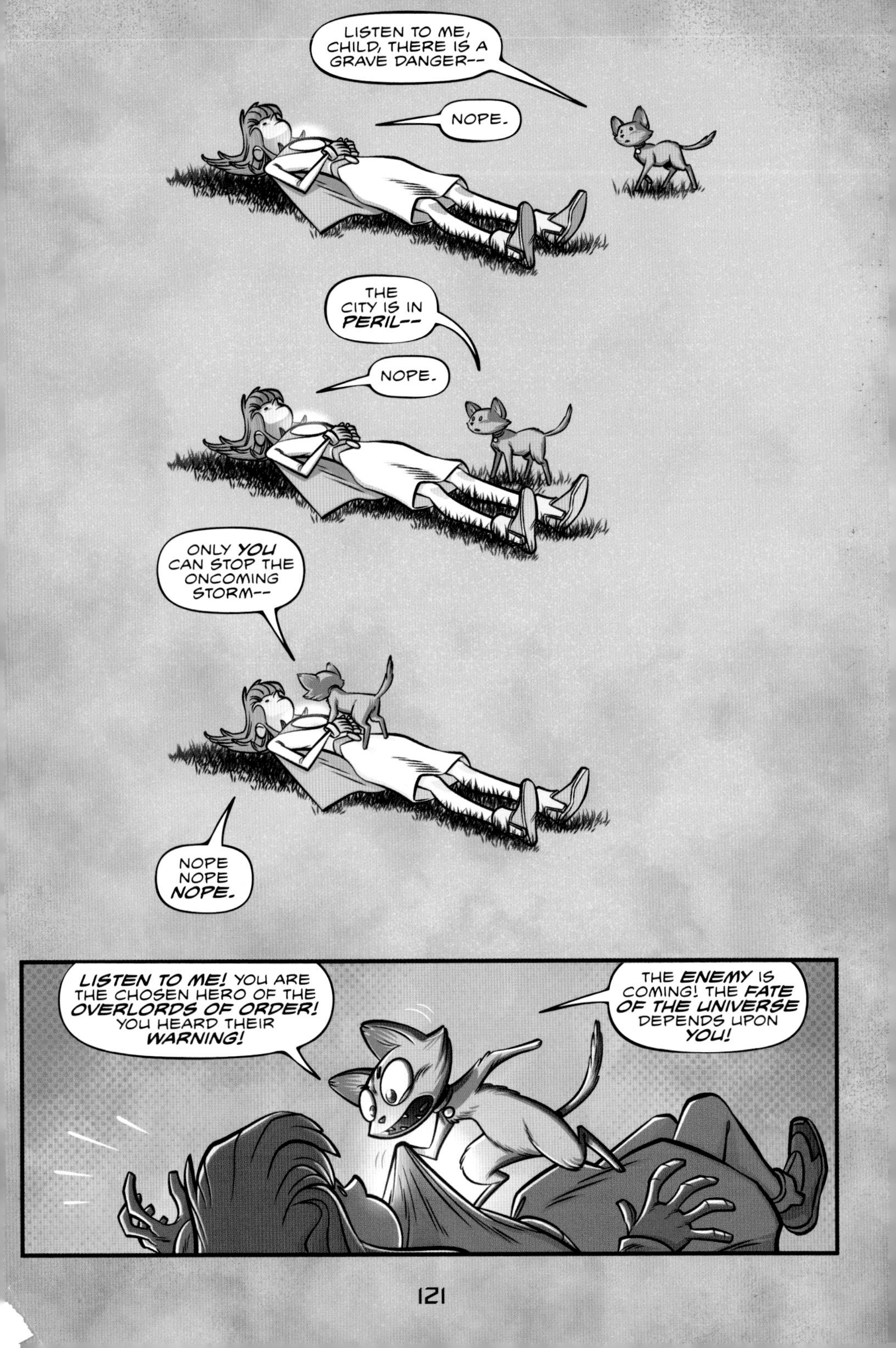
LISTEN TO ME, CHILD, THERE IS A GRAVE DANGER--
NOPE.
THE CITY IS IN PERIL--
NOPE.
ONLY YOU CAN STOP THE ONCOMING STORM--
NOPE NOPE NOPE.
LISTEN TO ME! YOU ARE THE CHOSEN HERO OF THE OVERLORDS OF ORDER! YOU HEARD THEIR WARNING!
THE ENEMY IS COMING! THE FATE OF THE UNIVERSE DEPENDS UPON YOU!

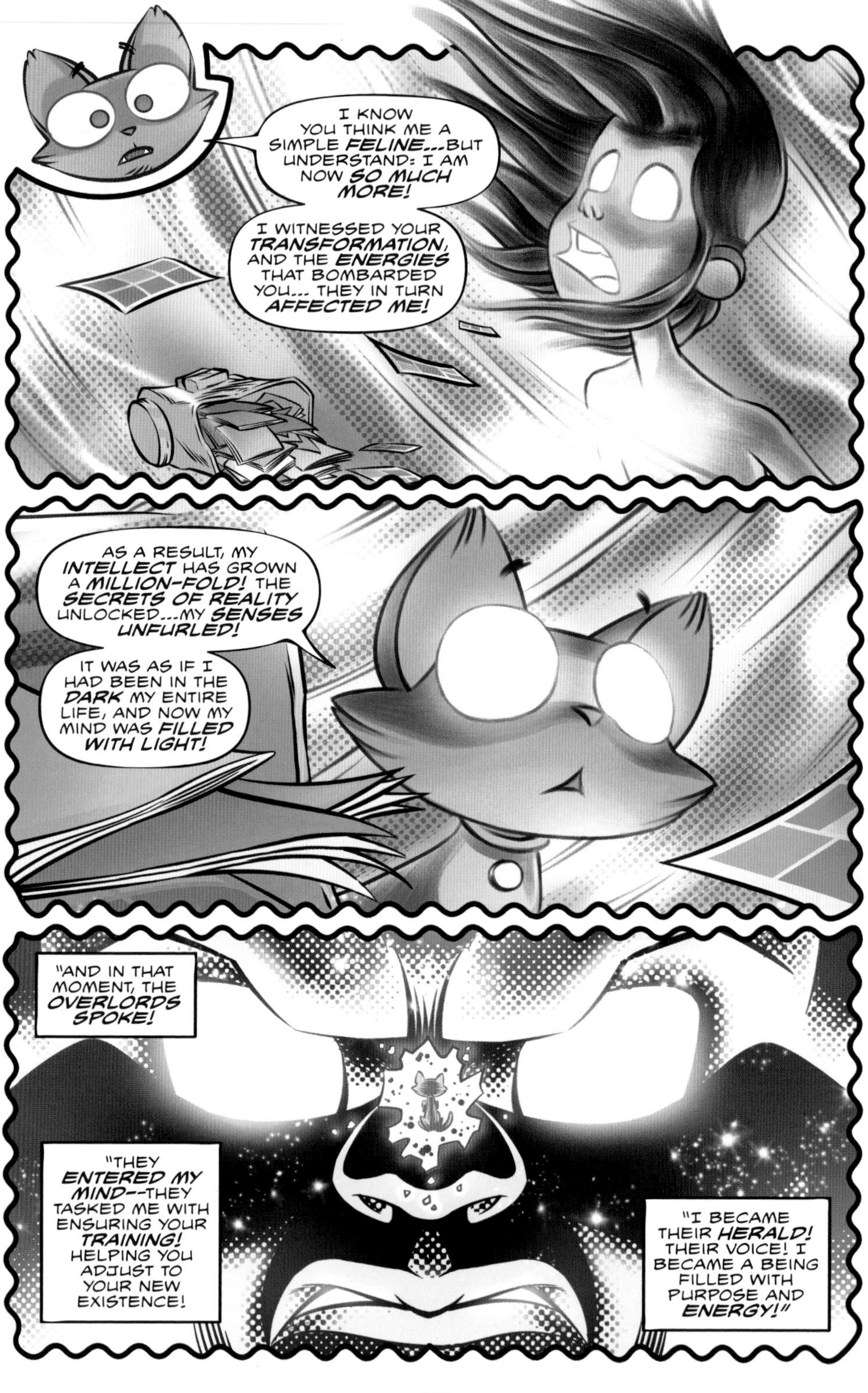
I KNOW YOU THINK ME A SIMPLE FELINE...BUT UNDERSTAND: I AM NOW SO MUCH MORE!
I WITNESSED YOUR TRANSFORMATION, AND THE ENERGIES THAT BOMBARDED YOU... THEY IN TURN AFFECTED ME!
AS A RESULT, MY INTELLECT HAS GROWN A MILLION-FOLD! THE SECRETS OF REALITY UNLOCKED...MY SENSES UNFURLED!
IT WAS AS IF I HAD BEEN IN THE DARK MY ENTIRE LIFE, AND NOW MY MIND WAS FILLED WITH LIGHT!
"AND IN THAT MOMENT, THE OVERLORDS SPOKE!
"THEY ENTERED MY MIND--THEY TASKED ME WITH ENSURING YOUR TRAINING! HELPING YOU ADJUST TO YOUR NEW EXISTENCE!
"I BECAME THEIR HERALD! THEIR VOICE! I BECAME A BEING FILLED WITH PURPOSE AND ENERGY!"

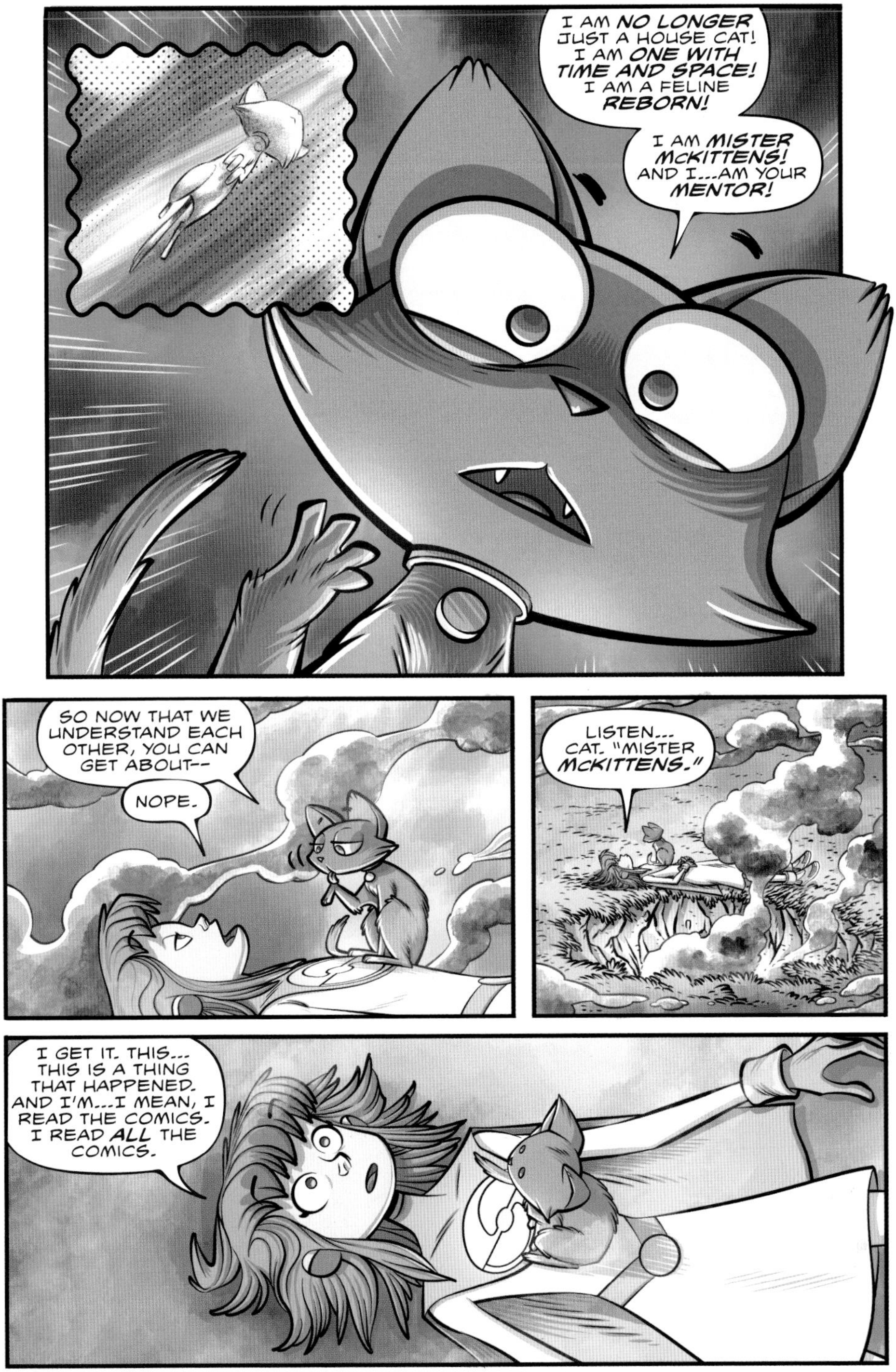
I AM NO LONGER JUST A HOUSE CAT! I AM ONE WITH TIME AND SPACE! I AM A FELINE REBORN!
I AM MISTER McKITTENS! AND I...AM YOUR MENTOR!
SO NOW THAT WE UNDERSTAND EACH OTHER, YOU CAN GET ABOUT--
NOPE.
LISTEN... CAT. "MISTER McKITTENS."
I GET IT. THIS... THIS IS A THING THAT HAPPENED. AND I'M...I MEAN, I READ THE COMICS. I READ ALL THE COMICS.

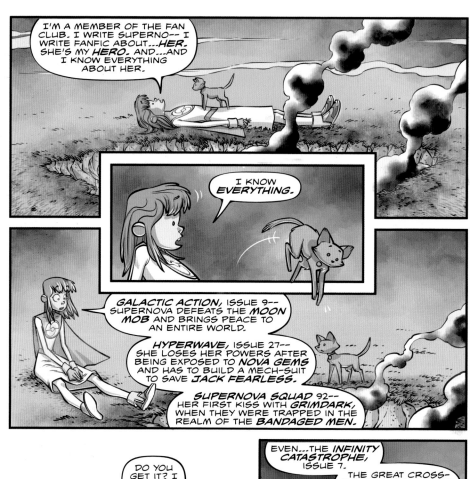

I'M A MEMBER OF THE FAN CLUB. I WRITE SUPERNO-- I WRITE FANFIC ABOUT...*HER*. SHE'S MY *HERO*. AND...AND I KNOW EVERYTHING ABOUT HER.

I KNOW *EVERYTHING*.

GALACTIC ACTION, ISSUE 9-- SUPERNOVA DEFEATS THE *MOON MOB* AND BRINGS PEACE TO AN ENTIRE WORLD.

HYPERWAVE, ISSUE 27-- SHE LOSES HER POWERS AFTER BEING EXPOSED TO *NOVA GEMS* AND HAS TO BUILD A MECH-SUIT TO SAVE *JACK FEARLESS*.

SUPERNOVA SQUAD 92-- HER FIRST KISS WITH *GRIMDARK*, WHEN THEY WERE TRAPPED IN THE REALM OF THE *BANDAGED MEN*.

DO YOU GET IT? I KNOW IT *ALL*.

EVEN...THE *INFINITY CATASTROPHE*, ISSUE 7.

THE GREAT CROSS-OVER BATTLE AGAINST *MEGA-CHRONOS, EATER OF TIME*.

HER *LAST STORY* EVER.

I KNOW HOW HER *STORY ENDS*.

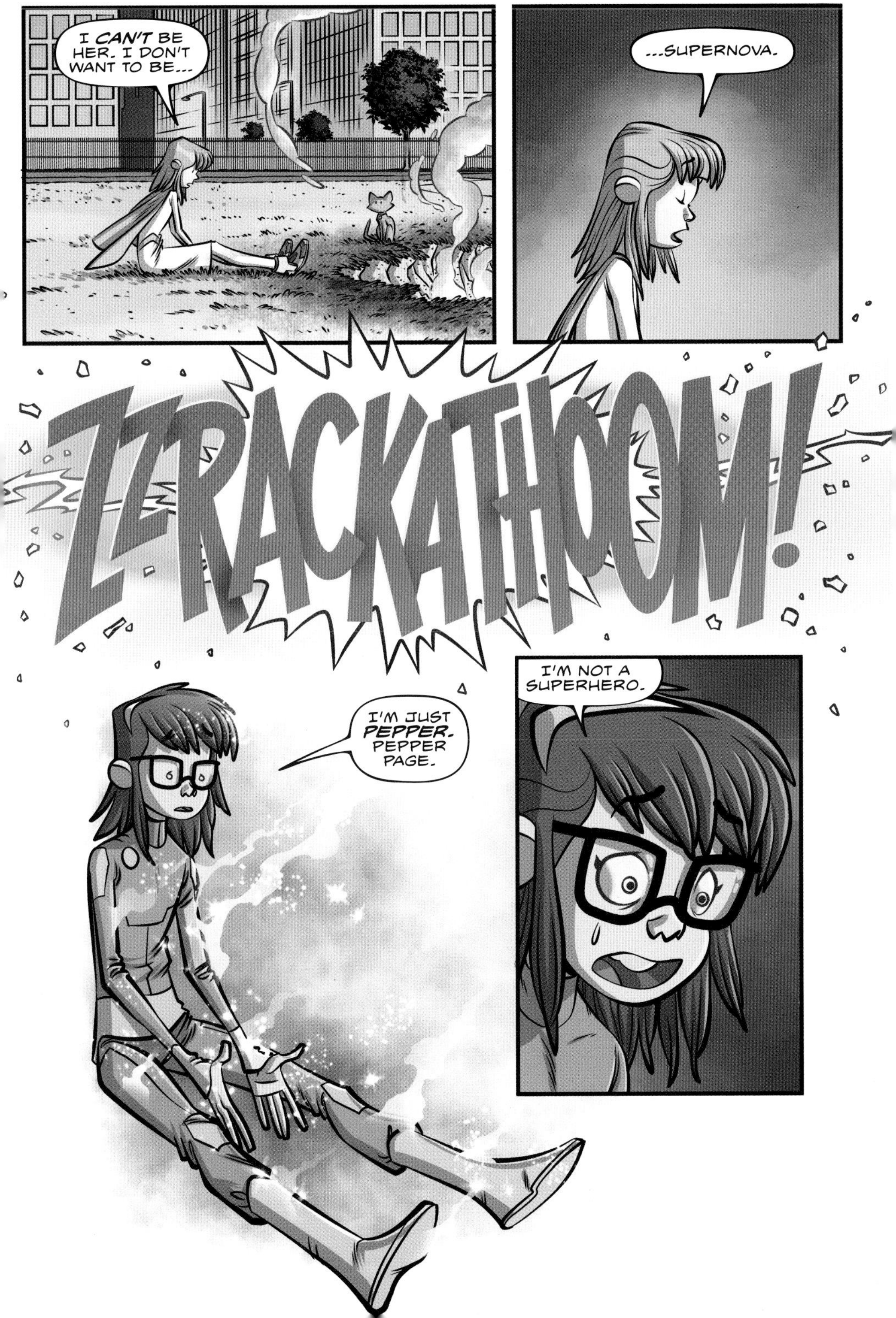
I CAN'T BE HER. I DON'T WANT TO BE...
...SUPERNOVA.
ZZRACKATHOOM!
I'M JUST PEPPER. PEPPER PAGE.
I'M NOT A SUPERHERO.

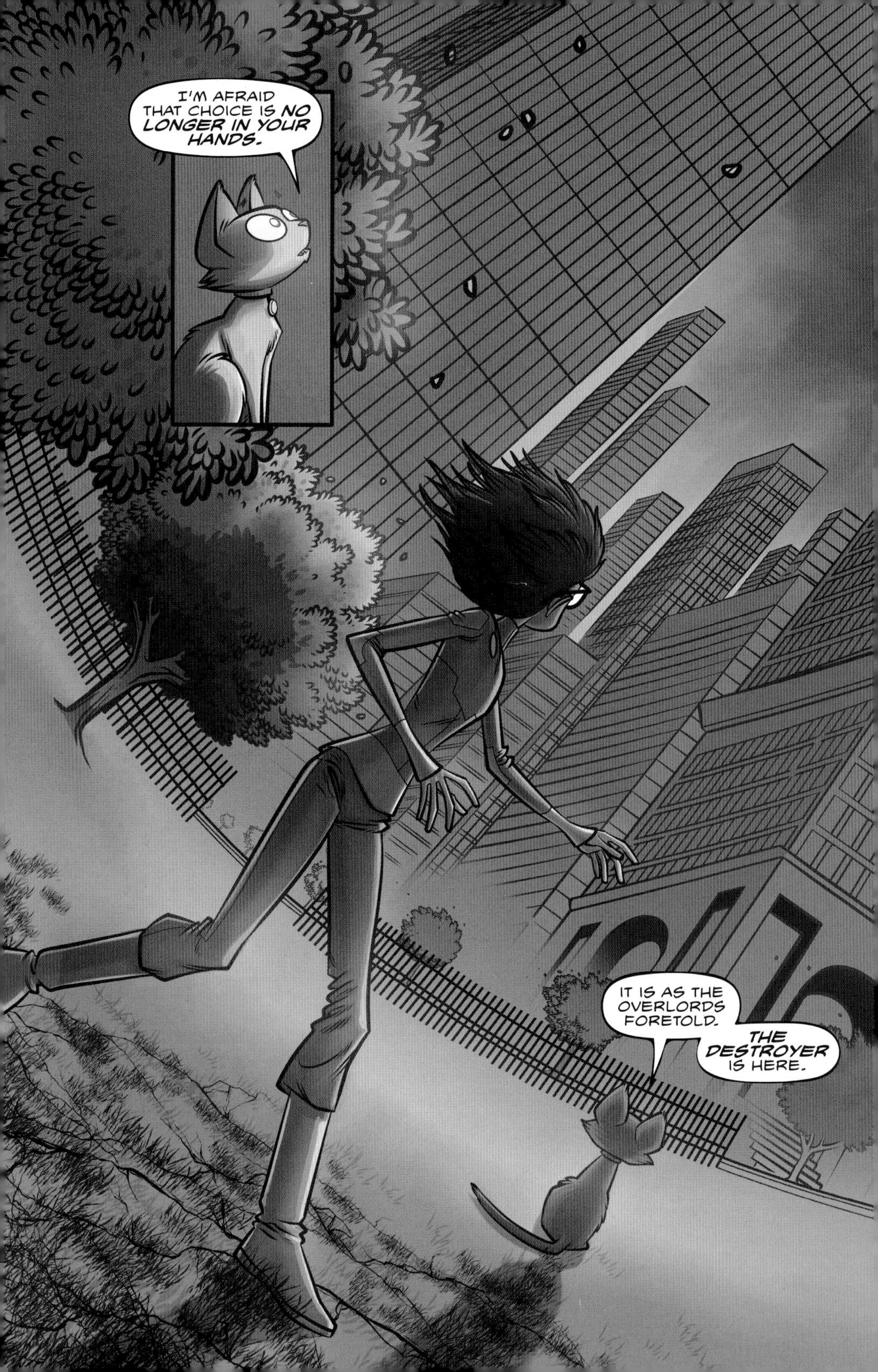
I'M AFRAID THAT CHOICE IS NO LONGER IN YOUR HANDS.
IT IS AS THE OVERLORDS FORETOLD. THE DESTROYER IS HERE.

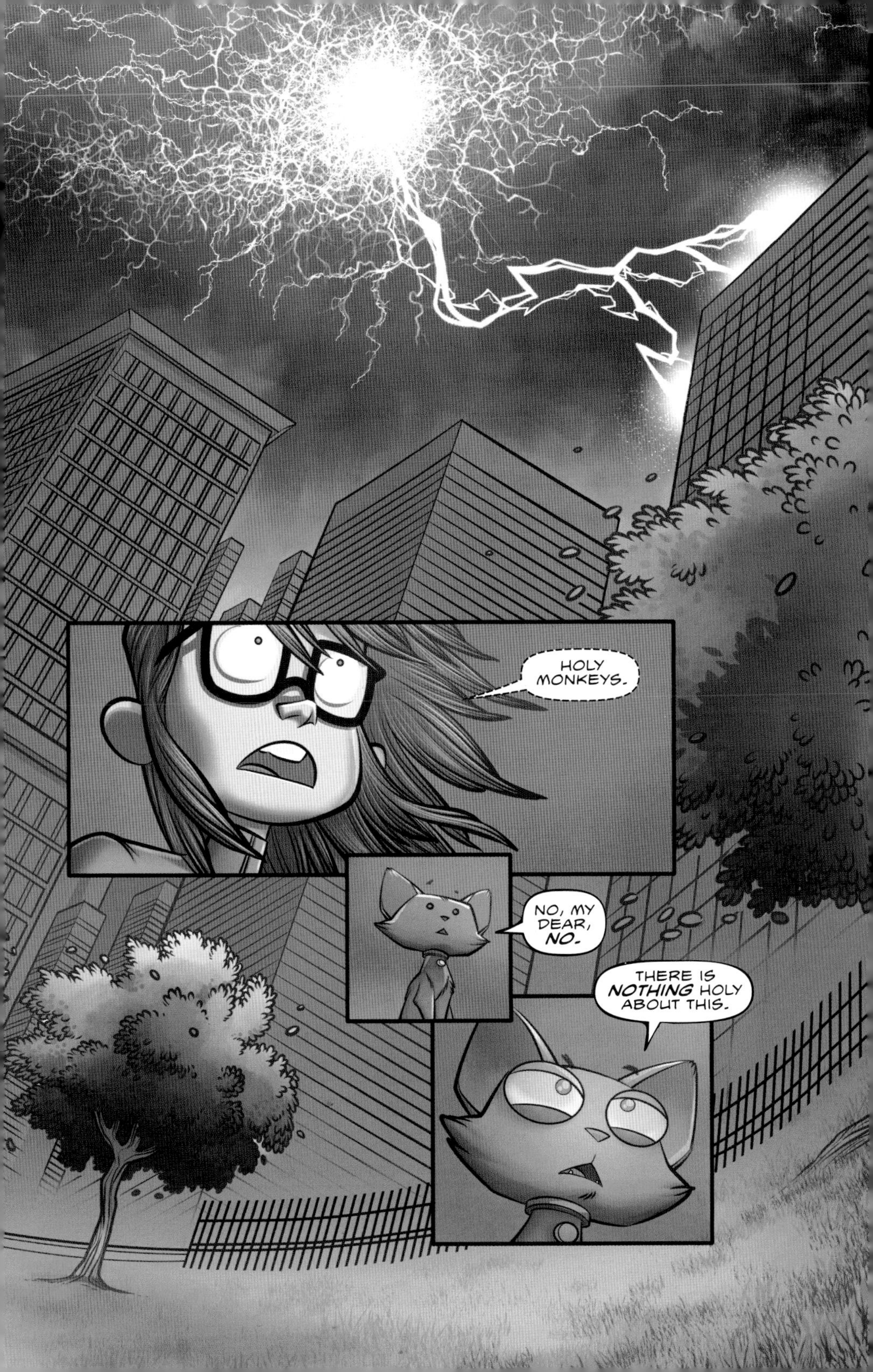
HOLY MONKEYS.
NO, MY DEAR, NO.
THERE IS NOTHING HOLY ABOUT THIS.

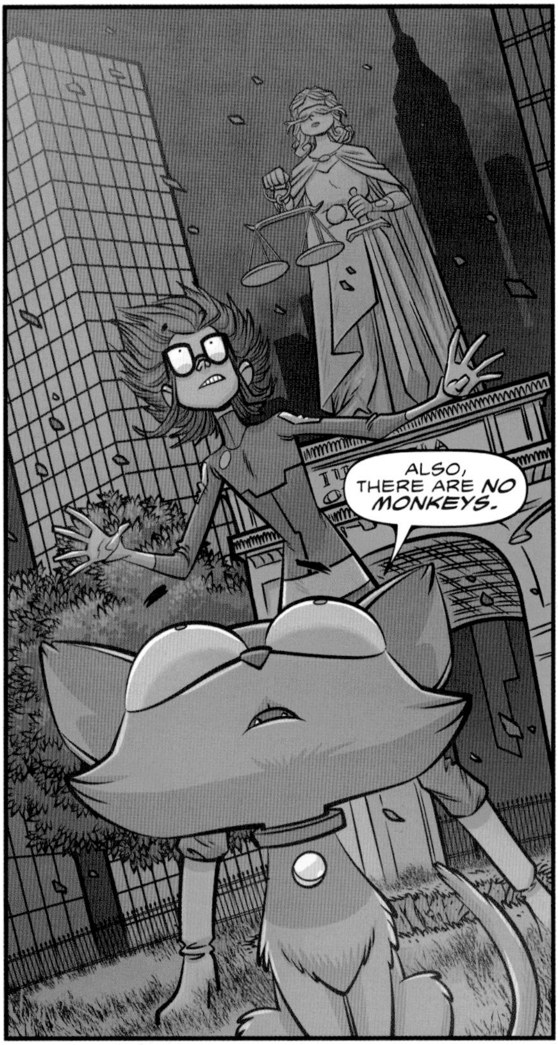
ALSO, THERE ARE NO MONKEYS.

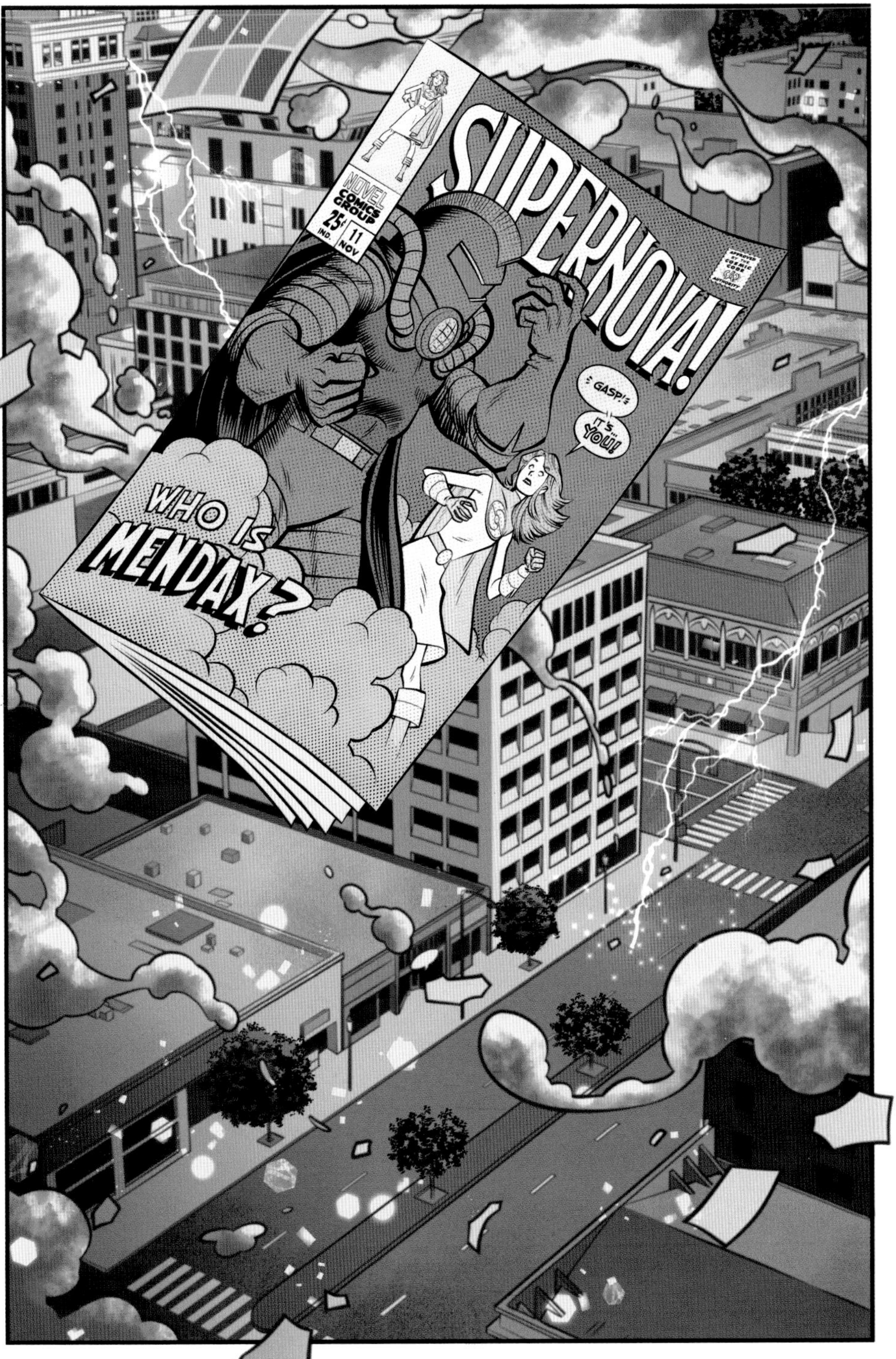
NOVEL
COMICS GROUP
25¢
IND.
11
NOV
SUPERNOVA!
APPROVED BY THE COSMIC CODE AUTHORITY
GASP!
IT'S... YOU!
WHO IS MENDAX?

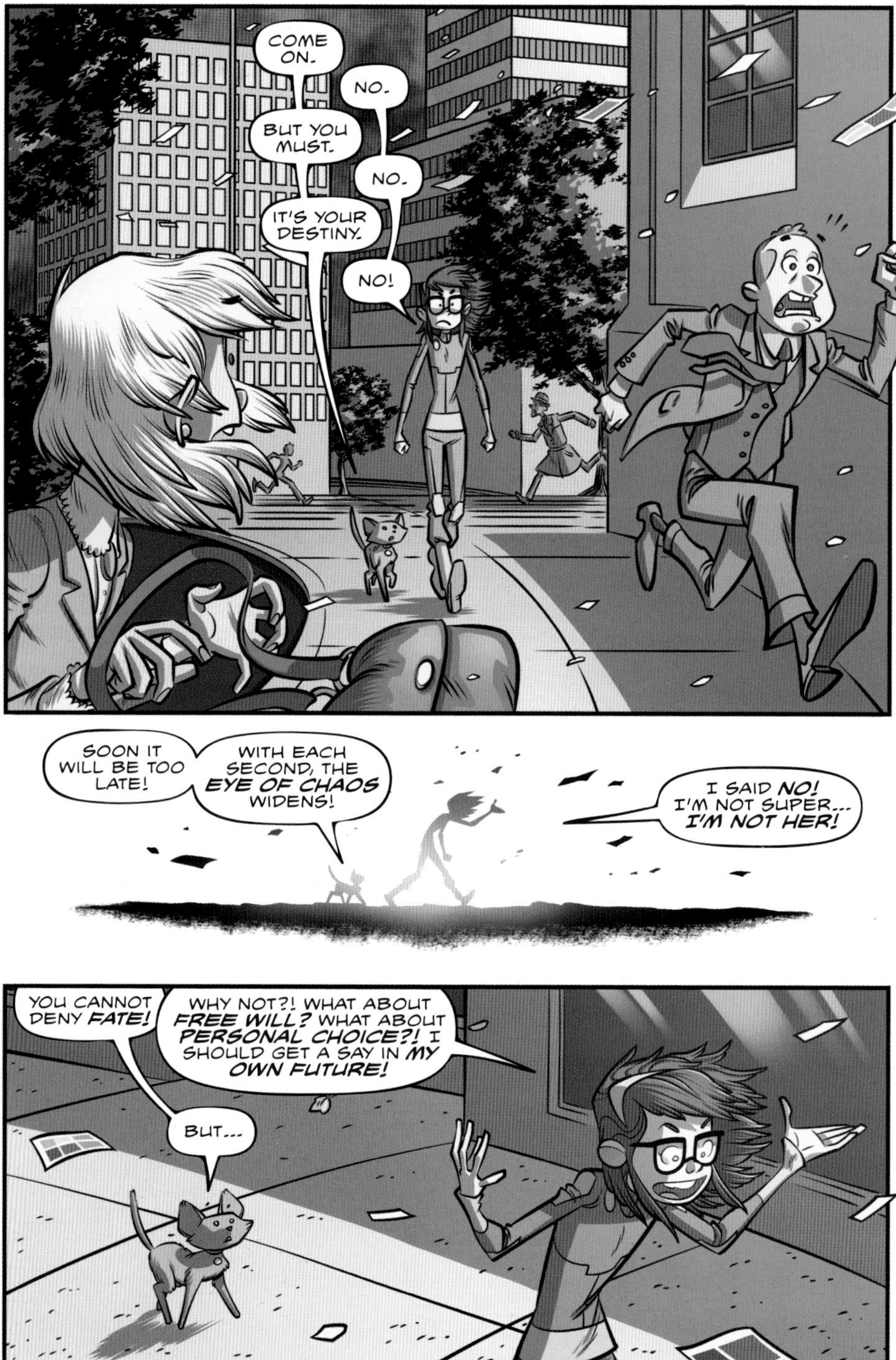
COME ON.
NO.
BUT YOU MUST.
NO.
IT'S YOUR DESTINY.
NO!
SOON IT WILL BE TOO LATE!
WITH EACH SECOND, THE EYE OF CHAOS WIDENS!
I SAID NO! I'M NOT SUPER... I'M NOT HER!
YOU CANNOT DENY FATE!
WHY NOT?! WHAT ABOUT FREE WILL? WHAT ABOUT PERSONAL CHOICE?! I SHOULD GET A SAY IN MY OWN FUTURE!
BUT...

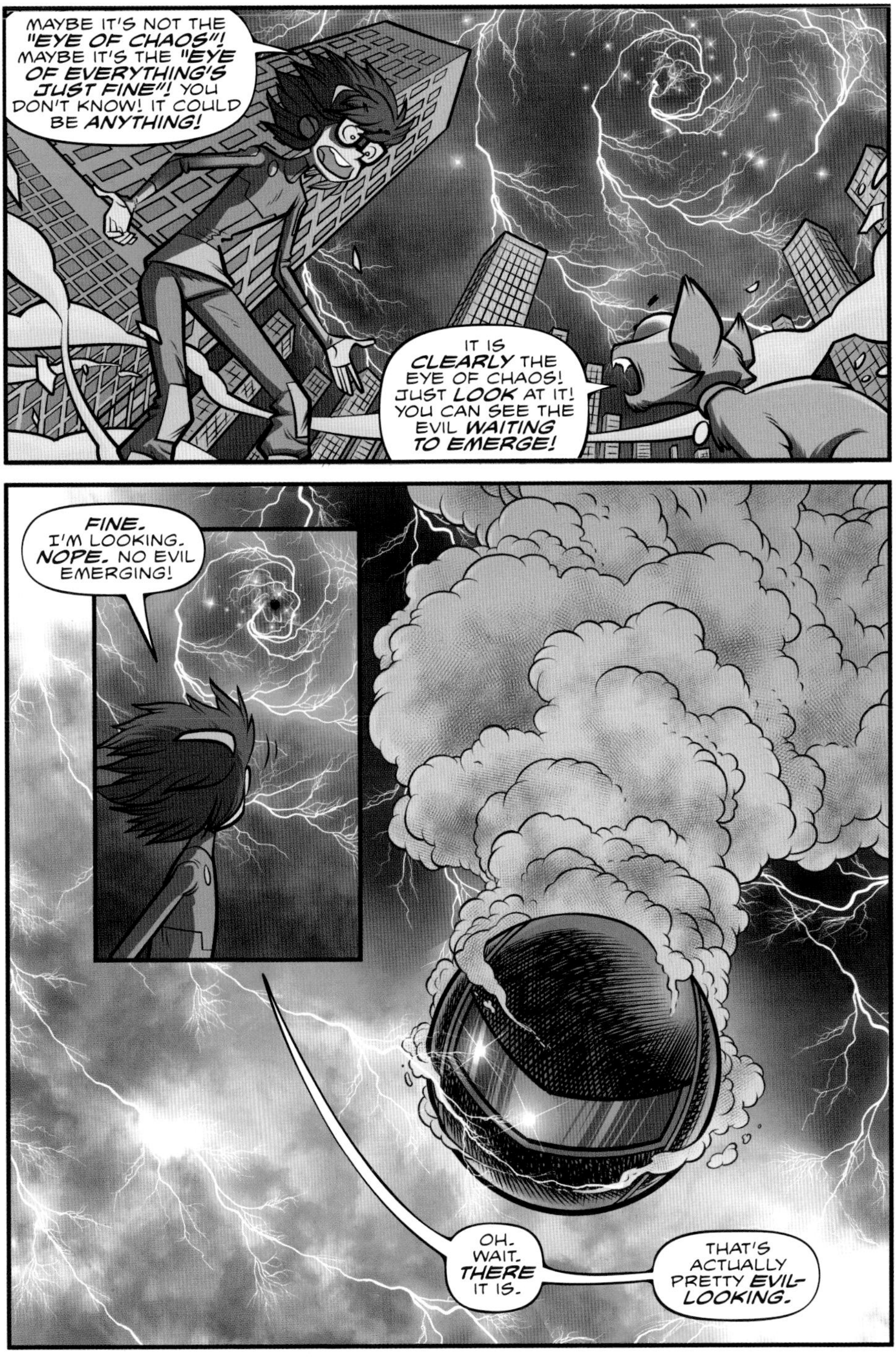
MAYBE IT'S NOT THE "EYE OF CHAOS"! MAYBE IT'S THE "EYE OF EVERYTHING'S JUST FINE"! YOU DON'T KNOW! IT COULD BE ANYTHING!
IT IS CLEARLY THE EYE OF CHAOS! JUST LOOK AT IT! YOU CAN SEE THE EVIL WAITING TO EMERGE!
FINE. I'M LOOKING. NOPE. NO EVIL EMERGING!
OH. WAIT. THERE IT IS.
THAT'S ACTUALLY PRETTY EVIL-LOOKING.

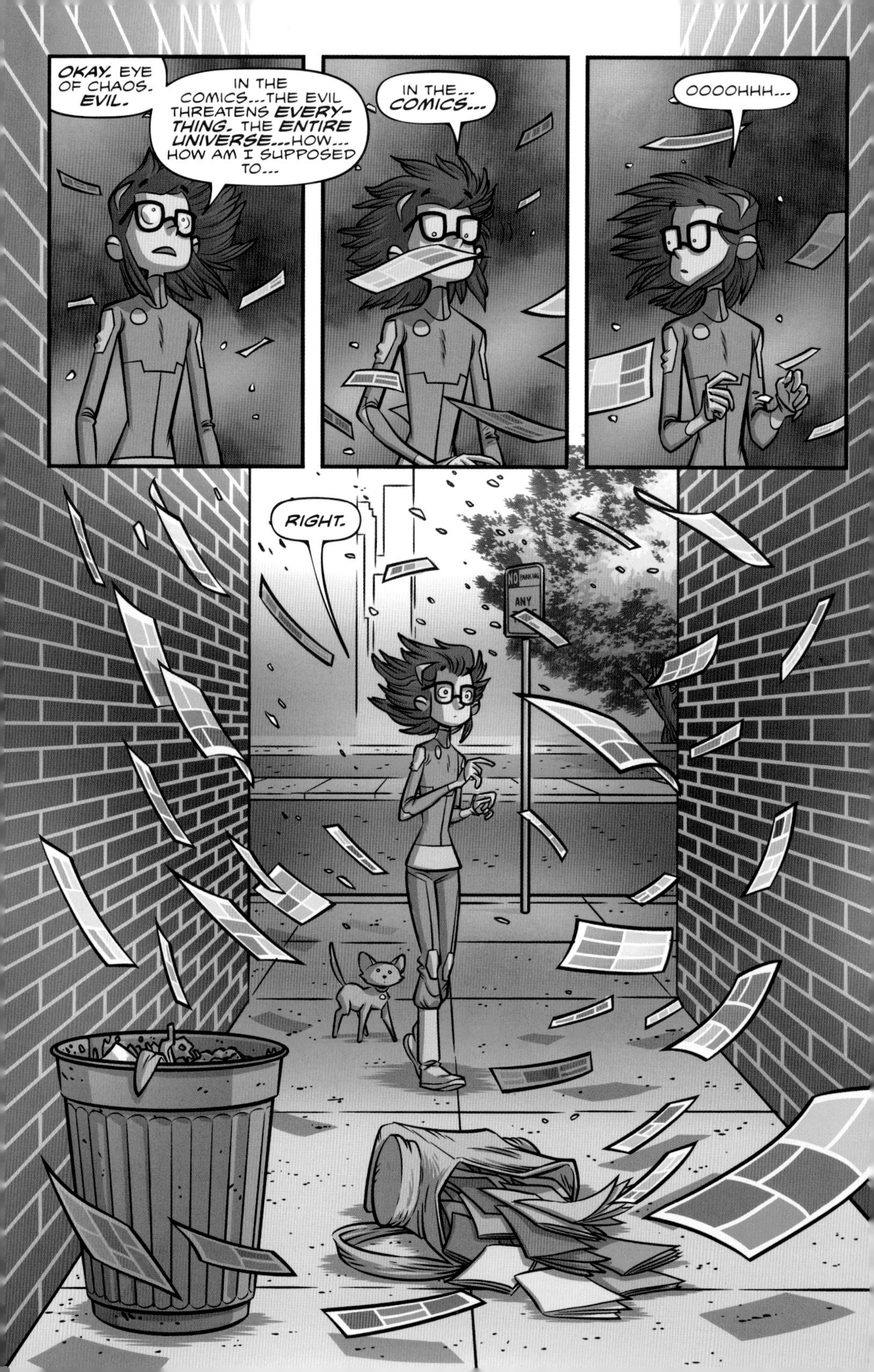

OKAY. EYE OF CHAOS. EVIL.
IN THE COMICS...THE EVIL THREATENS EVERYTHING. THE ENTIRE UNIVERSE...HOW... HOW AM I SUPPOSED TO...
IN THE... COMICS...
OOOOHHH...
RIGHT.
NO PARKING ANY

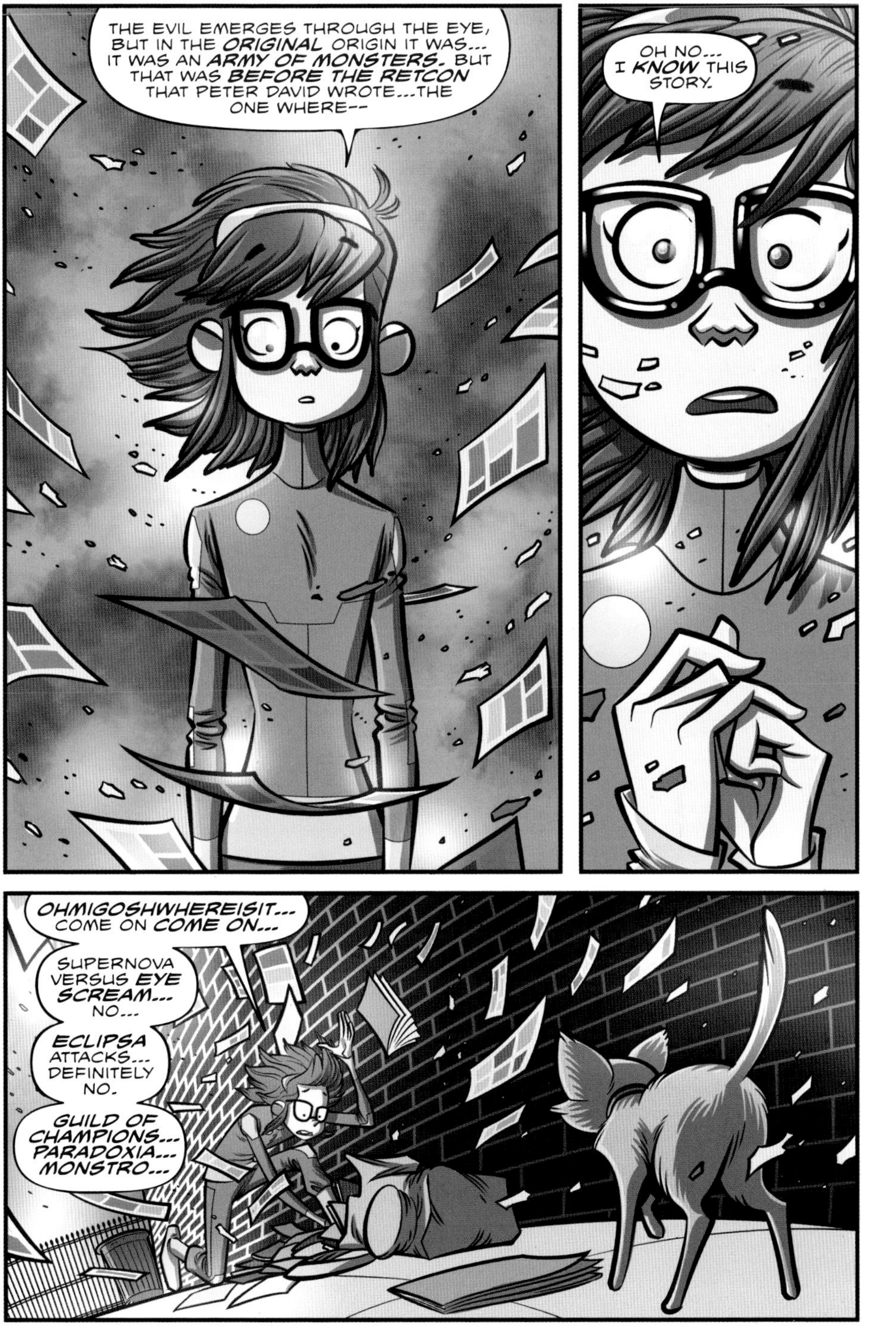
THE EVIL EMERGES THROUGH THE EYE, BUT IN THE ORIGINAL ORIGIN IT WAS... IT WAS AN ARMY OF MONSTERS. BUT THAT WAS BEFORE THE RETCON THAT PETER DAVID WROTE...THE ONE WHERE--
OH NO... I KNOW THIS STORY.
OHMIGOSHWHEREISIT... COME ON COME ON...
SUPERNOVA VERSUS EYE SCREAM... NO...
ECLIPSA ATTACKS... DEFINITELY NO.
GUILD OF CHAMPIONS... PARADOXIA... MONSTRO...

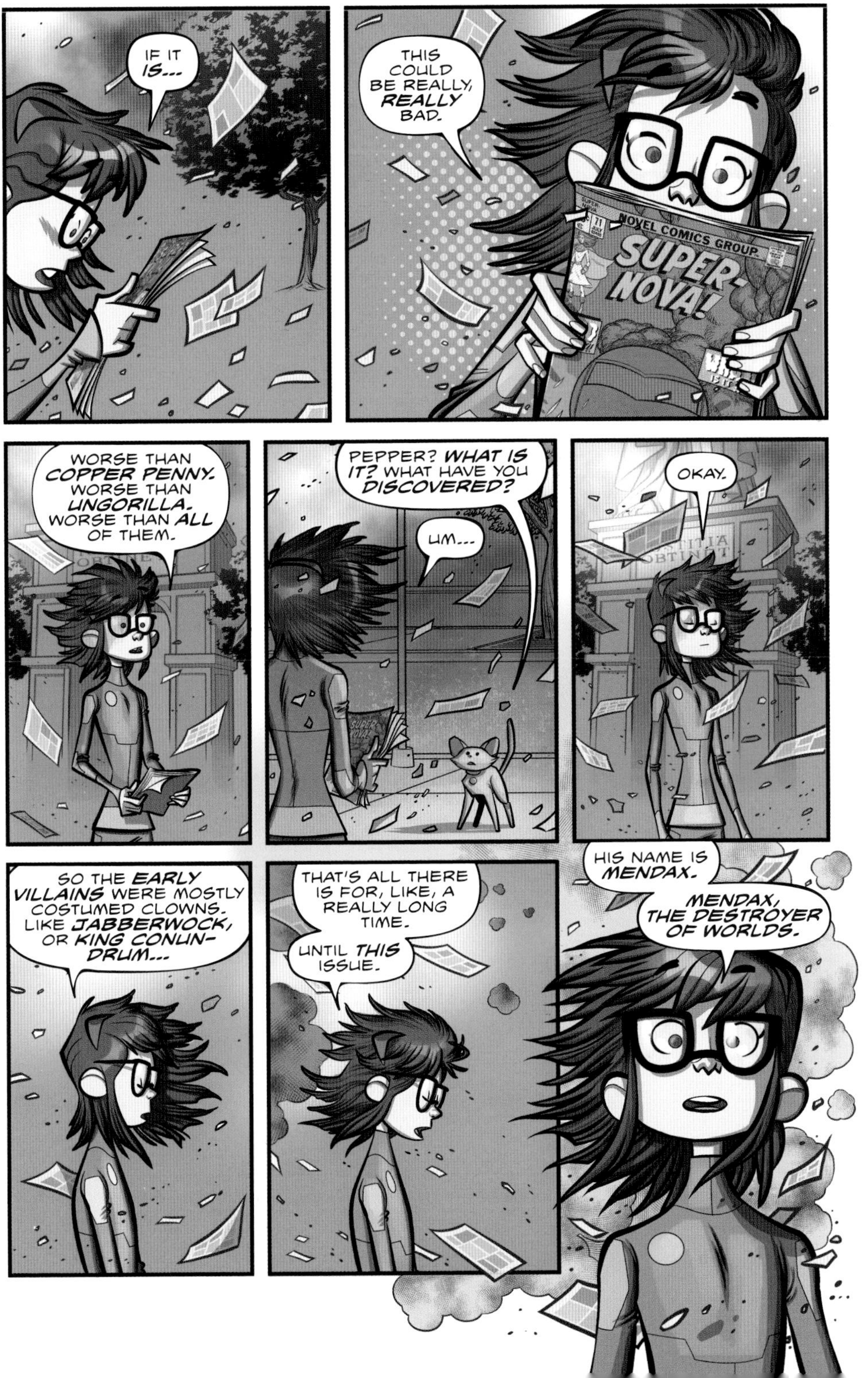

IF IT IS...
THIS COULD BE REALLY, REALLY BAD.
NOVEL COMICS GROUP.
SUPER-NOVA!
WORSE THAN COPPER PENNY. WORSE THAN UNGORILLA. WORSE THAN ALL OF THEM.
PEPPER? WHAT IS IT? WHAT HAVE YOU DISCOVERED?
UM...
OKAY.
SO THE EARLY VILLAINS WERE MOSTLY COSTUMED CLOWNS. LIKE JABBERWOCK, OR KING CONUN-DRUM...
THAT'S ALL THERE IS FOR, LIKE, A REALLY LONG TIME.
UNTIL THIS ISSUE.
HIS NAME IS MENDAX.
MENDAX, THE DESTROYER OF WORLDS.

136

PEPPER... YOU *MUST* SAY THE *NAME.* YOU *MUST* SAY IT *NOW.*

I DON'T *WANT* TO.

PEPPER... *PLEASE...*

THE SHIP IS *OPENING.* NO NO *NO....*

IT'S... IT'S....

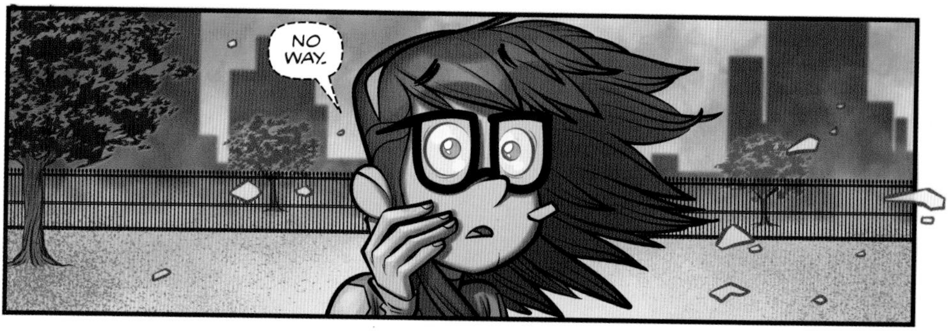
NO WAY.

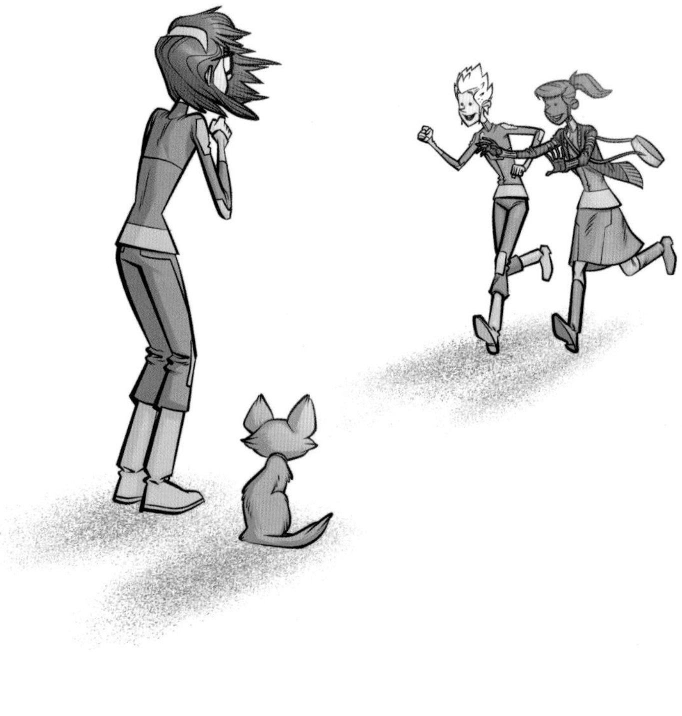

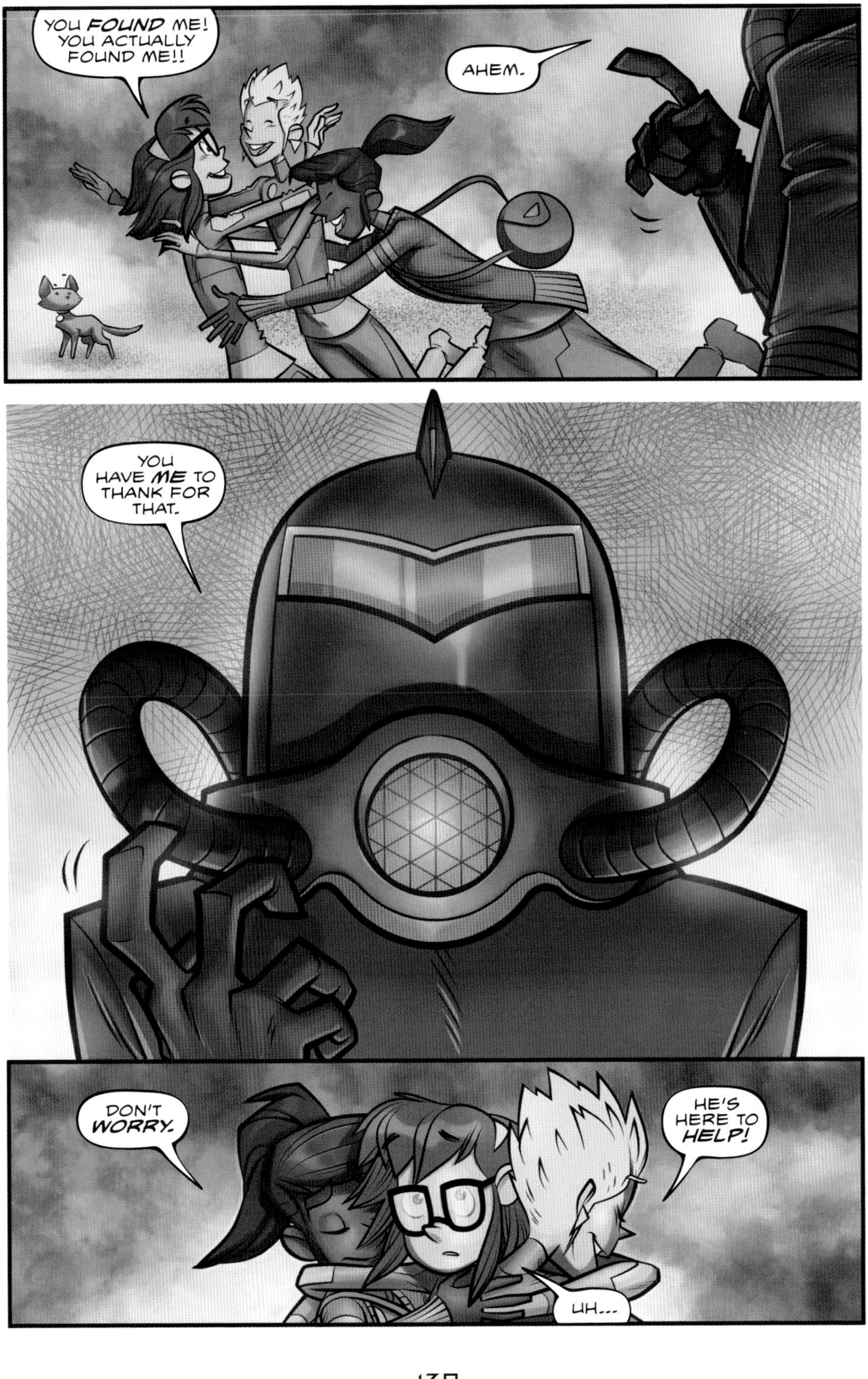
YOU FOUND ME! YOU ACTUALLY FOUND ME!!
AHEM.
YOU HAVE ME TO THANK FOR THAT.
DON'T WORRY.
HE'S HERE TO HELP!
UH...

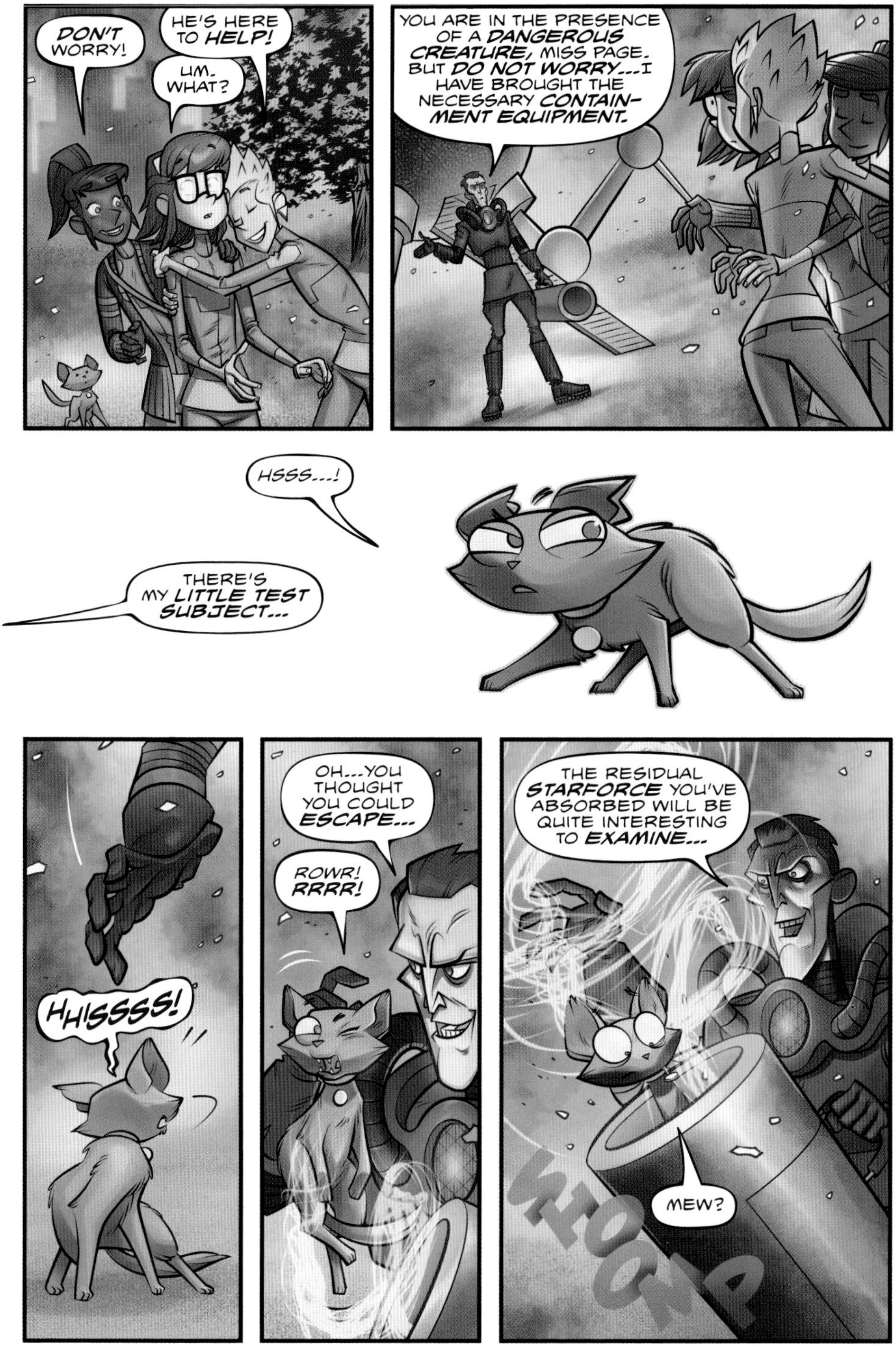
DON'T WORRY!
HE'S HERE TO HELP!
UM. WHAT?
YOU ARE IN THE PRESENCE OF A DANGEROUS CREATURE, MISS PAGE. BUT DO NOT WORRY...I HAVE BROUGHT THE NECESSARY CONTAINMENT EQUIPMENT.
HSSS...!
THERE'S MY LITTLE TEST SUBJECT...
HHISSSS!
OH...YOU THOUGHT YOU COULD ESCAPE...
ROWR! RRRR!
THE RESIDUAL STARFORCE YOU'VE ABSORBED WILL BE QUITE INTERESTING TO EXAMINE...
MEW?
WHOOMP

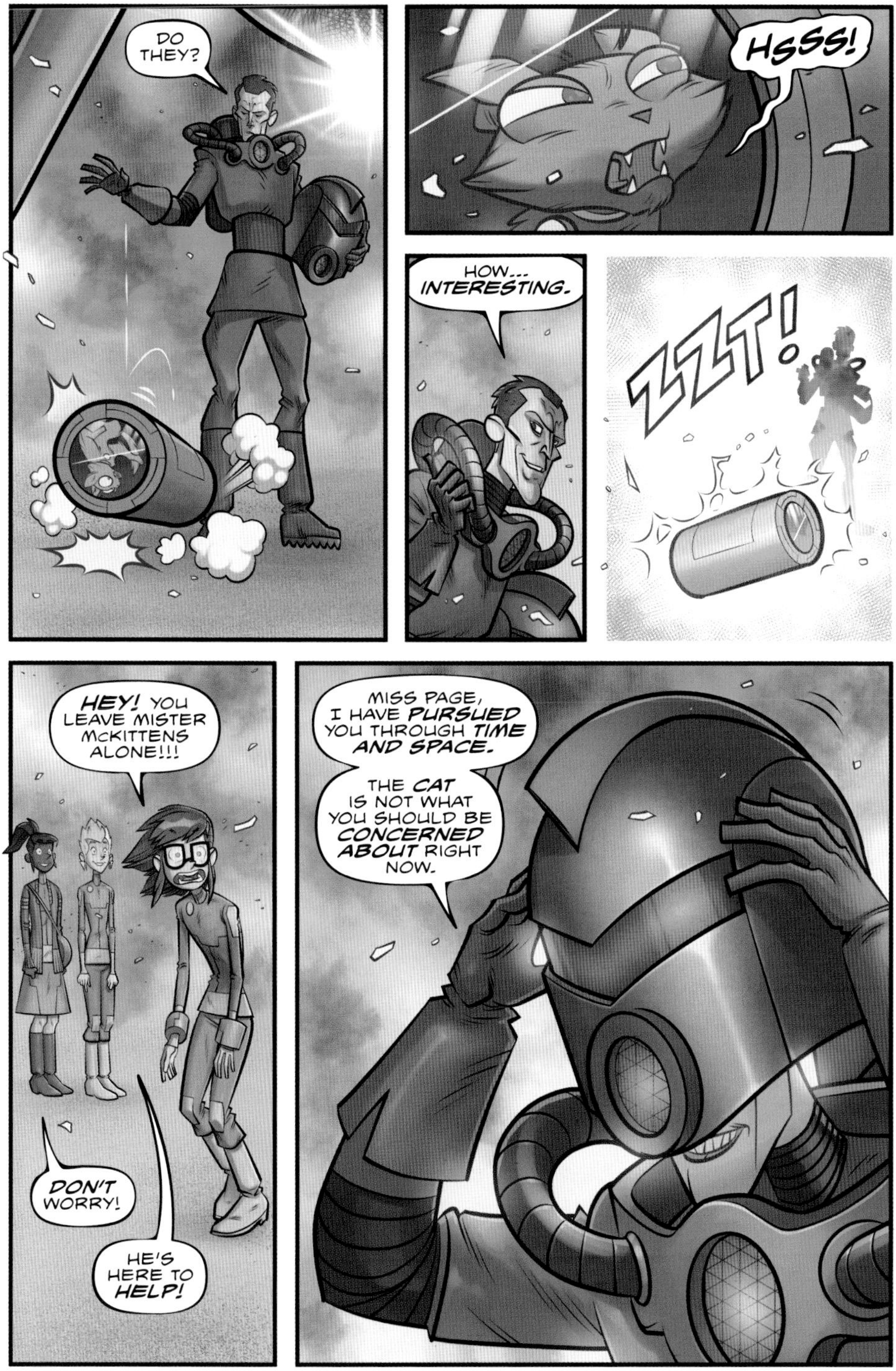
DO THEY?
HSSS!
HOW... INTERESTING.
ZZT!
HEY! YOU LEAVE MISTER McKITTENS ALONE!!!
DON'T WORRY!
HE'S HERE TO HELP!
MISS PAGE, I HAVE PURSUED YOU THROUGH TIME AND SPACE.
THE CAT IS NOT WHAT YOU SHOULD BE CONCERNED ABOUT RIGHT NOW.

144

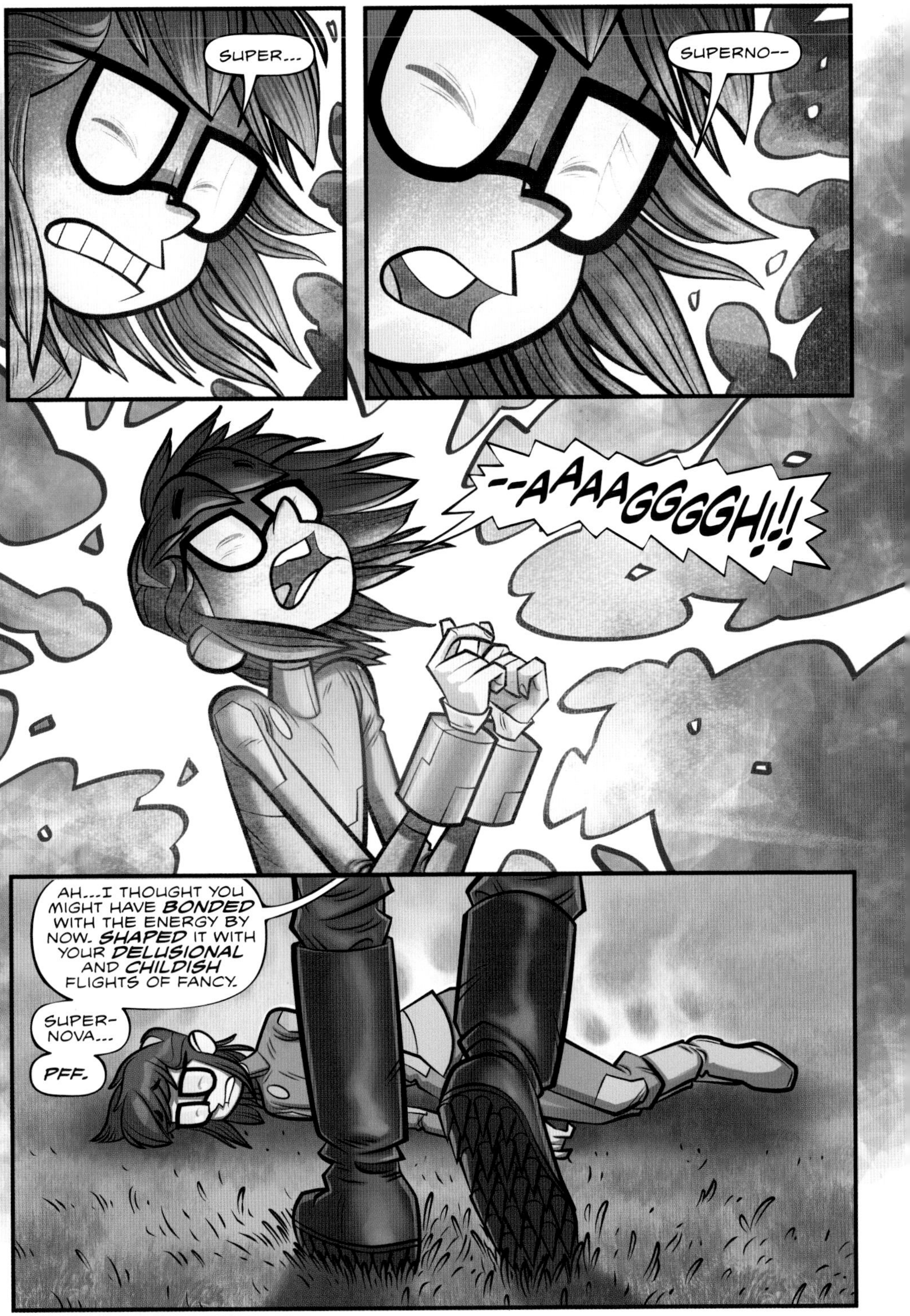
SUPER...
SUPERNO--
--AAAAGGGGH!!!
AH...I THOUGHT YOU MIGHT HAVE BONDED WITH THE ENERGY BY NOW. SHAPED IT WITH YOUR DELUSIONAL AND CHILDISH FLIGHTS OF FANCY.
SUPER-NOVA...
PFF.

DON'T BE A **FOOL.**

ANY ATTEMPT YOU MAKE IN ACCESSING THE **POWER WITHIN YOU**...WILL RESULT ONLY IN **PAIN.**

DON'T WORRY!

TALLY... ZOLA...

HE'S HERE TO **HELP!**

PROFESSOR KILLIAN...

YOU'RE SUPPOSED TO BE A **TEACHER!**

HM. YES. I SUPPOSE I **AM.**

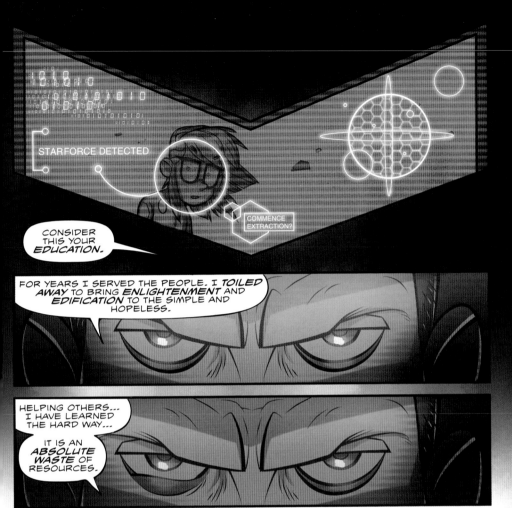

STARFORCE DETECTED

COMMENCE EXTRACTION?

CONSIDER THIS YOUR *EDUCATION.*

FOR YEARS I SERVED THE PEOPLE. I *TOILED AWAY* TO BRING *ENLIGHTENMENT* AND *EDIFICATION* TO THE SIMPLE AND HOPELESS.

HELPING OTHERS... I HAVE LEARNED THE HARD WAY...

IT IS AN *ABSOLUTE WASTE* OF RESOURCES.

I ASSUME *THIS* IS FAMILIAR TO YOU?

STARSTRUCK

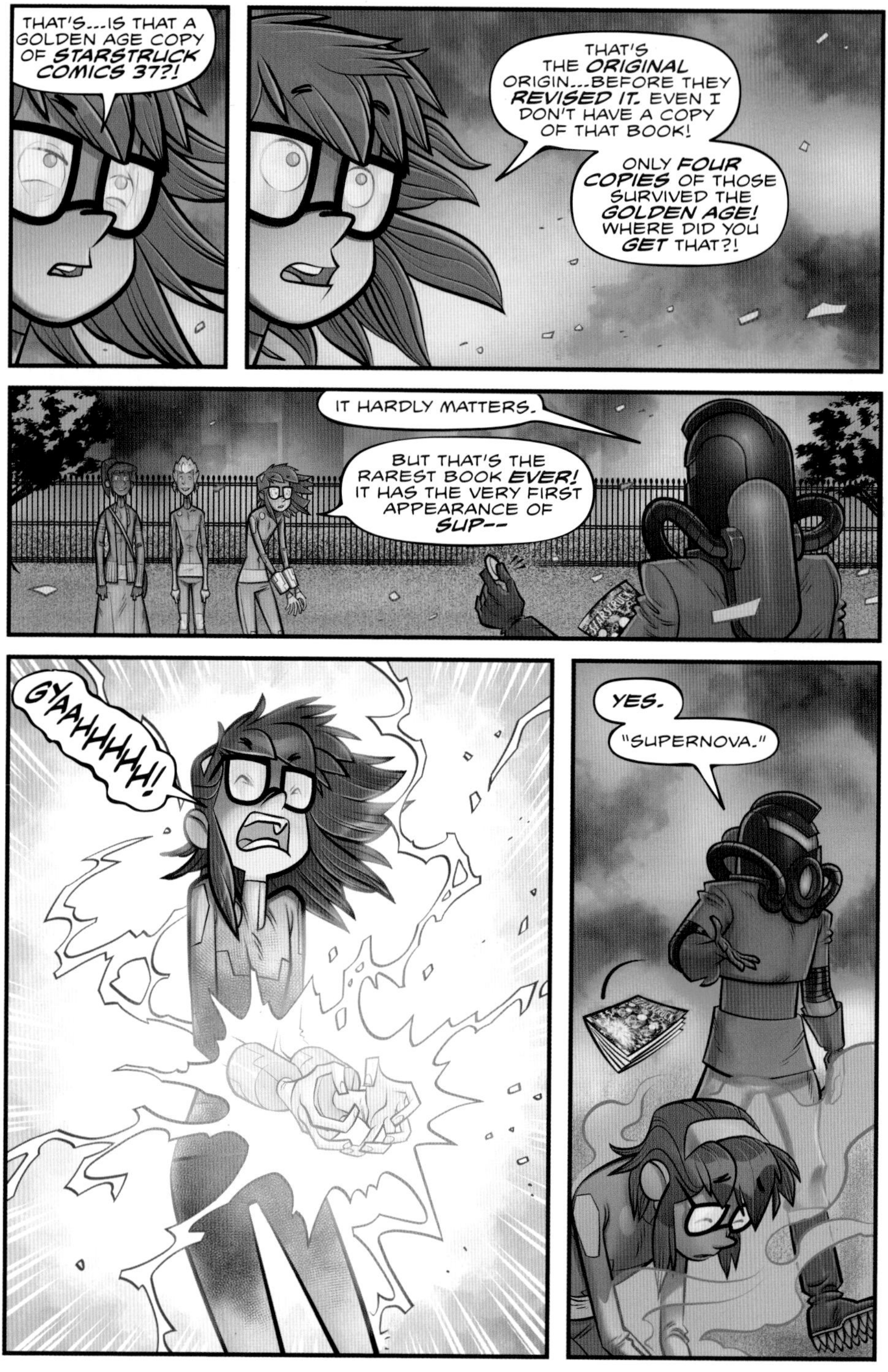
THAT'S...IS THAT A GOLDEN AGE COPY OF STARSTRUCK COMICS 37?!
THAT'S THE ORIGINAL ORIGIN...BEFORE THEY REVISED IT. EVEN I DON'T HAVE A COPY OF THAT BOOK!
ONLY FOUR COPIES OF THOSE SURVIVED THE GOLDEN AGE! WHERE DID YOU GET THAT?!
IT HARDLY MATTERS.
BUT THAT'S THE RAREST BOOK EVER! IT HAS THE VERY FIRST APPEARANCE OF SUP--
GYAAHHHHH!
YES.
"SUPERNOVA."

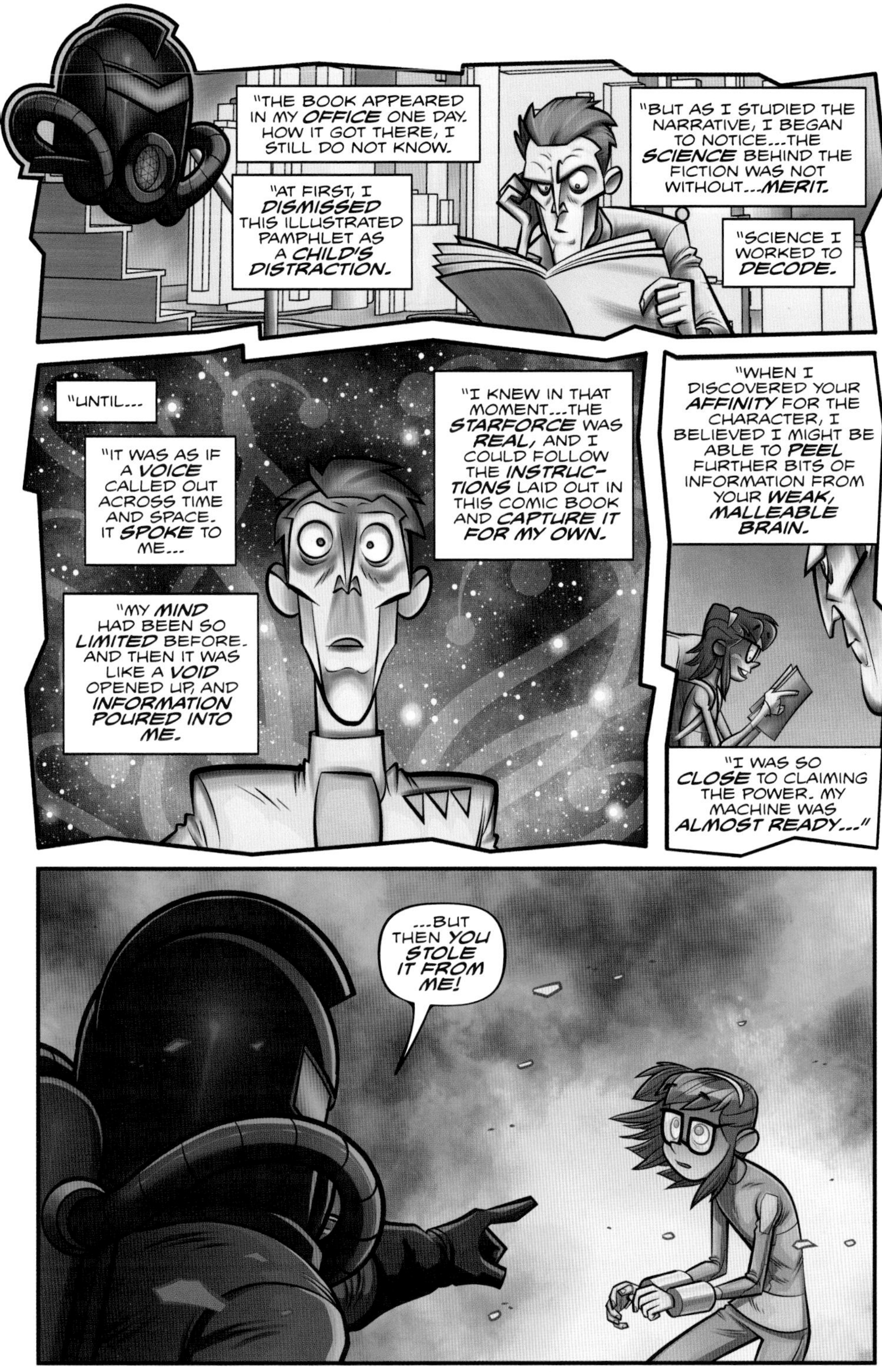
"THE BOOK APPEARED IN MY OFFICE ONE DAY. HOW IT GOT THERE, I STILL DO NOT KNOW.
"AT FIRST, I DISMISSED THIS ILLUSTRATED PAMPHLET AS A CHILD'S DISTRACTION.
"BUT AS I STUDIED THE NARRATIVE, I BEGAN TO NOTICE... THE SCIENCE BEHIND THE FICTION WAS NOT WITHOUT... MERIT.
"SCIENCE I WORKED TO DECODE.
"UNTIL...
"IT WAS AS IF A VOICE CALLED OUT ACROSS TIME AND SPACE. IT SPOKE TO ME...
"MY MIND HAD BEEN SO LIMITED BEFORE. AND THEN IT WAS LIKE A VOID OPENED UP, AND INFORMATION POURED INTO ME.
"I KNEW IN THAT MOMENT... THE STARFORCE WAS REAL, AND I COULD FOLLOW THE INSTRUCTIONS LAID OUT IN THIS COMIC BOOK AND CAPTURE IT FOR MY OWN.
"WHEN I DISCOVERED YOUR AFFINITY FOR THE CHARACTER, I BELIEVED I MIGHT BE ABLE TO PEEL FURTHER BITS OF INFORMATION FROM YOUR WEAK, MALLEABLE BRAIN.
"I WAS SO CLOSE TO CLAIMING THE POWER. MY MACHINE WAS ALMOST READY..."
...BUT THEN YOU STOLE IT FROM ME!

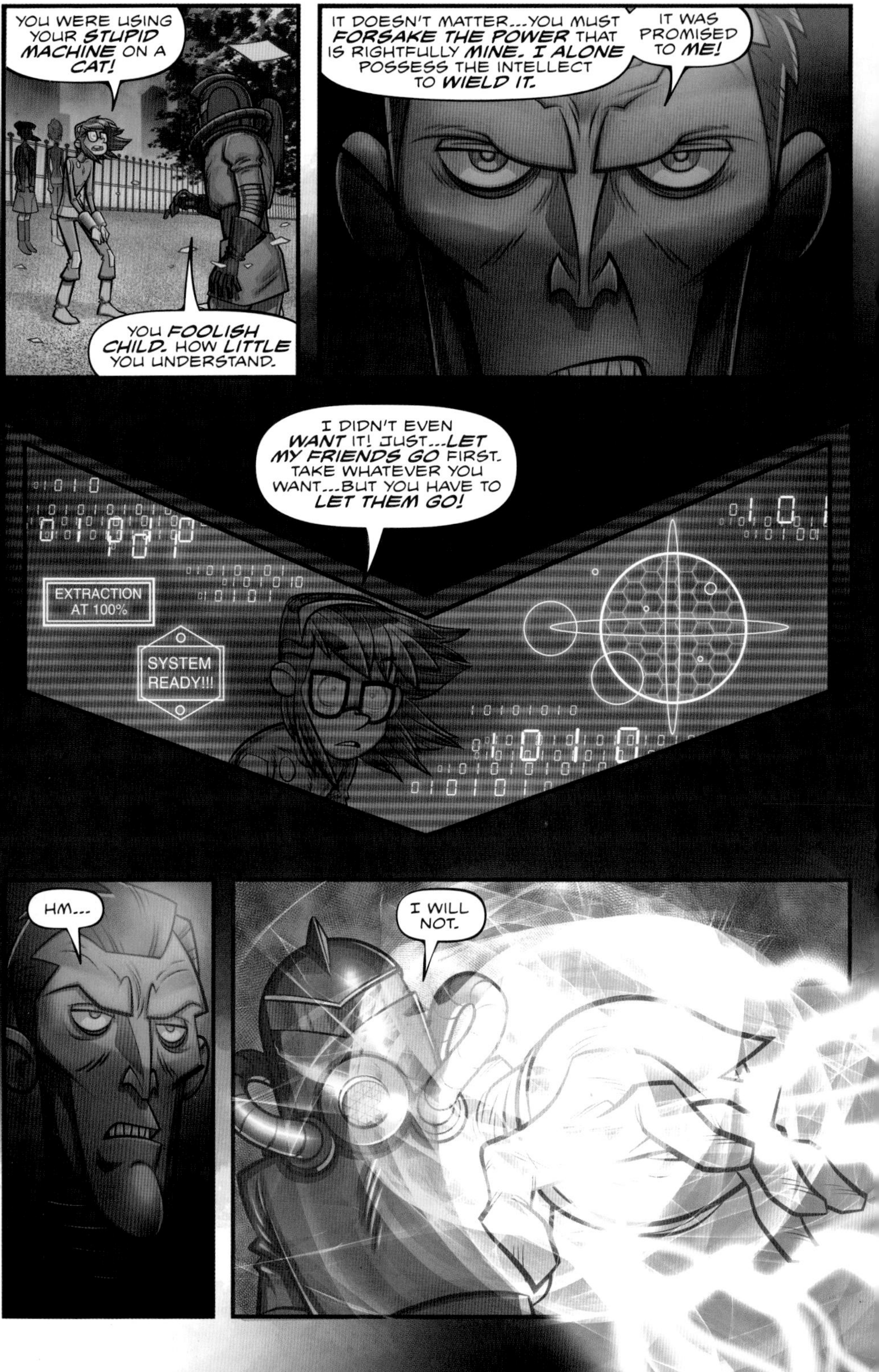
YOU WERE USING YOUR STUPID MACHINE ON A CAT!
YOU FOOLISH CHILD. HOW LITTLE YOU UNDERSTAND.
IT DOESN'T MATTER...YOU MUST FORSAKE THE POWER THAT IS RIGHTFULLY MINE. I ALONE POSSESS THE INTELLECT TO WIELD IT.
IT WAS PROMISED TO ME!
I DIDN'T EVEN WANT IT! JUST...LET MY FRIENDS GO FIRST. TAKE WHATEVER YOU WANT...BUT YOU HAVE TO LET THEM GO!
EXTRACTION AT 100%
SYSTEM READY!!!
HM...
I WILL NOT.

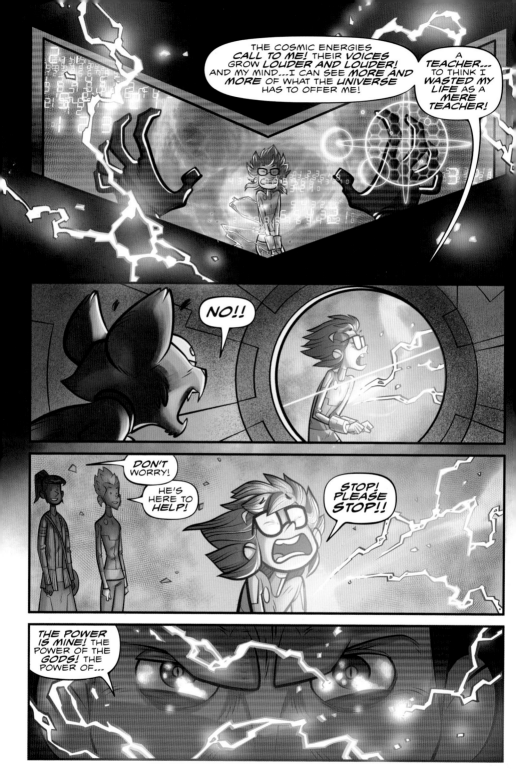

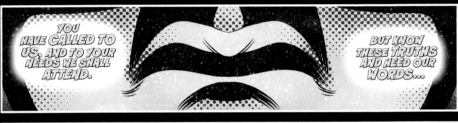

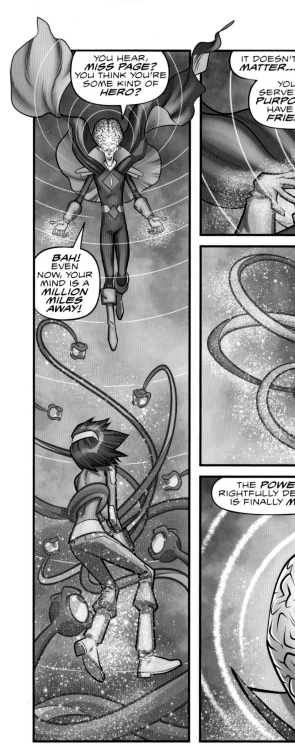

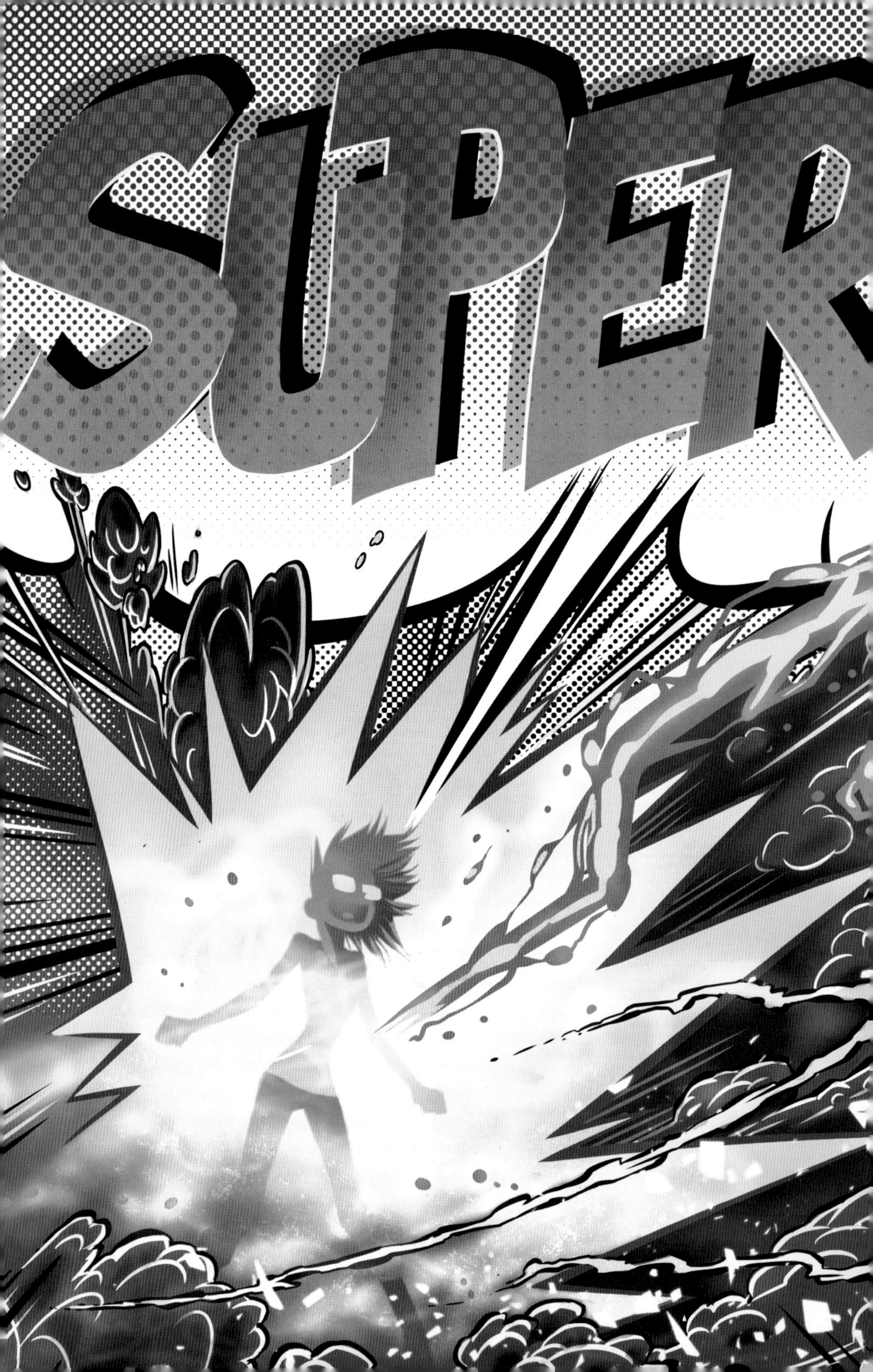
SUPER

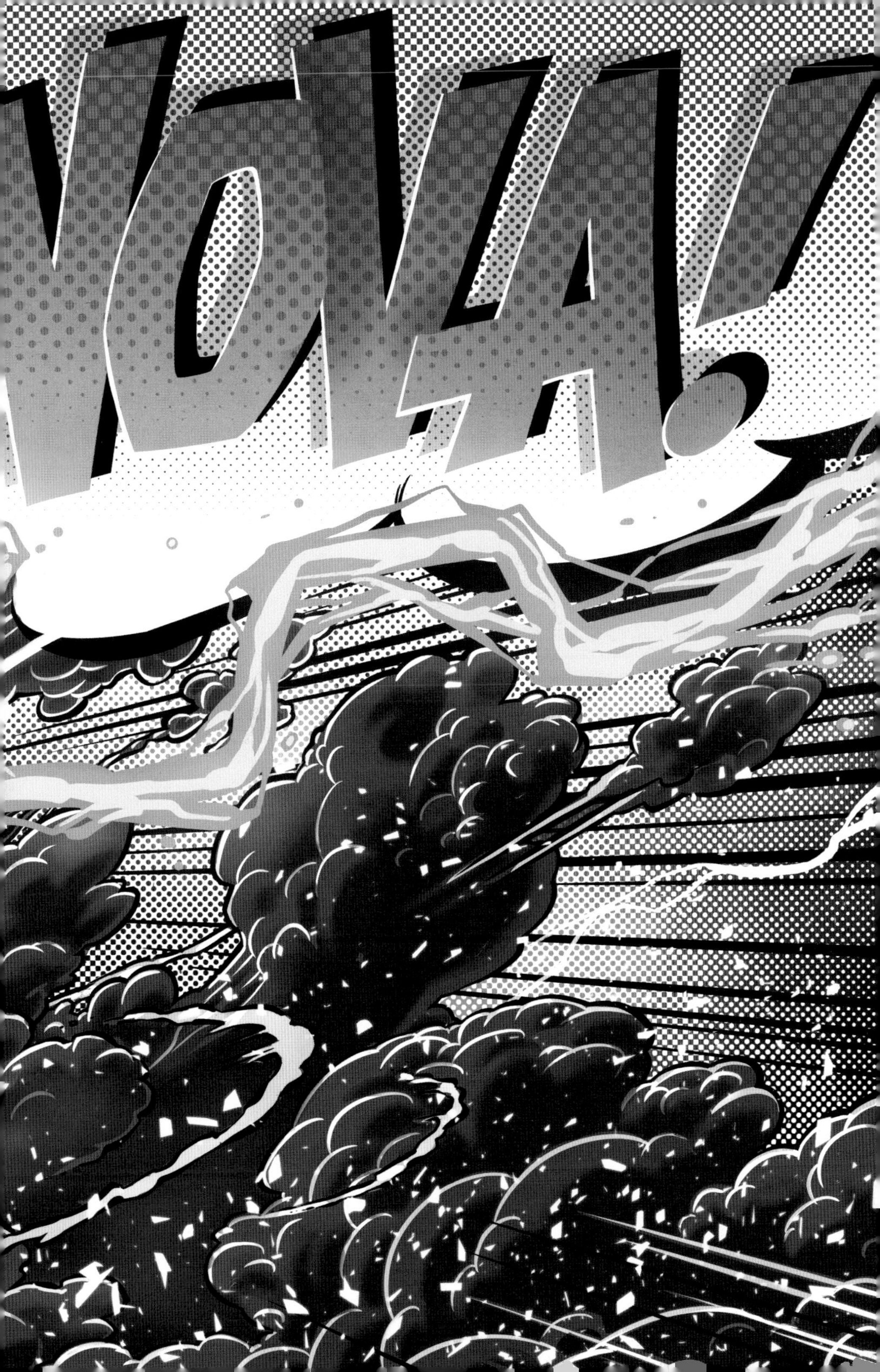
VOLA!

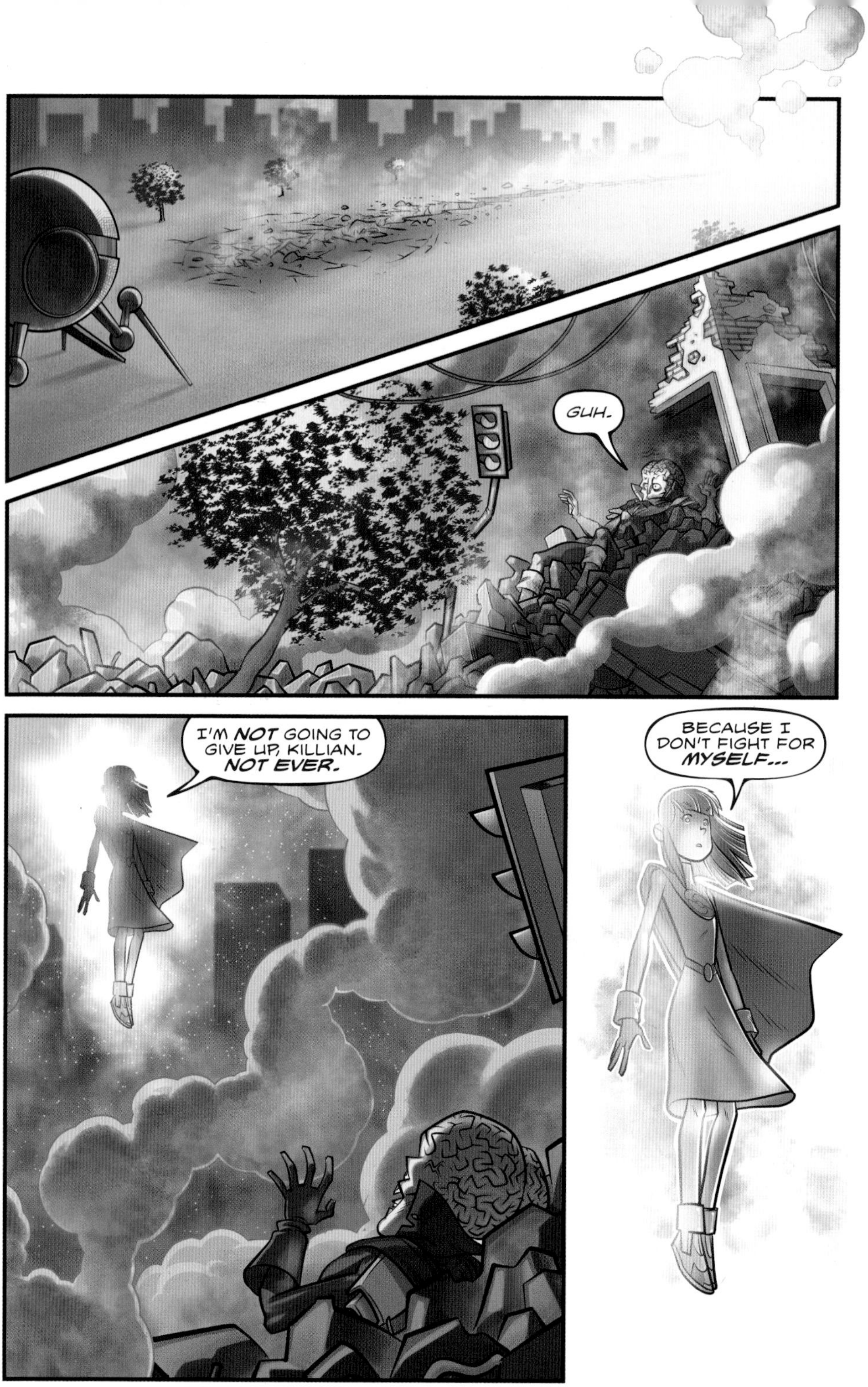
GUH.
I'M NOT GOING TO GIVE UP, KILLIAN. NOT EVER.
BECAUSE I DON'T FIGHT FOR MYSELF...

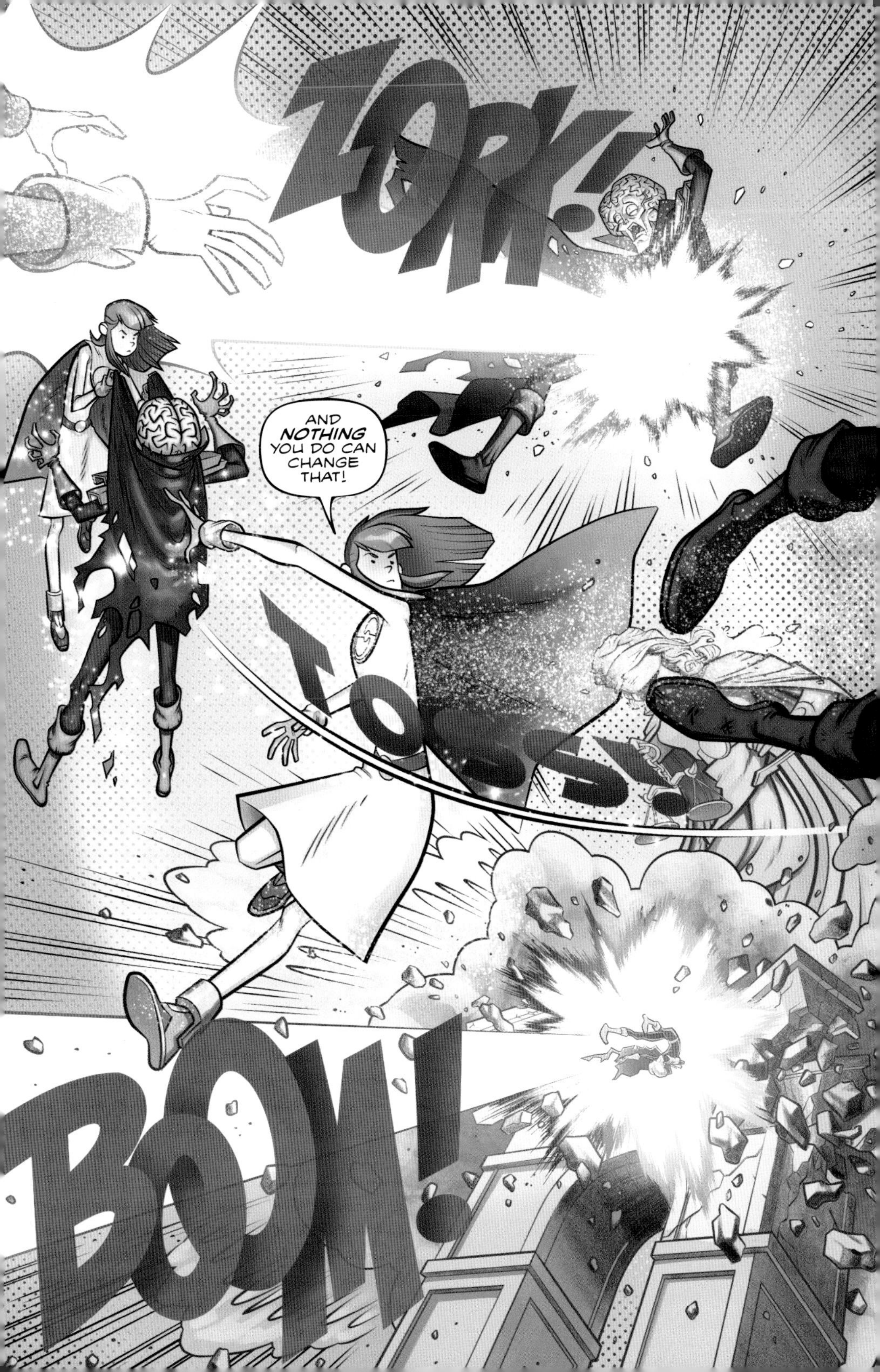
ZORK!
AND NOTHING YOU DO CAN CHANGE THAT!
TOSS!
BOOM!

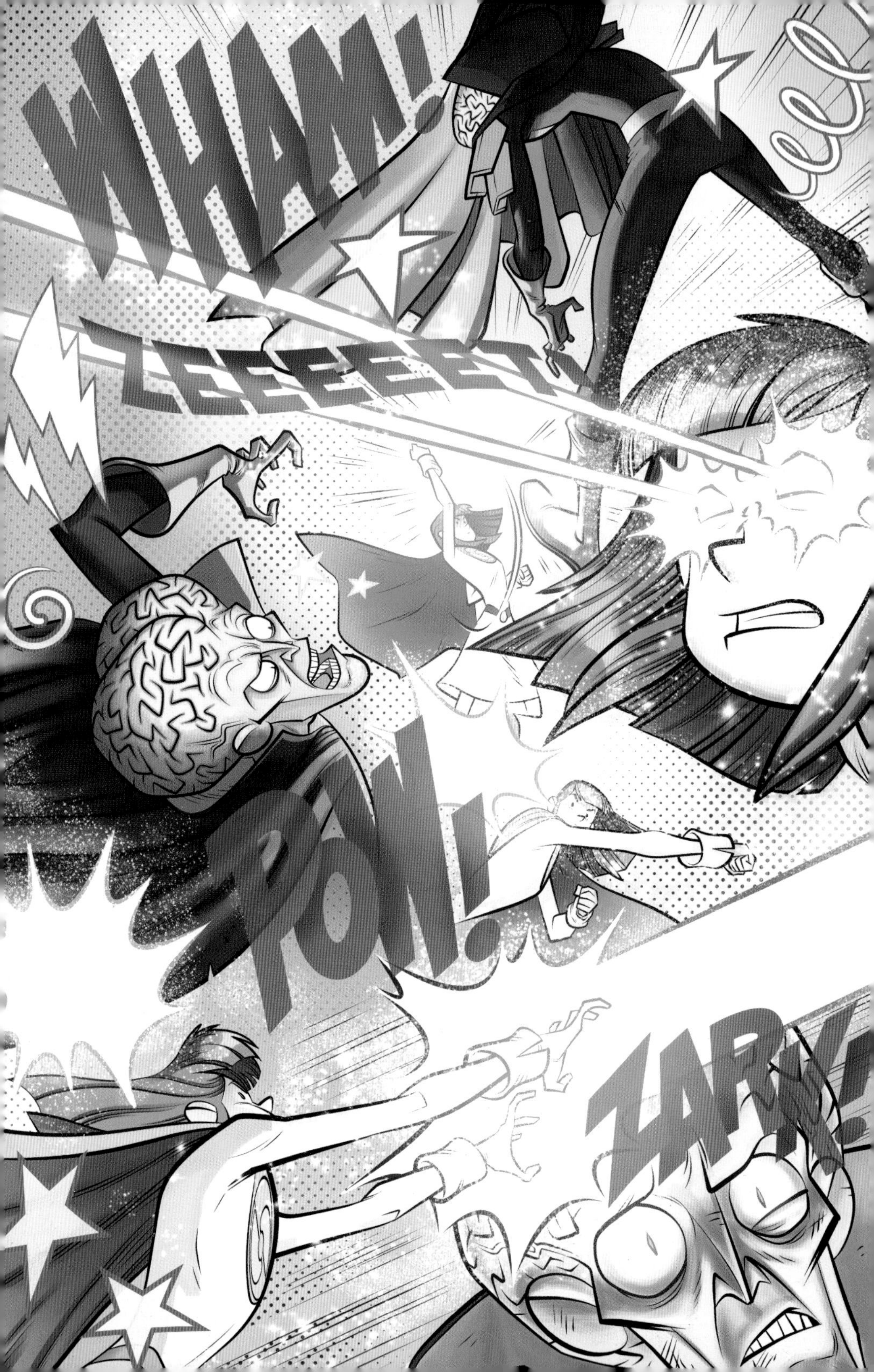
WHAM!
ZEEEEET!
POW!
ZARK!

168

169

GLK!

BLURG!

WHAT--?

THERE'S *NO WAY* YOU COULD HAVE *DEPROGRAMMED* THEM WITHOUT ACCESS TO MY *SHIP!* HOW--?

THAT CAT! IT MUST BE *HIM!*

NO MATTER. SOON I WILL *RETURN HIM* TO MY OPERATING--

KLIK

170

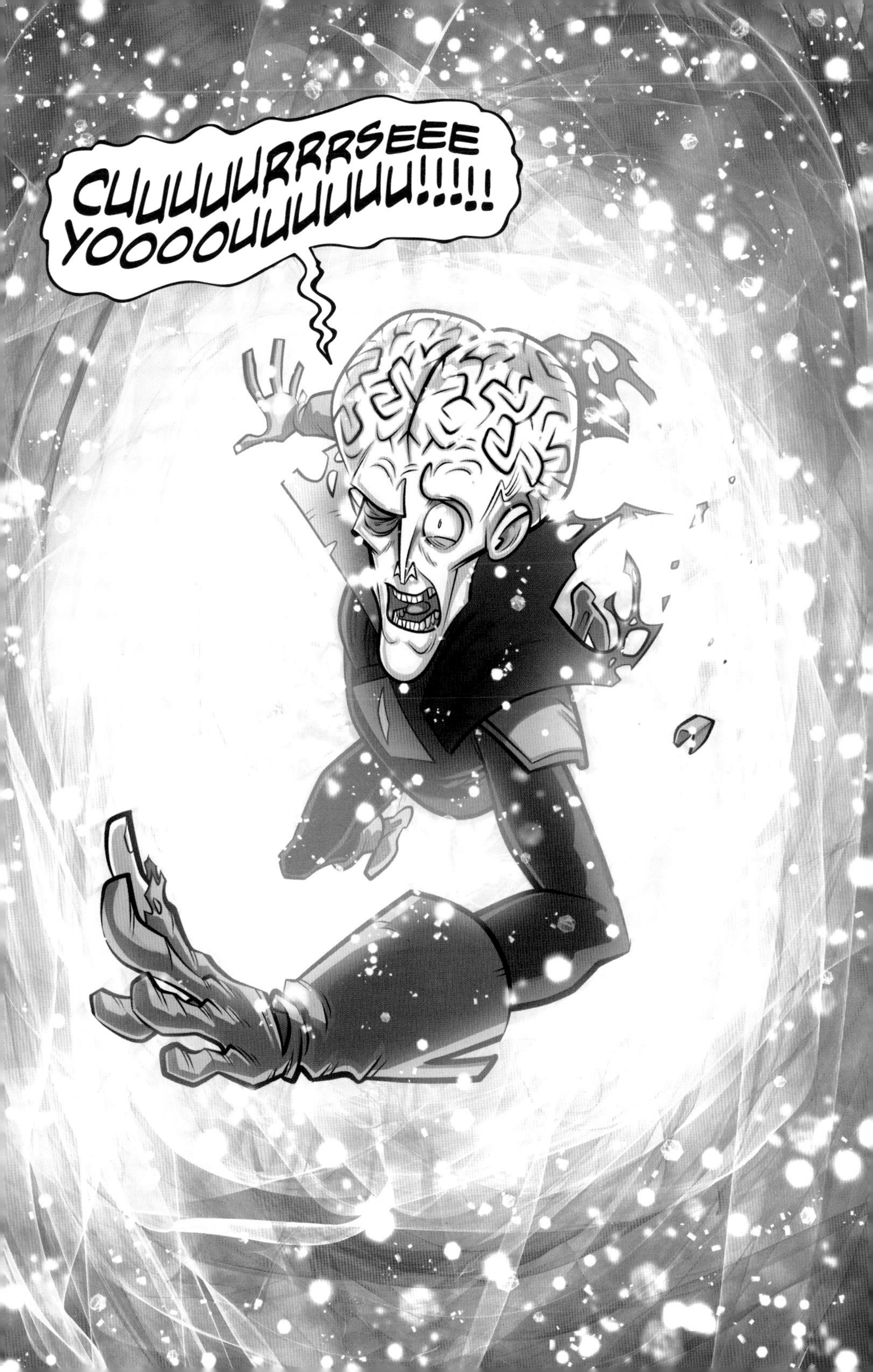
CUUUUURRRRSEEE YOOOOUUUUUUU!!!!!

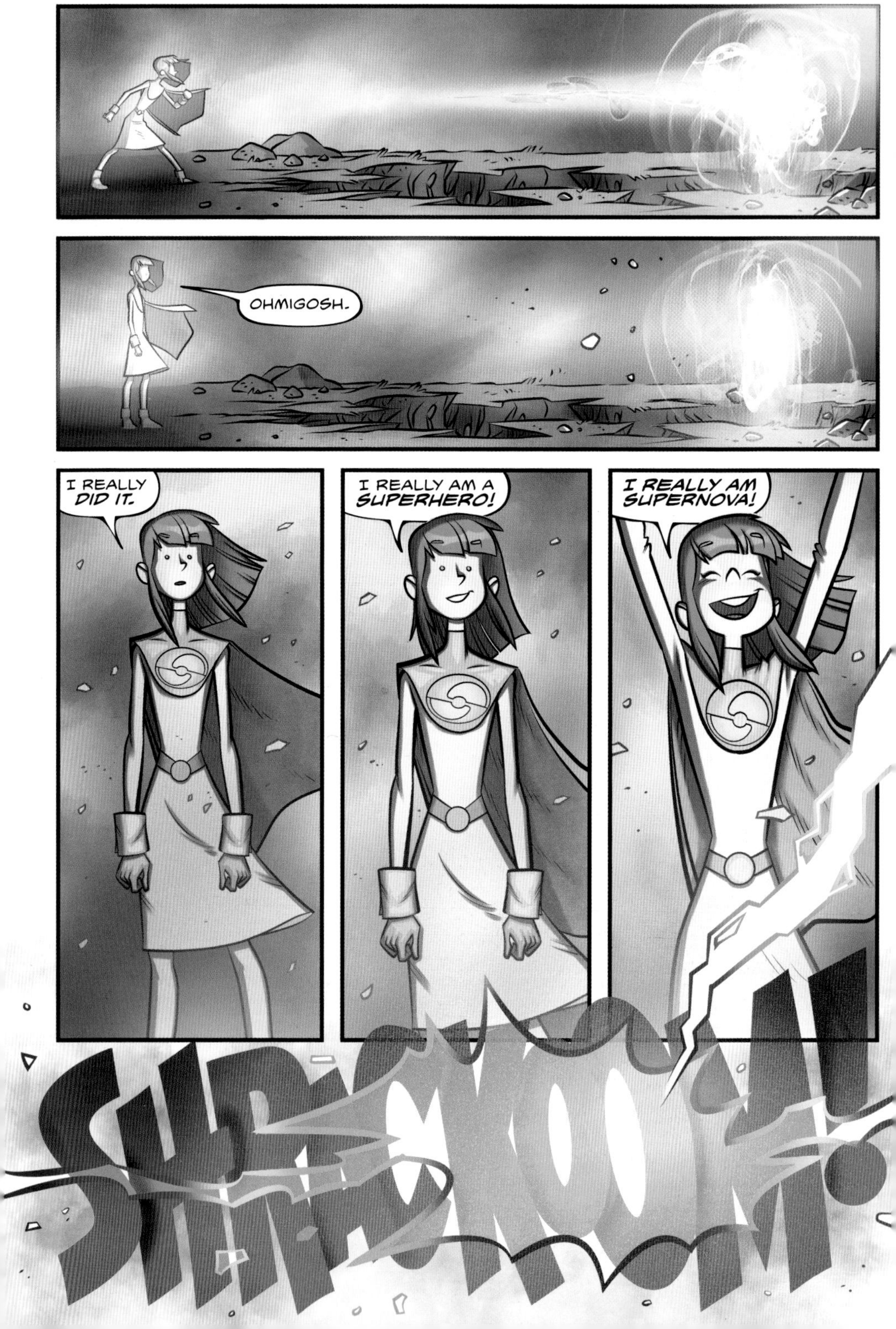
OHMIGOSH.
I REALLY DID IT.
I REALLY AM A SUPERHERO!
I REALLY AM SUPERNOVA!
SHRAKOOM!

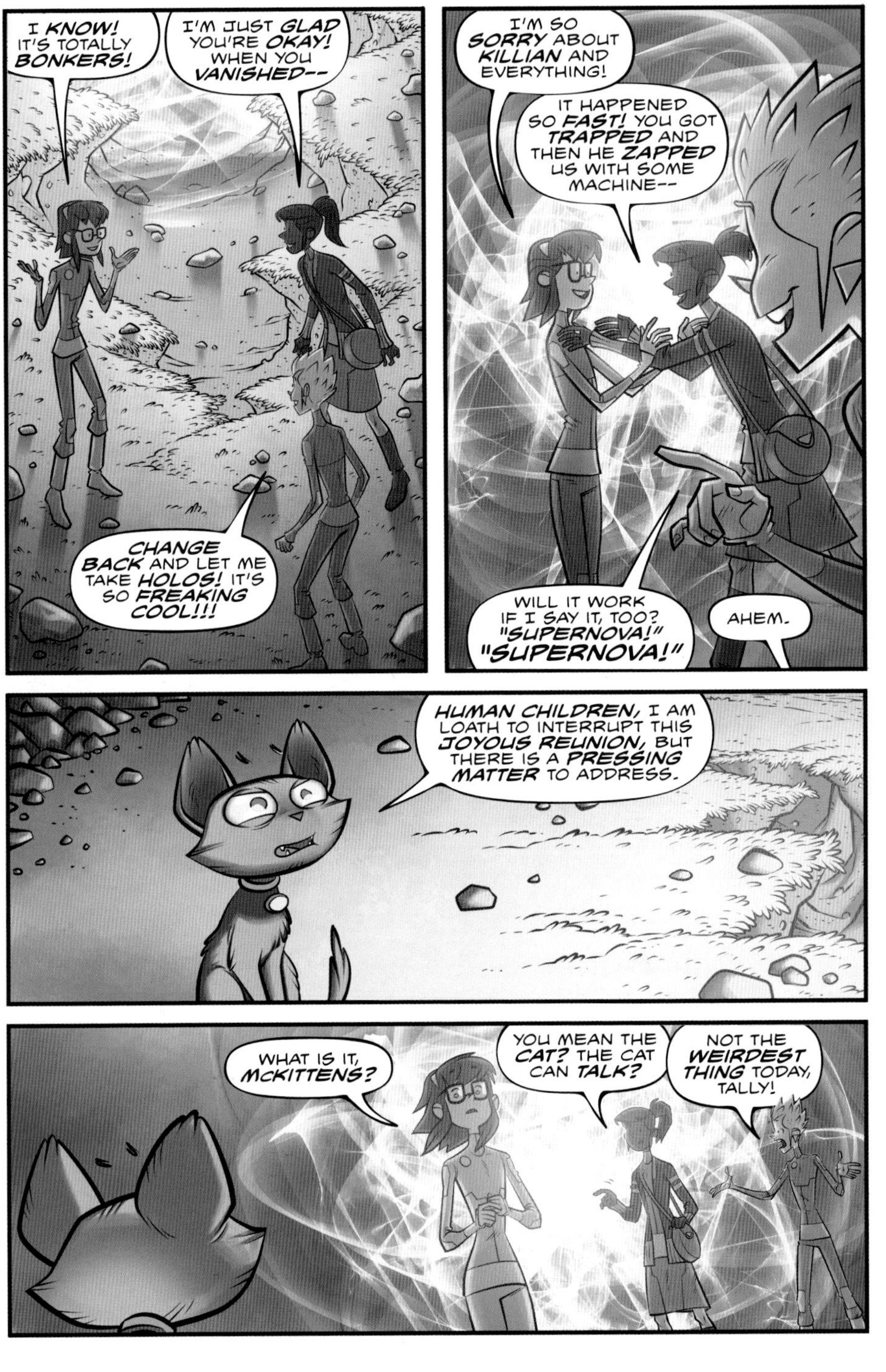
I KNOW! IT'S TOTALLY BONKERS!
I'M JUST GLAD YOU'RE OKAY! WHEN YOU VANISHED--
CHANGE BACK AND LET ME TAKE HOLOS! IT'S SO FREAKING COOL!!!
I'M SO SORRY ABOUT KILLIAN AND EVERYTHING!
IT HAPPENED SO FAST! YOU GOT TRAPPED AND THEN HE ZAPPED US WITH SOME MACHINE--
WILL IT WORK IF I SAY IT, TOO? "SUPERNOVA!" "SUPERNOVA!"
AHEM.
HUMAN CHILDREN, I AM LOATH TO INTERRUPT THIS JOYOUS REUNION, BUT THERE IS A PRESSING MATTER TO ADDRESS.
WHAT IS IT, MCKITTENS?
YOU MEAN THE CAT? THE CAT CAN TALK?
NOT THE WEIRDEST THING TODAY, TALLY!

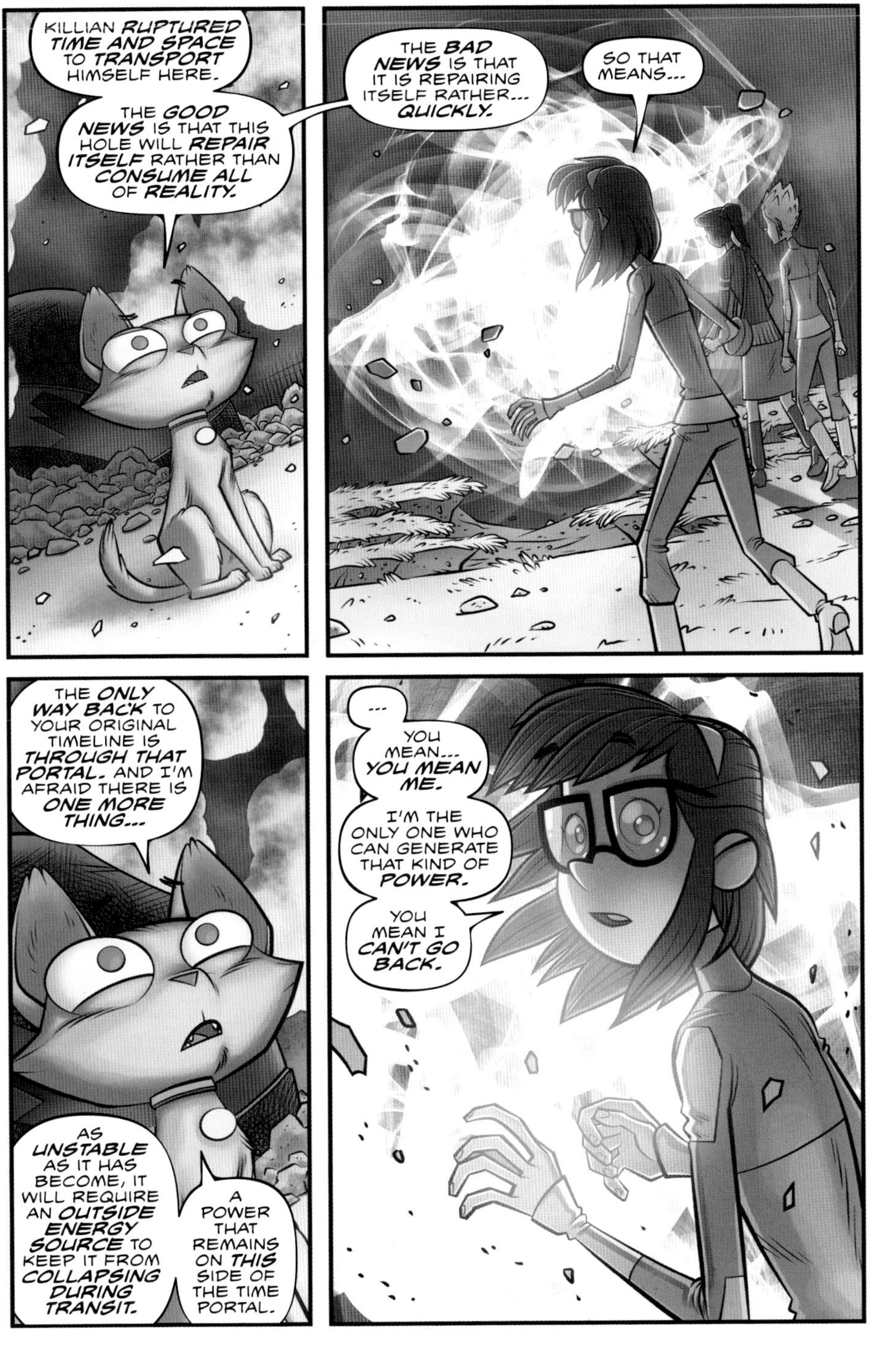
KILLIAN RUPTURED TIME AND SPACE TO TRANSPORT HIMSELF HERE.
THE GOOD NEWS IS THAT THIS HOLE WILL REPAIR ITSELF RATHER THAN CONSUME ALL OF REALITY.
THE BAD NEWS IS THAT IT IS REPAIRING ITSELF RATHER... QUICKLY.
SO THAT MEANS...
THE ONLY WAY BACK TO YOUR ORIGINAL TIMELINE IS THROUGH THAT PORTAL. AND I'M AFRAID THERE IS ONE MORE THING...
AS UNSTABLE AS IT HAS BECOME, IT WILL REQUIRE AN OUTSIDE ENERGY SOURCE TO KEEP IT FROM COLLAPSING DURING TRANSIT.
A POWER THAT REMAINS ON THIS SIDE OF THE TIME PORTAL.
...
YOU MEAN... YOU MEAN ME.
I'M THE ONLY ONE WHO CAN GENERATE THAT KIND OF POWER.
YOU MEAN I CAN'T GO BACK.

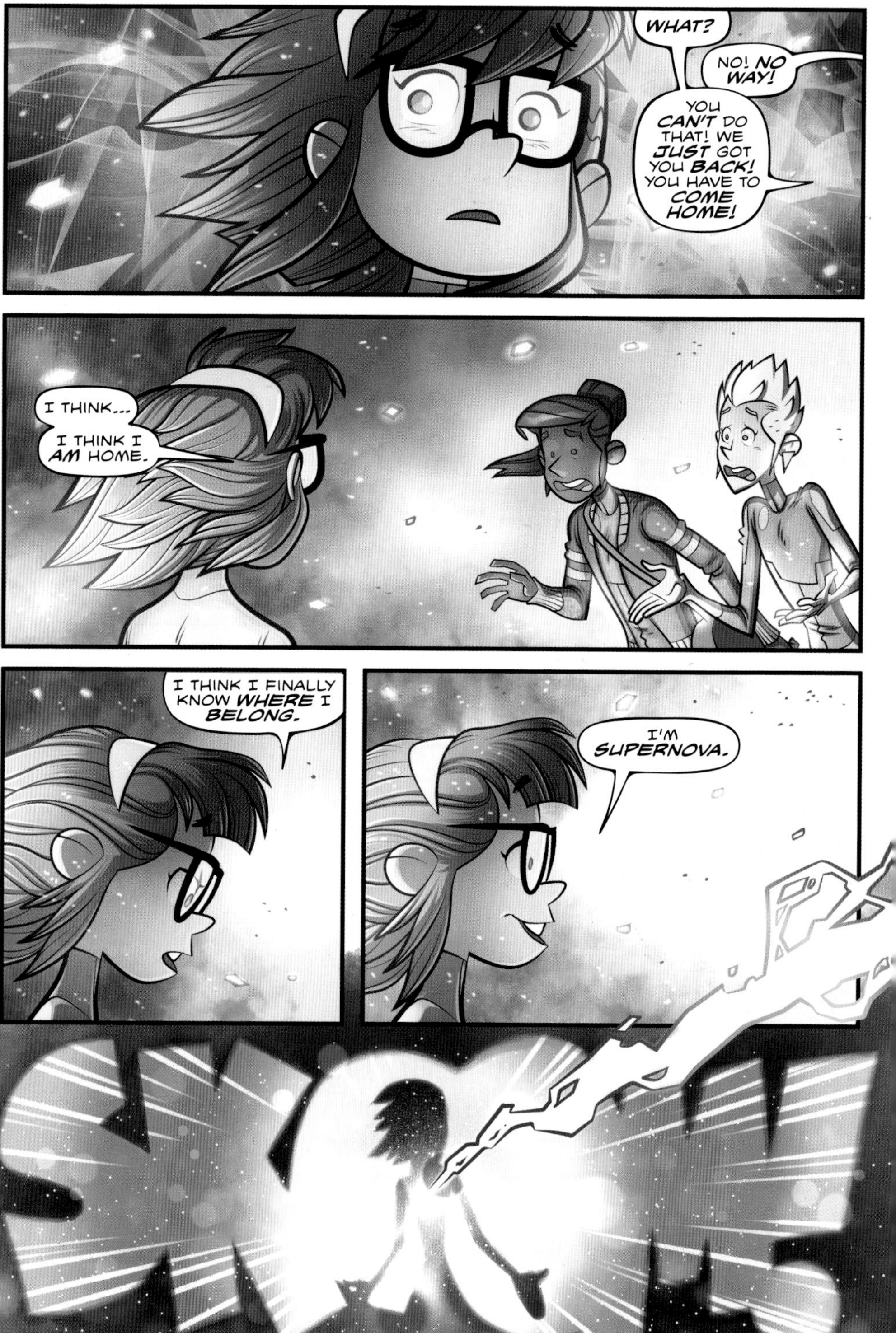
WHAT?
NO! NO WAY!
YOU CAN'T DO THAT! WE JUST GOT YOU BACK! YOU HAVE TO COME HOME!
I THINK...
I THINK I AM HOME.
I THINK I FINALLY KNOW WHERE I BELONG.
I'M SUPERNOVA.

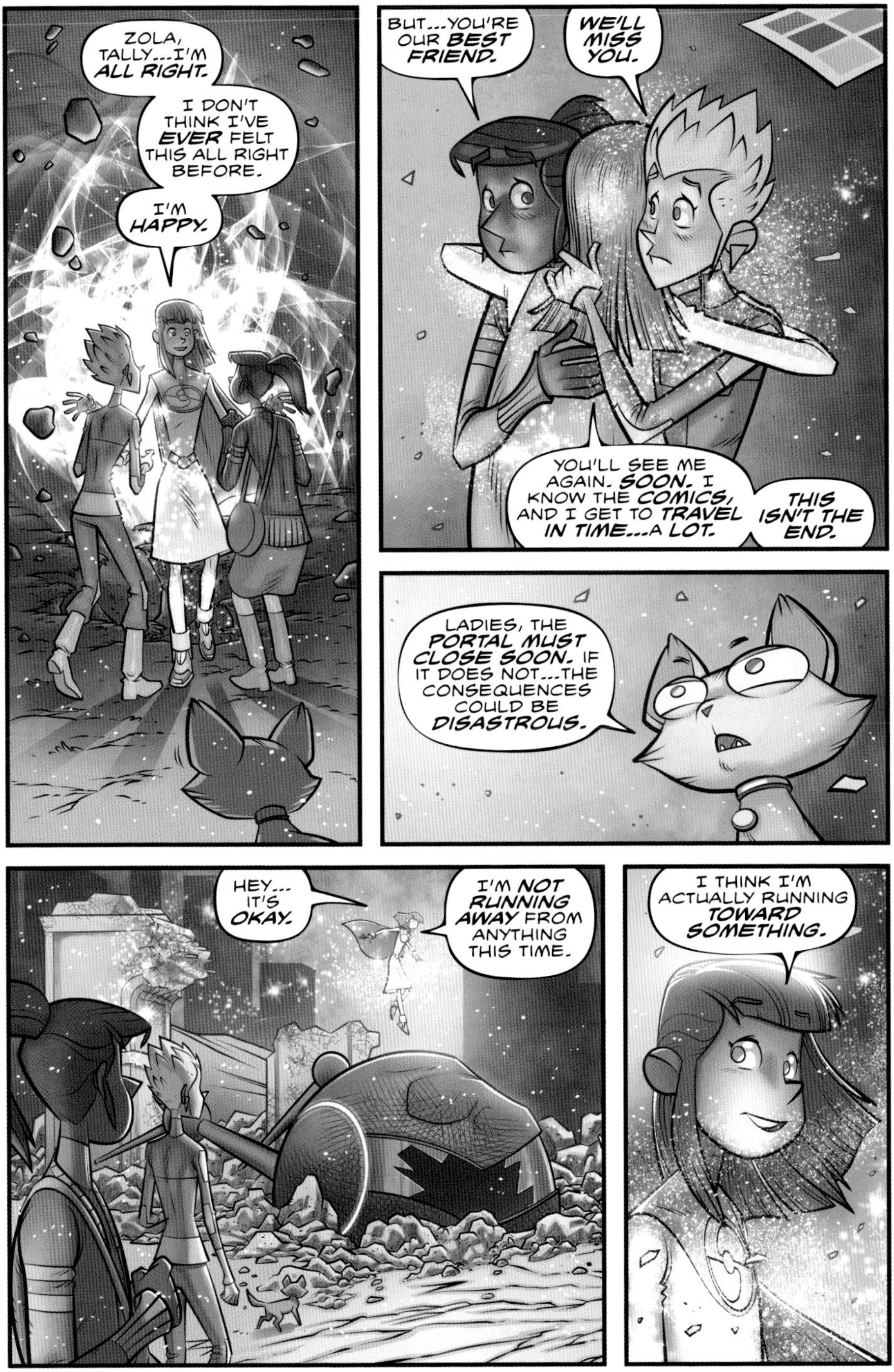
ZOLA, TALLY...I'M ALL RIGHT.
I DON'T THINK I'VE EVER FELT THIS ALL RIGHT BEFORE.
I'M HAPPY.
BUT...YOU'RE OUR BEST FRIEND.
WE'LL MISS YOU.
YOU'LL SEE ME AGAIN. SOON. I KNOW THE COMICS, AND I GET TO TRAVEL IN TIME...A LOT.
THIS ISN'T THE END.
LADIES, THE PORTAL MUST CLOSE SOON. IF IT DOES NOT...THE CONSEQUENCES COULD BE DISASTROUS.
HEY... IT'S OKAY.
I'M NOT RUNNING AWAY FROM ANYTHING THIS TIME.
I THINK I'M ACTUALLY RUNNING TOWARD SOMETHING.

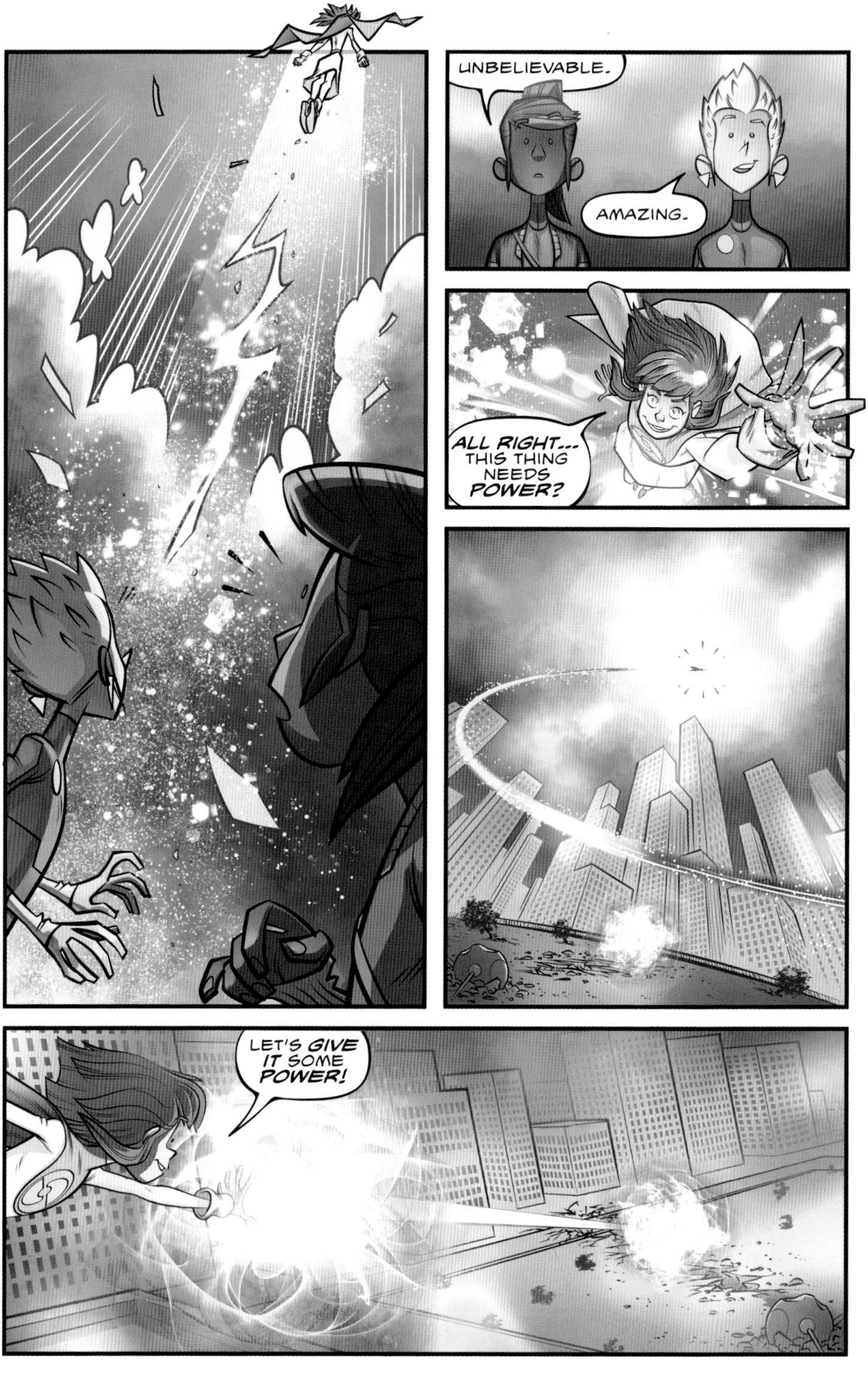
UNBELIEVABLE.
AMAZING.
ALL RIGHT... THIS THING NEEDS POWER?
LET'S GIVE IT SOME POWER!

IT'S JUST LIKE SHE SAID ON THE BUS!

SHE'S PUNCHING IT... WITH RAINBOWS.

AND IT'S AWESOME.

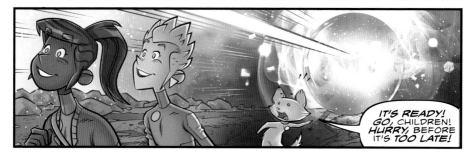

IT'S READY! GO, CHILDREN! HURRY, BEFORE IT'S TOO LATE!

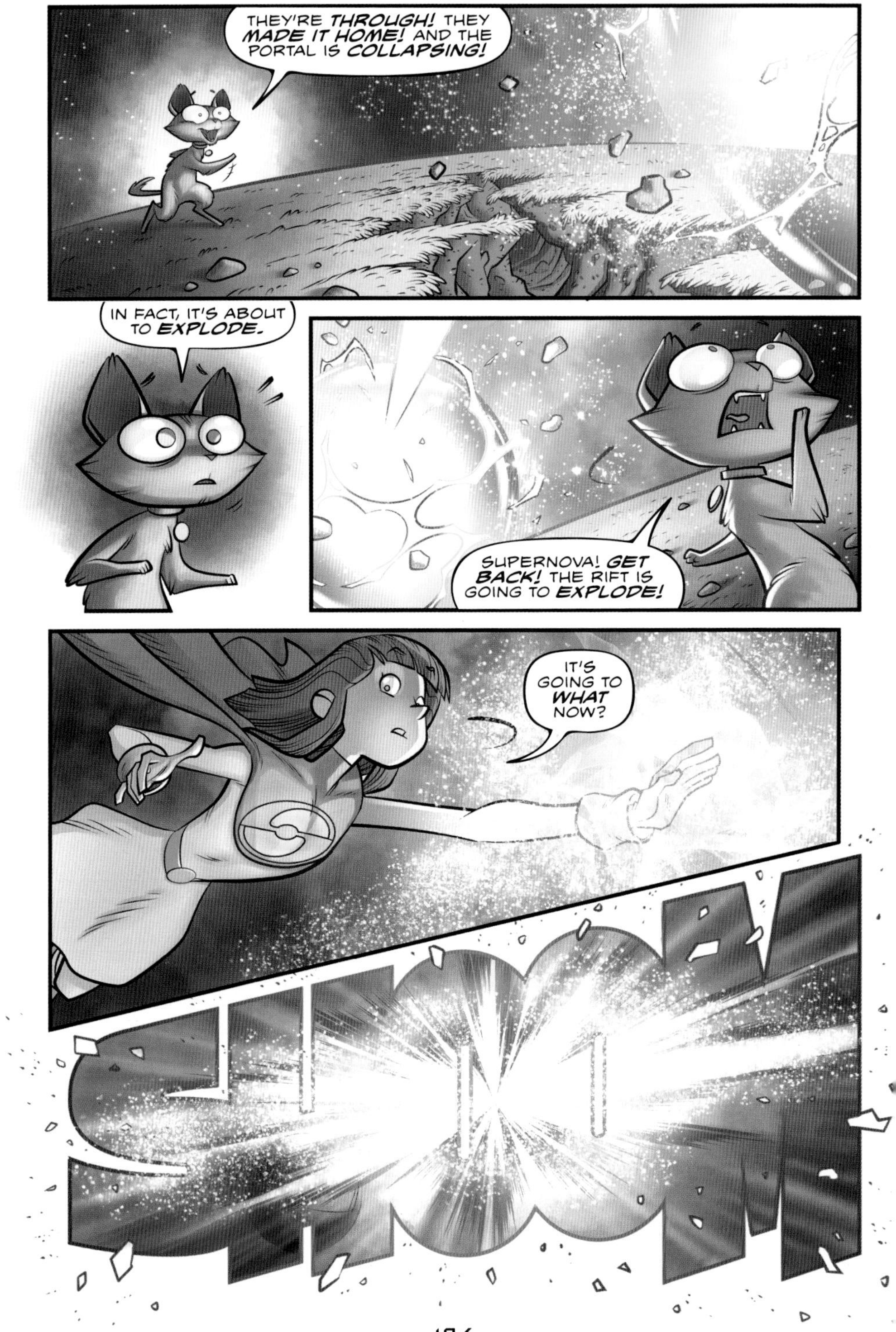
THEY'RE THROUGH! THEY MADE IT HOME! AND THE PORTAL IS COLLAPSING!
IN FACT, IT'S ABOUT TO EXPLODE.
SUPERNOVA! GET BACK! THE RIFT IS GOING TO EXPLODE!
IT'S GOING TO WHAT NOW?

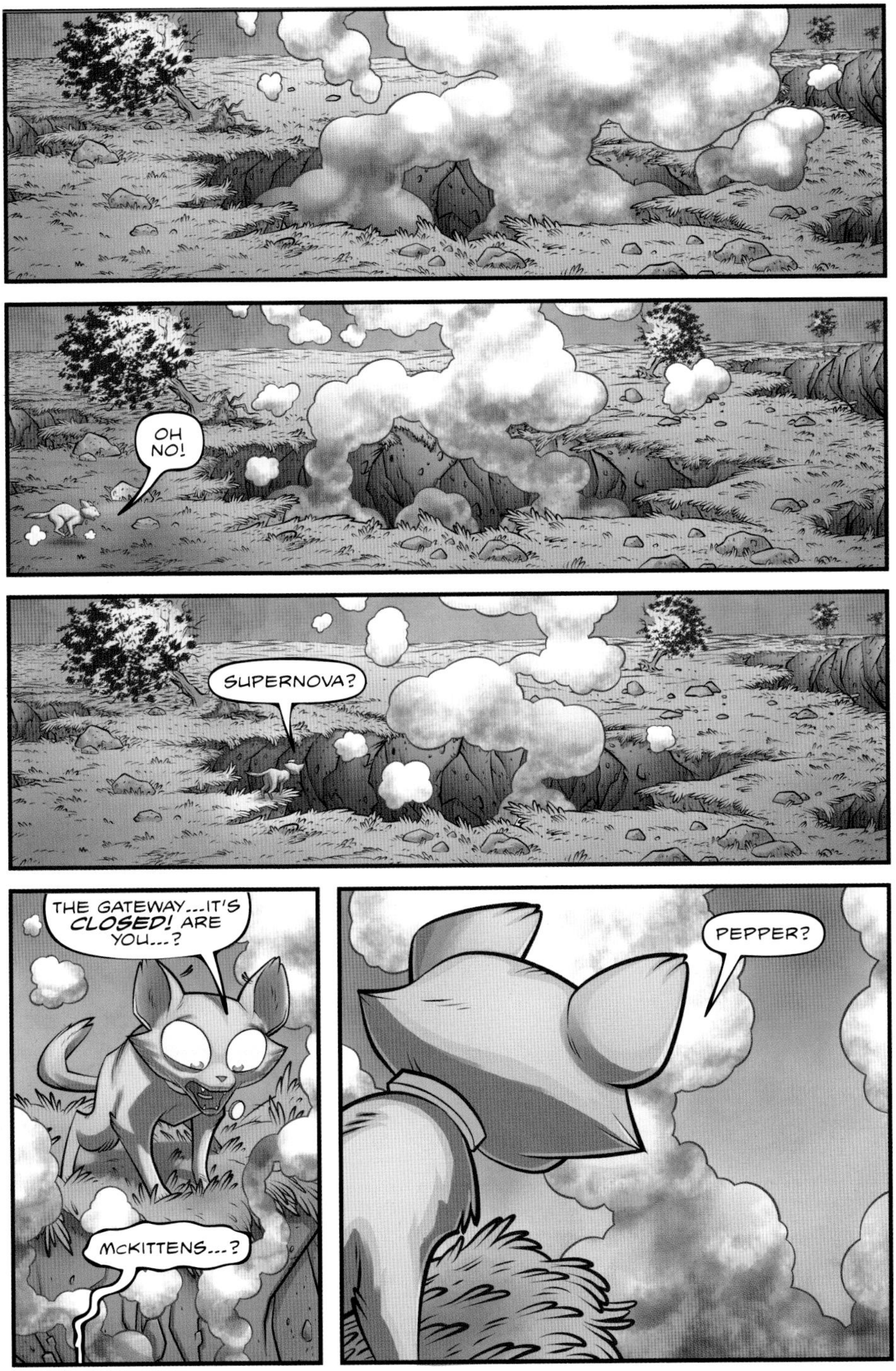
OH NO!
SUPERNOVA?
THE GATEWAY...IT'S CLOSED! ARE YOU...?
McKITTENS...?
PEPPER?

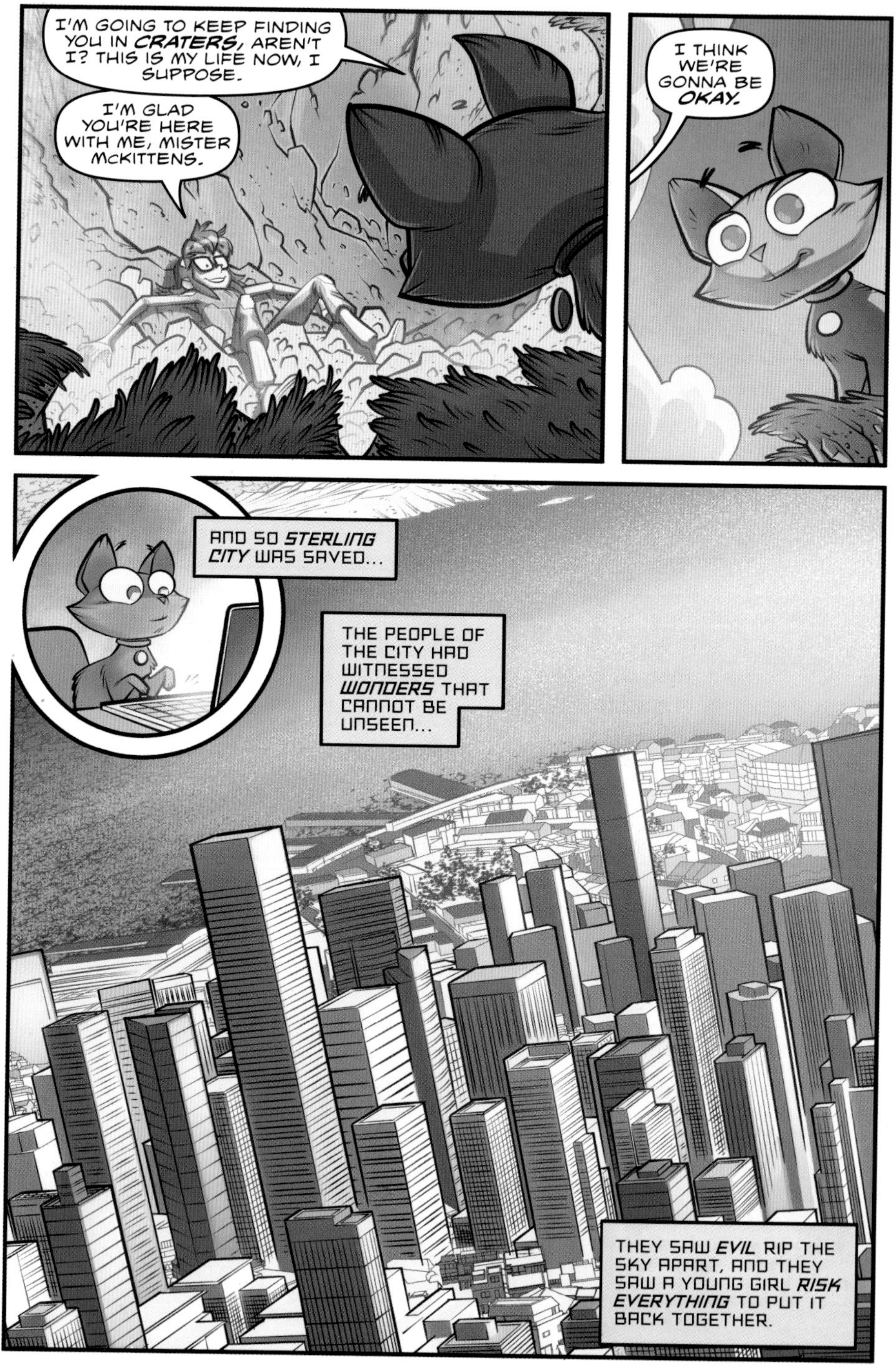
I'M GOING TO KEEP FINDING YOU IN CRATERS, AREN'T I? THIS IS MY LIFE NOW, I SUPPOSE.
I'M GLAD YOU'RE HERE WITH ME, MISTER MCKITTENS.
I THINK WE'RE GONNA BE OKAY.
AND SO STERLING CITY WAS SAVED...
THE PEOPLE OF THE CITY HAD WITNESSED WONDERS THAT CANNOT BE UNSEEN...
THEY SAW EVIL RIP THE SKY APART, AND THEY SAW A YOUNG GIRL RISK EVERYTHING TO PUT IT BACK TOGETHER.

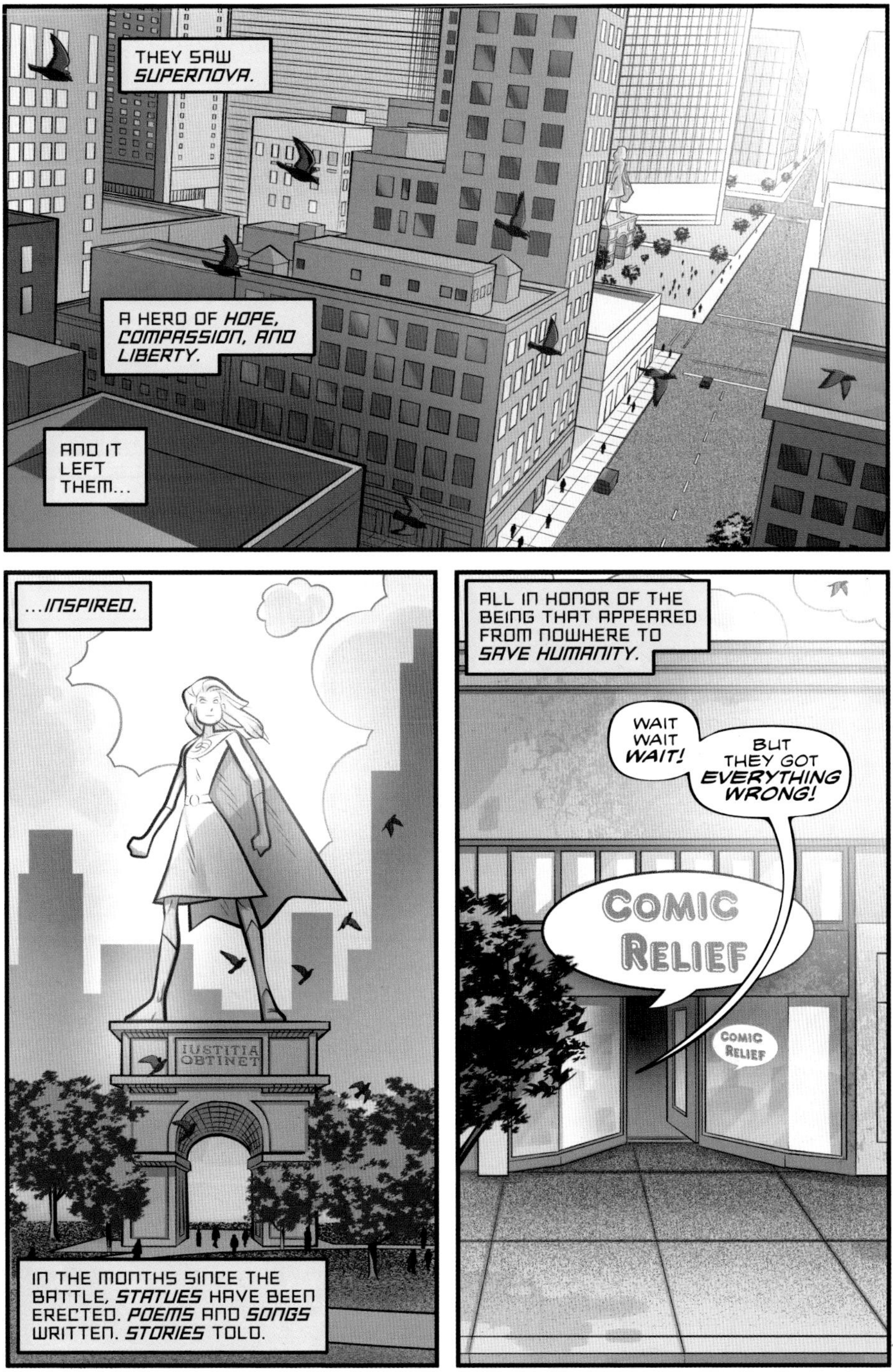
THEY SAW SUPERNOVA.
A HERO OF HOPE, COMPASSION, AND LIBERTY.
AND IT LEFT THEM...
...INSPIRED.
IUSTITIA OBTINET
IN THE MONTHS SINCE THE BATTLE, STATUES HAVE BEEN ERECTED. POEMS AND SONGS WRITTEN. STORIES TOLD.
ALL IN HONOR OF THE BEING THAT APPEARED FROM NOWHERE TO SAVE HUMANITY.
WAIT WAIT WAIT!
BUT THEY GOT EVERYTHING WRONG!
COMIC RELIEF
COMIC RELIEF

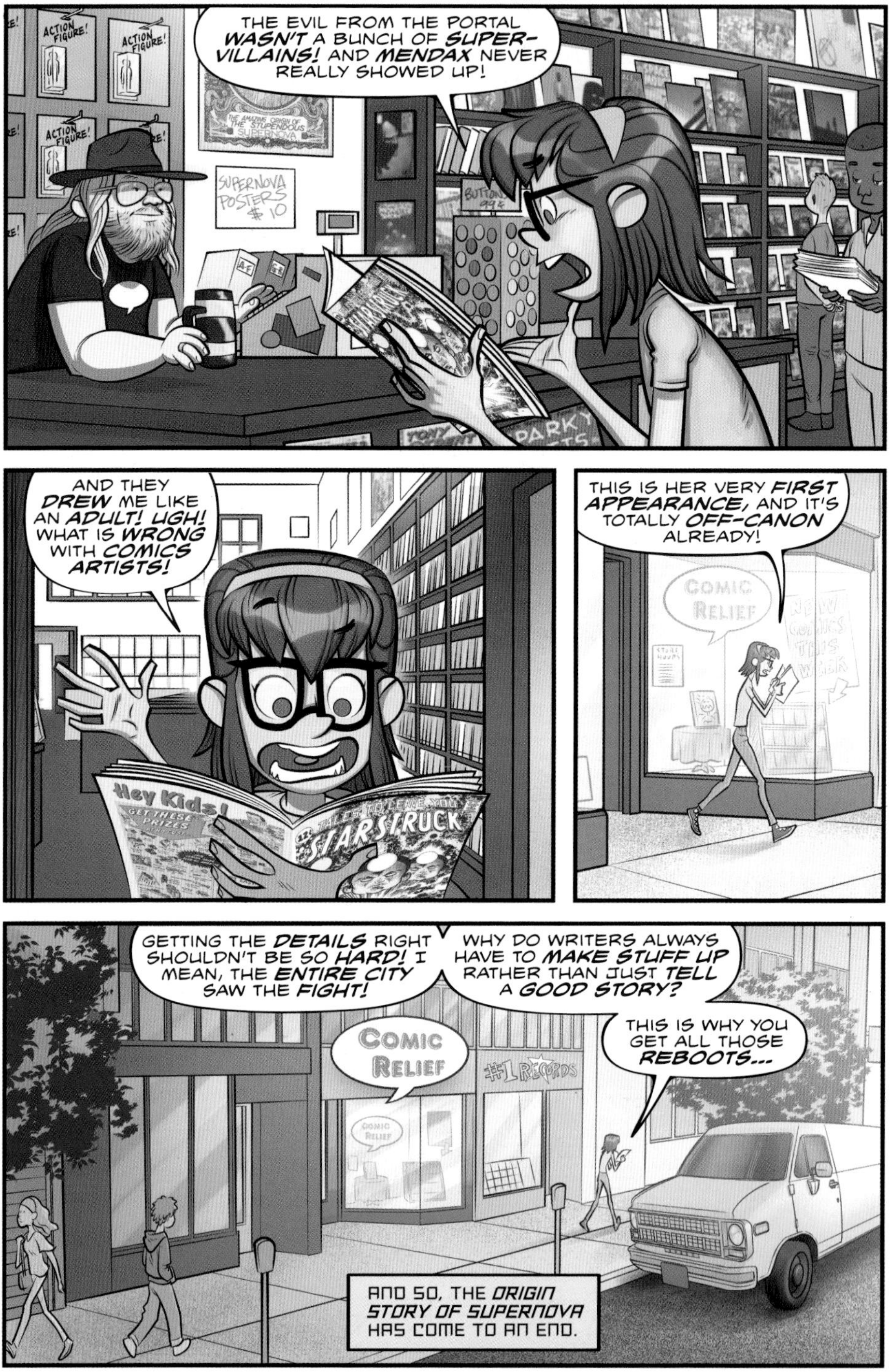

ACTION FIGURE!
THE AMAZING ORIGIN OF THE STUPENDOUS SUPERNOVA
SUPERNOVA POSTERS $10
THE EVIL FROM THE PORTAL WASN'T A BUNCH OF SUPER-VILLAINS! AND MENDAX NEVER REALLY SHOWED UP!
AND THEY DREW ME LIKE AN ADULT! UGH! WHAT IS WRONG WITH COMICS ARTISTS!
Hey Kids! GET THESE PRIZES
STARSTRUCK
THIS IS HER VERY FIRST APPEARANCE, AND IT'S TOTALLY OFF-CANON ALREADY!
COMIC RELIEF
GETTING THE DETAILS RIGHT SHOULDN'T BE SO HARD! I MEAN, THE ENTIRE CITY SAW THE FIGHT!
WHY DO WRITERS ALWAYS HAVE TO MAKE STUFF UP RATHER THAN JUST TELL A GOOD STORY?
THIS IS WHY YOU GET ALL THOSE REBOOTS...
COMIC RELIEF
#1 RECORDS
AND SO, THE ORIGIN STORY OF SUPERNOVA HAS COME TO AN END.

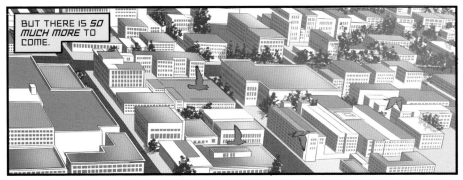

BUT THERE IS *SO MUCH MORE* TO COME.

HEROIC *ALLIES*... SINISTER *ENEMIES*...

ADVENTURE... INTRIGUE... *DANGER.*

ALREADY IN THESE LAST FEW MONTHS, *PEPPER* HAS MADE *GREAT STRIDES* IN HER ROLE AS *SUPERNOVA.*

STERLING HIGH SCHOOL

A *WEEK* AFTER KILLIAN'S SHIP WAS DESTROYED, SUPERNOVA DEFEATED THE ICY EVIL OF THE *CORRUPT CRIMINAL* CALLED *EYE SCREAM.*

A WEEK AFTER *THAT,* SHE UNCOVERED THE MALEVOLENT UNDERTAKINGS OF THE MASTER MAGICIAN KNOWN AS *HYPNOTICA.*

THE *TOY BRIGADE* WAS BROKEN. *KING CONUNDRUM'S* PUZZLES WERE ALL SOLVED. THE *MUFFIN MAN'S CRIME KITCHEN* CLOSED.

ORDER BALANCED AGAINST *CHAOS.* JUST AS THE *OVERLORDS* WANTED.

BUT IN THE SPIRIT OF *BALANCE...* A SUPERHERO IS NOT THE ONLY THING THAT *PEPPER PAGE* SHOULD BE.

AND SO WE ARE *HERE...*

PEPPER NICKNAMED IT *"THE LOCKER OF SOLACE."*

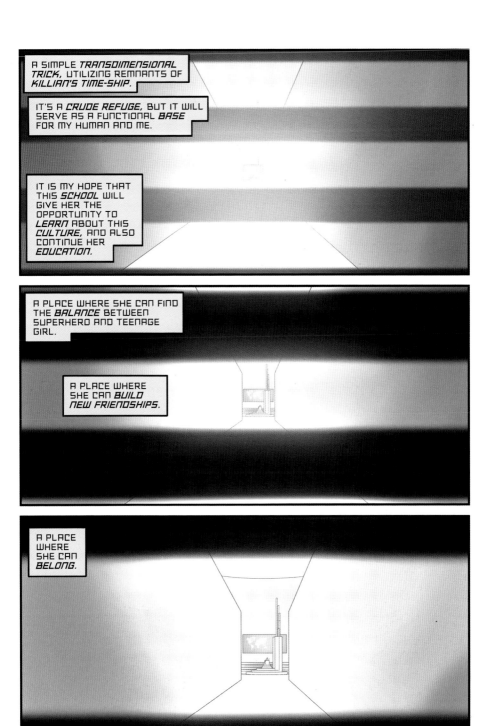

A SIMPLE *TRANSDIMENSIONAL TRICK*, UTILIZING REMNANTS OF *KILLIAN'S TIME-SHIP.*

IT'S A *CRUDE REFUGE*, BUT IT WILL SERVE AS A FUNCTIONAL *BASE* FOR MY HUMAN AND ME.

IT IS MY HOPE THAT THIS *SCHOOL* WILL GIVE HER THE OPPORTUNITY TO *LEARN* ABOUT THIS *CULTURE*, AND ALSO CONTINUE HER *EDUCATION.*

A PLACE WHERE SHE CAN FIND THE *BALANCE* BETWEEN SUPERHERO AND TEENAGE GIRL.

A PLACE WHERE SHE CAN *BUILD NEW FRIENDSHIPS.*

A PLACE WHERE SHE CAN *BELONG.*

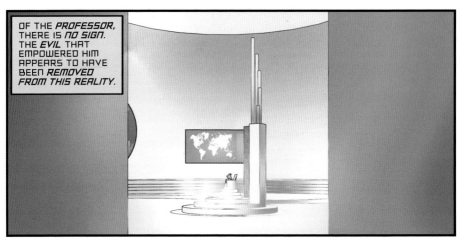

OF THE *PROFESSOR*, THERE IS *NO SIGN*. THE *EVIL* THAT EMPOWERED HIM APPEARS TO HAVE BEEN *REMOVED FROM THIS REALITY*.

BUT THE *COMIC BOOKS* PEPPER CARRIED THROUGH THE TIME STREAM PROMISE *ONE THING*...

...THERE WILL *ALWAYS* BE A NEED FOR A *HERO*.

PEPPER BELIEVES THAT THESE *PULP-PRINTED* STORIES THAT SHE HAS COLLECTED WILL SERVE HER AS A *MAP TO HER OWN FUTURE.*

I MAY BE BUT A *SIMPLE CAT,* ALBEIT ONE GIFTED WITH *COSMIC POWER* BEYOND RECKONING...

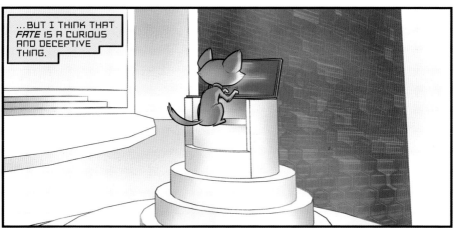

...BUT I THINK THAT *FATE* IS A CURIOUS AND DECEPTIVE THING.

AND THAT THE TRUE *SCOPE* OF AN ADVENTURE MUST BE LIVED...IT CANNOT BE *CONTAINED* TO PANELS AND PAGES AND DRAWINGS.

LIFE IS MEANT TO BE *LIVED;* THE *PATHS UNCOVERED* AS YOU GO.

AND IN THE CURIOUS STORY OF *PEPPER PAGE...*

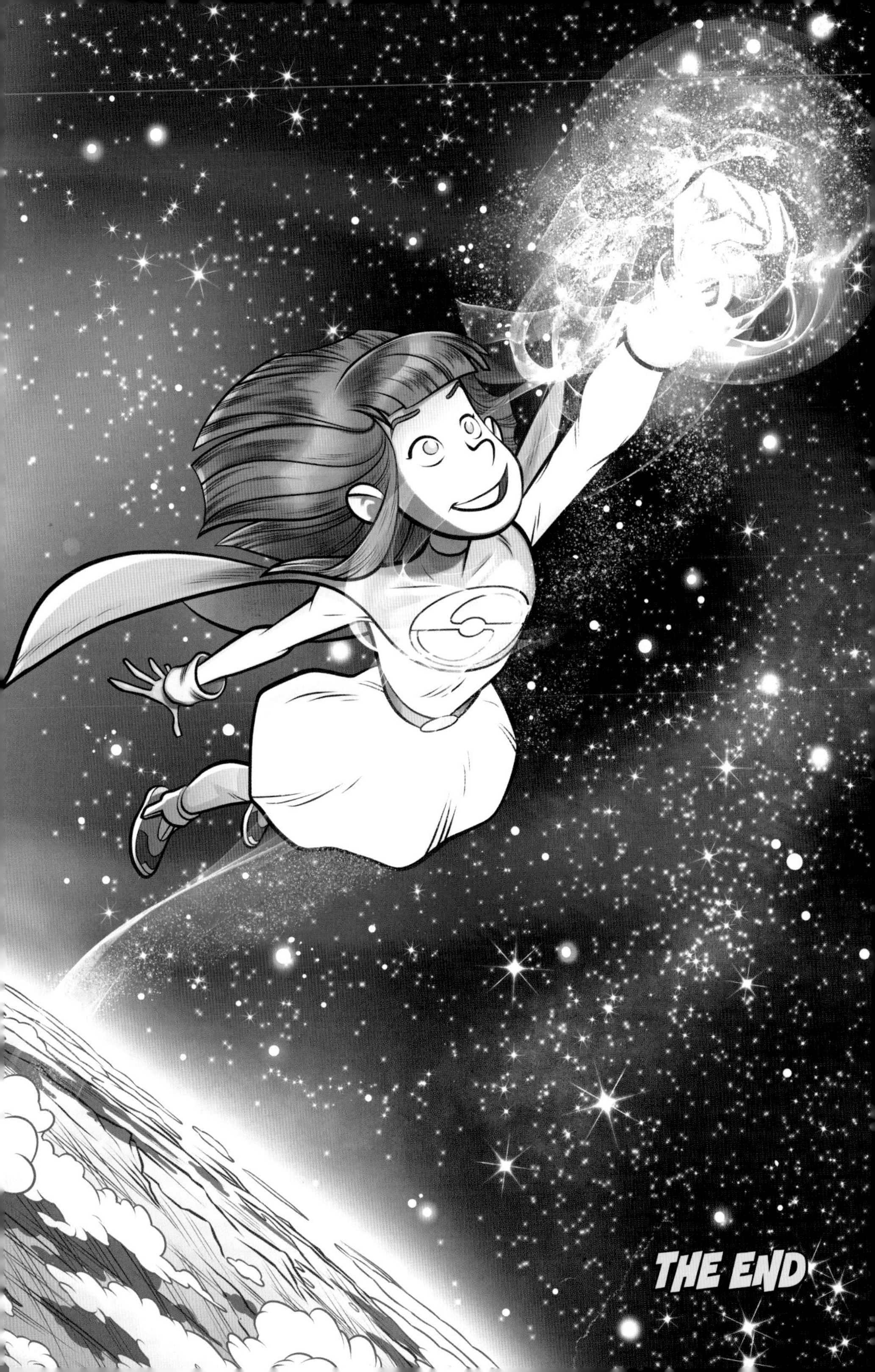
THE END

AND LOOK AT ALL THESE *COMIC BOOK COVERS!*

THE ARTIST MADE A *TON* OF ART THAT YOU BARELY EVEN SEE IN THE *STORY!*

BUT I LIKE IT BECAUSE IT MAKES THE WORLD OF *SUPERNOVA* SEEM *SO REAL!*

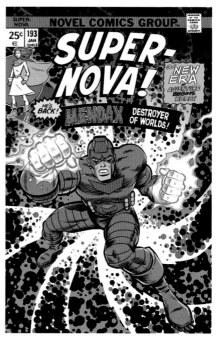

...THE END?

FOR STEVE B, WHO HAS ALWAYS BEEN
THERE FOR US, AND DANNY ADAMS, WHO WAS LIKE
A FATHER TO ME AND WILL BE MISSED —*LQW*

FOR ERIN, WHO MAKES ME BELIEVE IN
SUPERHEROES MORE EVERY DAY —*EMJ*

:01

First Second

Published by First Second
First Second is an imprint of Roaring Brook Press,
a division of Holtzbrinck Publishing Holdings Limited Partnership
120 Broadway, New York, NY 10271
firstsecondbooks.com
mackids.com

Library of Congress Control Number: 2020911248

Our books may be purchased in bulk for promotional, educational, or business use.
Please contact your local bookseller or the Macmillan Corporate and Premium Sales Department at
(800) 221-7945 ext. 5442 or by email at MacmillanSpecialMarkets@macmillan.com.

FIRST EDITION

First edition, 2021
Edited by Calista Brill and Steve Behling
Cover and interior book design by Sunny Lee
Printed in China by Toppan Leefung Printing Ltd., Dongguan City, Guangdong Province

The book is penciled with a vintage 1950s Wearever brand mechanical pencil on
20# Hammermill Copy Plus 8.5" x 11" copy paper, and the final art is digitally inked and
painted in Clip Studio Paint and Photoshop.

ISBN 978-1-250-21692-2 (paperback)
1 3 5 7 9 10 8 6 4 2

ISBN 978-1-250-21691-5 (hardcover)
1 3 5 7 9 10 8 6 4 2

Don't miss your next favorite book from First Second!
For the latest updates go to firstsecondnewsletter.com and sign up for our enewsletter.

BY ART WE LIVE